**"I've missed you, little darlin',"
Levi said, smiling down into his
daughter's face. "Did you miss
me, too?"**

More than anything in the world, Claire thought,
observing the way he ~~held his daughter~~. *And more
than you'll ever know*

With more than a little ~~effort, she forced~~
down her feelings. S~~he didn't want Levi to know~~
what she was thinkin~~g.~~

That was all she needed to do, Claire ~~reminded~~
herself. If Levi had a clue as to what she was
thinking, he would take that to mean that he could
move back into their apartment and just like that, it
would be business as usual.

Would that be so bad? She questioned herself.

Yes! Yes, it would be that bad. She'd be back to
spending all of her time taking care of the baby and
missing Levi while he'd be spending all his free time
away from her.

Supposedly securing their future if she were to
believe him.

She had to remember how that felt, missing him.
Being taken for granted, she silently counseled
herself.

But all that—staying angry—required effort. Effort
that was hard to maintain when part of her kept
longing for the touch of his hand, the feel of his lips
on hers.

MONTANA
★ COUNTRY LEGACY ★

THE BEST MAN'S SECOND CHANCE

———— ⚒ ————

USA TODAY Bestselling Author
Marie Ferrarella

Donna Alward

Previously published as *Do You Take This Maverick?*
and *The Cowboy's Valentine*

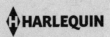

Special thanks and acknowledgment are given to
Marie Ferrarella for her contribution to the
Montana Mavericks: What Happened at the Wedding? continuity.

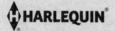

Recycling programs
for this product may
not exist in your area.

ISBN-13: 978-1-335-18991-2

Montana Country Legacy:
The Best Man's Second Chance
Copyright © 2020 by Harlequin Books S.A.

Do You Take This Maverick?
First published in 2015. This edition published in 2020.
Copyright © 2015 by Harlequin Books S.A.

The Cowboy's Valentine
First published in 2015. This edition published in 2020.
Copyright © 2015 by Donna Alward

This edition published by arrangement with Harlequin Books S.A.

For questions and comments about the quality of this book, please contact us at CustomerService@Harlequin.com.

Harlequin Enterprises ULC
22 Adelaide St. West, 40th Floor
Toronto, Ontario M5H 4E3, Canada
www.Harlequin.com

Printed in U.S.A.

CONTENTS

USA TODAY bestselling and RITA® Award–winning author **Marie Ferrarella** has written more than two hundred and fifty books for Harlequin, some under the name Marie Nicole. Her romances are beloved by fans worldwide. Visit her website, marieferrarella.com.

Books by Marie Ferrarella

Harlequin Special Edition

Matchmaking Mamas

Forever, Texas

The Fortunes of Texas: The Lost Fortunes

The Fortunes of Texas: The Secret Fortunes

The Montana Mavericks: The Great Family Roundup

Visit the Author Profile page at Harlequin.com for more titles.

DO YOU TAKE THIS MAVERICK?

Marie Ferrarella

To
Gail Chasan
Who Is Always
In My
Corner
Thank You

Prologue

"I don't see what you're so mad about."

Levi Wyatt stared at his wife of two years in absolute confusion. The second he had opened the door and walked into their room, Claire had lit into him, reading him the riot act.

Granted, it was almost dawn and he had never stayed out anywhere *near* this late before, but that was no reason for Claire to be so upset.

This was definitely a side of his wife he had never seen before.

Industrious, ambitious and hardworking, Levi rarely, if ever, took any time off from his job at the furniture store. As the recently promoted store manager, most of the time he even worked on the weekends, but this weekend—the Fourth of July—he'd taken off to escort Claire to a wedding in Rust Creek Falls. He could have skipped it, personally, but it seemed to be really important to Claire that he attend, too. Her grandparents were putting them up for the weekend at the boarding house that they ran.

The wedding was held in the town's park, and it was a great afternoon. The ceremony was crowded and joyous, the reception even more so. A few of the attendees had decided to get up a little friendly game of poker. Levi wasn't quite sure why, but he was *really* tempted by the game, so he'd joined in.

Since he, Claire and their eight-month-old daughter, Bekka, were all spending the weekend at the boarding house, he felt that Claire wouldn't lack for company while he was gone. Especially since Melba Strickland, Claire's grandma, had graciously offered to babysit so the couple could enjoy the wedding together. This seemed to be the perfect opportunity for him to knock off a little steam.

Besides, he noticed that Claire was busy talking to a woman she knew at the reception when he'd allowed himself to be lured away by the promise of a little harmless diversion.

It was only supposed to be for an hour—two tops.

It had run over.

Way over.

But that still wasn't any reason for Claire to explode this way.

"Oh, you don't, do you?" Claire cried heatedly. Up until this point she had managed to keep her ever-growing discontent under control. She'd never allowed Levi to even catch a glimpse of it, just as she wouldn't dream of letting him see her without her makeup on or with her hair looking anything but perfect. For Claire, it was all about maintaining the illusion of perfection. It always had been.

But tonight, for some reason, she was feeling rather light-headed, although all she'd had to drink at the reception was some of the wedding punch. Despite her petite frame, punch wouldn't affect her like this, she reasoned.

Still, because of her light-headedness, her discontent had slipped out of its usual restraints, and before she knew it, the second Levi had walked into their room at the boarding house, she was giving it to her husband with both barrels.

"No," Levi answered, standing his ground and waiting for Claire to say something that made sense to him, "I don't. I've been working really hard lately, putting in some really long hours. I came to the wedding because *you* wanted to come and when this poker game came up, I didn't see the harm in taking a little time off—"

"Didn't see the harm?" Claire echoed incredulously. Her eyes narrowed into angry, accusing slits. "No, you wouldn't, would you? Well, I'll tell you what the harm is. The harm is that you just walked off and left me— *again.*" Not wanting to wake up anyone at the boarding house, she struggled to keep from shouting at him, but it wasn't easy.

"Again? What *again*?" he demanded, stunned. "Claire, what are you talking about? When did I leave you?"

Was he serious? He couldn't possibly be as clueless as he was pretending to be, could he?

"When *didn't* you leave me?" Claire countered, her anger all but running over like a boiling pot of water. "You're always going off out of town to some sales meetings or other. And if it's not a meeting, then it's a *seminar*." She said the word as if it was a lie that he fed her. "I never get to see you anymore," she complained.

Levi felt his own temper surging, something that almost *never* happened. Ordinarily, he could put up with his wife's fluctuating moods, but right now he felt as if he'd had more than he could stand.

"You're seeing me now." Levi spread his hands wide, as if to highlight his presence. "I'm standing right here," he pointed out.

Was he mocking her? His attitude just kept fueling her anger. "You know what I mean."

"No, I *don't* know what you mean," he told her, feeling more and more bewildered and put upon by the second. "I'm going to those sales meetings and seminars because my job demands it. I'm doing it for you and the baby," Levi stressed.

But Claire saw it differently. "You're doing it to get *away* from me and the baby."

Levi blew out a long breath as he gave up. There was no reasoning with her. "You're tired, you don't know what you're saying," Levi concluded, feeling rather desperate. He just wanted this to stop.

Her big brown eyes—eyes he had fallen in love with the first time he saw her—were all but shooting daggers at him. "Oh, so now I'm just crazy?"

Where had that come from? "I didn't say that," Levi insisted.

She was twisting everything, he thought helplessly. He felt as if he had stepped into quicksand and was sinking fast, no matter how hard he tried to pull himself free.

"Maybe you didn't *say* it but that's what you implied," Claire retorted haughtily. "And who could blame me if I was crazy—which I'm *not*," Claire underscored. "The only one I get to talk to all day is a colicky, crying baby. Don't get me wrong, Levi, I love Bekka, but you're never around." It was an angry accusation, one she dared him to deny.

"Yes, I am," Levi insisted. "I come home to you every night," Levi told her.

"Sure, you come home," she jeered. "You come home to fall into bed, dead asleep before your head hits the pillow."

"I put in long hours, Claire, and I'm tired," Levi tried to explain.

Claire's back went up as she instantly took offense at what she thought he was implying. "Oh, and I don't and I'm not?"

Levi threw up his hands, thoroughly frustrated. He had stayed longer at the game than he had intended and lost money, to boot. He hadn't meant for any of that to happen. He wasn't really sure *why* it had happened. But he knew that her anger was way out of proportion.

"Look, let's not get into this now," he pleaded. "I'm sorry, okay?"

"No, it's not okay—and you're not sorry," she told him angrily. "But I am. I'm sorry I ever met you. I'm sorry I ever married you!"

Levi was close to being speechless. "Claire, what are you saying?"

Heightened fury was all but etched into her fine features and had colored her cheeks to a bright shade of pink.

"What I'm saying is that it's over," she retorted furiously. "I made a mistake. We *both* made a mistake. We should have never gotten married in the first place."

All this because he stayed out playing poker too long? He couldn't believe what he was hearing. "Claire—"

"Get out!" she cried. Circling him, she put her hands on his back and started pushing him out the door into the hallway. "Get out now!"

"Claire—" It was all Levi could get out of his mouth. He was completely stunned and unable to even understand how they had gotten to this impasse so quickly.

"Now!" she yelled, managing to shove him out all the way only because she had caught him so completely off guard.

The second he was across the threshold and in the hall, Claire pulled off her wedding ring.

"Here, I don't want this anymore, either!" she cried, throwing her wedding ring at him.

The next second she slammed the door shut behind him.

He heard the *click* and knew she'd flipped the lock. Claire had the only key.

Levi stood there in front of the door to their room for several moments, dazed and wondering if he was hallucinating all this for some reason. What had just happened seemed to have come out of nowhere.

This trip was supposed to have picked up Claire's spirits. Instead, he felt that he had just witnessed his marriage falling apart.

What the hell had just happened here? Levi wondered. He hadn't a clue.

As he walked away from the door, Levi heard Bekka beginning to wail from inside the room.

"You and me both, kid," he murmured under his breath. "You and me both."

Chapter 1

Almost a month had gone by since the disastrous night of the wedding, and Levi *still* didn't know exactly what had happened. What he did know was that he wanted his wife back.

He missed her.

Missed the baby.

Missed being a married man more than he had ever thought possible.

In one all-too-quick swoop his orderly world had fallen into a state of formless chaos, and he absolutely hated it. He felt directionless. When he and Claire had been together, his life had had purpose, he'd had goals. Now he was just blindly going from one end of the day to the other. He still showed up for work at the furniture store every morning, but he lacked his usual energy, feeling lost and so alone that he literally ached.

Without Claire, absolutely nothing seemed to make any sense to him anymore.

Initially, as he had walked back to his truck right after Claire had thrown him out, his own anger at what he felt was her uncalled-for reaction to his late arrival continued to grow—along with his confusion. Why had she blown a gasket? After all, he'd just been playing poker with some of the guys he'd met at the wedding, not playing around with some little flirt.

He knew lots of men who took any opportunity to cheat on their wives, claiming that marriage hemmed them in, and that they needed something besides the "same old piece of stale cake" to get their adrenaline flowing.

But he wasn't like that. And he certainly didn't feel that way about his marriage.

The moment that he had first laid eyes on Claire in that cute little sundress she'd been wearing the day they met, peering into the show window of the furniture store where he worked, he had fallen for her like the proverbial ton of bricks. He'd even taken the initiative and gone outside the store to tell her that the set she was looking at was on sale. It really wasn't. He'd made that up just to have an excuse to talk to her.

Had she actually wanted to buy that set, he would have had to come up with the difference out of his own pocket, but he was so taken with her, he would have done it and gladly. The way he saw it, it would have been more than worth it to him.

From that day forward, Claire Strickland had always been the only girl for him. He'd loved her so much, he'd been willing to wait until she graduated from college before they got married. In fact, he'd insisted on it. First the degree, then the ring. Because it was best for her, and he didn't want to be the reason she had dropped out of college. From the first moment he met her, it had always been about what was best for her. He felt that she brought out the best in him.

And now he had lost her…and he wasn't even sure *why*.

He could still see that look on her face as she'd pushed him out of the room. She'd been so angry at him, and he hadn't done anything to warrant that degree of fury. One of the men in the game had actually bet and lost the house he was living in. Now *that* was stupid.

What would have been her reaction if he'd done something like *that*?

Trying to be optimistic, Levi had hoped that whatever had gotten her angry to this degree would blow over once they got back home.

But when they *did* get back home—she'd had her grandmother drive her and Bekka home while he'd driven himself—he'd found that his belongings had all been thrown out on the lawn in front of their apartment.

This, in addition to having thrown her wedding ring at him, made the message clear.

It was over.

Except that he didn't want it to be.

Desperate, thinking that maybe she needed a little bit of time to come around, he gave Claire her space. By definition, that required his staying out of her way, so he'd bedded down in the storeroom at the furniture store. He alternated between that and spending the night in his truck. It was August so at least he didn't have to worry about cold weather. But that was small consolation in the face of what was going on in his life.

With each passing day, he kept hoping that Claire would relent and take him back. But she never came to the store, never answered the phone when he called, even though he called her at least three times a day, if not more. For all intents and purposes, Claire was acting as if he didn't exist.

And it was killing him.

Frustrated, Levi decided that enough was enough and went to the apartment where they'd lived for the past two years for a face-to-face confrontation with Claire.

But as he drove up, he saw that there were no lights on in the window to greet him, and he had a very uneasy feeling as he unlocked the front door.

Holding his breath, praying he was wrong, Levi cautiously walked in.

"Claire? Claire, it's me. Levi. Your husband," he added uncertainly. Nothing but silence answered him. "Claire," he called out, "where are you?"

Still nothing. Nothing but the hollow echo of his own voice.

Growing progressively more agitated as well as aggravated, Levi went from room to small room, looking for his wife, for his baby. Finding neither.

"Come on, Claire, this isn't funny anymore. Where *are* you?"

Nervous now, he debated calling Claire's parents. He didn't want to worry them, but then on the other hand, there might be a chance that they knew where their daughter and granddaughter were.

They might even be staying with her parents, for that matter.

He took out his cell phone and was all set to press

the appropriate numbers on the keypad, but then he paused, thinking. Maybe calling her parents wasn't such a good idea after all.

Claire's parents, Peter and Donna Strickland, had initially been very hesitant about their daughter getting involved with someone who was several years older than she was and who didn't have a college education. It had taken him a bit of doing to win them over.

But after her parents saw how much he really loved their youngest daughter, how he'd treated her as if she were made out of pure spun gold, they came around and gave their blessings. The older couple, who had been going strong for the past thirty years, had one of those rare, really happy marriages and according to Peter Strickland, they saw no reason why Claire and he couldn't have one, too.

If he called them, asking after Claire, then her parents would realize that they were having marital problems. He had a feeling that Claire *wouldn't* tell her parents what was going on. Because if she did, it was as good as admitting that their initial concerns about her getting married had been right. That he *wasn't* good enough for her. And even though she might actually believe that, he knew Claire well enough to know that she wouldn't readily admit that fact to her parents.

Who did that leave? he thought as he wandered around the empty apartment.

There were her two older sisters, Hadley and Tessa, but they were both professional career women who lived and worked in Bozeman, Montana, too. If Claire called either one of them, asking to be taken in, that would be as good as admitting failure, and she wouldn't do that. There was just the slightest bit of competitiveness among the sisters—at least as far as Claire was concerned.

No, she wouldn't call either one of her sisters, either. She would have rather died than allow her sisters to know that her marriage was in jeopardy.

But she had to call somebody, Levi reasoned. Claire couldn't opt to go it alone. She had the baby to think of.

The answer suddenly came to him. Of course. Claire would have turned to her grandparents for emotional support.

Her grandmother, Melba, was a lively, full-steam-ahead woman who had raised four children, including Claire's father, and had still managed to be a business-woman. She and her husband, Gene, ran the Strick-land Boarding House, where he and Claire had stayed when they'd attended the wedding that had ultimately torn them apart.

Claire admired her grandmother, so it was only natural that she would turn to the older woman. And, as he recalled, the crusty Gene Strickland really doted on his granddaughter and her baby girl, too.

Levi was by nature a private person. He had never gone to anyone with his hat in his hand before, pleading his case, but then, he'd never been in this sort of a situation before, either. He wanted his wife and his daughter back in the worst way. Getting them back meant more to him than his pride, even though the latter was a difficult thing for him to swallow.

But he'd do it. To get Claire back into his life, he'd do whatever was necessary.

Levi slowly looked around the apartment. Claire's clothes were gone. The closets were empty on her side.

He knew that since Claire *was* gone, he could stay here again. The familiar surroundings were infinitely more comfortable than bedding down in the storeroom or utilizing the flatbed of his truck.

But staying here wasn't going to get him any closer to Claire. He needed to go into work every day—taking any more time off was out of the question since the store was introducing a new line of furniture and he was needed to handle whatever problems might come up. That meant that in his off hours, he needed to maintain close proximity to Claire. So he needed to stay somewhere close by to where she was staying.

And that, he concluded, would most likely have to be at the boarding house. There'd been a couple of vacancies there last month when they were there for that damn wedding.

And even if there hadn't been, her grandfather was the type to find a way to make room for his granddaughter and his great-granddaughter even if it meant that *he* had to go sleep in his car. Gene Strickland would have thought nothing of it if doing so meant helping out Claire.

He needed to go see her grandparents, Levi decided. Her grandmother wasn't exactly a fan of his—the woman had made no bones about telling him that she thought Claire was too young to get married the first time she met him. But he did get along with Gene. If he could win the man over to his side in this, he'd have a fighting chance of winning Claire back, he reasoned.

Taking one last long look around, Levi closed and locked the front door behind him—fervently hoping that it wasn't for the last time.

* * *

How had she gone from feeling like a fairy-tale princess to being Cinderella before the fairy godmother had come into the picture in such a short amount of time?

Claire asked herself that question for the umpteenth time since she had come to her grandparents, asking if she could move into the boarding house until she could get on her feet again.

She could remember the way her grandmother had looked at her that day. Melba Strickland had never been what could be called a sentimental woman by any stretch of the imagination. But the woman was fair and she was family, which was what Claire felt she needed at a time like this.

At the time, her grandfather, a somewhat crusty bear of a man, had asked her, "What's wrong with your place?"

That was where she had broken down and cried. "I don't have a place anymore, Grandpa. I've left Levi."

"Left him?" Taking the fussing Bekka into his own arms, Gene cooed a few syllables at the baby, calming her down, and then looked at his granddaughter incredulously. "Don't you just mean that you've had a lovers' spat?"

Claire shook her head, unable to speak for a moment. When she finally could, she showed the two her bare left ring finger and said, "No, not a *lovers' spat*, Grandpa. Levi and I are separated." She took a ragged breath, telling herself that saying the words didn't hurt—but it did. She felt as if a jagged knife had just ripped through her heart. "We're getting divorced."

"Now hold on there, that's a big word, honey," Gene had told her. "Do you know what it means?"

Melba had frowned at her husband, annoyed. "Of course she knows what it means." And then she turned toward her granddaughter. "What happened, Claire? Did he disrespect you?" Her expression suddenly darkened. "He didn't lay a hand on you, did he? Because if he did, your grandfather is going to kill him."

Claire had struggled to keep her sobs from surfacing. "No, he didn't lay a hand on me, Grandmother."

"Then what happened? Why are you divorcing him?" Melba had demanded in her no-nonsense tone.

But Claire just shook her head, waving away the question. She had no intentions of reiterating the incident. She knew she'd break down before she even got to the middle of the story.

"It doesn't matter what happened. We're getting divorced. It's over," she told her grandparents with finality, her voice catching at the end.

For a moment she thought she was going to burst into sobs, but she managed to get herself under control at the last second.

Melba shot her husband a knowing look that all but shouted, "I told you so."

"I *knew* you were too young to get married." Although it was a declaration, there had been no triumph in Melba's voice. "You haven't had a chance to live yet. After graduating college, you're supposed to sample life a little. Travel. Do things, not tie yourself down with a marriage and a baby." She looked at her granddaughter knowingly. "Neither one of you was ready for that, especially not you."

"Melba," Gene warned, giving her a look that told her to keep her piece.

As headstrong and independent as ever, Melba was

not about to listen. Hands on her hips, the diminutive woman turned on her husband. "Don't *Melba* me, Gene. She *wasn't* ready."

The steely older woman looked at her granddaughter, then, after a moment, she enfolded the girl in her arms. Melba's intentions were obviously good, but it still made for a rather awkward moment.

"Oh, Claire," Melba said with a sigh, "you wound up setting yourself up. Marriage isn't some magical, happily-ever-after state. At best it's an ongoing work in progress."

"I'll say," Gene chuckled, his chest moving up and down with the deep rumble. It managed to entertain Bekka, who in turn gurgled her approval. "The first hundred years are the hardest, honey," he told his granddaughter with a twinkle in his eye. "After that it gets easier. But you have to invest the time."

Claire had sniffled then, doing her best not to cry. Doing her best to face the rest of her life stoically. "That's all water under the bridge, Grandpa. I threw Levi out." That had been two days ago. "It's over."

Melba's dark eyebrows drew together in a puzzled single line. "If you threw Levi out, what are you doing here?"

Claire shook her head. "Well, it's his apartment. I can't stay there now. Everywhere I look—the kitchen, the closet, our bedroom—I can see him. It's just too hard for me to take."

Gene had glanced over toward his wife as if he knew that Melba was obviously going to say something that would echo the voice of reason—and be utterly practical. But Claire didn't need *practical*. What she needed—rather desperately, if the look in her eyes was any gauge—was understanding.

In order to forestall his wife and whatever it was that she was going to say, Gene quickly spoke up, trying to stop whatever words were going to come out of Melba's mouth.

"Claire-bear," he said, addressing his granddaughter by the nickname he'd given her when she was about a month old, "You can stay here as long as you like. As it so happens, we've got a couple of vacancies, and it's been a long time since your grandmother and I have heard the sound of little running feet."

"Bekka is only eight months old, Grandpa. She doesn't even walk yet, much less run," Claire reminded her grandfather.

What her daughter did do, almost all night long, was fuss and cry. Another reason that she felt so worn out, hemmed in and trapped, Claire thought, struggling not to be resentful.

Her hostile feelings were redirected toward her husband. If he had been there to share in the responsibility, if he would have taken his turn walking the floor with the baby, then she wouldn't have felt as exhausted and out of sorts as she did.

"But she will," Gene was telling her. "She will and when she does, we'll be there to make sure she doesn't hurt herself, won't we, Mel?" he said, turning toward his wife.

"Sure. And the boarding house will just run itself," Melba commented sarcastically.

Gene shook his head as he looked at his granddaughter. "Don't mind your grandmother. She always sees the downside of things. Me, I see the upside." He winked at Claire. "That's why our marriage works."

"That's why your grandfather is a cockeyed optimist," Melba corrected.

For the sake of peace, Gene ignored his wife's comment. Instead, he said to Claire, "Like I said, you can stay here as long as you like." He turned toward the staircase, still holding Bekka in his arms. "Come on, we'll get you and the princess here settled in."

"I'll pay for the room, Grandmother," Claire had said, looking over her shoulder at Melba.

"You'll do no such thing," Gene informed her. "Family doesn't pay."

"But family pitches in," Melba had interjected. "We'll find something for you to do here at the boarding house, Claire."

"Anything," Claire had offered.

"How's your cooking?" Melba asked her. "I need someone to pick up the slack when Gina is busy," she elaborated, referring to the cook she'd recently hired. "I'm giving having someone else handling the cooking a try. I've already got a lot to keep me busy."

"Anything but that," Claire had amended almost sheepishly. "I'm afraid I still haven't gotten the hang of cooking." And then she brightened. "But I can make beds," she volunteered.

"This is a boarding house, Claire, not a bed-and-breakfast. People here make their own beds," Melba informed her matter-of-factly.

"Don't worry," Gene had said, putting one arm around his granddaughter's shoulders as he held his great-granddaughter against him with the other, "We'll come up with something for you to do until you find your way."

Claire had sighed then, leaning into him as she had done on so many occasions when she had been a little girl, growing up.

"I hope so, Grandpa," Claire said, doing her best to sound cheerful. "I really hope so."

Chapter 2

Gene Strickland tried to ignore it, but even after all these years of marriage, he hadn't found a way to go about things as if everything was all right when it wasn't. His wife's scowl—which was aimed directly at him and had been an ongoing thing now for the past two weeks—seemed to go clean down to the bone. There was no use pretending that it didn't.

So he didn't even try.

Pushing aside the monthly inventory he was in the process of updating in connection with the boarding house's current supplies, Gene asked, "Okay, woman. Out with it. What's got your panties all in a twist like this?"

Brooding dark brown eyes looked at him accusingly from across the large scarred oak desk they both shared in the corner room that served as an office.

"As if you don't know," she muttered under her breath, but clearly enough for Gene to hear.

"No, I don't know," he'd informed her. "I'd like to think that I'd have the good sense *not* to ask if I knew. I've been with you long enough to know that lots of things set you off and right now, I don't want to risk bringing up any of them."

Melba pursed her lips as her eyes held his. "You're coddling her."

"Her?" Gene echoed innocently.

"Yes, *her*. Claire," she finally said. "Don't play dumb with me," Melba warned. "You know damn well that I'm talking about our granddaughter, Gene."

Unable to properly focus on the inventory while his wife was talking, Gene put down his pen and shook his head. This whole thing with Claire had hit Melba hard, he thought. He had a feeling that his wife blamed herself for not speaking up more to change Claire's mind about marrying so young. Or, at the very least, getting Claire to wait another year or so before leaping into marriage. But they all knew that the young never listened to the old, he thought, resigned.

Melba needed to change her opinion about Claire's marriage as well.

Especially since he was going to have to let her in on a secret he would have rather not had to divulge. However, if Melba found out about this on her own—and she had a knack for doing that—then Claire and Levi's marriage might not be the only one in trouble.

"Claire's going through a really rough patch right now, Mel."

"I know that," the old woman snapped. "And she needs a backbone to get through it, not to be treated as if she was made out of spun glass and could break at any second. She *needs* to toughen up." The very thought of a fragile granddaughter exasperated Melba beyond words. "Her parents were just too soft on her. If it were me, I would have never given my permission for those two to get married two years ago."

"Two years ago she wasn't a minor anymore, Mel," Gene gently reminded her. "Legally, she could make her own decisions," the man pointed out.

Melba threw up her hands. "And look how great that turned out for her," she huffed.

Gene thought of the newest boarder he'd just taken in—without his wife's knowledge, certainly without her permission.

Time to lay some groundwork, he told himself.

"Story's not over yet, Mel. There's a second act coming. I just know it. Just remember," he told her, making eye contact with the woman he had slept beside for five decades, "not everyone has an iron resolve like you." Gene leaned over and kissed his wife's temple.

"Don't try to sweet-talk me into going soft, Gene Strickland," Melba snapped—but with less verve.

It was obvious that even that small a kiss had her lighting up in response. They had a connection, she and Gene. The kind that poets used to celebrate in their works. And spats or not, the warranty on that connection hadn't expired yet.

"I wouldn't dream of it," he told her with a straight face. "As a matter of fact, I'm appealing to the businesswoman in you."

Melba looked at her husband, somewhat confused. Where was all this going? "What's that supposed to mean?" she wanted to know.

"Well, you're a savvy businesswoman, aren't you, Mel?" he asked.

"I like to think so," she said guardedly, watching her husband as if she expected him to pull a rabbit out of a hat or something equally as predictable, yet at bottom, magical. "Okay, out with it. Just where are you going with this?"

He built the blocks up slowly. "Being a good businesswoman means that you like to make money, true?"

"Yes, yes, we already know this," she told her husband impatiently. Everyone knew she loved making money, loved the challenge of running the boarding house efficiently. Having half a dozen adults—or so— in one place presented a great many hurdles to clear. But so far she was managing to run the place very successfully. "Get to the point. Sometime before next Christmas would be nice."

He approached the heart of this matter cautiously, determined to set up a strong foundation first. "A good businesswoman wouldn't allow personal prejudices to get in the way of her making a good-size profit."

Though Gene had argued against it, Levi had insisted on paying more than the usual going rate for the room. Most likely in an effort to appeal to the entrepreneur in Melba when she learned of his being there.

"A good-size profit," she repeated. "What are you getting us into, Gene?" she wanted to know, eyeing her husband suspiciously. Usually, she could rely on him to ultimately come through at the end of the day, doing nothing to jeopardize their way of life or their income. But he was making her nervous now with his vague innuendos. Just exactly what did the man have up his sleeve?

"Making money in what way?" she asked her husband when he didn't answer her question.

"By renting out the last available room in the boarding house for more than the usual rate," he told her with just a shade too much innocence to satisfy Melba.

"What are you trying to say, Gene? Come on, spit it out," she ordered. "Just who is it that you're renting out this last room to?" she demanded. And then, just before her husband could give her an answer, a look of horrified indignation washed over the older woman's features. "Oh no, you can't mean to tell me—"

Her voice had gone up so high that it completely vanished at its peak.

Wanting to get this out and then, hopefully, put to rest, Gene supplied the name that Melba seemed incapable of uttering.

"Levi. Claire's husband. Yes, I rented it out to him," he told her with an air of finality that let her know that she was not allowed to toss the young man out on his ear under *any* circumstances.

Melba glared at him. "Have you gone and lost your mind, Gene?"

The heated accusation did *not* surprise him. "Not that I know of, no. Last I checked, it was still where it was supposed to be. Right between my ears—same as yours, Mel."

"Then why aren't you using it?" Melba wanted to know. Because the man was certainly acting as if he had lost his mind.

"I thought I was," he told her simply. "Not to mention my heart," he added pointedly.

"Claire came here to get away from that man," Melba

reminded her husband. "Or did you somehow forget that little fact?"

"No, I didn't forget that," he replied calmly. "And since when did you condone cowardice?" Gene wanted to know.

The accusation instantly stirred her up. "What are you talking about?" Melba demanded heatedly. "I am most certainly *not* condoning cowardice."

He gave her a skeptical look. "Then what would you call letting her run away from her situation instead of facing up to it and trying to resolve it?"

Melba's scowl deepened, even though it didn't seem physically possible for it to become any deeper than it already was. She debated giving her husband the silent treatment, but the words were burning on her tongue, and she knew she'd have no peace until this was resolved and she said what had been—and still was—on her mind.

"You and I both know that she married too young," she said to Gene.

Gene gave her a knowing look. "As I recall, she was the same age as you were when we got married." Apparently, that little fact had escaped his wife.

"Don't compare us," Melba retorted. "I was years older emotionally."

He tended to agree with her—although there were times when he felt Melba was too young to make competent decisions even at this age. Not that he would ever dare to tell her that.

"Be that as it may," Gene told her, "Levi's a good man, Mel, and he loves her." It was clear that he believed the couple should take another shot at recapturing the magic that had brought them together and had existed in the first months of their marriage.

"Love alone never solved anything," Melba retorted.

Gene gave her a sly, knowing look. "Maybe not, but it sure gave us something to look forward to on those cold, long nights. Remember?"

Melba pressed her lips together and swatted her husband's arm. She could feel her cheeks warming. "Behave yourself, Gene."

Gene chuckled, amused. "You don't really mean that and you know it," he told her.

The impish, sexy look he gave her melted the years away and brought them both back to a time when the only aches they felt involved their hearts and striving to be together over her parents' wishes otherwise.

Rising from his side of the desk, he circled around to where his wife was sitting. Hands bracketing her shoulders, he brought her up to her feet before him. Melba was a small woman. Her bombastic personality made him forget that at times. In reality, Gene all but dwarfed her when he stood beside his wife.

Height difference notwithstanding, Melba filled up his whole world and had from the moment he'd first met her.

"Give him a chance, Mel," he requested. "Give *them both* a chance to work this out."

Melba thought of how hurt Claire had been when she first came to them. How hurt she still seemed to be. "And if she doesn't want to?" she challenged.

"I have a feeling that she does," Gene told her confidently. He saw the skeptical look come over her face and said, "They have a daughter and four years invested in one another, two of them as a married couple. They've simply run into some turbulence just like a lot of other couples, but abandoning ship isn't the answer. If they do, if they don't try to make this work, they'll never forgive each other—or themselves."

Melba frowned, looking at her husband as if for the first time. "Since when did you get to be such a hopeless romantic?" she wanted to know.

That was an easy one to answer. "Since I married the most beautiful girl at the dance," he told her.

Melba huffed and shook her head. Her husband's answer both surprised her and pleased her, but she couldn't let him see that. If she did, she felt that she'd lose the upper hand in their relationship.

"Fine, Levi can stay," she informed him. "But he pays rent like everyone else," she warned. This wasn't a charity mission she was running here, she thought.

Levi had been one step ahead of Melba, Gene now thought. Insisting on paying more than the usual rate had been very smart of him. "I told you, that was already part of the deal."

Melba looked far from pleased. The scowl on her face not only remained, it deepened, too. "One wrong move and he's out of here."

"Understood." Gene paused, allowing her to savor her moment before he decided to bedevil her a little and asked, "Define *wrong move*."

She was at a disadvantage and not thinking as clearly as she should, Melba realized. Her mind was already on other matters that concerned the boarding house.

She chose the vague way out.

"You'll know it when you see it," she snapped. "Now I have to see if Gina has gotten dinner started," she told him, referring to the boarding-house cook. To that end,

Melba shrugged off her husband's large, capable hands from about her shoulders. "One wrong move," she repeated warningly just before she left the room.

"Hard to believe that woman once had what I took to be a soft heart underneath all that," Gene said out loud to the other occupant of the area once his wife had left the room.

Turning around he looked at the young man he knew had been standing in the shadows of the hallway until the matter of his staying at the boarding house had been resolved. He was a little bit afraid of Melba—as were they all.

"But she does," Gene affirmed.

Levi looked off in the direction the woman had gone in. "She doesn't like me very much, does she?"

It wasn't a question so much as an observation on Levi's part.

"She likes you fine, boy," Gene assured him. "What she doesn't like is the situation. She's very protective of the people she loves, kind of like a lioness guarding her cubs. And there is no second-guessing her moves." He looked pointedly at his granddaughter's husband. "Consider yourself warned."

Levi nodded. "Yes, sir. And I appreciate you taking my side in this," he said with genuine gratitude and feeling.

"Not taking sides," Gene corrected the younger man. "Just facilitating things so that they can move ahead if that's what's in the cards. I think that little girl loves you," Gene told the young man who had come to him with his hat in his hand as well as his heart on his sleeve. "The problem is that she just got really overwhelmed by everything.

"People figure that getting married and having babies is no big deal—but it is. It's a *huge* deal, and there's a lot of adjusting to be done by everybody. You impress me as a sensible, hardworking young man, and I can tell that you love Claire—just like I can tell that she loves you. But she expected that life would go on being one great big party, and that's just not so. Marriage takes work and sacrifice. That's the part people forget about. If you find someone you love, there always comes a time when you have to fight for them. And that's a good thing in the long run because nothing that's precious gets that way if it's too easy."

Levi nodded. "I'm willing to fight for Claire until my dying breath."

"Nobody's talking about dying, boy," Gene told him, clapping one hand against Levi's broad shoulders. "Now come with me. I've got some things in the basement I need moved around and brought up to the kitchen. I could use a hand with them."

"Absolutely," Levi responded eagerly, wanting nothing more than to try to pay the man back in some small way for his kindness in allowing him this chance to win back the only woman he had ever loved.

Not a day went by when Claire didn't regret all the hot words that just seemed to fly out of her mouth on their own accord that fateful morning after the wedding reception. Most of all, she regretted throwing Levi out—and throwing her wedding ring at him. But she had been so angry and so hurt that he had preferred a stupid card game to being with her, she'd lost all reason. She'd been so furious, she was almost blinded by it.

At first she'd been so angry, she felt justified in leaving his phone calls unanswered.

But then he'd stopped calling.

Which meant to her that he had stopped caring. Because if Levi cared, he would have upped the number of his calls, not stopped them so abruptly. If he cared about her, truly cared, he would have come looking for her and wouldn't have stopped—not to eat or drink or sleep—until he found her. And then he would have gone on to move heaven and earth to win her back.

Since none of that, heretofore, had happened, nor did it appear to be happening, it just told her that she was right.

Levi *didn't* care anymore.

Well, if he didn't care anymore, then she didn't, either.

Except that she did.

She cared so much, she literally hurt inside. Which just served to make her feel as if she was a fool. Only a fool pined for someone who wasn't worth it, she argued over and over again.

What she needed to do, she told herself at least once a day, was to forget all about Levi and just move on, the way normal people did.

But how could she forget about him when every time she looked down into her daughter's face, she saw traces of Levi?

How could she move on when every morning began with thoughts of Levi? And every night ended that way, as well?

How could she forget about Levi when, in her head, she kept hearing his voice? Seeing his face? Everywhere she turned, she could swear he'd been there, or even *was* there.

She felt haunted, and with each day it was just getting worse, not better.

"Okay, today is the first day of the rest of your life, and you are going to stop this," Claire ordered her reflection in the mirror over the bureau. "You are going to take your adorable baby and march right out that door and into the rest of your life. A life without boundaries and without Levi."

Easier said than done, a little voice said in her head.

Still, she couldn't just live her life standing here in this room, staring at her reflection, too afraid to venture out.

"The hell I am," she declared out loud with enthusiasm.

So resolved, she took her baby daughter into her arms, rested Bekka on her hip and walked out of her room and into the rest of her life, or so she wanted to believe.

Unfortunately, as she all but marched into the hallway, she also walked straight into the person she was trying most to avoid.

She walked straight into Levi.

Chapter 3

Caught completely off guard, Claire shrieked.

Her breath caught in her throat as she felt her heart—
an organ she had become painfully aware of in the past
month—slam against her rib cage.

Stunned, she blinked, fully expecting Levi to fade
away, a mere wistful product of her overactive imagination.

He didn't fade away. Levi remained exactly where he
was, standing in front of her, holding on to her shoulders to keep her from falling.

He'd been hoping to run into her, but not quite like
this and definitely not so literally.

Reacting automatically, Levi had grabbed his wife
by the shoulders to steady her. That turned out to be a
good thing, seeing how if he hadn't, Claire would have

probably stumbled backward and fallen while still holding Bekka tightly against her.

Holding on to Claire like this did more than just prevent a very unfortunate accident from happening. The exceedingly brief contact once again brought home the fact that he'd missed her. Missed his wife acutely. Missed the sight of her, the *feel* of her. The very first time he'd laid eyes on her, he'd *known*. Known that Claire Strickland was the one for him. Known that there was something very special going on between them.

The chemistry that all but sizzled whenever they were close to one another was just too hard to miss and too intense to ignore. At that moment he'd realized that he would have rather waited forever for Claire than settled for anyone else, no matter how willing she might have been to be in a relationship with him.

Claire was completely shaken. It took everything she had not to visibly tremble. Ever since she had thrown her husband out of her life, her nights had been filled with Levi.

Filled with dreams of him, with memories of him.

Filled with overwhelming longing for him.

In the privacy of the room she and Bekka were living in, she'd allowed herself to cry over a precious relationship that she believed in her heart had died—and it was her fault.

Bumping into Levi like this, in the last place in the world she'd thought that she would see him, her first reaction was a surge of sheer joy, not to mention that every fiber of her being had instantly—physically—responded to the very sight of him. At that moment she would have thrown her arms around Levi's neck if her arms had been free.

The next moment her sanity, as she chose to view it, returned.

Luckily for her, she realized, her arms were filled with baby, so she couldn't go with her first impulse. That allowed her second impulse to take root and swiftly take over. Her second impulse belonged to the young woman who had felt hurt and abandoned that fateful night a month ago. It belonged to the young woman whose husband was absent a good deal of the time—not to mention that the one time he wasn't absent, he'd turned his back on her, choosing a stupid poker game over her company. That made the whole thing even worse because he'd abandoned her without so much as a second thought, as if she were some inconsequential afterthought in his life.

As that realization had taken root, Claire felt that she had to be worthless and unattractive in his eyes. This despite the fact that she had *always* made sure that she was her most attractive before he laid eyes on her in the morning. Even before she'd said "I do" she was determined not to turn into one of those wives who allowed herself to let her appearance go after the wedding.

To that end, Claire made sure that she was always up before Levi so that she could put on her makeup and be flawlessly beautiful when her husband looked at her first thing in the morning.

It wasn't always easy, but she'd managed. Her makeup was flawless. The same went for her hair. Not a single strand was out of place, despite the demands of motherhood, made that much more acute by a colicky baby.

Claire's first priority was to make sure that she was

just as attractive to her husband on an everyday basis as she had been the first time he'd seen her.

And where had that gotten her? Abandoned for the first night they'd had baby-free in eight months, that's where, she thought angrily.

The honeymoon, Claire thought not for the first time, was definitely over and so was, by default, their marriage.

Claire pressed her lips together, suppressing a sob. She just wished she didn't still want Levi so damn much. Levi was a fantastic, thoughtful lover. She had no need to go through a litany of others to know just how very special he was. Her heart—and her body—told her so.

But even so, she refused to allow herself to be a needy woman in that respect.

Refused to allow Levi to see the advantage he had over her.

Finally finding her voice, she demanded, "What are you doing here?" as she shrugged out of his grasp.

The second he was sure that Claire was steady on her feet, he dropped his hands from her shoulders. Making eye contact with his daughter, he winked at her.

Placing her hand so that she blocked the baby's line of vision, Claire turned so that Bekka was against her and not between them.

Levi squelched the protest that rose to his lips. The only way he was going to get Claire back was not to antagonize her any further. That entailed walking on eggshells, but, seeing what was at stake, he was up to it. He had to be.

"I'm staying here for a while," he told her.

Claire's eyes widened in disbelief. Levi had never

lied to her before—but he had to be lying now. There was no other explanation for what he had just said.

"No, you're not," she cried. Why was he messing with her mind like this? Wasn't it enough that he had ripped her heart right out of her chest?

"Yes, I am," he contradicted. "I convinced your grandfather to rent a room to me."

Claire felt as if someone had just literally yanked a rug out from under her feet and sent her crashing down to the floor.

Her grandfather wouldn't do that to her—would he? As early as this morning, she would have confidently maintained that her grandfather wouldn't rent Levi a room because he knew how much it would upset her—not to mention that allowing Levi to stay at the boarding house would effectively negate the very reason she was staying here instead of in the two-bedroom apartment that she had shared with Levi.

But now, looking at the confident expression on her estranged husband's face, she no longer knew if what he was telling her was a pack of lies—or actually the truth.

The look in her eyes dared him to continue with what she viewed as his fabrication. "Why would my grandfather do that?" she demanded.

It took everything Levi had in him not to just sweep her into his arms and kiss her, baby and all. But he knew he couldn't force this. For now he had to be satisfied with giving her his most sincere look as he pleaded his case, laying it at her feet. "Maybe your grandfather sees how much you mean to me."

Was he still doing this? Still perpetuating the lie he had tried to sell her in the wee hours of the morning when he had come stumbling in after the wedding re-

ception had long been over? She was no more inclined
to believe him now than she had been then.

Less, in fact.

There was no way she was going to let Levi think
that she bought his story.

"Ha! If I meant anything to you, you'd be around
more often, not working at all hours, going out of town
for so-called meetings at the drop of a hat and going off
to play poker when we were supposed to be spending
time together on our first free night in months."

"We *were* spending time together," Levi insisted.
"We went to the wedding together."

How gullible did he think she was? "*I* was in a room
with a crying baby while *you* were at a poker table surrounded by your friends and playing cards until dawn.
Just how is that being *together*?" Claire demanded hotly.
Bekka began to fuss, and Claire automatically started
to rock the baby to try and soothe her.

"Okay," Levi conceded. "But up to that point, we
were together," he reminded her.

Stressed out, Claire began to pat the baby's bottom,
trying desperately to calm her down.

"That *was* the whole point," she informed Levi.
"After the wedding we were supposed to spend some
quality time together," she insisted. "My grandparents
were taking care of Bekka. You and I were supposed
to spend a nice, romantic evening together."

"How was I to know that? You didn't tell me," Levi
pointed out.

Claire stared at him, stunned. He couldn't have been
that thickheaded—could he?

"I shouldn't *have* to tell you," she cried. "You're supposed to have *wanted* that on your own, not had me force-feed you your lines or hold up a cue card for you."

The only way he could think to backtrack out of the potential explosion in the making he saw coming was to apologize. So he gave it a shot.

"Look, if I messed up, I'm sorry—"

"If? *If?*" Claire echoed incredulously. "You most certainly *did* mess up, no *if* about it."

She was getting him exasperated again, hitting the ball totally into his yard and then not allowing him to retrieve it or hit it back. He should have expected as much, he thought.

Mentally, Levi counted to ten, telling himself that he had to be calm or he would wind up losing any chance he had to get Claire back.

To get Bekka back.

He missed them both like crazy.

"Claire," he said as evenly as possible, "I'm trying to apologize here."

Her eyes were like small, intense laser beams, trained on his every move. "I'm glad you told me because I wouldn't have known otherwise," she informed him.

"You're making it really hard to be nice to you," he told her, his anger getting the best of him, at least for the moment.

"Then don't bother," Claire snapped coldly. She was forced to raise her voice because Bekka had started to wail again. The increased volume only made the baby cry more. "Because it's not going to get you anywhere. Apologies have to be sincere, and I can see now that every single word out of your mouth is nothing but a fabrication, a lie."

"What are you talking about?" Levi cried, completely confused. "When have I lied to you?"

Claire tossed her head, wanting desperately to get away from him and wanting, just as desperately, to never have gotten to this point in the first place. This wasn't the way she envisioned her life when she'd watched Levi slip the ring on her finger two years ago.

"You said you loved me," she accused.

"How is that a lie?" he wanted to know. "I *do* love you."

"No, you don't!" Claire cried. "If you loved me, you'd be home more often at night and you certainly wouldn't have picked poker over me."

He closed his eyes, searching for strength. How did he get through to her? "That again," he retorted. "I didn't pick poker over you—"

"Oh, someone put a gun to your head then, telling you to deal or they'd blow your brains out, is that it?"

"It wasn't a choice between you and poker," Levi insisted. How could she possibly think that? "You're not in the same league."

Was that supposed to make her happy? Claire looked at her husband coldly, doing her very best not to allow her mind to drift, to make her think back and relive exciting, intimate moments with him just because of their proximity. "Thanks."

Her icy tone ripped through him, and Levi threw up his hands in total disgust. "I just can't win with you, can I?"

"No, because I see right through you," she informed him, her voice cold enough to freeze a cup of hot coffee. Just then, as if she was aware that she had lapsed into another long, quiet moment, the baby began to cry. "Now look what you've done. You've agitated the baby," she accused.

"Me?" he said, stunned at the way she could shift blame onto someone else's shoulders so easily. "You're the one who's shouting."

Claire made no effort to back down or back off. The baby grew louder with each passing second. "If I'm shouting it's so I can get the words through your thick skull."

He sighed, shaking his head and struggling not to have his temper snap. "You're impossible."

"Right back at you!" she retorted.

Levi strode away before he said something he was going to regret and couldn't take back.

"That's right," she taunted, hurling the words at his back. "Run. That's all you ever do. You're never willing to talk things out, to own your mistakes. It's just easier for you to run away from any confrontation."

Don't say it, don't say it, Levi counseled himself, afraid that if he did open his mouth, he wouldn't be able to control the words that would come flying out. There was no doubt about it. Claire knew how to press all his buttons. Press them until he believed that all the negative thoughts she was spouting and hurling at him were his own, and all the detrimental things that Claire had said against him she actually believed to be the gospel truth.

There was a child to think of, Levi reminded himself. He couldn't just put this all behind him and walk out. Besides, he didn't *want* to. What he wanted was his life back.

Not today, Wyatt. Not after that little run-in, a voice in his head mocked him.

But where did that leave them?

They were at an impasse, he thought. But one of them was going to have to give in if this was ever going to be resolved.

Walking away, Levi paused for a second to look over his shoulder at his wife and daughter. Even as angry as she made him, he couldn't help thinking how much he'd missed having them in his life.

How empty his life seemed with the realization that he didn't have them to come home to anymore.

That had to change.

But how?

He wasn't about to come crawling over to her side. After all, a man did have his pride.

But pride was a cold thing to take to bed with him, Levi thought unhappily.

Besides, there had to be more to this. She couldn't be this angry over a stupid poker game—could she? He needed to get her to do more than just shout at him. He had to get her to come around—and really talk to him about what she was feeling,

Squelching the desire to march back to her, take her into his arms and kiss her until she forgot all about this stupid argument and all the stupid things she was saying to him, Levi forced himself to keep walking.

This was all probably just a ruse on her part anyway. Her so-called accusations were just an excuse she was using to stay away from him because she was disappointed in him.

He'd failed her somehow, and by failing he'd inadvertently shown her that he just wasn't good enough for her. That he couldn't give her the kind of comforts she had grown up with. Even if he tried to approximate the

kind of life she'd had before she married him by working his way up the ladder and earning more money, she
complained that he was never home. And if he kept the
hours that she wanted him to, if he was home earlier,
then he couldn't give her any of the things she'd come
to expect in her day-to-day life.

Either way, Levi thought glumly, he was doomed.

He had to get his priorities straight. He needed to
find a way to fix all this and soon, otherwise, he was
going to lose her for good.

Levi didn't know how much longer he could put up
with living without his girls. Living without seeing
Claire and Bekka every day.

There *had* to be a way to fix all this. There just *had*
to be.

"Grandpa, can I see you for a minute?" Claire asked,
standing in the doorway of Gene's cubbyhole of an office.

Gene rose to his feet. For the time being, what he
was working on was temporarily forgotten.

"You, princess, can see me for a whole hour if you
like," he told her cheerfully. Joining them, he asked,
"And how are my two best girls this morning?"

Claire thought of her run-in with Levi a few minutes
ago. "Stunned and confused," she told him.

Bushy eyebrows drew together, forming a squiggly
line worthy of a fat caterpillar.

"Come again?" Gene asked. "Are you stunned and
confused, peanut?" he asked Bekka.

Responding to the sound of his deep, resonant voice,
the baby cooed at Gene, making him laugh with un-
abashed pleasure.

"Grandpa, she can't talk," Claire informed the older man flatly.

"Maybe you can't understand her, but she can talk," he assured Claire with a touch of whimsy. "Look at her expression," he said pointedly. "That little girl is definitely trying to communicate."

"And so am I," Claire said to her grandfather in barely curbed exasperation.

Faced with this situation, Gene sobered slightly. "Go ahead, princess. I'm listening."

Claire's frown deepened. "Levi is staying here at the boarding house."

He had a feeling that Claire knew she wasn't telling him anything that he wasn't already aware of. He didn't bother feigning surprise at her news.

"Yes, I know."

She stared at the older man in disbelief. How could he have betrayed her this way? Unless Levi was lying about this, too. She found herself fervently hoping that he was. Otherwise, this was really going to shake her faith in her grandfather.

"He said you rented him a room." Maybe there was some other explanation for his being here.

The next moment her grandfather dashed that slim hope. He nodded his head. "I did."

Her mouth all but dropped open. "Why?" Claire demanded.

"Well, I couldn't very well not rent it to him," Gene replied seriously. "That would be prejudicial."

Claire's big brown eyes widened. She couldn't believe her ears. "Are you saying you were afraid he'd report you to the sheriff?"

Wide shoulders moved up and down in a vague

shrug. He went with the excuse his granddaughter had unknowingly come up with.

"You never know," he told her.

"Grandpa, this is Levi," she reminded him. "He wouldn't do that. Levi *likes* you."

"He also likes you," Gene told her. "A *lot*. And all he wants is a chance to prove it."

Claire couldn't believe her ears. "You're taking his side, Grandpa?" she cried, appalled.

"Like I told your grandmother, I'm not taking any sides, I'm just making sure that both sides get a chance to be heard."

"I don't need to 'hear' anything," his granddaughter informed him. "Besides," she reminded the man, "weren't you the one who once told me that actions speak louder than words?"

"I might have said that," he allowed, then went on to remind her, "I'm also the one who said everyone deserves a second chance."

"If you mean Levi, I *gave* him a second chance." She was working herself up. "I gave him *lots* of second chances, and he blew them all."

"He's been skipping out on you to play poker on a regular basis?" Gene asked innocently.

"No," she admitted reluctantly. As upset as she was about this situation, she wasn't about to lie about it to her grandfather.

Her grandfather looked at her pointedly. "Then what?" he wanted to know.

She was referring to Levi going out of town for meetings and seminars as well as coming home late and falling asleep on the couch before she could get his dinner warmed up. But she had no intentions of going into all that now.

Besides, she had a feeling that her grandfather would be taking Levi's side in that, saying he saw nothing wrong in a man trying to better his family's lot by putting in all those long hours at work.

"I don't want to talk about it," she informed her grandfather and with that, she turned on her heel and hurried away to find her grandmother.

At least her grandmother sided with her, Claire thought.

Or at least she hoped so.

Chapter 4

Holding a fussing Bekka in her arms, Claire went in search of her grandmother. Between feeling betrayed by her grandfather and being subjected to her baby's incessant crying, her nerves felt as if they were stretched as far as they could go. She was beyond stressed out.

"Come on, Bekka. Please stop," she begged.

Bekka went on crying.

At her wit's end, Claire finally found the object of her search in the kitchen. Melba was going over a menu change with the cook. Gina tapped the older woman on the shoulder and pointed behind her.

The moment she realized that her granddaughter was there, Melba paused, telling the cook, "We'll talk later." With that, she waited for Claire to join her.

"Is it true?" Claire asked without any preamble.

"Is *what* true?" Melba wanted to know, peering over

the tops of her rimless glasses at her distressed grand-daughter. And then she smiled, tickling Bekka under her chin. "Hi, peanut," she cooed.

"I just found out that Grandpa rented out Jordyn Leigh's old room to Levi," Claire complained, refer-ring to the young woman who'd moved out last month after marrying her longtime best friend, Will Clifton, a rancher from Thunder Canyon. They'd apparently tied the knot during the reception of the wedding she and Levi had attended last month.

"Yes, I know," Melba replied matter-of-factly with a dismissive shrug. She wasn't exactly happy at inviting this turmoil onto her home turf, but maybe Gene was right. Maybe Levi should be given another chance to make things right between him and Claire. Her grand-daughter certainly wasn't happy with the current state of her marriage.

Claire had come looking for sympathy. That her grandmother had had knowledge of this beforehand—and *hadn't* warned her—all but left her speechless.

It was all she could do not to have her jaw drop open.

"You *know*?" Claire cried, surprised. "Then it's actu-ally all right with you?" She stared at her grandmother, dumbfounded.

Claire made no attempt to hide the fact that she felt deeply wounded by what she viewed as an act of be-trayal. It didn't matter that she was having ambivalent feelings about throwing Levi out, that part of her was actually happy about this odd turn of events that was throwing her husband and her together. What mattered was that the rest of her was more than a little upset by the same set of circumstances. Her grandparents were supposed to be on her side; they were supposed to be protecting her, shielding her, not tossing her headfirst into the lion's den.

Levi had hurt her, and she didn't want him thinking that it was no big deal. Nor did she want him to think that all he had to do was turn up on her doorstep and she would forgive him.

The truth of it was that she wasn't sure *what* to feel, but because of what she had told her grandparents—that she'd left Levi because he neglected her and took her for granted—she felt that her grandparents were supposed to be supportive of her. They were supposed to present a united front and most certainly shun Levi because of the thoughtless way he had treated her. Whether or not he was paying them rent didn't change anything. They most certainly shouldn't have allowed Levi to take up residence in the very house where she was staying.

What were they *thinking*?

"I didn't say that," Melba pointed out calmly. "Your grandfather did what he did—renting the room out to Levi—without consulting me."

Claire immediately jumped on what she took to be the rightful implication. "Then you can overrule Grandpa on this, right?" she asked eagerly.

Having Levi here would just heighten her ambivalent feelings, making her go back and forth mentally like some sort of a virtual Ping-Pong ball. It would be for the best to have him leave here. She needed her space so she could make a decision about her future. She couldn't do that with Levi around. Seeing him only reminded her how much she wanted him to hold her, to kiss her, to— He had to go, she thought, agitated. If he didn't, she knew she was liable to do something very stupid.

"You can tell Levi that he's not welcomed here and has to get out," Claire concluded.

Melba gave her a reproving look. "You know I can't very well do that, Claire. According to your grandfather, Levi paid twice the going rate for a month in advance."

"Just give the money back to him," Claire insisted as if it was the simplest thing in the world. "Tell him he has to leave," she pleaded.

Melba gave her granddaughter a long, thoughtful look. "Claire, your grandfather happens to think that Levi deserves a second chance. And I happen to think that your grandfather usually displays good judgment, so he just might be right about your husband."

"Ex-husband," Claire corrected, exasperated. Why was everyone against her? It was hard enough steering clear of Levi. If he was on the same floor as she was, she was doomed.

Melba paused. "You're already divorced?"

Claire flushed as she struggled to quiet her baby. "Well, technically, no," she admitted, "but—"

Melba took the baby from her, patting the baby's bottom and murmuring something soothing into the tiny ear. As if by magic, Bekka began to settle down.

"Then *technically*, you are still married," Melba told her, "which makes Levi your husband, not your ex-husband."

Claire blew out a breath, surrendering—temporarily. "Technically, yes," she conceded grudgingly, clinging to the word.

Melba studied her for a long moment. Claire was so different from her two older sisters. Those girls took after *her*, Melba thought. They were professionals, fo-

cused and driven, unlike Claire. She understood Hadley
and Tessa. Claire was harder for her to read.

But she was trying. Lord knew she was trying.

"What are you afraid of, Claire?" Melba gently asked
her granddaughter.

"Afraid of?" Claire repeated, somewhat confused by
the question. "I'm not afraid of anything."

The more she thought about it, the more convinced
Melba was that she was right. Claire was most definitely afraid of something. And she had a sneaky feeling she knew what.

"Oh, yes, you are. You're acting as if you're afraid of
being in the same room with Levi. As if, if you remain
around Levi, those walls you've built up against him
are going to come crumbling down around you, allowing Levi to come back into your life."

Claire waved her grandmother's words away. Indignant and upset at her grandmother's assessment of
her, she tossed her head. "You're just imagining things,
Grandmother."

Melba's eyes met hers. "I am, am I? Well, if I am,
it doesn't really harm anything to have Levi here now,
does it?"

Claire squared her shoulders. "I just don't want him
around here," she insisted.

"Why?" The single word seemed to burrow straight
into Claire.

She was used to being backed up and getting her way
when it came to her family. Losing that crutch left her
bewildered and at loose ends, not to mention very un-
steady. "Because I don't," Claire stubbornly insisted.

The look Melba gave her made her fidget inside.
Furthermore, she looked on with envy at the way her

grandmother seemed to be able to quiet Bekka down with no effort at all.

"That's not a reason, Claire."

"It is for me," Claire maintained.

"Well, sadly for you, you don't run Strickland's Boarding House," Melba crisply informed her. "Your grandfather and I do. My advice to you is either make the best of this—or make yourself scarce whenever Levi comes around. By the way, your grandfather is putting that boy's strong back to use while he's here, so you'll be seeing him around a lot during the evening hours."

She couldn't have been on the receiving end of worse news. After a full day of boredom and longing, her resistance to Levi would have the strength of shredded, wet tissue paper.

"I thought you of all people would be on my side," Claire lamented.

"I *am* on your side, Claire," her grandmother informed her in her no-nonsense voice.

Claire knew she was pouting, but she couldn't help herself. "Doesn't feel that way to me."

Melba allowed a small sigh to escape. The girl had a lot of growing up to do, she thought.

"Someday, when you get to be around my age, you'll see that I was right and you'll thank me."

Claire's frown deepened by several degrees. She felt utterly abandoned and at a loss as to what to do and how to proceed. "If you say so," she said without any sort of enthusiasm.

Melba's eyes met her granddaughter's. "I do," the older woman said with conviction. "It's either that," her grandmother went on, "or admit that I was right in the first place."

At this point Claire was utterly confused as to what her grandmother was referring to. "Right about what?" she wanted to know.

"That you were too young and too immature to get married."

Her grandmother certainly didn't pull any punches, Claire thought, dismayed. Well, she wasn't about to admit that the woman was right about that, because she wasn't, Claire thought fiercely. About the only thing she was willing to admit at this point was that Levi had no idea how to treat a wife, how to make her feel loved, rather than inconsequential.

And everything else was beside the point as far as she was concerned.

It felt as if everyone was ganging up on her. There were tears gathering in her eyes, and she had to blink hard to keep them from sliding down her cheeks. She focused on making the tears go away.

Taking a defensive stance, Claire raised her chin pugnaciously. "I was the same age you were when you got married. Grandpa told me so," she added in case her grandmother was going to dispute the fact.

As if to prove that she was a good mother, Claire took the baby from her grandmother and back into her arms. The second she did, Bekka looked discontented. Within moments, she began to fuss again. Claire's heart sank. What *was* it that she was doing wrong?

Meanwhile, Melba looked entirely unaffected by the comparison that her granddaughter had brought up. "Only chronologically."

"Well, yes, chronologically," Claire agreed, clearly puzzled. Her grandmother was trying to confuse her, she thought. "What other way is there?"

"Emotionally," Melba readily answered. "At the time," she recalled, "I was a great deal older than you emotionally—*and* I was fully prepared to take on the responsibility of raising not just one child but eventually four of them—in short order. You can't say the same thing," Melba said with what Claire felt was unnerving certainty. "Raising one child seems to have confounded you."

Inwardly, Claire shuddered at the very mention of four babies. As much as she loved Bekka—and she loved her a great deal—the thought of two children, much less four, had her breaking out in a cold sweat.

She couldn't deny the fact that Bekka was proving to be hard enough for her to deal with. It seemed to her as if, ever since the baby had come into her life, she hadn't had a moment's peace or even a real moment to herself. Every minute of every day seemed to belong to Bekka. Even when the little girl was sleeping, Claire found herself waiting for the next go-round of crying and fussing to begin.

Or, at the very least, the next round of breast-feeding to get underway. Her only function seemed to be to serve the baby.

Claire felt as though she was being held prisoner by an eight-month-old. Even when, in those rare moments Bekka wasn't fussing, it was only a matter of time until she would begin again.

There was no denying that Claire felt as if she was on some giant, endless treadmill that was only moving faster and faster with each passing moment.

And she couldn't keep up.

Bekka was becoming more and more vocal—again.

Why couldn't she get the baby to stop crying? Claire wondered with a barely suppressed ragged sigh.

"I guess it's time to go feed her again," she said, resigned.

But as she turned to go, Melba moved suddenly in order to get in front of her, her arms outstretched. "Why don't you let me take care of that?" she suggested then nodded toward the back porch. "Go get yourself some fresh air. Take a walk."

Claire didn't understand what her grandmother was saying. "Are you telling me that you're going to feed Bekka?"

Melba didn't see why her granddaughter looked so befuddled about this. "That's exactly what I'm telling you."

"How?" Claire wanted to know. "I'm breast-feeding her, Grandmother." She would have been willing to bet that it had been a very long time since the other woman had been in her position. "No offense, but you *can't* feed her."

"Yes, I can," Melba contradicted. Resting the baby on her hip, she went toward the refrigerator. Opening the door, she reached toward the shelf that had several bottles all prepared and lined up in a row. Claire could only stare at them. "I'll warm up some formula for the baby."

"Formula?" Claire echoed in surprise. They'd had this discussion earlier, and she had vetoed the idea. Apparently, her grandmother was every bit as headstrong as her grandfather had warned her that she was. "I thought we agreed that Bekka's too young for that."

"*You* agreed, I didn't. Bekka is the *perfect* age for that. What are you going to do?" Melba wanted to know.

"Breast-feed that child until she's ready to go off to college?"

"No, of course not," Claire retorted, rolling her eyes at the ludicrous suggestion. "But—"

"No *but*," Melba said firmly, shutting her down. "I raised four children," she said, citing her credentials. "Each of them was on the bottle by the time they were six months old. If you ask me, Bekka's way overdue. You don't want her being socially arrested, now, do you?"

"No," Claire replied in a small voice, confusion reigning all through her. What did one thing have to do with the other? she wondered.

Melba looked at her granddaughter knowingly. "Then stop using the child as an excuse."

Further lost than ever now, Claire could only stare at her grandmother. "What do you mean as an excuse? I'm not using her as an excuse."

Melba saw it different. "Oh, yes, you are." And then she gave Claire an example. "'I know what you're thinking. You feel as though you can't make a move anywhere, can't go out of the house because your baby needs you 24/7." Melba gave her youngest granddaughter a knowing, penetrating look. "The truth is, she doesn't. And you *can* leave her side here and there for a bit. So do it," Melba encouraged. "While it's very true that a baby does shake up your life, there are still parts of that life that belong exclusively to you, so reclaim them. Now go. I've got a great-granddaughter to feed," she told Claire, shooing her granddaughter out of the kitchen with her one free hand.

Claire stopped short just beyond the entrance to the kitchen.

Except for the few hours that she and Levi had attended the wedding, Bekka had either been in her arms or within arm's reach since the day she was born. The baby's crib was set up in their bedroom and during her own waking hours, Claire carried the baby around with her almost everywhere. If she did set the child down, she was always close by at all times.

To have her arms empty like this and to have Bekka out of her line of sight felt very strange.

It also, heaven help her, felt liberating, Claire thought.

So she did as her grandmother had suggested. Leaving the boarding house, she took a walk around the area, keeping close by—just in case she was needed. Old habits were hard to break.

It was August, which meant that, for the most part, the weather was hot and humid—not unlike the summer that she had first met Levi, Claire caught herself nostalgically remembering.

No, don't do that. Don't get all sentimental on me now, she chided herself. *That's not going to help anything.*

Her head began to hurt.

Admittedly, Claire thought as she walked slowly around her grandparents' property, she was very confused about her situation. Part of her felt she'd been justified in the way she'd reacted to Levi's absences, and especially to that night after the reception.

That was the part of her that felt that there was no turning back from what she'd done, throwing him out like that. Levi was going to come to his senses, decide that he could do a lot better than to tie himself down to a woman who was, for all intents and purposes, a shrew who could only find fault with him rather than to be grateful for the virtues he displayed.

There wasn't a chance in hell that this was going to have the happy ending she was hoping for. Levi was definitely *not* going to want her back after the way she'd treated him.

He was probably here not to try to win her back, but to make her regret what she had done. Regret it and see what she had lost by tossing him out.

That meant that Levi was probably here out for revenge.

Her headache was getting worse.

Not only that, but it felt as if there really was this internal Ping-Pong game going on, and her feelings kept going back and forth like the ball being lobbed over the net.

In all honesty, she didn't know just which side of the net the ball really belonged.

She needed to get back, Claire told herself. The baby had been with her grandmother long enough. She couldn't just pass Bekka along as if she was some sort of a doll. She was a flesh-and-blood child.

Bekka was *her* responsibility, not her grandmother's or her grandfather's.

Holding Bekka in her arms—even when the baby insisted on fussing—was the only time that everything felt even marginally right, Claire thought.

Until she could figure her life out, she was going to hold off on making any major decisions.

She had spent enough time away from her baby, she told herself, quickening her pace.

When she got back into the kitchen, Claire found that neither her grandmother nor her baby were there.

She quickly made her way around to the back of the house and exited through the rear door onto the porch.

Even as she began to push the door open, she heard the sound of voices.

One belonged to her grandmother, and the other voice—Claire cocked her head even as the answer came to her—belonged to Levi.

Moving quickly, Claire's first thought was to retrieve her baby. But even before she could reach Levi and Bekka, she could see that, instead of fussing and crying, the little girl was smiling and cooing.

There was some formula staining her dimples—dimples that the little girl had in common with her daddy, Claire thought ruefully. Despite Bekka's less than pristine appearance, she hadn't seen the baby looking this contented in more than a month—since the last time she had observed Levi and their daughter together.

He had a way with her, Claire admitted grudgingly.

Levi glanced up just as she approached them. He appeared to look just a tad sheepish, but he made no attempt to stop feeding the baby or to get up and surrender their daughter to her.

From out of nowhere, Melba came up directly behind her.

"They look good together, don't they?" her grandmother observed.

Claire fisted her hands at her sides as she turned toward the woman. "I thought you said you were going to feed her."

"I was, but then Levi came over and asked me if I'd mind if he held Bekka for a few minutes. A loving father shouldn't have to ask for permission to hold his own baby daughter," Melba told her, "so I let him take

Bekka and feed her." Small brown eyes narrowed as she looked pointedly at her granddaughter. "Do you have a problem with that?"

"No, ma'am, I don't," Claire replied quietly.

"Good, because you shouldn't." She looked from Levi to Claire, making up her mind. "All right, since the two of you are here now, I'll leave my great-granddaughter in your so-called 'capable' hands—try not to argue around her. She might be too young to talk, but she's not too young to hear or to be affected by the sound of raised voices and misbegotten accusations," Melba informed them pointedly.

The next moment the woman turned on her stacked heel and walked away.

Chapter 5

Gently rocking his daughter in his arms as he continued feeding Bekka her bottle, Levi silently watched Melba Strickland walk away.

"Tough lady, your grandmother." There was admiration in his voice.

"Yes," Claire agreed. "Grandmother's been known to be tough as nails."

But Melba only held his attention for a moment. The little beauty in his arms had more than garnered the bulk of it. He could feel his heart swelling as he looked at her. They had been apart for thirty days. How much had he missed out on in thirty days?

He had a feeling that it was a lot. Every moment was precious at this point of his daughter's development. He didn't want to miss any more.

"I can't believe how much she's grown," Levi murmured, more to himself than to the woman standing near him.

Claire's attention had been focused on her grandmother and the fact that the woman was truly acting as if she saw nothing wrong with Levi invading the boarding house like this.

She turned now to look at Levi quizzically. "Grandmother?"

"No," he laughed. Lookswise, Claire's grandmother hadn't changed a hair since he'd first met her four years ago. "Bekka. She looks like she's beginning to really fill out. And there's personality in those eyes of hers. She's going to be a regular heartbreaker when she grows up." As she continued to suck enthusiastically on her bottle, Levi smiled down into his daughter's face. "I've missed you, little darlin'," he told her. "Did you miss me, too?"

More than anything in the world, Claire thought. observing the way he was with Bekka. *And more than you'll ever know.*

With more than a little effort, she blocked and shut down her feelings. She was *not* about to own up to what she was thinking or say the words out loud.

That was all she needed to do, Claire upbraided herself. If Levi had a clue as to what she was thinking, he would just take that to mean that he could move back into their apartment and just like that, it would be business as usual.

Would that be so bad? she questioned herself.

Yes! Yes, it would be that bad. She'd be back to spending all of her time taking care of the baby and missing Levi while he'd be spending all his free time away from her.

Supposedly securing their future if she was to believe him.

She had to remember how that felt, missing him. Being taken for granted, she silently counseled herself.

But all that—staying angry—required effort. Effort that was hard to maintain when part of her kept longing for the touch of his hand, the feel of his lips on hers.

Seeing him with Bekka certainly didn't help.

Watching Levi with their infant daughter tugged at her heart in a way she'd never anticipated. The feeling sliced through her insecurities and her hurt.

It also did something else she hadn't anticipated.

It made her feel just the slightest bit jealous.

Her baby was responding to Levi the way she didn't to *her*. Bekka was cooing and making a host of other contented noises whereupon when she held Bekka, all the baby did was fuss and cry.

Maybe the baby really *was* picking up on her stress levels, Claire thought. But in that case, it also meant that Levi *wasn't* stressed in the least about their estranged situation.

And that, in turn, meant that he just didn't care about either.

If that was the case, why was she standing here, looking at him like some lovesick simpleton? Didn't she *know* any better by now?

Bekka was finally finished with her bottle. Setting it aside, he put the baby over his shoulder and patted her back the way he had learned surfing YouTube videos that were meant for new dads.

"You should put something on your shoulder," Claire advised coolly. "She'll spit up on it."

"That's okay," he told her, making small, concentric

circles on the baby's small back, intermittently patting it, as well. "The shirt's washable."

His heart swelled just holding his daughter like this. She felt so tiny, so dependent on him. So precious. He'd never thought that he could fall in love so quickly, so completely, and yet this little girl held his heart in the palm of her hand. He'd fallen in love with her even faster than he had fallen for her mother, he thought.

It went without saying that he would do anything for Bekka, anything to keep her safe and warm. And happy. He also didn't want to spend another day without her, much less another month.

There had to be a way.

Searching for a way to initiate "peace talks" with his estranged wife, he glanced up and saw a rather strange expression on Claire's face. One he couldn't really begin to read.

"What?" he asked.

Watching the way Bekka responded to Levi, she was beginning to feel threatened. And left out.

"I'd like my daughter back, please," Claire said primly as she reached for Bekka.

"*Our* daughter," Levi emphasized. "Bekka's *our* daughter."

She wasn't about to be lectured to by this absentee father. Not after all the lonely hours she'd put in, caring for Bekka by herself.

"Oh, so now she's *our* daughter, is she?" Claire demanded hotly.

"What are you talking about?" Levi asked. He could feel another fight brewing. Why did she insist on doing that? On picking fights when all he wanted to do was to make up and go from there? "She's always been our daughter."

She had her hands on Bekka, but Levi was still holding her. "Then why were you never around to help take care of her?"

"It wasn't *never*," he corrected defensively.

"Well, it certainly felt that way. Every time I could have used your help, you weren't there," she accused.

"That's because I was earning money to provide for Bekka *and* for you." Because he was afraid that Bekka could turn into the main component in a tug of war, he relinquished his hold on his daughter, albeit reluctantly. He would have been willing to hold her all day if he could.

Claire rested the baby against her shoulder while she glared at Levi. "Ah, yes. Saint Levi, working all those long hours to bring home a paycheck. Why is it that other fathers seem to be able to keep regular hours while you're gone from dawn to midnight, using any excuse not to come home?"

Now she was just making things up, Levi thought, frustrated. "That's not true and you know it," he told her, struggling not to raise his voice. He didn't want to make Bekka cry. "I got a promotion so I have to put in longer hours. I've got a lot of new responsibilities, as well as my old ones. If I start telling the boss I can't attend those meetings and seminars he keeps sending me to, he'll replace me with someone who can. Tell me, what good will I be doing Bekka or you if I can't pay for a roof over your heads?" he wanted to know.

He thought that would finally be the end of it—but he should have known better.

She narrowed her eyes as she looked at him. "At least we'd both know your face."

"Come on, Claire," he said in disbelief, "that's not fair."

"Fair?" she echoed incredulously. "I'll tell you what's *fair*. *Fair* is taking your turn walking the floor with a shrieking baby. *Fair* is taking turns changing her diaper, giving her a bath, watching out for her so she doesn't bump her head. *Fair* is giving me someone to talk to once in a while besides a fussing infant."

"Why don't you call your sisters, talk to them?" he suggested.

She could also just as easily have called her mother, but he had a feeling that her pride was keeping her from admitting to her mother that she found motherhood to be far more difficult to deal with than she'd thought—just as her mother had tried to get her to realize that it would be.

Claire was just too stubborn for her own good, he thought.

"What, you mean call them instead of you?" Claire asked in disbelief. "I love my sisters. But I don't have anything in common with them, other than the fact that we all have the same blood running through our veins. They can't understand why I'd want to get married—which in their eyes means tied down, and I can't understand why they'd rather go it alone—at least, I didn't understand why until our marriage fell apart," she amended.

She didn't know what she was talking about, he thought angrily. "It *didn't* fall apart," Levi insisted.

"Oh, no?" What universe did this man live in? "Then

what would you call this?" she demanded, waving her hand around to indicate the three of them.

Levi responded without hesitation. "A bump in the road."

"A bump?" she repeated, dumbfounded. "This isn't a *bump*, it's a whole mountain range."

He looked at Bekka. She'd drifted to sleep, but was now beginning to stir again. "Lower your voice," he ordered softly. "Before you make her cry again."

Why was *she* always to blame for everything? Especially when the fault was with him. "Maybe it's *you* that's making her cry again."

Taking a breath, he tried once more, even though he could see failure coming from a mile away. "Look, Claire, I'm trying to apologize here." *Again*, he thought with a mounting feeling of hopelessness threatening to cave in on him.

"Apologize?" she asked incredulously. "Is *that* what you're doing? Well, trust me, you're doing a really terrible job of it. As a matter of fact, this is probably the worst apology in history," Claire informed him haughtily.

With that, she turned on her heel and marched back into the boarding house. She didn't stop walking until she got to their room.

Still holding Bekka in her arms, she locked the door to ensure that Levi couldn't get in. Then she put Bekka down in her crib. Her grandfather had gotten it down from the attic when she'd arrived, announcing that she'd left Levi and was staying with them. She drew some comfort from the fact that, according to her grandmother, the crib had once been her father's. It gave her a sense of continuity.

Once Bekka was lying safely in her crib, Claire threw herself facedown on the bedspread and sobbed her heart out.

She hated this. Hated fighting with the only man she now knew she had ever really loved. Most of all, she hated thinking that there was no saving her marriage.

There had to be. But what if Levi decided that she wasn't worth his changing? What if he had been staying away from her on purpose? Using any excuse he could come up with?.

Her tears flowed faster. And her heart ached more.

"I see it's not going as well as you'd like," Gene Strickland commented as he came up behind his grandson-in-law.

The older man had been privy to the latter half of the exchange between his granddaughter and Levi, taking care to stay out of sight until it was finally over.

He had a feeling that one of them would need a shoulder to cry on—or at least a sounding board.

He wasn't entirely wrong.

Levi turned around to face the older man. "The way I'd like?" he repeated. "Sir, it's not going well in any manner, shape or form," Levi lamented, trying very hard not to allow despair to swallow him up whole.

"Strickland women are not the easiest people to live with at times," Gene agreed sagely. "They can be stubborn and pigheaded," he admitted. "But they can also be loyal and loving. Just don't give up, boy," Claire's grandfather counseled.

"Oh, I have no intentions of giving up," Levi told the man. "But I'm afraid the problem is that Claire doesn't think I'm good enough for her."

If he knew his granddaughter, the reverse was probably true. She probably worried that Levi thought he was too good for her. The family loyalty he'd mentioned kept him from saying that.

Instead, Gene asked, "Where did you get a fool notion like that?"

The origin of his insecurity in this case wasn't hard to trace. "Well, her parents had their doubts about me because I didn't have a college degree like she has."

"A college degree," Gene repeated, scoffing. "That's just a pretty piece of paper. It's what's in here—" he poked a thick finger in the middle of Levi's chest "—that counts, not some piece of paper with fancy lettering. Give me a man who's graduated from the school of hard knocks instead of one who's graduated from some snobbish 'institution of higher learning' any day. Besides, Claire's folks like you. If they knew what was going on, they'd be right here in your corner, egging you on. Telling her to come to her senses."

Levi looked at the man, stunned. He thought the whole town knew about their situation. Strangers were stopping him in the street to share their advice.

"Wait. Her parents don't know?" Gene shook his head in response. "That makes them practically the only ones who don't know," Levi said. "It feels like everyone in town knows and has an opinion about whether or not Claire and I should get back together. God knows I've heard enough of them."

Gene shrugged his wide, squat shoulders. "It's a small town," Gene told him. "Not much happens here by way of entertainment. Folks get bored. I've seen them make bets on how much snow's gonna fall on the first foot of the front step in front of the general store in a given amount of time."

The word *bets* caught Levi's attention. "Are they making bets on my marriage?"

"Wouldn't surprise me," Gene confessed. And then he waved his hand at the whole enterprise. "Don't pay them no mind," he advised. "What counts is how you and Claire-bear feel about your marriage."

Levi turned the nickname over in his mind. Claire-bear. Right now she seemed to be more "bear" than "Claire."

"How do I get her back, Mr. Strickland?" Levi asked unabashedly.

"Patience," Gene said. "And the name's Gene," he told Levi, offering him a friendly grin. "My advice is just be the best you that you can be and always make her feel loved. That's important to a woman," Gene emphasized.

"What if that's not enough?"

"It will be," Gene promised. "That girl was always falling in and out of love when she went to college," he recalled.

Was that supposed to make him feel better? "Then I'm doomed," Levi lamented.

"No, you're not," Gene contradicted. "Like I said, she was always falling in and out of love, but that summer when she came by and told us about you, she lit up like a Christmas tree. I swear there were stars in her eyes. I knew there and then that you had to be the one—and you were."

He sure didn't feel like *the one* right now—unless it meant "the one who got dumped."

"I don't know about that, Mr. Strickland," Levi said

quietly, then amended, "I mean, Gene," when the man looked at him expectantly.

"You ever hear that story about the race between the rabbit and the turtle, boy?" Gene asked sagely.

Who hadn't? "Yes, sir," Levi replied respectfully.

"Then you know that that cocky rabbit was all flashy and confident, telling the turtle he was wasting his time competing and should just pull out and quit right at the start. But that turtle didn't pay any attention to that blowhard rabbit. He just kept doing what he was doing, making his way to the finish line by putting one foot in front of the other and damn, if he didn't make it to the finish line before the rabbit, who was busy taking bows and losing sight of the prize. Be that turtle, boy," he said, daring him to be otherwise. "Don't give up until you cross that finish line. In the meantime, I've got more things I need brought up from the basement. You up for it?" he wanted to know, looking at the young man.

In his opinion, it was the very least he could do for the older man after the latter seemed to have taken a shine to him this way. "Yes, sir."

Gene clapped his hand on his grandson-in-law's back. "That's my boy."

At least her grandfather was on his side, Levi thought. Now if he could only get Claire to feel the same way…

Claire took her meal in her room that night, afraid that if she left it, she would immediately run into Levi, and she just didn't feel as if she was up to that.

The truth of it was, her resolve felt rather shaken, and she was afraid that she would just give up and go back with him. The past four weeks would have all been for nothing.

And everyone would think she had no backbone. She *had* to leave Levi—whether or not, deep down, she really wanted to.

Even her grandmother was giving her her space, Claire thought, not altogether sure she was happy about that turn of events. What if the woman had just given up on her instead? Then what would she do?

As it turned out, Melba gave her until the following morning to deal with whatever feelings she needed to deal with, then let herself in with her pass key.

Walking in, as big as day, she took Claire completely by surprise.

"You scared me, Grandmother," Claire cried, one hand covering the heart that had almost leaped out of her chest.

"I'm not that bad-looking yet," Melba said, disgruntled.

"I didn't mean that," Claire told her, quick to correct any misunderstanding. "I thought you were Levi."

"Levi's gone," Melba said flatly.

The news completely stunned her. "Gone? You mean he's given up?" The thought that he had devastated her. Didn't he care at all? One try and that was it?

"Why?" Melba asked, peering at her closely. "Would you be upset if he had?" Checking the baby's diaper, she made a quick decision and began to change Bekka right then and there.

"Yes. No," Claire amended quickly. "I just thought that since he was here, he'd try harder. Guess he didn't think I was worth it."

"Don't know what he thought," Melba answered

crisply. "Don't have the gift that way," her grandmother told her. "Just know that he had to go to work."

"Work? You mean he left for *work*? Does that mean he's planning on coming back?" Even she heard the hopeful note in her own voice.

"If he's not, he's gonna run out of clothes pretty quick because his suitcase is still in his room," Melba said matter-of-factly, tossing out the dirty diaper.

"Oh." With the immediate threat over, Claire went back to her ambivalent, confused state.

"What that means is that you can come out of hiding," Melba told her, picking the baby up and cradling her in her arms.

"I wasn't hiding," Claire protested.

"Listen to her, Bekka," Melba said to the baby. "She wasn't *hiding*," Melba repeated the word in an animated voice. "Sure she was, wasn't she?" Melba looked up at her granddaughter, her eyes narrowing. "You've got makeup on, don't you?"

"Yes."

It was only eight in the morning. "You sleep in that stuff?"

"No, of course not," she lied, knowing what her grandmother would say if the woman knew that she actually did wear make up to bed so that Levi would always think she looked pretty. It had gotten to be a habit for her. She just continued doing it automatically. "I put it on this morning," she said.

Melba looked her over with a critical eye. "Who are you getting all dolled up for if you're avoiding that love-sick husband of yours?"

"Nobody," Claire lied. "You really think he's love-sick?"

Melba nodded her head. "Worst case I've ever seen."

But Claire pursed her lips together as she shook her head. "I think you're wrong."

Very thin shoulders rose and fell in quick, dismissive succession. "It's a free country. You can think whatever you want to think, even if you're wrong." And it was obvious that she believed that her granddaughter was wrong.

"If he was so lovesick, then why did he stay after the reception and play poker with his friends instead of coming home to me?" Claire challenged.

Melba frowned, unwilling to go another round with this scenario. "You think on that, honey. When you come up with the answer, you'll be ready to be a real wife. Now let's go. We're going to get you fed and then we're going to put you to work. Aren't we, angel?" she asked Bekka.

Bekka cooed in response.

"Good answer," Melba murmured.

Claire sincerely hoped so.

Chapter 6

Claire looked around at her surroundings, more than a little puzzled when her grandmother had stopped walking and turned around to face her.

"This is the kitchen," Claire said in a quizzical tone of voice.

This didn't make any sense. She'd already had her breakfast in the dining room. Why had her grandmother brought her here?

Melba laughed shortly. "Very good. What was your first clue?"

In the past month she had grown rather accustomed to her grandmother's sarcastic retorts. Claire scarcely took note of the older woman's flippant question. But there was something that she knew did need to be asked.

"I thought you said that after breakfast, you were going to find some work for me to do." She did want to be able to pull her own weight—and to prove to her grandmother that she was a responsible adult rather than just an overgrown child.

"I did and I am," Melba answered crisply. Taking Bekka from her granddaughter, she told the baby—in a far sweeter, softer voice—"You, peanut, are going to keep your great-grandfather company and out of trouble while I put your mama here to work."

Starting to leave, Melba paused to look over her shoulder at Claire. "Stay here," she ordered. "I'll be right back. Talk to Gina while I'm gone," she suggested, waving a hand toward the cook.

Her voice softened just a touch again as she walked out of the kitchen, talking to the baby as if Bekka understood and was hanging on every word.

Feeling a little awkward, Claire looked around the kitchen and offered a quick, small smile to Gina. The latter short, squat, energetic woman was standing by the industrial sink, washing all the dishes, glasses and cutlery that had just been put to use during breakfast. Because there was nothing else for her to do, Claire picked up a towel and began drying everything that Gina had just washed.

The sound of running water and the clanging of dishes was still not enough to really do away with the silence hovering in the room, so Claire tried making polite conversation with the other woman.

"Have you been working for my grandmother long?"

She realized only after the words were out of her mouth that she had failed to include her grandfather in that question. But that was because of the two, it was her grandmother who was the more dynamic of the duo and the one who was always very quick to act.

That, consequentially, made the woman stand out. Of the two, her grandfather was the slow and steady one, the one who was always dependable, while her grandmother was the bolt of lightning that lit up the sky and just as easily scrambled the brains of anyone who had the misfortune of getting in that lightning bolt's way.

"About two months, now," Gina answered, raising her voice in order to be heard above the clatter. Working with pots now, the noise grew louder, erasing the need for small talk.

But now that she had started, Claire just continued talking. "She can be a little tough," she conceded, wondering if the other woman was holding back because she was afraid she'd lose her job if she complained about her grandmother's bombastic personality.

Gina looked at her over her shoulder. She appeared to be weighing her words before she said, "She's a lady who knows her mind and knows what she wants."

In Claire's estimation, the vague description could easily cover a multitude of sins and transgressions. Gina was apparently being diplomatic.

Claire nodded her head. "And isn't afraid to go get it," she added.

"Being afraid is a waste of time," Melba said, coming up behind the two younger women.

Startled, Claire jumped. She hadn't expected her grandmother to be back so soon. For a heavyset woman, she moved rather noiselessly. Claire flashed her a spasmodic smile that vanished as quickly as it had appeared. "I guess you found Grandpa right away."

"No, I left Bekka in the living rooom in the potted plant stand." Her grandmother said the words so calmly, for one terrible second, Claire actually thought that the woman was being serious.

And then she realized her grandmother was merely being sarcastic. "Oh, you're kidding. Wow." Claire blew out a breath, attempting to steady her nerves. "For a second you had me really going there."

Melba paused to stare at her granddaughter, and then she shook her head.

"What goes through that head of yours, girl?" she wanted to know. But the very next moment the woman held up her hand like a police officer directing traffic, except that instead of the flow of cars, her grandmother's intention was to hold back any flow of words that might be coming her way. "No, never mind. Don't tell me. I'd rather not know. If I don't know, it won't depress me. Just in case you're unclear about your daughter's whereabouts, Bekka is with your grandfather. Whatever other faults he might have, your grandfather is an excellent babysitter.

"Now, after you finish helping Gina with the rest of kitchen cleanup, she is going to teach you some of the very basics so that you can start helping her prepare the meals here."

Claire stared at her grandmother, stunned. They'd already had this conversation weeks ago. "Grandmother, I can't cook," she protested with feeling. " We eat a lot of…frozen food," she said lamely, knowing what her grandmother was likely to say about *that*!

About to leave the kitchen, Melba turned and fixed her with a look that seemed to penetrate straight into her bones.

"Can't or won't?" Melba challenged.

"Can't," Claire answered in a very small, helpless voice.

It was obvious by her grandmother's expression that the woman thought otherwise. "When you lose a limb, you *can't* grow it back. It's not possible. That is *not* the case when it comes to cooking. Just because you're currently burning water when you boil it doesn't mean that you're doomed to keep repeating that mistake. You *can* learn how to cook and you *will* learn how to cook," she instructed. "You just need to have someone who is good at it teach you what to do. Gina here," Melba said, gesturing toward the other woman, "is the very best."

Gina smiled, somewhat dazed at the compliment. Everyone knew that it wasn't often that the woman had anything positive to say. This was a very rare moment.

"Thank you, Mrs. Strickland. But I'm not really very good at teaching someone," Gina politely protested.

Melba turned to look at the cook. She had just one word for her.

"Learn."

And with that, Melba left the kitchen. Her very bearing indicated that she expected any miracles that needed to be called into play to be done so, efficiently and quickly.

Gina looked far from happy about the situation, but at the same time she appeared to be stoically resigned to her fate.

"Did you really burn water?" Gina asked her new apprentice.

Claire flushed and stared down at her shoes as she nodded her answer. She took no pride in the fact that the answer to the question was affirmative. She silently nodded her head, thinking that there were really a couple of excuses—one weaker than the next—to be said in her defense.

No one had ever gone out of their way in any manner to attempt to teach her how to cook when she was growing up. Coupled with that was that she had never had the slightest desire to learn. When she was growing up, there was always someone to do the cooking. She ate without giving the meal's preparation a second thought.

When she was finally on her own, away at college, she subsisted on take-out foods and the occasional microwave specials that required from ninety seconds to six minutes of microwave time, no more. The meals were basically satisfactory with no fuss involved.

When she first married Levi, she'd made a couple of halfhearted attempts at cooking before returning to her tried-and-true avenues of provisions: takeouts and microwaveable meals.

Occasionally, Levi would cook or they would go out. Or at least they had gone out before Bekka was born. Having the baby around changed almost everything, including her eating habits.

Especially when Levi was away on business.

Without giving it much thought, Claire subsisted on sandwiches and microwavable meals.

"So, what *do* you know how to cook?" Gina asked her once the last pot had been washed, dried and put away some twenty minutes later. Her tone of voice indicated that she really didn't believe that the girl standing next to her wasn't able to cook *anything*.

Claire took a deep breath before answering. She did her best not to feel inadequate. "Nothing," she answered honestly.

"O-kay," Gina said, taking the response in stride. It

was clear that she was looking for something positive to be gleaned from this. "That means there's nothing to unlearn. Good. We'll start out with a clean slate."

Claire waited a beat longer, holding her breath. Expecting something more derogatory to be said in reference to her lack of any basic culinary skills.

When nothing followed, she released a long sigh of relief. She'd thought that Gina would say something belittling or snide about the fact that she had reached her present age of twenty-four without learning how to even scramble an egg properly—hers came out looking as if they'd been uncovered in a war zone.

A *major* war zone, Claire thought ruefully, remembering her last effort.

"Okay, so this is what we're going to do. We're going to start with the very basics and build up from there," Gina told her, giving the impression of mentally rolling up her sleeves. "Do you know how to make mashed potatoes?"

Claire pressed her lips together. She was well aware that she had to be coming across like some sort of an inept idiot. But she didn't know enough to bluff her way through this. She was forced to own up to the truth.

"No," she admitted.

"After today, you will," Gina told her so matter-of-factly that Claire found herself believing the older woman.

It wasn't easy, and he was tired enough to briefly consider just going back to his apartment right here in Bozeman and crashing there after the day he had put in at the store.

A day that required double duty from him in order

to be able to leave the store at something approaching regular hours.

But the apartment was as hauntingly empty as ever. He couldn't endure that. It was almost like living with ghosts. After all, they'd had some happy times living in the apartment before things began to go bad.

So, even though he had to push himself, Levi made his mind up and was driving back to Rust Creek Falls. He was doing it in order to at least be sleeping under the same general roof as Claire and the baby.

One baby step at a time in order to get back to where he once was, he told himself.

With one eye watching for any telltale signs of patrol cars hiding in the shadows, hoping to hand out speeding tickets, Levi wound up making remarkably good time with no mishaps.

Parking his vehicle in the first place he could, he hurried into the boarding house and toward the stairs. He was hoping to be able to at least take one peek into Claire's room to catch a glimpse of her and the baby.

If she let him.

But before he could even reach the staircase, Gene saw him and called him over into the sitting room. The second Levi started to approach, he saw that the older man was not alone.

Levi cut the distance between them quickly.

"Thought you might want to say hi to your best girl here," Gene told him. "Or at least one of them." The man amended his own statement with a wink. Lowering his face so it was next to the baby's, Gene coaxed, "Bekka, say hi to your daddy."

Drained though he was, Levi all but melted at the sight of his daughter. To him she was a ray of sunshine in a disposable diaper. His heart was instantly warm and overflowing with love.

"How's the most beautiful eight-month-old girl in the whole wide world?" Levi asked Bekka.

He picked his daughter up from the very frilly bassinet she was lying in. Gene had gone out and bought the bassinet for her the very first time Claire had brought the baby by for a visit. He'd said he thought it was a very worthwhile investment, even though Bekka would be quick to outgrow it.

"You can always save it for the next baby," Gene had told Claire. He'd had a hopeful gleam in his eye at the time.

In Levi's overjoyed estimation, his daughter looked as if she was excited to see him. Bekka began to wave her tiny fists around while she started to gurgle and coo. A series of tiny, interconnected bubbles were cascading from her lips, formed out of the formula that she'd had earlier.

The resulting mess didn't bother Levi in the slightest. In all honesty, the entire sight pleased him no end.

Taking out his handkerchief, he wiped the drool marks from his daughter's mouth and chin.

"I see your great-grandpa's keeping you fed," he told the baby with a pleased laugh. Mission accomplished, he shoved his handkerchief back into his pocket. "Did you miss your daddy?" He asked the baby the question as seriously as if he was addressing a ten-year-old. "I hate leaving you, baby, but Daddy has to go to work so that you can have all the formula that you want."

Picking Bekka up and holding her close, Levi heard his daughter continue to make a few more noises.

One noise in particular had him suddenly freezing in place.

His lower jaw dropped.

Stunned, he immediately turned toward Gene to see if the other man had heard it, as well, or if his imagination and overwrought state were just playing tricks on him.

"Did you hear that?" he asked in what amounted to a hushed whisper, afraid that if he voiced the question any louder, the moment would be gone.

"I did, indeed," Gene confirmed, beaming because he was thoroughly pleased with this turn of events. He had always liked his granddaughter's choice of a partner for all eternity.

"She said 'Da,'" Levi cried, utterly thrilled beyond words. And then his eyes shifted back to Gene, his witness in this joyous matter. "She did say 'Da,' right? I mean, you heard her say it. It's not just me, is it?"

Levi's state of ecstasy tickled the older man. He identified with it completely. There was just nothing to compare to the moment that a child suddenly chooses to identify you and bond with that identification. He remembered how it had been with his own boys.

"No, it's not just you and yes, I heard her say it," Gene told him with a laugh.

Another thought suddenly hit Levi. "Is that normal?" he wanted to know. "I mean, do babies her age actually talk?"

Maybe she was some sort of a prodigy, he thought, his mind already racing and making half-formed plans.

"Not so's you can carry on an actual conversation," Gene told him, "but some babies have been known to say a word or two. Or at least make sounds that *sounded* like words." Gene ran his hand lightly over the back of Bekka's exceptionally soft hair. "And this little princess here did say 'Da.' We both heard her. It's a red-letter day. Bekka said her first word."

The moment the impact of the older man's last sentence sank in, the extremely wide grin on Levi's lips faded a degree, replaced by a look of concern. "You can't tell Claire." It was both an instruction and a plea on Levi's part.

Gene didn't quite understand why that was so important to Bekka's dad. "Because you want to be the first one to tell her?" he guessed.

Levi shook his head. "No, no, I don't want to tell her. I don't want *anyone* to tell her. I don't want Claire to know," he insisted.

Gene's shaggy eyebrows drew together over his brow like two hairy spiders. "I don't think I understand."

"When we were still living together in the apartment, Claire spent a lot of her time with the baby while I was working. Her whole life was centered around feeding Bekka, changing Bekka, bathing Bekka—you get the picture," he said, halting the barrage of examples. "For Claire it was almost nothing but Bekka 24/7. After putting in all that time with the baby, to have Bekka's first word be 'Da' instead of 'Mama,' well, it'll just devastate her."

That Levi was so concerned about Claire's feelings was nothing short of touching, Gene thought. "Maybe you're underestimating her."

But Levi apparently didn't think so. "Claire's got feelings, and those feelings can get really hurt," Levi told the older man. "I don't want to take a chance that I'm actually right about this."

"What if Bekka says it in front of Claire? That could happen," Gene pointed out.

"We'll have to take our chances. Maybe she'll say 'Mama,'" Levi said hopefully.

Based on his own children, Gene had his doubts about that. "So you really don't want me to tell her?" Gene questioned. After all, a baby's first word was a really big deal for her parents.

"No," Levi answered. "It's just better if Claire doesn't know."

"What's better if Claire doesn't know?" Claire asked, picking that moment to walk into the room. She had put in close to five hours in the kitchen under Gina's tutelage, and she was utterly exhausted.

But on the outside chance that she might just bump into Levi tonight, she'd hurried to her room to freshen up her makeup and comb her hair into some sort of an attractive style—just in case. She didn't want Levi to *ever* see her looking anything but perfect. She was afraid that he would be disappointed if that ever happened. Her wobbly self-esteem couldn't handle the blow.

Claire looked expectantly now from one man to the other, waiting for an answer.

"I thought it was better if you didn't know that I broke a couple of speed limits getting here from work," Levi told her, improvising on the spot. "I didn't get a ticket, but just the same, I didn't want you getting mad that I broke the law. I guess I was really anxious to get back to you and the baby," he repeated, giving her the most soulful look he could.

"Well, you shouldn't do that," Claire told him. "Speeding tickets are expensive." Then a hint of a smile broke through and she added almost shyly, "But I do understand why you did it."

And it secretly did please her very, very much.

Chapter 7

Maybe she'd been too hasty, throwing Levi out of their apartment—and her life—the way she had, Claire thought a few days later. She was walking through the quaint streets of Rust Creek Falls, pushing Bekka in the carriage that she and Levi had picked out together a week before Bekka was born.

She remembered the day clearly because she had literally *begged* Levi to let her get out of bed for what had amounted to a rare outing. The latter half of her pregnancy had been exceedingly difficult for her, and the doctor had recommended complete bed rest just to remain on the safe side.

At first, surrounded with books and all the things she'd wanted to catch up on, bed rest had almost been welcomed. It was certainly no big hardship. However, after three months of looking at the same four walls, day in, day out, Claire felt as if she was in danger of going completely crazy.

Since she'd been feeling stronger and by her own assessment, hadn't been feeling violently ill in a long while, she had begged and pleaded with Levi to take her outside of their apartment.

To take her *anywhere* as long as it didn't involve those same four walls.

Eventually, Levi had reluctantly given in and agreed. But rather than allow her to walk outside, her chivalrous cowboy husband had carried her into their flatbed truck. Since he was trying to cheer her up, Levi hinted that he had a specific destination in mind. She'd badgered him, but he had remained steadfast and secretive until they finally got there.

He'd driven them over to a store that dealt exclusively in baby items, from furnishings to clothes to toys. The owner, a friendly man named Jamie Pierce, turned out to be someone Levi had met and struck up a friendship with at one of those seminars he had been required to attend. The upshot of that was that they got a really good deal on the baby carriage.

What she remembered from that day was not the deal, but the fact that Levi had carried her to and from the truck, and that he had surprised her with the baby carriage, one she had seen in a catalog and had wistfully been pining after for the past few months.

The carriage had come unassembled. Levi brought the box into their bedroom so that she could witness the process and offer her suggestions from the sidelines while he stayed up half the night putting all the carriage pieces together. She'd fallen asleep watching him. All she knew was that in the morning, when she woke up, the carriage had been assembled and Levi had already left for work. A simple calculation told her that he had gone to work on—at most—approximately three hours' sleep.

It struck her as truly selfless.

He was a good father, Claire thought now as she crossed the street. And not exactly that shabby a husband, either. Not everyone would have gone out of their way like that to indulge a frustrated, housebound pregnant wife.

What had she been thinking?

The answer was she hadn't been thinking. She'd been too quick to allow her emotions to dictate her actions, she told herself. Before acting on a whim like that, she should have counted to ten—and then ten more. Hardworking, loving men like Levi were hard to find. Tossing him aside like that was crazy.

She just hadn't been herself that July Fourth weekend.

Chewing on her bottom lip, she looked down at Bekka. The baby was still asleep, lulled by the soothing feel of the summer sun warming the area around her, if not her directly.

It was time to start heading back.

But unintentionally, she had just crossed the collective path of a group of Rust Creek Falls' senior citizens, otherwise regarded by some as the town's opinionated, unofficial Greek chorus. They behaved as if they were qualified—and actually obligated—to express their opinions on everything that transpired in the small town.

Today was no exception.

"Heard you gave that no-show husband of yours

his walking papers, dearie," Blanche Curtis, an older woman sitting on the extreme left of the bench in front of the One-Stop General Store said to her. The woman had gray hair, more than her share of wrinkles thanks to an unforgiving sun and looked as if she would be perfectly at home playing the wicked witch in a revival of *The Wizard of Oz.* "Good for you," she cried encouragingly. "That'll teach him to take you for granted.

"These men," she continued, casting a critical eye toward her seatmates on the other end of the bench. "They tell you that you're the moon and the stars to them, then they get you pregnant and pretty quick, they lose all interest in you. 'Time to move on to new challenges,'" Blanche said in disgust, shaking her head. "They're all about the hunt and conquest, nothing else."

"I'm sorry," Claire said, unable to get away because the woman was holding on to the side of the carriage with her long, thin fingers, "do I know you?"

"No, but I know you," the woman told her with an air of mystery. "Blanche Curtis," the woman told her, sticking out her hand. "I'm a friend of your grandma's," she added, as if that explained everything.

"If you're such a great friend, why are you trying to mess with her granddaughter's life and give her advice she doesn't need?" the man sitting on the far side of the bench wanted to know.

"I beg your pardon." Blanche sniffed indignantly. The woman sat up a little straighter, as if that could help her repel any unwanted criticism from the man on the end.

"Don't beg for my pardon, beg for hers," the man said, nodding his head toward Claire. Leaning both hands on the ornate head of his sleek, black cane, he slid forward on the seat just a tad. "Don't pay her any mind, Claire. She's been a bitter old woman since the third grade when Michael Finnegan picked Rachel White to be his square-dance partner instead of her. You put that family of yours together the first chance you get, young lady," the man advised. "A baby deserves to have both a mama and a daddy."

"Billy Joe Ryan, you do an awful lot of talking for a man with no brain," the woman who had introduced herself as Blanche angrily accused.

"Now, Blanche, leave the poor girl alone," a third member of the unofficial town philosophers' group, Homer Gilmore, said. "Can't you see that she's thinking about doing the right thing? Everyone deserves a second chance, even a husband," he said with enthusiastic conviction. And then he turned toward Claire. "You give that man of yours a second chance, Miss Claire," he advised nervously. "You'll be happy you did. You don't like being alone, right?"

Claire stared at the man who she vaguely remembered meeting once before, at the wedding reception. He seemed to be very convinced that she needed to forgive Levi. Why would it matter to him one way or another?

Didn't these people have anything better to do than to sit around, giving out unwanted advice?

"Better alone than being with a man who doesn't care just how much he hurts his wife with his actions," the fourth member on the bench, a woman she'd heard referred to as "Alice" at the reception, proclaimed.

Claire could only take in this unwanted commentary on her life in abject horror. Did *everyone* in this town have an opinion on her marital state and on whether or not she should take Levi back?

The very thought unnerved her and made her want to run for cover. Didn't these people have *lives* of their own?

Upset and protective of her family's right to privacy, Claire asked, "Is that all you people talk about? The state of my marriage?"

"Lately, it's been pretty much of an equal draw between your marriage and the weather," she heard a deep voice behind her saying.

Claire whirled around, startled. Her attention focused on the four people who had just rendered very public their opinions about the very private matter of her home life, Claire hadn't been aware of anyone coming up behind her until just now when he spoke.

When she'd swung around, she was still holding on to the handle of the baby carriage and brought it abruptly around with her. The result was that she came within a hair's breadth of whacking a man's legs with the carriage.

Sucking in her breath, she pulled the carriage to her and away from the man.

"I'm so sorry," Claire apologized then added in her own defense, "but you snuck up on me."

"Wasn't planning it that way. I'm Detective Russ Campbell," he told her. Even as he spoke, all four occupants of the bench seemed to lean forward in unison, obviously intent on hearing what was being said. Campbell was just as intent that they didn't. "Listen, is there anywhere that you and I could go to have a few words?" He left the choice up to her. "I'd like to ask you some questions."

What possible reason would an officer of the law have to question her? Claire couldn't help wondering.

Was this because of something that Levi had done, because, to the very best of her knowledge, she certainly wasn't guilty of anything.

Except for cooking, maybe, she silently amended.

"What kind of questions?" Claire wanted to know. Out of the corner of her eye, she saw that the four people on the bench seemed to have moved closer to the side where she and the officer were standing.

"The kind you wouldn't want the people around here to speculate about," Russ wisely replied.

Claire lowered her voice. "You mean it could get worse than this?" she asked incredulously.

The detective laughed at the naive question. "Can it ever," he said to her. "I believe the old expression that best summarizes this is, 'You ain't seen nothin' yet.'"

That was all she needed, Claire thought, to have the whole town talking and speculating about something in her life.

As if she didn't have enough to deal with.

"Okay, you talked me into it," she told him. And then she remembered. She had obligations now. She didn't want to give her grandmother any reason to think she was behaving irresponsibly. It was a matter of pride. "But will this take long? I have to be getting back to help out with lunch. I'm staying at the Strickland Boarding House," she added.

An easy smile curved the cop's lips. "Yes, I know. I was just getting ready to go over there to see you."

This was beginning to come together for her. "Oh, so I didn't just bump into you."

"Not exactly," he told her.

Claire turned her back to the bench and its occupants, not wanting to give the foursome an opportunity to eavesdrop. "You could come back there with me," she suggested. "We could talk on the way."

Russ glanced over his shoulder and saw four pairs of eyes watching them intently. However, he seemed fairly certain that none of the four would be willing to rise and follow behind them for the sake of satisfying any latent curiosity.

Russ nodded. "Sounds good to me."

Without bothering to say goodbye or anything else to the foursome, Claire started walking back to the boarding house, pushing Bekka's carriage in front of her.

The detective fell into step beside her.

"What is it you want to know?" she asked.

"On the night of the wedding that you and your husband attended, did you notice anything out of the ordinary going on at the reception?"

She certainly hadn't expected the detective to question her about the harmless wedding reception.

"Out of the ordinary?" Claire repeated, confused. Thinking back to that night, she felt that the goings-on at the reception had all been slightly out of the ordinary. The reception was one big party, and parties were all about people cutting loose. Since it wasn't just a wedding reception but also the Fourth of July, that was to be expected—wasn't it?

"Yes." Russ tried rephrasing his question. "Was anyone behaving suspiciously?"

Claire thought for a moment, but nothing really came to mind. "No, I don't think so."

Russ became more specific. "Did you by any chance notice anyone slipping something into people's drinks, or into the punch bowl?"

That was something she would not have just taken

notice of, but mentioned to either Levi or later on to her grandfather. But she hadn't observed anything of the kind.

"No, of course not." Did the man actually think she would have taken that in stride? "I would have said something if I'd seen someone doing that." And then she replayed the detective's question in her mind. "Why? Do you think someone was tampering with people's drinks at the reception?" she asked, horrified by the very thought and what it implied.

Russ didn't answer her directly. Instead, he asked her another question. "Think back to that night. Do you think that anyone had a reason to slip a mickey into your drink?"

Claire blinked. "*My* drink? Why would anyone slip something into my drink?" she wanted to know. There was no reason for the officer to think anything like that. She wasn't a threat to anyone. Nor did she have any enemies or even friendly rivals. "I was planning on going home with my husband when the reception was over."

"But you didn't," Russ pointed out.

"No, I didn't." It took effort to say that without a trace of bitterness. "Levi decided he wanted to join in a poker game some of the guys were getting up."

"Was that usual behavior for him?" Russ asked.

"Usual?" she echoed, not sure what the cop was asking.

Russ rephrased the question. "Does he go off to play poker a lot?"

"No, as a matter of fact, he's *never* done that." *See, even you have to admit that it was unusual for Levi to walk off and leave you like that. Something's just not right here.* "Do you think that someone slipped him something?"

"Do *you* think that?" Russ asked, turning the question back around on her.

"I don't know," she said helplessly. "Levi seemed normal enough. I mean, he wasn't slurring or weaving or anything like that." She got back to the officer's question. "What reason would anyone have to spike his drink?" Claire asked.

Russ tried to make himself clearer. He was still trying to clarify the situation for himself. "I don't think he was targeted specifically. I think that a lot of people might have been affected by the punch being spiked."

"So the punch *was* spiked?" she repeated incredulously. "But why would anyone want to do that?" Claire wanted to know.

That was the giant knot he was attempting to untangle. "That's what I'm trying to find out," Russ told her. "Did anything strike you as being odd that evening?" he asked again. "Anything overall?"

Claire pressed her lips together, thinking. "Well, now that you mention it…*I* felt kind of odd that evening. I mean, I'm small and it doesn't take much to make me feel light-headed, but even I can hold down one drink, or even two, without having the room go spinning around."

Russ stopped walking and looked at her. "And did it?" he asked her. "The room, did it go spinning around for you?"

"Yes," she admitted, recalling the unpleasant sensation. "It did. What does that mean?" she asked him. "I mean, aside from the fact that someone might have tampered with the punch. Why would someone do that? What was there to gain?"

The officer shook his head. "I don't really know. Yet," Russ added. "But I will," he promised. "I will."

Claire couldn't wait for Levi to come back to the boarding house that evening. All through her chores, as she assisted Gina with both lunch and the evening meal, her mind kept going back to the fateful night of the wedding reception.

But nothing enlightening came to her.

The officer had told her that he suspected someone had tampered with the punch, causing everyone who drank it to behave erratically.

But she hadn't.

And Levi hadn't.

Levi hadn't behaved erratically at all. He had just tuned her out and gone off with his friends. That was behaving thoughtlessly, she told herself, not erratically.

Right?

Stop giving the man excuses.

But what if that *had* been Levi's excuse? What if Levi's drink *had* been spiked? That meant that he hadn't been himself that night and couldn't be held account-able for just leaving her like that to go play cards with his friends.

Okay, that was *that* night, but what about all the other nights? The nights that he was out late "working" or away altogether, in another town, at some so-called "furniture" seminar—whatever *that* was.

And what if it hadn't been a seminar? What if Levi was entertaining an out-of-town guest? A party of one, emphasis on the word *party*?

The very thought that he might be cheating on her, that he had gotten tired of her and maybe struck up a "friendship" with some other younger, prettier, *single* woman began to prey on her mind, making her conjure up a host of terrible scenarios.

By the time Levi returned to the boarding house that evening, it was rather late. Even so, he made it a point to stop at Claire's room and knock on her door. When she didn't answer, he tried again.

There was still no answer.

He knew she wasn't downstairs in the common room because he'd checked there first before coming up.

Had she gone back home? If not that, then what? He'd thought that they were making progress, taking baby steps, but still making progress. But maybe he was wrong.

A feeling of desperation began to mount up within him as he knocked yet a third time. If she didn't answer this time, he was going to go look for her grandfather and—

The door opened. Relief flooded through him, but it was short-lived.

Claire was holding the door ajar, placing her own body in the way like a human doorstop. Levi couldn't get in unless he pushed her out of the way, which he wasn't about to do.

"Detective Campbell wants to talk to you," she told him coolly. Her body language made it crystal clear that he wasn't setting foot into the room.

"Detective Campbell?" he questioned, trying to put the name to a face. He failed. "About what?"

Claire drew herself up to her full height. "About the night of the reception."

That still really didn't answer his question. "What about it?" he wanted to know.

Claire's eyes met his. "He wants to know if you think you were drugged at the time."

"Drugged? You mean he thinks I took drugs?" Claire wasn't being very clear about this, he thought. "You know I don't do that kind of thing," he told her.

When she didn't immediately respond, telling him that she knew he would never take any sort of unlawful substance, that he was far too responsible to do something like that, Levi was quick to swear an oath. "May I never see my little girl again if I took so much as a larger dosage of aspirin, much less some kind of an illegal drug."

She regarded him for a very long moment, as if she was weighing several things. In the end, she relented. Sort of.

"I believe that *you* don't think you took any kind of an illegal drug, but maybe someone managed to slip you something without your knowledge." Cocking her head, she peered at him, as if a different angle could somehow give her a better perspective. "Would you even know?"

Having had absolutely no experience with any of that, he shrugged. "I guess that depends on what it was and what the dosage was."

"But offhand? What did you feel that night, after the wedding reception?" Claire pressed, wanting to see what he would say to her.

He thought about it for a long moment, trying to re-create the time frame in his mind. "Maybe I felt a little hyper and somewhat wired." That sounded so lame, he thought, but that was the best he could describe it. "All I know was that I was looking forward to playing poker."

Her eyes narrowed slightly. Well, now she knew. "But not to being with me."

Damn, she was doing it again, Levi thought. She was putting words into his mouth. "I never said that," he protested.

"You didn't have to," she informed him, her hurt galvanizing her again. "Good night!" she cried. Pushing him back, she slammed the door right in his face.

Chapter 8

She was doing it again, Levi thought glumly. Claire was shutting him out.

He thought that they were finally making progress, and now Claire was giving him the cold shoulder every time they were within a couple feet of each other.

To his overwhelming dismay, this had been going on for a couple of days now, and he was pretty much at his wit's end as to how to win her back or even how to wear her down so that they were back to where they'd been just a few days ago.

He had thought that whatever set Claire off the other evening would have faded away by now. That they would be back to that cautious two-step they were doing, dancing around the issues and the sensitive feelings that were involved while trying to slowly work their way back to where they'd been before this whole wedding reception/Fourth of July fiasco had ever happened.

But they weren't. At least, Claire wasn't.

As for him, he was more than willing to go down on bended knee to ask her forgiveness if that was what it took. He just wanted to get Claire past this hurdle and back on track. Back to being his wife and the mother of his beloved baby girl.

It was getting worse, not better. He missed being with Claire and the baby like crazy. Missed the silent comfort of their ordinary, day-to-day lives.

But each time they'd cross paths, Claire would deliberately and pointedly look away, as if looking at him caused her more distress and annoyance than she could bear.

There had to be something he could do to change that. But what?

The thought that he couldn't think of anything really bothered him as Levi stood near the front door of the furniture store. Knowing that he had a full day of work ahead of him, he managed to plaster a cheerful, albeit very hollow smile on his face.

It was hard for him to keep his mind on business when everything inside him felt as if it was in complete turmoil.

But he knew he had to continue this charade he was presently engaged in. If he didn't—if he allowed the situation to get the better of him and make him fall apart—he'd wind up putting his job in jeopardy, and that was totally unacceptable.

He couldn't dare risk losing his job. Besides having worked long and hard to get to where he was, working here at the furniture store represented the only source of income that he had. Without any income, he knew he was *sure* to lose Claire and Bekka.

The thought struck him as being ironic, since it was initially his job—and the long hours that it required him to keep—that had torn his little family apart in the first place.

There were presently several customers in the store, wandering through the various artfully arranged furnishings that he had personally staged and set up. Levi kept his distance from the potential clients, instinctively knowing that there was nothing that drove customers away faster than a salesperson who hovered, or worse, one who offered a running commentary on whatever piece they might be looking at.

He'd learned early on that customers appreciated being given their space to view and debate before they came to their final decision. If they needed any assistance of any sort, he knew for a fact that they would seek him out.

All he had to do was wait and make himself available to them.

If he was only certain that the same theory was true when it came to Claire. He swore she was like the proverbial wild card that could pop up in a hand at any time. He had absolutely no idea what she was thinking or what she was liable to do. All he knew with certainty was that he had to win her back. As to when and how, well, that was anyone's guess. He certainly didn't have a clue. All he could do was make himself available.

And pray.

His cell phone rang. Pulling it out of his pocket, he answered the phone before it could ring again.

"So how's it going?" the feminine voice on the other end of the line asked.

For just a moment he found the familiarity of his mother's voice comforting. But he wasn't a little boy anymore, and the days that she could make all things right were long gone.

"It's not, Ma," he said honestly. "It's stalled."

There was a long pause on the other end before his mother told him, "It's only stalled if you want it to be."

He refrained from telling his mother that he was attempting to move heaven and earth—and not getting very far doing it. "It's not that simple, Ma."

"It's also not as complicated as you're making it, Levi," Lucy Wyatt told him. "First of all, you have to give yourself permission to be happy. That doesn't mean working yourself to death," she added pointedly.

His mother, he recalled, always worried that he was working too hard. "I'm not, Ma."

Lucy dismissed her son's words. "Oh, if I know you, you are, Levi. And I blame myself for that. I shouldn't have allowed you to turn your back on furthering your education by going out to work right after high school graduation. I know that you did that strictly to help out your brothers, as well as me.

"You're a good boy, Levi," she went on. "Your motives were pure and noble when you took that job. But mine weren't. I should have known better. I shouldn't have accepted the money that you turned over to me." A deep sadness entered her voice as Lucy said, "I sold out your childhood for a paycheck. What kind of a mother does that make me?"

"You are a great mother, and I was hardly a child, Ma," he pointed out.

He could hear the tightness in her throat as she said, "That's right, you hardly were. And that was my fault. When your father walked out on us, leaving me to raise and provide for the three of you, I let you take those part-time jobs, turning a blind eye to what that would eventually mean. I allowed you to put in all those long hours working while your friends were out having fun, being young. You never got that chance."

He didn't want his mother berating herself for what had been his decision. "They were just being kids, Ma," Levi said dismissively.

"Exactly! Something you should have had a right to be, too," she insisted.

He didn't want her to beat herself up for what he felt was one of the better decisions of his life. "I'll do it the second time around."

"The second time?" Lucy repeated, bewildered. "I don't understand."

He laughed. "They say that when people get very old, they regress to their childhood and start behaving like little kids. I'll get to it then," Levi told his mother. "Don't worry about it."

But it was obvious that she did.

However, since it was also obvious that the conversation wasn't going anywhere with this topic, Lucy Wyatt switched back to the topic that had initially prompted her to call her son in the first place.

"So how's the campaign to win back your touchy wife going?"

"Ma—" There was a hint of a warning note in his voice. He and Claire might be having their problems, and he knew that his mother was on his side no matter what, but he couldn't just stand by and allow blame to be heaped on Claire's head this way.

"Sorry," Lucy apologized with little enthusiasm. However, it was clear that she had no intentions of antagonizing her son, either. "How's the campaign to win back your wife going?" she reworded.

Levi refrained from blowing out a long breath. He didn't want to call any undue attention to himself from any of the people currently in the store. "It's not."

Lucy's voice was filled with tenderness as she made her son this offer. "Honey, would you like me to talk to her for you?"

He felt a chill streaking down his back at the very thought of what she was saying. "God forbid. It'll set Claire off. No offense, Ma, but you're not exactly a disinterested party here."

Lucy had never been anything but honest when dealing with her sons. She respected them too much as human beings to indulge in any verbal games.

"No, I'm not. I'm a *very* interested party. You're a good person and you deserve the best, Levi. I just get upset when I see you being treated with anything but the utmost love and respect," she confessed.

She was putting him up on a pedestal again, Levi thought. She had to stop doing that and get more realistic. "I'm not perfect, Ma."

"Maybe not, but then neither is she," Lucy said loyally. "And besides, there's a baby's happiness at stake here. Bekka needs you in her life." Emotion throbbed in her voice as she told her son, "I won't have Claire painting you as the bad guy."

"She's not, Ma. Really," he told his mother. "Don't take this the wrong way, but please stay out of it." In a moment of weakness and at a very low point, he'd told his mother about their argument and his subsequent—and hopefully temporary—change of address. He more than regretted it now.

It was obvious that his mother wasn't buying his protests, but being his mother, she also didn't want to argue about it since it clearly upset him.

Lucy cast about for another way to help her oldest son. "Maybe if I got together with Claire's mother and father and talked to them… If I made them see that they really needed to talk some sense into their daughter's head—"

That would just make everything that much worse, Levi thought. Didn't his mother see that? She wouldn't have wanted anyone butting into her private affairs. "Ma, promise me you won't interfere." He was all but begging now.

"All right, as long as you promise me you won't give up trying to talk some sense into that girl. I don't want my granddaughter growing up without her father—or her father's mother," Lucy added.

That makes two of us, Ma, Levi thought. "I promise, and Bekka won't, don't worry."

"But I *do* worry," Lucy told her son. "I'm your mother. It's my job to worry. Now promise you'll call me the minute you two get back together."

"Yes, Ma," Levi replied dutifully. "I promise. Look, I've got to go. I'm at the store and I've got a customer who wants to make a purchase—"

"Look at you, making a sale without saying a word," Lucy commented proudly. "I hope your boss knows what a prize you are."

Levi rolled his eyes. He knew if he let her, his mother

could go on like that for hours, and he loved her for it. But not right now.

"He does."

"Maybe *he* can talk to your wife, since I can't," Lucy said with a touch of exasperation in her voice.

He knew he had to quit now while he still could. "Bye, Ma. I'm hanging up now," he told her, and then terminated the call.

Although the store did have customers—and one had even looked his way—no one had approached him, indicating that they were ready to talk business. He'd only said that to his mother to get off the phone. He had the uneasy feeling that not only wasn't his mother going to cease and desist, but she was also most likely going to attempt to broker some sort of mediation between himself and Claire.

There would be no way he would even remotely agree to anything his mother had in mind because he was certain that he would be risking having things become even worse than they were at the present moment.

His mother, unfortunately, had that way about her. Besides, what woman wanted to have her mother-in-law butting in to her life?

All he could do, Levi thought as he quietly observed the customers meandering through the various displays in the store, was to make himself as readily available as he could to Claire and hope for the best.

When he finally came back to the boarding house that night, he was just as wiped out as he had been all the previous nights. The drive back to Rust Creek Falls and the boarding house seemed to get longer every evening. But even though he was having trouble putting one foot in front of the other, he still stopped by Claire's room, hoping against hope she would allow him a glimpse of their daughter.

He had even brought flowers with him to smooth the path.

This time, when he knocked on Claire's door, it opened immediately. That it did caught him completely by surprise, especially since Claire had been turning a deaf ear to his knocking—no matter how hard or how long—on the previous last two nights.

When the door opened Levi unconsciously squeezed the bouquet he was holding a little harder, but made no effort to offer the flowers to her. In actuality, he'd temporarily forgotten that he was clutching them.

Claire was wearing a tank top that didn't quite cover her midriff, and she had on a pair of denim shorts that brought new meaning to the term *cutoffs*. The whimsical fringes that had resulted from the so-called "cut" barely covered what they were intended to cover, flirting outrageously with the eye of the beholder. In addition, the somewhat faded material clung to her curves as if it had been painted on instead of hastily sewn together in some shop.

Levi had to remind himself to breathe. Periodically. And deeply.

And then he looked more closely at the expression on her face. It didn't look like the kind of expression a woman wearing a sexy tank top and pulse-accelerating shorts would have on her face.

Something was definitely up.

"Your mother called."

The three little words swiftly brought down the

world he thought he was about to enter in less than three seconds.

"Oh, God," he groaned, afraid to begin to imagine the damage his mother had caused. "I'm sorry, Claire. I told her I didn't want her getting involved or saying anything to you, but my mother has always been a very headstrong woman."

"Nothing wrong with being headstrong," Claire told him then added, "It's probably your mother's best quality." Claire paused for a second before she got to the crux of her statement. "She told me a few things."

"I can just imagine," he said, bracing himself. "Look, whatever she said, I'm sorry. I didn't put her up to anything. As a matter of fact, I told her not to bother you. But she was never very good at listening to what people were saying. Especially if it wasn't exactly what she wanted to hear."

"Why didn't you tell me that you didn't go on to college because you felt you needed to provide for your mother and your two younger brothers?"

He shrugged, fervently wishing that for once in her life, his mother could have just backed off. He knew that she meant well, but he was already having enough trouble with this estranged situation. He didn't want Claire thinking that he'd deliberately had his mother cite something he had done for his family. He'd done it because he wanted to and felt it was the right thing to do. He hadn't done it to come off as some selfless martyr.

"The subject never came up," he answered vaguely.

For just a moment his answer had rendered Claire speechless. And then she found her tongue.

"The hell it didn't," she retorted. "The subject was

there every time I came home from college, every time I'd nag you about going to college yourself."

Levi shrugged, uncomfortable with the very nature of the subject.

"I didn't think you'd be interested in hearing the story," he told her.

The real truth was he was afraid that if Claire knew the whole story, she might look at him with pity because his father had abandoned him, leaving him to struggle and do the best he could for the ones he cared about.

But in his heart, Levi had felt he owed it to his mother and brothers. That if he could make life a little better for them, then he should. It helped him as much as it did them to make life more tolerable for his family.

The same way he now did for Claire and Bekka.

Right now he just wanted to put this whole subject behind him. "Claire, I know it's late, but I was hoping I could look in on Bekka for a couple of minutes. I promise I won't wake her up."

For a second he thought Claire was going to turn him down. And then she laughed softly.

"You won't have to," Claire told him. "Mother Nature beat you to it. Bekka's been wide-awake for hours now." She looked at Levi for a second. "Maybe she was just killing time while she waited to see her daddy."

He looked at Claire. That certainly didn't sound like the sarcastic, flippant woman he had come to know in the past few weeks. He would have said that he was dreaming—except that he knew he wasn't.

He told himself to stop wasting time before Claire realized that she was being kind and rescinded the implied offer.

"You don't mind if I see her?" he asked uncertainly.

"No, I don't mind," Claire answered in the same quiet voice. She gestured toward the baby lying in the portable playpen. "Go on, it's okay. Since Bekka lights up whenever you walk into a room, maybe it might be a good thing for her if you spent a little time with our little girl."

"Thanks," Levi said to her with feeling. Then he slanted another look toward Claire—a longer one as he tried to puzzle things out—and asked, "How do you feel about my spending time with her mother?"

Claire arched one eyebrow as she regarded him. "I wouldn't push it if I were you, Levi," she warned.

He raised his hands in a sign of complete surrender. "Message received. You don't need to say another word, Claire. My question is officially rescinded," he told her. And then, because he prided himself on always being truthful with Claire, he added, "I'm a patient man. I can wait until you decide to change your mind about that."

Because he had really left her no recourse if she was to save face, Claire told him, "I don't think there's enough patience in the whole world for that."

"We'll see," Levi said softly, more to himself than to her. "We'll see."

Claire gave no indication that she had overheard him. But she had.

And something very deep inside her warmed to his words.

Chapter 9

"Looks like you're going to be flying solo today, kid," Gene said to his granddaughter when she opened the door to his knock a couple of mornings later.

Gene had become his great-granddaughter's official babysitter while Claire was busy in the kitchen, helping Gina prepare meals for the other residents at the boarding house. Melba told her granddaughter that as far as she was concerned, she was killing two birds with one stone. Bekka was well taken care of while Claire was cooking, and Gene had something meaningful to do that "kept him out from underfoot."

Melba herself saw to it that she was everywhere at once, taking care of the myriad details that went into running the boarding house.

"Ah, there's my little playmate," Gene declared warmly as he walked into the room and crossed directly to Bekka's portable crib. Half a second later, the baby was in his arms and snug against his chest.

Claire still marveled how her usually crusty grandfather transformed into what amounted to a bowl of mush whenever he was around her daughter. It was as if he became an entirely different person if he got within fifteen feet of the baby.

However, this morning it was what he'd said as part of his greeting that had corralled her attention.

"What do you mean by *solo*, Grandpa? I don't understand." Even so, there was a tight feeling of uneasy anticipation in her stomach.

Patting Bekka's bottom in a soothing motion, Gene obligingly spelled it out for his granddaughter. "Gina called in sick this morning, so you're on your own," he explained. "Who's my best girl?" he asked in the next breath, cooing at the baby in his arms.

Bekka gurgled in response, as if she understood her great-grandfather's question.

"Sick?" Claire repeated. That nauseous feeling was beginning to spread. "What do you mean she called in sick?"

Gently swaying to and fro with the baby, Gene looked at his granddaughter as if he didn't understand exactly what she was questioning.

"Just that. I don't know any other languages to use, Claire-bear. Gina said she was sick and she's not going to be coming in today, so you're in charge of making breakfast, lunch and dinner—since the guests have become accustomed to this. Now do you understand?" he asked.

Her knees suddenly weak, Claire sank down on the

edge of her bed just in time. A second later her legs completely turned to liquid.

"Oh, God."

"Hey, it's not so bad," he said, attempting to encourage her. "Your grandmother says you're doing terrific."

Claire raised skeptical eyes to the old man's face. "Grandmother doesn't use the word *terrific* to describe *anything*, much less my halting progress in the world of cooking," she pointed out.

"Okay," Gene conceded reluctantly. "So maybe she didn't use that *exact* word, but she meant that one. You know your grandma. If she's not happy with or about something, we *all* know about it. Fast," he underscored.

Claire still looked stricken about the idea of cooking all those meals by herself. It wasn't that the boarding house was teeming with people, but right now *any* people were just too many for her to deal with.

"I don't even know where to start," she confessed to her grandfather.

"In the kitchen would be a good place," Gene told her with only a hint of a smile on his face. "Come on, princess and I will walk you there, Claire-bear," he offered.

Taking in a shaky breath, Claire let it out slowly. Crossing the threshold, she waited for her grandfather to follow, then locked her door, pocketing the key. "I feel like I'm about to walk my last mile to the execution chamber."

"Have a little faith in yourself, Claire-bear," Gene encouraged.

"I do," Claire countered. "Very little."

As they made their way down the hall to the stairs, Levi opened his door. He was dressed in a light gray suit and blue shirt and was obviously about to leave for work. His attention was instantly captured by the minuscule parade and especially by the distressed look on his wife's face.

Rather than extending a typical greeting to Gene, whom he considered a valuable ally, or pausing to say a few loving words of nonsense to his daughter, his attention was completely focused on Claire.

"Anything wrong, Claire?" Levi asked the inane question, even though he knew there *had* to be something wrong. As a rule, Claire did not sport an expression that looked as if she'd just lost her best friend, but she certainly did now.

Denial immediately rose to her lips, but Claire refrained from saying the words out loud. There'd been a time when she and Levi had been not just husband and wife but best friends, as well, and it was to her former best friend that she now spoke.

"Grandpa just told me that I'm supposed to make breakfast, lunch and dinner for the rest of the boarders today."

Gene had already informed him of Claire's new duties in the kitchen, telling him it was Melba's way of making Claire more domestic. "I thought you were doing that already."

Another shaky breath escaped her lips. "Not by myself, I haven't."

"Gina's sick," Gene volunteered.

"Oh, I see." He searched Claire's face, as if it could answer things for him that she couldn't. "But you've been working with Gina for the last couple of weeks, haven't you?"

There was a world of difference between doing

something under watchful, supervising eyes and going it alone as she was now expected to do. "Yes, but—"

Levi didn't let her finish. "Was she satisfied with what you were making?"

Claire raised and lowered her shoulder in a vague response to the question. She felt as if she was on very shaky ground here.

"I guess so…"

He wasn't finished yet. "Did what you made get served?"

She didn't have to think; she remembered each occasion. "Yes."

He smiled, lightly patting her shoulder. "Then you'll be fine."

Claire was far from being sold. "I don't know about that."

It looked as if Claire was going to need more support than just a few encouraging words, Levi thought. He weighed his options, although he already knew what he needed to do. "Tell you what. If you want me to, I'll stick around and help you with breakfast."

"Breakfast is from 7:30 to 9:30," Claire pointed out. That was two hours. More if she factored in the prep time.

"I know," Levi replied.

She expected him to offer a barrage of reasons why he couldn't hold her hand in this, not continue to offer to stay and help. "You'll be late for work." Didn't Levi realize that?

Again he surprised Claire by telling her, "I know that, too."

Was this the same man who was never home? Who seemed to be married to his job and chose it over her time and again? "You're actually willing to do that?" she asked in disbelief. "You're willing to be late for work just to help me out?"

He knew he was risking a lot, but at the same time, if he hadn't proven himself at work yet, then he never would, and there was something really important at stake here. He realized that now.

"You're more important to me than work, Claire." Putting his arm around her shoulders, he said, "Come on, let's go downstairs and get started."

Because he was offering to stay, she didn't feel nearly as threatened by his job as she previously had. Her perspective began shifting.

"No, that's okay," Claire said. "I don't need you to hold my hand. Go to work. You've got a long drive ahead of you."

Reaching the bottom of the stairs, Levi made no move to leave. "You're sure you'll be all right?" he wanted to know.

Claire nodded. There was even a small smile on her lips. "Yes, I'm sure. Besides, I've got a feeling that if I start falling behind, Grandmother will be there to pick up the slack. After all, that was what she used to do and she's too much of a type A personality not to try to take over if she thinks I need help."

"Okay," Levi said, scrutinizing her face closely. "Then I guess maybe I'll see you tonight."

"Maybe," she agreed, echoing what was the key word in his sentence.

He had almost reached the front door when she called after him. "Levi?"

One hand on the doorknob, he turned around to face

her. Had she changed her mind about accepting his help after all? "Yes?"

"Thank you."

The smile that bloomed on his lips made his face positively irresistible. It took Claire no effort at all to remember the effect he had had on her when they were first dating. She could remember hardly being able to keep her hands off him—and the feeling had been deliciously mutual.

"Don't mention it," he responded. Nodding at Gene, Levi left the house.

He'd held his peace all during the exchanges between his granddaughter and her husband, but now Gene felt he had to speak his mind. "You ask me, Claire-bear, you married a right nice fella."

She couldn't very well sling mud at her husband right now. "I guess he does have his moments."

Gene chuckled. "That he does, Claire-bear. That he does."

She knew where this was going, and she didn't have time for that discussion. Not the time, nor the heart to try to untangle what had gone wrong with a marriage that looked as if it should have been a triumphant success from day one.

Claire squared her shoulders and turned toward the kitchen in the rear of the first floor. "Yes, Grandpa, but it's the hours I'm thinking about, not the moments. See you after breakfast—I hope."

"Like that boy said—" her grandfather paused to kiss the top of her head "—you'll do just fine. It's breakfast. Nothing special."

"Right," Claire murmured under her breath as she

took small, measured steps to the kitchen. "Nothing special."

She had been making breakfast every morning now since her grandmother had put her to work in the kitchen. Melba had taken the mystery out of making French toast, blueberry pancakes and Belgian waffles, as well as showing her a number of different ways to prepare and serve eggs.

That should be more than enough to get her through breakfast.

"I can do this," Claire told herself as she finally walked into the kitchen—a kitchen that for some reason felt a lot bigger this morning than it had on previous mornings. "Get a grip, Claire," she instructed herself sternly under her breath. "You haven't poisoned anyone yet."

She tied her apron on, grabbed her whisk and began cracking eggs.

The second the store was locked up for the evening, Levi all but raced to his car. He was behind the wheel and on the road to Rust Creek Falls less than five minutes after he had double-checked that the security alarms had all been set.

There was a huge bouquet of flowers lying on the passenger seat next to him. In order not to waste any time stopping for them on the way home, he had bought the flowers during part of his lunch break. He'd used the rest of his break to work so that he didn't have to stay after hours, attending to myriad details and making sure that everything was taken care of.

Depending on how the day—meaning her cooking debut—had gone for Claire, the flowers were either to celebrate her success or they were to console her if the meals she made hadn't gone as she'd planned.

Either way, he'd gotten her favorites. Pink and white carnations. A whole avalanche of pink and white carnations. If nothing more, he was hoping to bring a smile to her face—and to help make her see that not only was he on her side, but he was also always thinking of her.

Which he was.

He was also always thinking about their separation. It was going on much too long, and it was beginning to really worry him. Levi was becoming really afraid that if he didn't do something about ending it, it would wind up dragging on much too long and could eventually lead to the one thing he couldn't bear to have happen.

A divorce.

He'd already been painfully rejected once in his life when his father had walked out on his family. While he knew that there had been a number of issues between his parents, issues causing them to argue long and loud, he had taken his father's abandonment of the family personally, feeling that if he had just done something right, said something right, he would have been able to change his father's mind and the man would have remained with them. Would have been the father they all needed.

But he hadn't managed to say something right, *do* something right, and his father had taken off for parts unknown—even to this day. His mother would never say as much, never even so much as *hinted* at this, but he acutely felt that his father's walking out on them had somehow been his fault.

And it all came vividly back to him again when Claire had thrown him out and then, within less than a week, had taken off with the baby to live in another town.

If he hadn't come looking for her, she would have most likely remained where she was and they would now be headed for divorce.

What makes you think you're not still headed there? the devil's advocate in him taunted.

But Levi had to believe otherwise, had to believe that with enough effort on his part, he could turn things around. Could make Claire change her mind about leaving him.

However, even with that effort, even desperately *wanting* to turn things around, for his own sanity he was holding a piece of himself back. It was a gesture of self-preservation. He really couldn't bear to put all of him out there and then, very possibly, get rejected.

If that happened, it would, quite simply, just kill him.

He wasn't brave enough to do that. Not right now. Not yet.

Perhaps not ever.

This way, if she *did* reject him, and he hadn't fully connected with her, then she hadn't rejected all of him because she never *had* all of him.

It was contrived, but it was the only way he had of preserving his peace of mind.

As he drove, Levi kept sipping the triple espresso he had in his cup holder, wanting not just to stay awake but to be wired, as well.

When he reached the boarding house in what amounted to record time for him, Levi felt as if he was ready to go ten rounds with whoever wanted to defend the middleweight boxing championship of the world.

On arrival, he parked at the curb some sixty feet away from the boarding house and all but sprinted to the front door—twice. The first time he was about to enter when he realized that he had left the flowers he had bought for Claire on the seat in his car. He hurried back for the bouquet, then swiftly retraced his steps back to the front door.

Walking in, he was greeted by the lingering, tempting scent of recently fried chicken.

He smiled to himself as he inhaled. It appeared that the flowers he'd brought were going to be of the celebratory nature.

Dinner was over, but he knew for a fact that the refrigerator was not off-limits, at least not for him because he was not only a boarder here at Strickland House, he was also family. Even Melba had grudgingly acknowledged that fact after she'd gotten over old Gene's going behind her back.

Levi peeked into the kitchen, not to see if he could sneak a late meal out of the refrigerator, but to see if Claire was still there.

She wasn't.

That meant, more than likely, that she was upstairs in her room. He'd passed by the common room on his way to the kitchen and hadn't seen her. Process of elimination had put her in her room. Unless she'd gone out for the evening, and he didn't want to entertain that thought unless he really had to.

Levi took the back stairs two at a time, humming and hoping for the best.

Chapter 10

To Levi's surprise, Claire's grandmother opened the door to Claire's room when he knocked on it.

"Yes?" she asked, her small dark brown eyes taking slow, complete measure of him as she deliberately kept him waiting out in the hall. As far as she was concerned, he had hurt Claire—intentionally or not—and she had yet to forgive him.

She stood blocking access to the room and was also blocking any view into it.

Levi managed to keep down his frustration. "I came to see how Claire's big day went."

Melba's expression was quizzical. "Big day?" she repeated.

"She was doing all the cooking by herself."

"Yes?" she asked expectantly.

"She seemed worried about handling the responsibility, and I just wanted to ask her how it went."

"It went," Melba said with a careless shrug. She was proud of Claire, but too much praise might make the girl relax and stop making the progress she was making lately.

She clearly wanted him to leave, but Levi wasn't ready to do that.

"Well?" he prompted. He tried again to peer into the room, but Melba only moved farther forward, pulling the door behind her.

Cutting off any hope for a view.

"Well, what?" she demanded.

That's not the way he'd meant the word. "Did it go *well* for Claire?"

Melba gave him another nonanswer of sorts. "Her grandfather's taking her out to the movies in Kalispell to celebrate," she said, mentioning the town that was some twenty miles away, "so what do you think?"

"The movies?" Levi echoed in surprise. When they were first dating, he and Claire used to go to the movies regularly. At the time he was thrilled to find out that they actually liked the same kind of films: action movies that still maintained a believable premise. But when the baby had come along, that had all stopped. He began picking up extra hours whenever he could.

He'd done the wrong thing for all the right reasons, he thought now.

"That's what I said."

"Have they left yet?" he asked.

"Yes," Melba told him with finality. "They have."

"No, we haven't," the deep voice behind him told Levi. "Claire was just helping me find my string tie—a man likes to spruce up a bit when he's escorting a pretty lady out in public," Gene explained, and then he chuckled. "But then, I don't have to be telling you that, do I?" he asked Levi.

Standing to one side in order to be able to look at both Levi and his granddaughter who was in the hall behind him, Gene quickly put two and two together and he had a suggestion he felt was in everyone's best interests. Although he had a feeling that Melba wasn't going to be crazy about it. But his wife, in this case, wasn't his first concern.

"Listen, honey," he said to Claire. "As much as I'd love to go to the movies with you tonight, I'm an old man and I'm liable to fall asleep right in the middle of all the excitement. You want to go with someone you can talk with about the movie as you're going home."

"That's okay, Grandpa, we don't have to go," Claire demurred, trying not to look disappointed. It had been a while since she'd had an outing, and the moment her grandfather had suggested it, she'd gotten excited.

"No, I insist you go." He looked at the young man his wife had herded into the hall. "Levi, can I get you to make sure my granddaughter has a good time tonight?"

"Eugene," his wife said sharply, her tone of voice taking him to task and silently threatening him with a whole host of things in that single utterance.

"Yes, sir," Levi replied eagerly.

Gene smiled broadly. "Knew I could count on you, boy. All right, then, it's all settled. And of course the movies are still on me," he added, taking out two bills and pressing them into the palm of Levi's hand. "I insist," he added when Levi opened his mouth to protest. "Now go out and have a good time, you two. Have her tell you all about how good the food turned out today," Gene prompted, all but pushing the two of them together and toward the stairs.

"We need to talk, Gene." Melba all but growled out the words.

"Have an especially good time," Gene instructed his granddaughter and her husband. "Hate to think I did this all for no reason," he added quietly.

"What movie were you going to go see?" he asked Claire as they went down the stairs. In the background, they could hear Melba beginning to berate her husband's "damn fool behavior." Levi cringed inwardly.

"Along Came Jones," Claire answered when they reached the bottom of the stairs. She turned toward him. "Listen, we don't have to do this—"

If their relationship had a chance of healing, Levi knew he was going to have to face things rather than hide his head in the sand, hoping things would work themselves out. It was up to *him* to work them out.

"You don't want to go to the movies with me," he guessed.

"No, that's not it," Claire began.

That was all the lead-in he needed. "Great. Then let's go," Levi told her, brightening.

"You *want* to go?" Claire asked, looking at him uncertainly.

"More than you can possibly ever guess," Levi answered then paused by the front door before opening it. "Why would you ask that?"

She'd had the feeling that things were just disintegrating between them. "Well, Grandpa did seem to twist your arm—"

He stopped her there. "Not that I noticed. We used

to do this all the time, remember?" he reminded her, referring to all the movies they had gone to see.

A soft, sentimental smile curved her lips. "I remember," she said almost wistfully. "It seems like a million years ago."

"Not quite that long," Levi replied. And, with any luck, the time line would grow shorter. Taking special care not to ignore her feelings, he told her, "If you don't mind going with me, I'd certainly love to go with you."

Claire recalled his actions just that morning. Levi had been willing to be late for work just to help her out if she asked him to. The offer meant the world to her and had left a very positive impression on her.

She smiled broadly. "Then I guess we're going to the movies."

Levi grinned in response. "I guess so," he agreed. And then he realized that he was still holding the bouquet. "Oh, I almost forgot. These are for you."

She smiled as she looked down into the bouquet. "Carnations. My favorite. I have to put them in water," she told him. "Wait right here," she said. "I'll only be a minute." But before she ran to the kitchen, she paused long enough to brush her lips against his cheek. "Thank you."

And then she hurried off to the kitchen.

She was back in less than five minutes. "All ready," she announced.

"Me, too," he told her.

With his hand at the small of her back, he escorted Claire to his truck. Stopping before the passenger door, he appeared to be a bit self-conscious as he said, "Not exactly a royal coach," even though she had ridden countless times in the truck. He opened the door for her and held it, waiting for her to slide in.

"One person's truck is another person's royal coach," she answered, getting in.

He closed the door then rounded the hood to get in on his side.

Claire waited until he buckled up, then asked him the question that had just occurred to her. "Do you know where the movie's playing?"

"In Kalispell," he replied then assured her, "I'll find it. It hasn't been that long since we've gone to the movies."

"More than a year," she told him, "but I think you'll find it faster if I give you directions."

Levi started up the truck. "Fire away."

As she gave him directions, he smiled to himself. For the duration of this isolated interlude, they were a team again.

There was definitely hope for them, he thought.

Nearly two and a half hours later, they walked out of the theater, the last of the credits scrolling on the screen as the musical score built up to a final crescendo before the movie screen lightened.

Levi had parked the truck three blocks away out of necessity. All the available parking spaces close to the movie theater had been filled.

As they began to cross the street, Claire stumbled over something. Levi managed to catch her by the hand at the last second, keeping her upright rather than having her unceremoniously sprawl out on the ground.

Caught entirely off balance, Claire sucked air in, her heart temporarily launching into double-time.

His free arm went around her, steadying her further, "You okay?" he asked, his eyes searching her face for signs of acute distress. There weren't any. But there definitely was discomfort.

"I just bruised my pride, nothing else," Claire assured him.

"Maybe you should hold on to me until we get to the truck," Levi suggested. Not waiting for an answer, he tucked her hand through his arm.

She knew he meant well, but this rattled her own self-image. "I'm not an invalid, Levi," she protested.

"Nobody said you were, but there're rocks scattered all around here and it's dark. Do it for my sake," he implored. "If I return you with a turned ankle or worse, more than likely your grandmother's going to skin me—and with great pleasure."

Claire laughed at the exaggeration. "Grandpa wouldn't let her."

He didn't see it that way. "Grandpa, in case you haven't noticed, is afraid of her—just like everyone else is."

"I'm not afraid of my grandmother," Claire informed him. Levi said nothing, but merely continued looking at her. "Very much," Claire finally added.

Levi laughed. "Your grandmother does cast a big shadow for such a little person," he observed.

"She lived in a house with five men. She had to do something to keep from being outnumbered and overwhelmed by them."

"Well, if you ask me, I think she definitely succeeded." Pulling out of the parking spot and then the parking lot, Levi turned the truck toward the Strickland Boarding House. "Almost seemed like old times, didn't it?" he asked Claire. He knew he definitely was having more than just one nostalgic moment.

Claire didn't respond immediately. But when she finally did, she had to grudgingly agree that he had a point. "Almost."

Levi decided to nudge her memory just a tad more. "We used to do this every weekend, remember?"

Claire suppressed a sigh. "I remember. I also remember we used to be younger," she added as if that was reason enough to put the memory away in a deep, dark box.

"Not *that* much younger," Levi insisted.

She begged to differ. But there was another, more important reason why they really couldn't recapture what once was. "And without a daughter to be responsible for."

"That does change things a bit," he had to agree, although if he had a chance to change things, he knew he wouldn't. He dearly loved that little eight-month-old responsibility.

Silence began to take away bits and pieces of the dusky evening. It grew in width and depth until Levi felt he couldn't tolerate it any longer.

"How did it get to be this complicated?" he wanted to know.

She thought that point had already been made. "We had a baby."

"That was supposed to make it better, not complicated," he told her. "There are lots of people with three, four and even five kids."

"Not many," Claire insisted. In this decade, large families were the exception, not the norm.

He disagreed. "Enough."

She closed her eyes, not wanting to get into an argument and spoil what had been, up to this point, a really nice evening. "I don't know how those women do it."

"It's not just the women," he pointed out.

She turned and looked at him. "Ninety-nine percent of the time, yes, it is. The men, if they're in the picture at all, only get to see what life with a kid is like for a limited amount of time. Unless they're stay-at-home dads—something that there's few and far in between— they have no idea what it's like to spend all your time with a crying kid, day in, day out."

She looked at Levi's profile. He was being quiet. Had he even heard what she'd just said? Or was he simply ignoring her?

"Nothing to say?" she asked him.

"I was just thinking," he told her.

She braced herself. "About what?"

He turned to face her. "That maybe we should trade for a day or so."

She didn't understand what he was talking about. "Trade?"

"Yes." The more he thought about it, the more he felt they should give it a shot. "If I gave you a crash course on what I do and my boss okays it, you could come in and do my job, and I'd stay with Bekka and try to do what you do."

She noticed that he hadn't said he could do it, he'd used the word *try*. Did he mean it or was he just attempting to be polite about the situation? And why did he think she needed a crash course in what he did while he could just walk into her life without any effort?

"You sell furniture," she pointed out. "What's so hard about that?"

"I'm the store manager. That entails more than just

selling furniture," he told her. He went over only a few of the things he was required to keep tabs on. "That includes payrolls, dealing with customers' complaints and at times their various requirements, as well. It includes making sure that what the customer asks for, he also needs."

He was making it sound complicated. "What does that mean?"

"Well, for instance, I had a couple who wanted to get a five-piece sofa set—wife just fell in love with the model we had on the floor. But their living room was way too small to adequately accommodate it. Which is what I told them after I'd gone to look it over."

She couldn't remember ever getting that kind of service. "You went to their apartment?"

He nodded then explained, "That was all part of the service that helped put my store over the top in sales. I'm not saying that you can't do it, I'm just saying that you can't walk into my job cold. But I could coach you, get you ready—and then if you find that you're into something that you weren't sure how to handle, you could always call me and I'll talk you through it."

That sounded just like him, she thought. But it also didn't sound fair to him. "Isn't that cheating?"

That didn't make any sense to him. "Why would it be cheating? It's only common sense."

He was being so nice, she was starting to feel guilty not only about the way she'd been treating him but even about the way she'd resented him for being able to leave each morning while she felt stuck, tethered to their apartment while dancing attendance to a colicky, teething baby.

She was being quiet again, Levi noted. That wasn't usually a good sign. Luckily, they were home.

He pulled up into an available spot. "We're here," he announced.

Claire blinked. It took a couple of seconds for his words to sink in. When she looked outside the truck, she saw that they had returned to the boarding house without her even realizing it.

It was intensely dark, with only a couple of lights still on within the house. Beyond that, there was no illumination.

They might as well have been the last two people left alive in the world for all the signs of life she saw outside the car window.

Which was possibly why she did what she did next.

Chapter 11

Although Levi had parked his truck and turned off the ignition, neither he nor Claire made any attempt to get out of the vehicle.

It was as if they both knew that the second either one of them opened the door on their side and got out, the evening—and the almost magical time that they had just spent with one another, recapturing "old times"— would dissolve into the night.

And when it did, they would once again be that separated couple contemplating the very real possibility of turning their separation into a permanent state by getting a divorce.

Claire didn't want to face any decisions, didn't want to think of what might be ahead or dwell on just what she had already lost and stood to lose if she went forward with her initial threat.

Quite simply, she wanted to preserve this moment in time, wanted nothing more than to have it go on indefinitely.

Wanted, she realized, Levi to want her as much as she found herself wanting him. If possible, she was more attracted to him now, at this moment, than she had been when she'd first met him.

It was with this on her mind that she leaned into Levi. Not by much, but then, considering the limited space around her, it didn't really take all that much. Even a fraction of an inch brought her into his space, brought her closer to his aura.

Taking a steadying breath, she detected just the slightest hint of the soap that Levi favored.

Something clean and woodsy.

His eyes on hers, Levi matched her, small move for small move. Which was how their lips came to occupy almost the exact same space.

They couldn't avoid having them touch.

Ordinarily, given the circumstances, Claire knew she should have pulled her head back, thereby taking her lips out of range and deliberately avoiding his. She would have, with that one simple movement, evacuated the enticing danger zone.

Except that she wanted very much to be in that danger zone. Wanted very much to be kissed by Levi. Wanted, more than anything, to return that kiss a hundredfold.

More.

Her soul had missed him more than any words could begin to describe.

Her heart pounding, she moved *into* the kiss rather than away from it. And, as she moved into it, she kissed her estranged husband with every fiber of her being. Kissed him as if she had never thrown him and her wedding ring out onto the street.

Kissed him as if she still loved him.

Because she did.

Dazed, Levi felt as though he had just been struck by lightning—but he was definitely *not* complaining. If anything, he would have been celebrating and doing handstands—if he wasn't presently and deliciously otherwise occupied.

Very occupied.

Feeling a huge, electrical-like surge throughout his entire body, he leaned in over the truck's gearshift, taking no note of it as he took Claire into his arms.

Holding on to her because letting her go meant losing his soul.

Levi could feel his body heating up, could feel himself yearning for Claire the way he hadn't thought was humanly possible. A very large part of him felt that he wouldn't be able to breathe if he couldn't have her.

Get a grip, Levi, he sternly upbraided himself.

He didn't want to be guilty of overpowering her. Of making her succumb to the moment if she was only going to regret it later. There was more than just sex involved here, and he didn't want her thinking that *that* was what was foremost in his mind.

As much as his body felt incomplete without being sealed to hers, he didn't want to risk losing her permanently if he let her believe that all he wanted was to make love with her and that he would do anything that was necessary, would move any obstacle that might be in his way, to *get* his way with her.

He loved her too much for that.

And it was that very love that made him vulnerable to her.

Claire felt herself weakening more and more by the second. Within a couple more seconds, she knew she'd be all ready and primed to be taken by him right here, never mind that they were parked in front of her grandparents' boarding house.

There was too much riding on this for her to completely give in to the demands she felt inside. Doing so would only cloud the issue—attaining a better relationship in which they could communicate well enough to be able not to have things blow up between them the way they had since the July Fourth wedding. So she kissed the only man she had ever truly loved once more for the road—a very steamy, rocky road—and then she pulled back, albeit very reluctantly.

Clearing her throat so that she could sound like a human being when she spoke, rather than squeaking, Claire whispered, "I think we'd better be going in."

She was right.

He knew she was right, even as every muscle in his body loathed to back away. But there was no way, no matter how he felt, that he was about to force himself on her. It didn't matter that she was his wife, that in their brief time together they had made love countless times and with utter, complete abandon.

That was then, this was now.

This time around, she had backed away, indicating, by example, that he had to do the same. He wasn't about to cast a shadow on what they'd had—what he hoped they *would* have again—by pretending not to hear her or just getting it into his head to override her and simply take what was his.

Because that would destroy what they'd had and what he wanted them to have again.

Much as it pained him down to the very bottom of his soul, there were new rules to follow—and Levi was determined that he was going to follow them. This while fervently praying that she would come back to him soon because holding out this way for long was bordering on sainthood.

"Whatever you want, Claire," he replied solemnly.

Whatever I want, Claire thought, repeating his words in her head.

What I want is to rip your clothes off with my teeth and have you do the same to mine.

What I want is to make wild, passionate love with you until neither one of us can breathe.

What I want is for none of this to have ever happened so that we could just go on the way we had once been.

But that wasn't the reality they were faced with, Claire was forced to admit. She *had* thrown him out, and she *had* pulled up stakes and moved away with Bekka. She couldn't just undo that in the blink of an eye without looking like some kind of a flighty, bird-brained idiot. Why would he want to stay with a flighty, quick-tempered woman, even if her makeup was always perfectly applied and she never had a hair out of place?

The simple answer was that he wouldn't.

Pulling herself together, burying her desire until such time as she could effectively handle it and perhaps even give it a voice in her life, Claire nodded in response and opened the door on her side.

It would have been helpful if a blast of cold air had hit her, making her shiver and focus on trying to keep warm. But this was August, so the only air she detected was on the hot side, and it was more of a waft than a blast.

That was all she needed. The sensation of heat traveling up and down her body— reminding her how she had felt whenever Levi touched her and made her his.

Closing the passenger door behind her, Claire let out a long, shaky breath. And then she squared her shoulders and headed for the boarding house front door. She heard Levi getting out behind her on the driver's side.

"You don't have to walk me to my door," she told him without turning around.

Her very real fear was that if he came in with her, somehow or other, she would wind up pulling him into her room, ruining all her good intentions.

"I'm not," Levi answered. When she turned to look at him quizzically, as if she had just caught him in a lie, he pointed out, "I live here, too, remember?"

She'd actually forgotten for a second. What was the matter with her? She was too young to be courting senility.

Apparently, Claire decided, her rampant desires were wiping out everything else, including what there was of her thought process.

"Yes," she replied quietly. "I remember."

The hall light was the only lamp lit on the first floor, a clear indication that everyone had either gone to bed— or was making an evening of it somewhere else.

Claire went up the stairs to her room.

She was aware of Levi following her up the stairs. She knew he was just going to his room, which was down the hall from hers, but even so, she was waging a battle within herself, wrestling with the pros and cons of inviting Levi into her room for just a few minutes to see the baby. After all, it was his right.

Claire knew that he and Bekka would both enjoy the interaction. No matter what went down between her and Levi, good and bad, she couldn't deny that he was a fantastic father and that Bekka still lit up like a lighthouse beacon whenever he walked into their daughter's room.

But in her own present state, Claire thought, she lit up, as well.

Maybe even more so, Claire thought in semidespair.

Turning at the top of the stairs, in this position she was eye to eye with Levi. "If Bekka's awake, do you want to stop in for a minute and see her before you go to bed?"

It was *his* turn to light up like that lighthouse beacon.

"If you don't mind," he prefaced. "Sure."

He had to admit, ever since she had thrown him out, he was carrying around a very real fear that even if they got back together, she could easily reject him again. He had to safeguard himself from that.

Because emotionally he just couldn't bear another rejection.

Claire looked at him, puzzled. "Why should I mind? I just asked if you wanted to. If I *minded*, I wouldn't have made the offer."

"No," he agreed, thinking it over. She wouldn't play games where Bekka was concerned. "I guess you wouldn't have. Thanks," he told her with a wide smile.

Levi could always undo her with his smile. "Don't mention it," she murmured, feeling her heart beating in triple time.

The first thing she saw the second she unlocked her door was her grandfather. Gene quickly crossed over and told her in a whisper, "She just dropped off to sleep about ten minutes ago. That means you can get in about two hours of uninterrupted sleep before she's ready to roll again." Her grandfather looked from his granddaughter to the young man who had brought her back. "I suggest you make the most of it," he said just before he slipped out of the room.

It wasn't clear just who Gene was giving that advice to.

Levi took her grandfather's exit to mean that he should be leaving, as well.

"Well, I guess then I'd better—" Levi began, about to back out of Claire's room.

"You can still look at her if you'd like to," Claire told him. "It might even be a little easier to look at her with her asleep. This way she's not bouncing all over the place."

"You might have a point there," Levi said just before he tiptoed over to his daughter's crib. Leaning his arms on the railing, he looked down at the little girl's face. "She looks just like an angel, doesn't she?" he whispered to Claire as he continued gazing at the sleeping, cherubic face.

"God's clever use of deceptive packaging," Claire replied, amusement curving the corners of her generous mouth.

"Bekka will grow out of it and calm down," Levi predicted. "In about five years or so—give or take," he added with a fond laugh. It was obvious that no matter what she did and how old she got, she would always be his little girl, and he'd love her unconditionally.

Which made Bekka, Claire thought, one lucky little

girl. And by association, that made her lucky, as well, to have that kind of a loving father for her child.

"Hope you're right," Claire told him. They both stood there, looking down on what amounted to their most precious handiwork, for several moments.

When Levi took her hand in his, her breath caught in her throat. For a second she was afraid to move, afraid of encouraging him—more afraid of doing something to discourage him and chase Levi away.

"Gene said something about her staying asleep for a couple of hours. Does she?" Levi questioned.

Claire nodded. "Bekka's taken to sleeping for two hours at a time. She just started doing that the last couple of weeks. I was stunned," she admitted. "But thrilled at the same time."

"Then I guess you'd better listen to Gene and make the most of it. I should let you get your rest," Levi told her. "I'll see you in the morning," he added, forcing himself to cross to the door.

A sense of urgency washed over her. "Levi—"

When he turned around to look at her and hear whatever last minute words she wanted to send him off with, he found that he didn't have very far to look. Claire was right there, standing right inside his shadow.

"Claire?"

Even the way he said her name excited her.

In the very next heartbeat, she wrapped her arms around his neck, pushed herself up on her toes and then sealed her mouth to his.

Levi resisted.

Or at least he thought he did. That part transpired in far less than a heartbeat, after which time every noble intention he'd gathered together to help him stay strong and rise above his desires was utterly and effectively stripped away from him.

Before he knew what he was doing, Levi kissed her back. Part of him, a very small part, still struggled to do the right thing and pull back.

When he finally succeeded in creating a small space between them, he'd only been able to draw his head back a couple of inches from hers.

"Claire, are you sure—?"

"Stop talking," she instructed breathlessly.

Claire had no idea if she was strong enough to override the kind of logic he might throw at her. All she knew was that her whole body was burning for him. It felt as if it was vibrating like a freshly struck tuning fork, all because of the very delicious feel of his body pressed against hers.

She had no doubt that come morning, she was going to regret this.

Perhaps a little.

Most likely a lot.

But right now what she would definitely regret was letting him return to his room, leaving her to crawl into her own bed.

Alone.

Heaven help her, she *needed* him.

Chapter 12

The ache that came over Levi, instant and acute, reminded him of every single second that he had gone without making love with Claire. But despite the keenly felt desire, a shaky but irrefutable logic still managed to prevail.

For the second time in as many minutes, he drew his lips away from Claire's, leaving her confused and bereft, if the expression on her face was any indication of what she was experiencing.

"The baby," he murmured thickly.

Claire instantly understood what he was referring to, understood the conscientious objection that he was raising.

Moving over to the crib, which was no longer located right next to her bed as it had been when she'd left for the movies—her guess was that her grandfather had had a premonition about the way the evening might wind up going and with that in mind had moved the crib as far away from her bed as possible—she picked up the baby blanket and spread it out so that it covered the entire length of the guard rail.

Spread out this way, the pink blanket would provide the only viewing surface Bekka would be able to look at if the baby should open her eyes while she and Levi were otherwise occupied.

Turning from the now-isolated crib, Claire smiled at the man who had won her heart just a few years ago, her smile clearly indicating that the mission was accomplished.

His concerns about Bekka laid to rest, Levi wasted no time pulling his wife back into his arms. Capturing her lips again, his hands eagerly roamed over all the stirring curves of her body.

Levi worshipped every inch of her and happily celebrated the very thought of their physical reunion to come.

"I've missed this," he breathed against the side of her throat, his breath quickly stirring her to an unimaginable fever pitch. "I've missed *you*, Claire."

Eager for that special form of frenzy that only he could create within her, Claire pushed Levi back against her bed, and quickly began tearing at his shirt, working his belt loose and then urgently tugging at his slacks, drawing them down off his taut hips and hard, muscular thighs.

She had him half-undressed before he had pulled down her tank top and the strapless bra that she wore beneath it.

Her shorts came next, leaving her in what could be

rated as the skimpiest of all-but-transparent hot-pink thong panties.

The thong's life expectancy swiftly plummeted down to zero in less than thirty seconds as he slid his fingertips beneath the thin elastic on either side of her hips. And then, in the blink of an eye, the thong and her hips parted company, and she was lying on top of him, completely nude.

Wrapping his arms around her and covering her mouth with his own, Levi reversed their positions and she was suddenly beneath him.

He took great care to balance his weight on the length of his arms and his elbows even as his lips reacquainted themselves with the length and breadth of her skin.

Levi kissed her everywhere, making her head spin, her heart race and her body prime itself for him. The yearning she experienced was almost unbelievably urgent and ever so overwhelming.

She wasn't sure just how she managed to get the remainder of his clothes away from his body, but she finally accomplished that, eager to give as good as she got.

But Levi had always been the master at this game. She had come to him with limited experience, and he had uncovered such mind-blowing pleasures for her that she knew without being told that what she had with Levi was something indescribably precious and wonderful.

Levi kept on kissing her until he had reduced her to a pulsating mass of desire. And then she felt his lips withdrawing from hers only to leave their imprint on her neck, her shoulders, the swell of her breasts and then her newly taut belly.

The muscles quivered beneath his lips and hot, stirring breath. Claire arched into his lips, eager to absorb every nuance, every pass that he made.

Levi went farther down.

Deeper.

Priming her soft, inner core, his tongue wove magic, creating havoc even as it coaxed one climax after another from her.

It was all sweet agony.

Claire chewed on her lip. It was all she could do not to cry out. Only the fact that her cries would wake up the baby held her in check.

Grabbing fistfuls of bedding in her hands as she tried to anchor part of herself to reality, Claire arched higher and higher, eager to experience the full impact of the sensations that Levi was so expertly creating within her.

She fell back, exhausted, only to feel his lips forging a path back up to hers. Claire was sure that there was nothing left within her, nothing to give, nothing to absorb.

She was miles beyond tired.

And then he moved her legs apart with his knee and entered her.

Levi did it slowly, gently, as if he didn't want to take a chance on hurting her even though they had made love this way countless times before, often several times in the space of a few hours.

And yet, she realized, Levi treated her like a virgin bride.

And in so doing, he'd caused her to fall in love with him all over again.

Almost in slow motion, Levi managed to create paradise for her, bringing her closer and closer to the ultimate climax, the ultimate moment that they could both share.

She didn't want slowly.

Claire raced to that wondrous sensation eagerly, knowing that Levi was there to share it with her, to feel everything she was feeling.

That made it twice as special as it had been before.

Clinging to him, Claire climbed up to the very pinnacle of the mountain they were trying to scale.

And then, just like that, they skydived down back to the ground together.

Claire clung to him on the way down, as well, unwilling to give up even a second of the experience or draw into herself before it was time.

She truly wanted to have him there, beside her, guiding her and protecting her. Doing all the things that had made her fall in love with him in the first place.

When the euphoria finally abated, moving back into the shadows, Claire was more than a little reluctant to release her hold on it.

But whether or not she did it, the sensation still receded, vanishing into the ether until there wasn't even a trace of it left.

Claire sighed, burying her face in Levi's shoulder, not wanting to engage with the world just yet.

Levi could feel her turning into him, could feel him wanting her in response. He felt every breath she took and released.

Damn, but she was stirring up things again, making him want her again.

Making him ready to stay the night and pick up all the threads of his life and arrange them the way they had once been.

Closing one arm around his wife to keep her against him, Levi kissed the top of her head. "I have *missed* that," he murmured with great feeling into her hair.

Raising her head ever so slightly so that she could look up at him, Claire said in a hushed whisper, "Me, too."

He wanted to keep on talking, to somehow get her to tell him—no, to promise him—that his period of exile from her life was over. That she was willing to pick up and resume their lives just where they had left them.

To hear that would have meant the world to him, perhaps even put his uneasiness to rest, at least for a while. But he knew that if he said any of this to her, it left him open to the possibility that she could say no, then continue to say that nothing had really changed between them despite this quick visit to happier days.

Because if she said that, it would most likely crush him, and right now he was far too vulnerable to risk that. He hadn't managed to properly build up his walls, his defenses against the possibility of hearing things that would leave devastating holes in his soul.

So he said nothing and just held her in his arms for as long as he could.

The silence enveloped her.

At first she thought nothing of it. But ever so slowly, it began to make her feel uncomfortable.

Awkward.

Made her feel as if, now that the sexual tension had been addressed and depleted for the time being, they were suddenly being thrown back to the lives they'd been living a few short hours ago.

"Is something wrong?" she heard herself finally asking him.

"No," Levi denied a bit too quickly, belying his thought process. "Why? Do you feel something's wrong?" he asked, throwing the ball back into her court.

"You're not talking."

"Funny, I thought I heard myself talking. I could have sworn that was the sound of my voice just now. Oh, wait, there it goes again," he said, hoping to get his point across to Claire. To make her laugh.

Instead of amused, Claire looked a little frustrated. "You know what I mean."

"No," Levi was forced to admit since he didn't believe in lying. "Not usually."

She propped herself up on her elbow to look at him from a better angle. "We just made love."

"I know," he replied with a solemn expression. "I was there."

"And now you're pulling back," she pointed out.

He balked at the criticism, even though he knew, in his heart, that she was right. "I'm right here," he contradicted.

"Physically," Claire emphasized. Didn't he see the difference? "I'm talking about what you have inside." She jabbed an index finger into his chest.

Levi fell back on logic, the way he always did. "What I have inside is a whole bunch of organs, which still seem to be working at maximum capacity."

She closed her eyes and sighed. Opening them again, she said, "I'm talking about your spirit."

"Spirit," he repeated. "As in ghosts?"

Levi was deliberately baiting her, wanting to see where this was going and just what she truly felt about what had happened. Because he would have liked nothing more than to hear that this meant they were going to get back together. That she missed them being a couple as much as he did.

He was well aware that in each relationship, one person always loved more than the other. It was a given as far as he was concerned. But what he couldn't bear was if it turned out that he was the only one in this relationship. He wouldn't be able to stand it if she was going to turn her back on him and willfully abandon him the way his father had.

He knew he wouldn't be able to live with that or bear up to that.

"No, not as in ghosts," she said, a slight glimmer of anger creasing her brow, tainting her reaction to him and to what had just happened here between them. "As if what we're both carrying within us—what makes us fall in love," she added before he could jump back on that ridiculous analogy about inner organs and whatnot, "doesn't really exist." She drew herself up, holding the sheet against her breasts. "Didn't you *ever* love me?" she wanted to know.

"Of course I did—I do," he amended when he realized that he'd framed his answer using the past tense. All he was doing was following her lead, but he knew if he pointed that out, she'd lash out at him, claiming that he was just being argumentative.

Claire looked unconvinced—but she also looked as if she *wanted* to be convinced.

"If you love me, why did you go off that night to play poker with the guys instead of coming home with me to *play* something else?"

At this point he honestly didn't know, but saying

that sounded like a cop-out, so he tried to come up with something that sounded plausible.

"You were busy," he began, thinking of the woman at the wedding that Claire had been talking to.

"I have never been too busy for you—unlike you for me," she said with renewed feeling.

"*When* was I ever too busy for you?" he wanted to know.

Was he kidding? "Almost every day—when you don't come home from work," she added, in case he was too obtuse to understand her meaning.

"That's just it. Work. It's *work*, it's not personal—"

She sniffed, showing contempt for his answer, clearly unconvinced. "It certainly felt personal to me. And it would to you, too, if *you* were on the receiving end of what I've had to put up with," she informed him.

It was happening, Levi thought.

He could feel it.

They were slipping back into the quagmire comprised of her grievances about his behavior. If he didn't get up and leave now, she was just going to start going over the entire litany of his faults and shortcomings.

The second she started, any headway that he'd felt being made while they were making love would swiftly become null and void—as if it had never happened, he thought. He would rather leave now and retain a shred of what he felt had transpired between them than to stick around and watch it all come crashing down and burn.

Again.

Sitting up, he swung his legs down on the opposite side of the bed, rose and began picking up his clothing. He began to pull on his slacks and shirt.

Levi was dressed within a couple of minutes.

Claire remained sitting up in bed, watching him. Stunned and speechless. When she finally found her tongue, she demanded, "What do you think you're doing?"

He spared her a fleeting glance. "Putting my clothes on."

She could see that. What she wanted from him was to know *why* he was putting his clothes on.

"Just like that?" she demanded.

"Only way I know how to get dressed," he said, his voice devoid of feeling.

Her eyes narrowed. "That's not what I meant."

He shrugged. "Guess you're just going to have to work on being able to communicate your thoughts better."

He was criticizing her. They'd just made love and she'd thought—she'd thought—

Angry tears filled her eyes,

Damn, nothing had been resolved, she told herself. She was a fool to think that a few loving moments made everything all right.

"Get out," she ordered, pointing at the door. To underscore her command, she threw a pillow at him.

He ducked out of the door and closed it before the pillow could come in contact with him.

Chapter 13

Claire had thrown him out.

Again.

Levi knew in his gut that it was just a matter of time before she would issue a full-scale rejection, banishing him from her life just as she had after that blasted wedding they'd attended.

Except that this time it could very possibly be permanent.

And if that happened, she would be, in essence, abandoning him.

Abandoning him just the way that his father had abandoned him.

Because he wasn't worth loving.

Wasn't worth sticking around for and trying to iron out the snags that had occurred in the fabric of their relationship.

And he obviously wasn't worth the effort to even *attempt* to set things right.

It was the story of his life, Levi thought glumly as he sat in the dark in his room. He might as well bail rather than stick around and have the point driven home that much more sharply.

Even so, it still hurt, he thought. It hurt like hell.

It was his fault, Levi realized, staring into the darkness. His fault for thinking that he could actually have a woman like Claire in his life. His fault for thinking that a woman like Claire could love him—and that he had an actual shot at building a solid life with her and their daughter.

On some level, he'd known all along that this was liable to happen.

That was why he'd done what he could to consciously hold a piece of himself back when they made love. Because if he held back, then maybe he wouldn't be completely destroyed if she turned her back on him and left him again.

All in all, it was a decent protective, working theory. But in reality, his defense mechanisms weren't nearly as effective as he needed them to be.

He still felt vulnerable and completely stripped down to his skin.

He was just going to have to harden himself, because as long as he remained in the Strickland Boarding House, there was a good chance that he and Claire would run into each other, that their paths would cross no matter how careful he was to keep away from her.

His path, Levi thought, was clear. He was going to have to pack up and leave as soon as he got back from work tomorrow.

* * *

But the following evening, when he arrived back at the boarding house, Levi felt far too exhausted to face the prospect of packing, so he put off leaving the boarding house—and Claire—until the following day.

But the evening that followed that one brought with it the same set of circumstances, the same reluctance on his part and consequently, the same results.

So did the day after that.

And the day after that.

Levi made peace with the idea that he wasn't going anywhere for a while, telling himself that it was easier to do nothing and remain in limbo, than to take an inevitable step that would, he felt, irrevocably close a chapter of his life. A chapter, he was sure, he would never be able to open again.

Claire slipped back into her room. Breakfast was finally over. She'd been working on automatic pilot for days now, and she was drained.

Her room was empty and so quiet, the silence all but vibrated around her as well as within her. Her grandfather, bless him, had happily taken over the care and feeding of Bekka, as he did every day while she went off to the kitchen to help feed the masses.

She was very grateful for his help, but as her grandmother had pointed out, he enjoyed caring for Bekka and playing with her, so it wasn't exactly a hardship for him to watch the baby. Besides, it made him feel useful, as well as happy.

Claire had to admit that she envied her grandfather his happiness.

Happiness.

It was something she felt that she would never experience again. Finding out that she'd been right all along in her dealings with Levi didn't make her feel the slightest bit better or vindicated.

This was one time she would have given *anything* to have been wrong. But Levi had proven that she'd been right by his glaring absence from her life.

Ever since she was in her teens, she'd been insecure when it came to her looks. Marriage didn't change anything. It certainly didn't change her thinking. All along she had felt that she wasn't pretty enough to hold on to a man like Levi.

Levi was sharp, clever and so handsome that it almost hurt. What would he want with someone like her? Why would he tie himself down with her? Especially long-term? In a desperate effort to ensure that he would remain in her life, she had gone out of her way to be certain that Levi would never see her without her makeup on, or with her hair uncombed—not even once.

A case in point was the day she had gone into labor. She hadn't called him to take her to the hospital before she had checked her hair and her makeup in the mirror—and touched up her lipstick as well as spraying a fine mist of cologne into her hair. She wanted to look picture-perfect each and every time he looked at her.

So that he wouldn't be tempted to leave her.

Granted, that did make her life that much harder, but she'd wanted to be sure that if he left—as he now indeed had—it wouldn't be because he wanted to find someone more attractive than she was.

But it seemed now that he had grown tired of her anyway.

Even when they had made love that last time, here

at the boarding house, she had felt that Levi was definitely holding back, holding a part of himself in check, just out of her reach.

She had wanted to give Levi her all, but after sensing that, she had suddenly shut down and backed away herself.

Two could play the "stranger" game, she thought. If Levi wanted to treat her like someone he barely knew, well, she could do the same with him.

But behaving this way was taking a terrible toll on her, making her usually sunny disposition all but vanish entirely. She managed to sound upbeat when dealing with some of the other residents in the boarding house. And she was fairly certain that she had fooled her grandfather and even her more suspicious grandmother, but it was far from easy.

Which was why she was here in her room, seeking out a little space and trying very hard to rally her spirits which had, over the past few days, plummeted down to a subbasement level.

Thinking of what she'd had and now apparently had lost, Claire couldn't keep the tears from surfacing. However, since she was alone, she let them come, hoping to get all the sadness out of her.

Claire threw herself facedown on her bed, gathered her pillow to her and just cried. She stifled her sobs by burying her head in her pillow.

She wasn't sure just how long she remained like that, crying her heart out. She knew that she'd cried so hard and so long, she was virtually exhausted.

That was when she heard the knock on her door.

Caught off guard, she remained silent, hoping that

whoever was on the other side of the door would think she wasn't in and would just go away.

But they didn't go away.

The second round of knocking had her pulling into herself even more, determined to wait it out. The last thing she felt like doing was talking.

To anyone.

Shutting her eyes, she braced herself to wait the person out.

She wasn't prepared for the door to suddenly be opened.

The second it began to move, Claire popped up into a sitting position. She rubbed the heels of her hands against her eyes, trying to clear away as much as she could of the telltale trail of tears.

She was just lucky she wasn't one of those women who spent a great deal of time on her eye makeup. If she had, she was certain she would have looked like a raccoon right now. Instead, at most, she would be showing some puffiness beneath her eyes, which could mean any one of a number of things, not necessarily a sign of the heartbreak she was experiencing.

The next second, her grandmother walked in, pocketing her pass key.

"Why aren't you answering your door?" Melba Strickland wanted to know.

Scowling, with one hand on her ample hip, the woman looked very formidable despite her short stature.

Claire looked down at the rumpled bedspread on the bed. "Sorry," she mumbled. "I guess I must have fallen asleep and didn't hear you."

The scowl on Melba's face deepened more than just a fraction.

"Okay, then." Melba sniffed, closing the door behind her. Coming into the room, she took her granddaughter's chin in her hand and carefully scrutinized both sides of her face. "And just when, exactly, did you take up lying to your grandmother?" she wanted to know.

Nerves caused adrenaline to go surging through her system. She wasn't any good at this, but since she'd laid the groundwork, she felt she needed to see it through. "I'm not lying. I'm…"

"Experiencing a lapse in good judgment?" Melba supplied.

Feeling very vulnerable in her present position—she was looking up at her grandmother as if she were down on her knees—Claire got off her bed.

"Is there something I can do for you, Grandmother?" she asked, doing her best to sound calm.

"Yes," the woman answered in a no-nonsense tone of voice. "You can stop feeling sorry for yourself."

Claire's defenses went into high gear. "I'm not feeling sorry for—" Claire stopped. Oh, what was the point of trying to deny it? Her grandmother had this eerie ability to see right through her. "How can you tell?"

Melba snorted. "I'm old and I've seen it all, Claire-bear." Narrowing her eyes, the older woman stared at her granddaughter's face again. "This have anything to do with that exiled husband of yours?" she asked.

Claire waited a couple of beats before asking, "If I said no, would you believe me?"

Melba's eyes held hers. Her face was devoid of any telltale expression. "What do you think?"

She knew her grandmother well enough to give up any attempt at denial. "Then I won't say no."

Melba nodded her head. "Good thinking. And speaking of thinking—or not thinking—just what is going on with you two?" Melba asked. Her tone indicated that she wouldn't put up with any attempts to weasel out of answering her. "A week ago, it looked as if things were getting back on track between you and Levi. Now you're involved in some kind of elaborate game of hide-and-seek—except that neither one of you is seeking." When Claire didn't say anything, Melba ordered, "Out with it."

It was useless to beat around the bush. So she didn't. "He doesn't want me anymore."

"Honey, if that were the case, that man would have been long gone. Nobody's holding a gun to his head, making him stay here—and he *is* still here," her grandmother pointed out.

Sitting down on Claire's bed, the woman looked expectantly at her until Claire followed suit and sat back down on the bed beside her.

"Let me make myself clear," her grandmother began. "Levi Wyatt wouldn't have been my first choice for you—or my second, for that matter. But he does seem to be crazy about Bekka, and any fool can see that man loves you. Ever since you've crawled into that shell of yours, your furniture cowboy seems to have gotten downright mopey. Now, just what makes you think that he doesn't love you anymore?"

Claire took a breath as she looked away. "I'm just not pretty enough," she muttered.

"What?" Melba said sharply.

As if this was easy for her to admit, Claire thought. But she knew that her grandmother would just chip away at her until she had the whole story. Telling her the story right off the bat was just saving her a lot of grief.

"I tried very hard to look perfect for him—I've never let him see me without my makeup. Not even once," Claire said with just a touch of pride. "But that doesn't seem to be enough. I'm just not pretty enough or interesting enough to hold on to him."

Melba stared at her for a moment that grew so long, it became almost intolerable.

And then she spoke. "So what you're telling me is that you married a shallow jerk."

"No!" Claire cried, horrified at the label her grandmother had just slapped on Bekka's father. "He's not a shallow jerk!"

Melba looked far from convinced. "Well, only a shallow jerk is going to stop loving someone because they decided that the woman they married wasn't as *pretty* as they thought she was. Is Levi *that* shallow?" her grandmother wanted to know, her sharp brown eyes pinning Claire down, daring her to defend the indefensible.

"No, he's not," Claire declared loyally. "But I'm still not pretty enough to hang on to him."

Melba sighed, shaking her head. Her granddaughter had *so* much to learn. "Honey, there are a lot of things that go into making and maintaining a good marriage— being pretty doesn't even make the top twenty. Surface beauty doesn't last, and unless it goes beyond being skin-deep, being pretty is not good for anything except maybe making makeup commercials.

"Now, that young man you married is not a rocket scientist, but he's pretty sharp, which means he's got a good head on his shoulders and some decent set of values to guide him." Her grandmother's eyes held hers. "The man doesn't want a picture-perfect wife. He wants a loving wife. One he can talk to and reason with.

"There's no such thing as perfect anyway. Best you can hope for is someone who tries their best to be a good husband—or a good wife," Melba said pointedly, looking at her granddaughter. "Now, let me let you in on a little secret. Marriages aren't made in heaven. They're made right here on earth and played out here, as well.

"Nothing good is ever gotten easily. You have to work at it, fight for it, sacrifice for it. That's when you really get to appreciate what you have. Someone hands you something on a silver platter, you might like it and enjoy it for a little while, but that doesn't come close to the way you feel after you've fought the good fight and won something. It also becomes a lot more precious to you. Now, stop hiding in your room and see if you can make that young man want to go on putting up with you."

Claire wished she could, but the sinking feeling in her stomach told her there was no point in even trying. "It's too late."

Melba rose to her feet. Holding her granddaughter's hand, she brought Claire up with her. "It's only too late if one of you is dead, and unless he's expired on his way to work, your man is alive and well and coming back here tonight. The only way that man is going to leave you is if you chase him away. So *stop chasing him away.*"

Claire shook her head. "You're wrong. I can feel him holding back—"

"Well, yeah," Melba agreed. "Of course he's holding back. If you thought someone was going to use your heart for flamenco practice, you'd hold back, too.

"Look, you've already declared your marriage dead—you've got nothing to lose by approaching Levi, and everything to gain." When her granddaughter made no move to leave the room, Melba delivered her ultimate threat. "Just remember, you're not too big for me to take over my knee."

Claire laughed shortly, thinking her grandmother was kidding. "I'm not a kid anymore, Grandmother," she pointed out. "I'm an adult."

"You're an adult," the older woman echoed. Melba's eyes narrowed again as she focused in on her granddaughter. "Fine. Then prove it."

Chapter 14

Claire looked at her grandmother, confused. "I don't understand. What do you mean, *prove it*? What are you telling me to do?"

Melba huffed, exasperated. Shutting the door again, she proceeded to answer her granddaughter's question. "I'm telling you to *act* like an adult. When Levi comes home tonight, go up to him and apologize for your part in this fiasco that's gotten so completely out of hand. Own up to your mistakes—it takes two to have an argument, not just one person."

Frowning, her eyes swept over Claire. "And for heaven's sake, let him see you the way you really are, not like this." She waved her hand to indicate Claire in her entirety. "Not like some girl who's ready to be on the cover of some fashion magazine. If he loves you, then he loves *you*, not your shade of lipstick, or the eye shadow you have on." Melba's gaze was highly disapproving. "Or that powder you use to hide any so-called flaws you think you have.

"The man married *you*, not a makeup case. Give him a little credit," Melba insisted, surprising Claire. She'd been under the impression that her grandmother did *not* approve of Levi. This sounded as if she was in his corner. "Besides," Melba continued, "there's nothing wrong with the way you look. What *is* wrong is your insecurity."

Melba abruptly stopped herself from going on. "Now, despite what you're probably thinking, I'm not here to lecture you. I just want to wake you up to what you stand to lose if you don't get a grip on your behavior." Blowing out a breath, Melba glanced at her wristwatch. "Time for you to stop feeling sorry for yourself and get back to the kitchen, Cinderella. Until she's feeling better, Gina's going to need your help."

Melba opened the door and stepped out into the hallway. Claire was quick to pull herself together and follow her out of the room. "And while you're working," Melba added as a parting shot. "*Think* about what I just said. Think very, very hard."

"Yes, ma'am," Claire murmured.

Heading in a different direction than her granddaughter, Melba spared her one last look and just shook her head without saying another word.

Claire had no idea how to read her grandmother's parting expression, but the woman had certainly given her a great deal to think about. She supposed that her grandmother did have a point. She had married a man, a *real* man, not some prince charming who only existed in fairy tales.

Since he was real, she owed it to Levi to let him see her the way she really looked. He'd earned the right. Levi had followed her here even after she'd thrown him out. That *had* to count for something, she reasoned. Maybe he did really love her and not just the image she had been projecting every day and night since that first day that they met.

It wasn't Levi who had set her on this path of always projecting a picture-perfect image. She had been like this ever since she could remember. She had never allowed herself to appear dirty or messy in public, never left the house unless she passed her own inspection, critically looking herself over in a full-length mirror.

What that amounted to was always being neat, always making sure that her clothes, her makeup and her hair were all impeccable. The idea of looking anything less than exceedingly attractive was just unthinkable to her. She didn't even own a pair of sweatpants or a pair of sneakers.

Her grandmother was right, Claire thought grudgingly. It was time to let her hair down.

In more ways than one.

Claire began to watch the clock, counting the hours and the minutes until Levi came back to the boarding house from the furniture store. Although it had taken a lot of courage, she had made up her mind. She was going to unveil herself, to show Levi the *real* Claire, flaws and all.

And then she was going to pray that he didn't find the real her a turnoff.

Levi stared straight ahead at the dark road in front of him. With little or no traffic before him, the road was numbingly hypnotic. The second he had hit the road tonight, he'd made up his mind.

This was going to be the last time he'd make this run.

It was time to face the facts, pick up his marbles and, in effect, "go home." There was no point in continuing to beat his head against the wall. It wasn't going to change anything, wasn't going to give him the outcome he'd been hoping for.

He and Claire weren't going to get back together again.

For him to pretend otherwise was just another way of prolonging his pain. He'd been stalling these past few days, stubbornly and futilely delaying the inevitable.

He might not be a college graduate, he thought ruefully, but he was certainly bright enough to take a hint and read the signs—especially if Claire was beating him over the head with one of them.

His marriage was over.

The sooner he came to terms with that, the sooner he would...

Would what?

Heal? he asked himself, mocking the very thought.

Heal for what reason? So that he could someday fall for someone else and get to go through this all over again? So he could set himself up for another fall ? No, living through this brutal experience once was more than enough for him.

Even the most thickheaded of creatures eventually learned their lesson, and it was time for him to learn his. In this case, his lesson was that he was the kind of man who was destined to be abandoned time and again. His father hadn't wanted to stick around. Who knew? Maybe his mother wouldn't have, either, if it wasn't for the fact that she also had two younger sons besides him at home.

Levi pressed his lips together. That wasn't fair, and he knew it. He was just allowing the situation to get the better of him.

He had tried, really honestly *tried*, to be the best husband and father he could be. But without an example to follow, he admittedly was just blindly moving through his days, doing what he *thought* was the right thing without really knowing if he was succeeding.

Levi laughed shortly at himself.

Obviously, he *hadn't* succeeded because if he had, he would have been home in his apartment with Claire and the baby, and all this would have been moot.

And it wasn't.

Levi blinked to clear his vision and focus. He'd been so preoccupied with this new course of action he was plotting for himself that he hadn't realized that he'd driven the entire way back.

The route had gotten to be so automatic for him that he'd just driven without watching, and he was now parked behind the boarding house.

For a second he just remained where he was, not wanting to move, not wanting to begin implementing what was to be the last leg of his failed union with Claire. And then he shrugged. He supposed he might as well get this over with.

He had to view this the way he viewed removing a Band-Aid from a wound. He had to strike fast and keep it neat. That would help keep the pain at a minimum.

Who the hell was he kidding? The pain wasn't going to be kept at a minimum. The pain was going to be devastating. But it still had to happen.

Opening the front door, Levi glanced in the direction of the dining room and then the kitchen. The pull he experienced to just walk to either one of the rooms in hopes of seeing Claire was strong, but he forced himself to ignore it.

Why prolong his agony? No matter what, it was going to end the same way. He had to do what he had to do and do it like a man, not like a whimpering child.

So instead of going to either room with the hopes of catching a glimpse of Claire, he went straight to the front stairs and headed up to the second floor and his room.

He had things to pack.

Claire frowned as she craned her neck and looked out of the kitchen and down the hall. She could have sworn she'd heard the front door open and then close again. At this hour, that had to be Levi. This was about the time that he'd been coming in the past few weeks.

Then again, maybe he'd stayed at the store longer, she thought. Doing some of that overtime he always talked about.

But would he do that, considering how things were between them right now? she asked herself, playing her own devil's advocate. No, she was fairly sure that he wouldn't.

That meant that perhaps he'd already come home and had just gone up to his room. He could very well be up there at this moment.

Gina looked in her direction and obviously noticed her preoccupation. "Something wrong?" Gina asked.

Claire had noticed that as a rule, Gina did not pry.

That the older woman was even asking this question meant that she wasn't masking her feelings very well.

Even so, her first reaction was denial. "No, nothing's wrong." And then Claire paused, rethinking her words. "Well, maybe," she admitted, vacillating.

And then she made up her mind. What was she doing, standing here, talking to Gina, when she could be upstairs, saving her marriage? It was no contest.

"I'll be right back," she told Gina, stripping the apron off and leaving it slung over the back of one of the chairs.

Gina nodded, as if she understood the chaotic thoughts that were bouncing off one another in her head.

"Take your time," Gina advised. "We're almost finished here anyway."

Claire fervently hoped that the statement couldn't also be applied to her own situation with Levi.

Hurrying out of the kitchen, Claire passed her grandfather holding her daughter in his arms just outside the door.

"Look who's here, Bekka. Your mama's rushing to see you—"

"Grandpa, I need a few more minutes," she began, not really sure how to frame the problem she was currently facing.

Fortunately, in her grandfather's eyes, she could do no wrong, and he was more than willing to do anything she wanted him to.

"No problem, Claire-bear. That just means more time for me to spend with the princess here." He cuddled his cheek against the baby's. "Isn't that right, princess?"

Bekka made some sort of a cooing noise, as if she

understood the question that had been put to her and was agreeing with her great-grandfather.

Claire breathed a sigh of relief. She needed a few minutes alone with Levi if she was going to convince him that she meant what she was saying.

Patting Gene's arm just before she flew up the stairs, she said, "Thank you, Grandpa. You're the best!"

"Tell your grandmother that," he told her, calling up the stairs after her disappearing form.

"I will," she called back. "I promise."

Mentally, she was already far away from the conversation with her grandfather.

Never superstitious, Claire still crossed her fingers. *Just let this go well, please*, she prayed.

Claire stopped just a few steps short of her husband's door. Taking a deep breath, she tried the doorknob.

Expecting to find it open, she turned the knob only to discover that it didn't give. Levi had locked his door. Since when?

A chill zipped up and down her spine, making all of her feel cold.

This was a bad sign, she thought, looking at the door.

Releasing the doorknob, Claire began to turn away. And then, out of nowhere, she heard her grandmother's voice in her head. It was mocking her.

Giving up already? You're no granddaughter of mine if you do.

"Oh, yes, I am," Claire caught herself saying out loud. She had to watch that, she silently upbraided herself. She didn't want anyone thinking she was talking to herself.

The next moment she knocked on Levi's door. "Levi?

Are you in there?" She knocked again, more loudly this time. "Levi?"

There was still no answer.

Her pulse quickened. She was making a fool of herself, Claire thought. She was standing out here, knocking on his door, and he probably wasn't in.

And, if he *was* in, then that was even worse because it meant that he was ignoring her.

Well, what did you expect? That he was just going to be standing in the shadows, pining away for you until you gave him the time of day? Give it up.

Her heart ached as she turned away from the door. Claire had taken a total of three steps toward the stairs when she heard the door behind her opening.

Hope suddenly renewed and bursting out inside her, she swung around to see if it was Levi, or if someone else had opened their door to see what all the commotion was about.

It wasn't *someone else*, it was Levi.

A very solemn-looking Levi with flat, unreadable eyes.

This isn't good, a little voice in her head whispered.

All that meant was that she had to make this good, that same voice told her.

The problem was, she wasn't sure if she could anymore.

"Is something wrong with Bekka?" Levi asked, concerned. He couldn't think of any other reason why Claire would come to his door, looking for him.

Levi had given her an excuse to use, and she almost ran with it. But then she stopped herself. The truth. She needed to stick with the truth. That was the only way this was going to work between them.

Levi respected the truth. What he didn't respect, she recalled, were women who played silly games. That was one of the first things he had ever said to her, telling her that he was grateful that she didn't believe in playing games.

"Nothing's wrong with Bekka," she told Levi quietly. And then she took a deep breath and said, almost all in one breath, "There's something wrong with me."

The concern on his face instantly multiplied a dozenfold. Taking her hand in his, Levi asked her, "Are you sick?"

Granted, she felt a little light-headed, but that could have been due to any one of a number of reasons. And right now it would be squandering the moment if she talked about anything else but what she needed to get off her chest.

"May I come in?"

"Sure." Levi stepped back and opened his door. "Sit," he instructed, gesturing toward the bed. One question came swiftly on the heels of another. "Do you want a glass of water? Do you want me to call your grandmother—?"

"No. And no," Claire told him with finality. "I don't need water or my grandmother. What I need is you," she told him slowly, as if she was testing out each word on the tip of her tongue before she said it out loud.

Since he had come to the boarding house and registered for a room just to be near Claire and the baby, he'd allowed his spirits to rise up more than a dozen times, only to have them come crashing down time and again. This time, he kept a tight rein on them.

"I don't understand."

She opened her mouth to explain, then stopped. For

the first time Claire looked around the room he'd been living in these past few weeks.

Claire noted that he had both his suitcases on the bed, opened. They were both more than half-filled. Her uneasiness increased.

"Going on a trip?" she asked, doing her best to make her voice sound innocent.

His eyes met hers and held them for a long moment. "Going back," he corrected. "To the apartment."

"You're leaving?" Claire asked numbly, even as something in her head was screaming not to allow that to happen.

"Yeah," he confirmed, shutting the door behind her. "I guess the plus side of that will be that I won't be bothering you anymore."

"What if…" Her voice suddenly evaporated, and she had to concentrate on finding it again. Clearing her throat, Claire tried once more. "What if I said I wanted you to bother me?"

Levi stared at her, wondering what was going on and why she'd say something like that when she couldn't possibly mean it.

"I'd say that nothing would make me happier—but we both know that you're just yanking my chain. I'm not going to hang around here and hope that I wear you down. I don't want you by default. I want you because you want to be with me. Because you love me at least half as much as I love you.

"But I know that I can't make you love me," he continued, his spirit flagging, "and—"

"What about the other night?" she wanted to know, pulling out all the stops. "We made love, and that was pretty special."

"It was more than that."

Pretty special seemed like such a tiny, meaningless phrase to apply to what had transpired between them. "But it's still not enough," Levi told her. "I want more than just chemistry, Claire. More than just Fourth of July rockets exploding between us. I want—I *need*— the whole package."

He looked at her for a very long moment, framing the last of his summation. "Most of all, I don't want to constantly have to worry that you're going to leave me. That it's just a matter of time before I come home one night to find that you've packed up and left with the baby. Part of me says I should be happy with what I can get, but I can't live that way anymore, Claire. It's just not fair to—"

"You're right," Claire agreed wholeheartedly, jumping the gun and filling in his last word. "It's not fair to you."

That wasn't what he meant. He felt that the way it stood, it was an unfair situation for the both of them, not just him.

"I didn't say that—"

"Well, you should have," she told Levi, cutting him off. And then she had an idea. "Can I use your bathroom for a second?"

The request seemed to come completely out of nowhere and threw him for a second.

But then Levi shrugged and indicated the closed door to the tiny powder room. "Sure. Go ahead. It's right through there. I'll just get back to my packing," he told her, turning away.

She'd almost left then. Seeing the suitcases and

watching him get back to packing, her courage plummeted strongly.

But then she squared her shoulders and silently told herself, *It's now or never. Grandmother had it right. If something was worth having, it was worth fighting for.*

She closed the powder room door behind her.

Chapter 15

Ordinarily, this would be exactly the time when she would touch up her makeup, make sure that she was, visually, the very best version of herself that she could possibly be. That would involve making sure that her dress—or a skimpy top and abbreviated shorts—showed her off to her best advantage.

She'd also make sure that her hair was combed into a lustrous sheen if she was wearing it down, and if it happened to be up, she would strategically dispense colored-crystal clips discreetly throughout.

That was her total package, and it left no man un-affected.

But tonight, here in Levi's tiny powder room, there were no crystal hairclips, no extra, secret little rituals that helped her create this complete picture of perfection she was usually so desperate to project. Beneath it all, she was certain that she was downright plain.

Claire stared at herself in the framed mirror that took the place of the outside of a medicine cabinet. Then she turned on the faucet and scrubbed her face clean, dried off with a towel and looked back into the mirror.

Well, there she was, Claire thought, just as God had created her. Maybe not entirely a plain Jane, but certainly not a "Jane" who was guaranteed to take a man's breath away.

"Okay," she told the reflection in the mirror. "Time to face the music and show the man what he really wound up getting when he said *I do*."

"Claire?" Levi's voice came through the bathroom door, calling out to her.

Claire froze.

Could he possibly have caught a glimpse of her through a crack in the door?

Turning, she looked at the door that separated them. There was no crack evident. Claire told herself to calm down.

"Yes?" she asked a little hesitantly.

"Who are you talking to?" Levi wanted to know.

"Just myself," she answered. Then so he wouldn't think she was crazy, she added as an explanation, "Working up my courage."

The reply puzzled him more than it answered anything. "Courage for what?"

Putting her hand on the doorknob, Claire slowly turned it. The resulting sound of the tongue leaving the groove, allowing her to open the door, seemed to echo extra loudly in her head, like a final warning sound. She knew that once she stepped out of the powder room and into his bedroom, there would be no turning back.

Her breath seemed to shorten, and the whole procedure felt as if it was taking place in slow motion.

"For this," she told him in a small, hollow voice. Her mouth felt as dry as a desert as she came out and stood before him.

Levi looked at her. He shook his head, not in disapproval but in complete confusion.

"This?" he repeated, completely mystified. "What are you talking about, Claire?"

She couldn't believe that he didn't see it. He had to be pulling her leg. Either that, or the man was so used to her, he wasn't "seeing" her the way she really was, but the way he perceived her in his mind.

"This," she repeated more insistently. She swept her hand up and down in the vicinity of her face. By the look on Levi's face, he still wasn't seeing it. How could he not? "Don't tell me you don't see it," she said incredulously.

He still had no idea what she was talking about. "What I'm seeing is my wife."

"And—?" she asked, trying to lead him to what she believed was the most important part of this soul-searching moment.

"And she looks nice," Levi concluded. But by the exasperated look on Claire's face, that wasn't what she wanted to hear. "Okay, no more games, Claire. What is it you want me to say?"

She threw up her hands, giving up. "I'm not wearing any makeup, Levi. *None,*" she cried. Just how blind *was* he?

He nodded his head, although his expression didn't change. He didn't appear to be a man who had suddenly experienced enlightenment. "I can see that. And I like it better."

That was *not* what she was expecting. "What?"

"I like it better," he repeated. "You look, I don't know, cleaner, fresher." And then he smiled as he said, "Prettier. All that makeup, it always made me feel like I was supposed to be taking you out to some expensive restaurant. It also made me feel that you were just killing time with me until someone better came along, someone who could give you a fancy lifestyle that I couldn't afford—yet," he added, because he fully intended to, someday.

She was having trouble coming to terms with his reaction to her soul-baring experiment. Cocking her head, she tried to read between the lines. Tried to discover if this man was on the level.

"You're actually telling me that you like me *better* this way?"

He didn't want to hurt her feelings or insult her, but the truth was the truth.

"I suppose I am. You look more genuine," he confessed. Since his answer was obviously not making her very happy, he was quick to add, "Not that you're not beautiful with all the stuff on your face, but you just look more…real."

They'd been married nearly two years. Before that, they had been together for two years. And she had never let him see her without her makeup in all that time. "If you felt that way, why didn't you say anything sooner?" she wanted to know.

"Tell you I thought you had on too much makeup?" Levi questioned. "Claire, I might not be the sharpest knife in the drawer, but I'm not a complete idiot, and

I don't harbor a death wish. I know better than to tell a beautiful woman she's being heavy-handed with her makeup. Besides, it seemed to make you happy, and I wasn't going to criticize something that made you feel good about yourself."

Claire felt as if she was shell-shocked. She wanted to be sure she absorbed this properly. "So you really, truly *like* me this way?"

"*Like* is a very weak word," Levi pointed out. "I *love* you this way."

Her eyes searched his face to make sure that she'd heard him correctly. And then they strayed to his bed and the opened luggage on it.

"If that's the case, why are the suitcases still out?" she asked.

Since she had let down her hair, so to speak, he felt it was safe to be honest with her the way she was asking him to be. "Because I can't live with the uncertainty anymore."

It was her turn to look confused. Older and more sophisticated than she was, he had always struck her as the pillar of confidence. This was all news to her. "Uncertainty?"

Levi blew out a breath. This was harder than he imagined. "I was sure that you were going to leave me again the very next time we have an argument."

"You're right," she answered simply.

"Then you *were* going to leave the very next time we had an argument?" Maybe he should be putting that in the present tense, he thought. The pain that caused him hurt his heart.

"No," she corrected, "you're right that you shouldn't have to live this way. Let's just call that our period of adjustment—we were ironing out the kinks of being two married people with a baby. A baby always adds a lot of extra stress until we both learn how to successfully juggle your job, our lives and the baby's needs. And while we're talking about our faults—" She paused for a second, biting her lower lip as she thought about what she was going to say and how to word it.

"I was wrong."

Levi had the distinct feeling that they were waltzing around not one issue but a number of them. "Wrong about what?"

Since she was apologizing, she might as well give it to him with all the trimmings. There was nothing to be gained by being evasive.

"Wrong about getting so upset because you went to play poker and hang out with some of the local guys. Adults need 'playtime,' too," she told Levi encouragingly.

Levi's mouth dropped open as he stared at his wife. "You're serious?"

She nodded. "Completely. I guess…sometimes it takes me a while to come to my senses. I just felt abandoned every morning when you went off to work, leaving me with the dirty dishes, a crying baby and my ever-depleting feelings of self-worth."

Stunned, he rounded the side of the bed and came closer to Claire, his suitcases and the clothes he was putting into them temporarily forgotten about. They could always be packed later.

She'd caught his attention with an almost throwaway line. The line made absolutely no sense to him. "Why would your feelings of self-worth be depleted?"

There were a lot of answers to that. She gave him

the simplest one. "I couldn't even calm down a baby. My grandfather's better at it than I am."

There were reasons for that. "Number one, your grandfather helped raise four boys, and he tells me that the more experience you have with kids, the easier it is to raise them. You were learning how to deal with all that at your own pace," he told her encouragingly. "And I guess I wasn't all that supportive."

He expected her to agree. When she didn't, he began to feel that maybe there was hope for them after all.

"You were trying to make sure that you were earning enough money so that Bekka never needed anything. It couldn't have been easy, pushing yourself like that. Especially when all you had to come home to was a complaining wife."

Feeling a certain lightness had him playfully teasing her. "Hey, don't be so hard on my wife. She had her reasons." He paused, looking at her closely. "So I guess maybe we do have a chance of making this work?" He ended with a question, but there was definitely a hopeful note in his voice.

Her smile was from ear to ear. "I sure hope so. Oh, Levi, I am *so* ready to go home."

He took her into his arms, wrapping them around her as he brought her close to him. "I think we already are home."

She looked at him, puzzled. "Here?" she questioned, looking around the tiny room.

"I'm going to talk to your grandparents, see if maybe we could get one of the larger rooms for the three of us and stay on for a while." He told her his news, news that had all but seemed irrelevant this morning, but now it could very well be the key to straightening out their lives. "The furniture chain is opening up a new branch in Kalispell, which is a lot closer for me so I won't be gone as long as I used to be each day."

She nodded, taking it in. It all sounded like maybe their lives were finally coming together. "And I could go on working here at the boarding house. Grandmother wants me to be the assistant cook. I really didn't think I could manage the job, but it seems to be coming together," she told him proudly. "Cooking is working out pretty well for me. Even my grandmother can't find anything to complain about with my cooking. Or, if Grandmother decides to go back to cooking here herself—she mentioned that she misses doing it, and Gina and her husband are considering moving to Bozeman, to be closer to their kids, so who knows what might happen. And, if Grandmother does go back to cooking here, I could get a part-time job at the day care."

He laughed, enjoying his wife's enthusiasm. "Hey, you can do anything you set your mind to."

She was fixated on her part in this new plan. "I'm thinking if I had that part-time job, then maybe you wouldn't have to work as many hours as you do—and we could spend more time together as a family."

He smiled into her eyes. "Sounds good to me. *Really* good," he told her, lightly kissing her temple, creating a delicious warmth within her. "Let's make a deal," he told her.

"A deal?" She wasn't sure where he was going with this. She wasn't leery—she loved him—but she tried to brace herself.

He nodded. "Whatever we do from here on in, we're going to make our decisions together. As a family. None of this stoically taking on more than we should and then expecting that the other person's going to be all right with it without at least hearing the argument for it. Does that sound like something you can live with?" he asked her.

"As long as I can live with you, that's all I care about." She felt as if a huge, huge boulder had been lifted from her heart. "And you're sure that you're okay with looking at me like this?" she had to ask one last time.

"Perfectly okay," he told her. And then he dead-panned, "I figure if I haven't been turned to stone yet, the odds are pretty good in my favor."

Claire doubled up her fist and punched him in the arm. He laughed, pretending to wince.

"There's my Claire," he announced, delighted. "You haven't done that in a long time."

"I could pummel you to the ground and make up for lost time," she offered.

"I think I'll take a pass on that for now. Besides, if you pummel me to the ground, how am I going to be able to do this?" he asked, kissing first one cheek and then the other.

"Good point," she murmured, feeling the kernel of excitement pop within her inner core and flowering into all the surrounding regions. "Wouldn't want to stifle your creative instincts."

"Speaking of creative instincts, how much longer do you think we can count on your grandfather entertaining Bekka and keeping her with him?"

"Indefinitely," she answered. "He usually hangs on to Bekka until I come to his room to collect her."

Levi's expression brightened. "So if we don't show up for a couple of hours to claim her—"

"Grandpa will be, as they like to say, 'in hog heaven.'"

Claire wasn't sure just what was going on. "Why are you asking about Bekka?"

He spared her a long, penetrating look. "Just wanted to be sure that she's not going to suddenly show up at the wrong time."

Claire laughed as she suddenly had a vision of their eight-month-old standing outside their door, plotting to get even for being left with a sitter.

"Not on her own, she wouldn't. She's only a little older than eight months, remember? Babies don't walk at eight months."

"But they do see."

"Yesss." She stretched out the word, waiting to see where he was going with this.

"I think her education should begin a little later, not now."

"You're planning to do something educational with me?" she asked innocently, humor dancing in her eyes.

"Not exactly educational," he allowed. "I think I'd place this in the realm of entertainment instead. Entertainment and pleasure." He smiled. "Think I could interest you in, oh, perhaps getting a sample?"

"I think you could interest me in getting a complete course in the subject."

"I was hoping you'd say that." Just before he kissed her, he framed her face with his hand. "God, but I have missed you."

"I'm right here, Levi. And I'm not going anywhere."

"Amen to that," he murmured just before he lowered his mouth to hers.

"I love you, Claire," he said against her mouth before there wasn't room for any more talk.

At the last possible second, she said, "I love you, too," sending the rest of their marriage off to a wonderfully promising start.

Epilogue

Her eyes still closed, Claire stretched beneath the sheet. Ever so slowly, she shed the confining restraints of sleep from her body.

It took her brain a beat to catch up.

When it did, the fact that her arm didn't come in contact with another body registered. The place beside her in bed was empty.

Her eyes flew open as the significance of that fact sank in.

Levi wasn't next to her.

After making love in his room last night, they had both gotten dressed and gone down together to her grandfather to retrieve Bekka. The old man offered to keep the little girl with him overnight, but they had politely refused. Neither she nor Levi wanted to be that obvious about their reconciliation—yet.

As if she somehow sensed that her parents needed more time together, the baby had fallen right to sleep the moment they laid her down and for once, she didn't wake up crying two or three times during the course of the night. Instead, she'd slept straight through, leaving Levi and her to reexplore the joys of sleeping in the same bed all over again.

Claire couldn't remember when she'd felt as happy as she had when she'd fallen asleep last night.

But this morning was a different story.

She woke up to an empty bed—and an empty crib, she suddenly realized. It was not only Levi who was missing, but it was the baby, too.

Bekka was nowhere to be seen.

Had the baby woken up sick? Had Levi taken her downstairs to her grandmother for help? Or maybe he'd driven Bekka over to the hospital.

Without telling her?

Why wouldn't he wake her up and tell her he was taking the baby to the hospital?

A panic began to set in, stealing her very breath away.

Throwing off the sheet, Claire was about to pull on the first clothes she found when she heard the door opening.

Levi walked in carrying Bekka in one arm while holding a mostly empty baby bottle in the other.

"Oh, look, Bekka, Mommy's up—and she's naked." Levi then quickly reversed his instructions. "Don't look, Bekka."

Flushing, although more from annoyance than embarrassment, Claire grabbed the robe that was on the floor at the foot of her bed. She assumed it must have slipped off during last night's activities.

"Where were you?" she wanted to know. "You had me really worried."

Levi placed the baby into her crib then joined Claire. He paused to brush his lips against hers.

"Nice to know you worry, but Bekka was fussing and I thought you deserved to sleep in a little bit, especially after that encore performance last night," he added with a wink.

"So you took her downstairs?" Claire asked, surprised.

"Had to eventually. That was where her formula was," Levi explained when she looked at him quizzically.

Claire decided that sounded as plausible as any other explanation. She turned her attention to the baby.

"She's probably soaking wet by now. I'd better change her—"

"Already done," Levi said, stopping her in her tracks.

Claire looked at him in amazement. "Boy, one day on the job and you've gotten better at it than me," she commented.

He was quick to negate her assessment. "That could never happen, not even if I was on the job a hundred years. All I want to do is help," he told her with sincerity.

"You help," Claire assured him. "Just by being here, you help a lot." Tightening the sash at her waist, she proceeded to make her bed. She was going to have to be in the kitchen soon, she thought as she worked her way around the perimeter of the bed.

When she got to Levi's side, she stopped dead. There

was a lump under the sheet just beneath his pillow. When she started to smooth it out, she discovered that the lump wasn't caused by a crumpled sheet, it was caused by a black velvet box. She looked at it, and then at Levi. "What's this?"

"Best way to find out is to open it," he told her casually.

Her hands were steady, but she was trembling inside as she slowly drew back the top of the box. Inside the ring box was her wedding ring, gleaming the way it hadn't in two years.

"My ring," she cried. Raising her eyes to his, she asked, "It *is* my wedding ring, right?"

"It is your wedding ring," he confirmed.

"But I looked everywhere for it," she told him, remembering how bitterly unhappy she'd been to lose it. "How did you—?"

"When you threw it at me, it fell onto the floor in the hall, and of course I picked it up so it wouldn't get lost. I held on to it hoping you'd want it—and me—back someday." Taking the box from her, he took the ring out and held it up to her. "Claire Strickland, will you do me the very great honor of becoming my wife—again?"

"Yes!" She threw her arms around him, hugging him tightly. "Oh, yes!"

Levi tugged at her sash and then slipped his arms in beneath her robe.

Claire forgot all about getting ready for work.

They both did.

* * * * *

Donna Alward lives on Canada's east coast with her family, which includes her husband, a couple of kids, a senior dog and two crazy cats. Her heartwarming stories of love, hope and homecoming have been translated into several languages, hit bestseller lists and won awards, but her favorite thing is hearing from readers! When she's not writing, she enjoys reading (of course), knitting, gardening, cooking...and she is a *Masterpiece Theatre* addict. You can visit her on the web at donnaalward.com and join her mailing list at donnaalward.com/newsletter.

Books by Donna Alward

Harlequin Romance

Destination Brides
Summer Escape with the Tycoon

Marrying a Millionaire
Best Man for the Wedding Planner
Secret Millionaire for the Surrogate

Holiday Miracles
Sleigh Ride with the Rancher

Cadence Creek Cowboys
The Last Real Cowboy
The Rebel Rancher
Little Cowgirl on His Doorstep
A Cowboy to Come Home To
A Cadence Creek Christmas

Heart to Heart

Hired: The Italian's Bride

How a Cowboy Stole Her Heart

Visit the Author Profile page at Harlequin.com for more titles.

THE COWBOY'S VALENTINE

Donna Alward

Chapter 1

The last place in the world Lacey Duggan expected to find herself was back at Crooked Valley Ranch.

It had only been a month since she'd shared the Christmas holiday with her brother Duke at the ranch they'd once called home. Those days were a lifetime ago. She'd never wanted to return to the small town of Gibson, Montana. Instead she'd made her life in Helena, working for the Department of Natural Resources and Conservation. She wasn't a farmer, or even much of an outdoor girl. Her work for the department was spent in an office. It wasn't that she didn't care; she genuinely enjoyed working with grant proposals and budgets. She just didn't need to be out there in hip waders or rubber boots doing all the digging around. The desk job suited her just fine.

Or at least it had. Past tense.

She stood on the porch of the main house, hesitating. All it would take was the slightest reach and she could open the door and step inside. But right now it seemed like too much to ask. The moment she did that was the moment she admitted every single aspect of her life had fallen apart. First it was the diagnosis that had killed her dreams. Then it was the divorce. She'd made it through both of those, holding on to what she had left—her job. Then came the kicker. The new budget had come down and her position had been made redundant. After six years in the same department, she was out of work.

And one-third owner of a ranch she didn't want.

A gust of wind swirled up the steps and around the porch, icy cold on her legs. This was ridiculous. It was just a door. It signified nothing, really. Except that it was warm in there and cold out here. With a frown she reached for the knob, only to have it ripped out of her hand the moment she touched it. She stared blindly as the door opened and a large figure stood in the doorway, blocking her from entering.

Quinn Solomon.

Her hand was still stretched out, hanging in thin air as she looked up to see the ranch manager staring down at her. Quinn. Quinn with the startling blue eyes and broad shoulders and long legs and cute daughter—and a low opinion of Lacey Duggan.

"Are you coming in or are you going to stand there all day?"

His harsh voice interrupted her assessment and despite the cold she felt her cheeks heat. "Sorry…"

"We're not paying to heat the outdoors. Get in here, you foolish woman."

Her pride blistered as she obeyed, sliding past him into the warmth of the foyer. The house wasn't huge but it was welcoming, and she dropped her purse on the floor and rubbed her arms a bit. Exactly how long had she stood out there?

She glanced up and met his probing gaze. "I didn't expect you to be here," she said, not meaning it to be an accusation, but it sounded like one just the same.

"I work here. My office is here. But don't worry, Lacey. I'll stay out of your way."

"I didn't mean it that way." She sighed. Duke and Quinn were good friends now, and she was sure her brother had told the ranch manager all about her situation, which was humiliating enough. "Look, Quinn, I'm not that happy about being here, either."

"I'm pretty sure I already knew that. So why *did* you come, Lacey?"

From the moment they'd met, he'd never beat around the bush with her. He always said exactly what was on his mind and she might have found that refreshing except that she was usually on the receiving end of a criticism. Her pride already smarting, she decided she'd meet bluntness with bluntness.

"The truth is, if I'd been wise and built up a better savings, I could have had cash flow to keep my place while I looked for another job. As it is, I had to cover my month's rent with my last paycheck and my unemployment won't kick in for another few weeks. My furniture is in my mom's garage while I figure things out, and I already feel like a big fat failure, so you don't have to go out of your way to exert your authority. I get it. You're the boss." She didn't even mention the car repair that had cost her nearly a thousand dollars. A thousand bucks might have at least afforded her a buffer. She couldn't seem to catch a break, and she'd die before going to Carter for money. She was pretty sure she was sick of the "throw good money after bad" speech.

He took a step closer, close enough that she could feel the warmth of his body emanating from beneath his plaid work shirt, smell the clean, fresh scent of his soap and see the particularly attractive bow shape to his lips. Determined, she stood her ground.

"This," he said darkly, "has absolutely nothing to do with my authority but a hell of a lot to do with yours. You own one-third of this ranch, but you've made it clear that you hate it and that it's a last resort for you. Forgive me if that doesn't make me feel all warm and fuzzy."

"I didn't mean it that way…"

He shook his head. "Yes, you did. And that's fine. Let's just not pretend it's anything other than what it is. You need a place that's free and Duke needs time to convince you to hang on to your third. My job? Is to run the place as if your family drama didn't exist."

She swallowed. He was absolutely right. Instead of appreciating the fact that she actually had an alternative, she was showing up with a big ol' resentful chip on her shoulder. It just so happened that Quinn seemed to be able to get her back up without even trying. He had from the moment they'd met.

"I don't want to keep you from your job, then," she replied, mollified. "I'll just get settled. And find Duke." She didn't know what would happen after that. She owned a third of Crooked Valley, but she knew absolutely nothing about running a ranch. What had her grandfather been thinking, anyway, leaving the place

to the three of them? Duke had been in the Army when
the will had been drafted, and Rylan…well, Rylan was
never in one place for long. She supposed leaving the
place to the three of them was the old man's way of
getting them on the ranch since he hadn't succeeded
in doing that when he was alive.

"Duke and Carrie are both out, moving the herd to
a new pasture. They won't be in until midafternoon."

"Oh."

"You're a big girl. I'm sure you can find a way to
amuse yourself. If you'll excuse me…"

She stepped aside, took off her coat and hung it on
a hook in the entry. Quinn, on the other hand, pulled
on boots, a heavy jacket, hat and thick gloves. "You'll
find the door's rarely locked here, Lacey. All you have
to do is turn the knob and come in."

It might have been a welcoming sort of sentiment if
it hadn't made her feel stupid and foolish. With a huff
she turned her back on Quinn and walked away, heading towards the kitchen and main living room. A few
moments later she heard the door open and close and
she finally relaxed her shoulders. Good riddance.

She had to admit, the house was cozy, despite its
size. The downstairs contained a huge kitchen, living
room, formal dining room, and the ranch office as well
as a half bath and large doors exiting onto a deck that
offered a view of rolling hills and the mountains in the
distance. Upstairs, as she'd learned at Christmas, were
four large bedrooms. All of them were vacant at the moment, though at Christmas they'd been partially occupied by her mom and stepdad, David, and her brother
Rylan who'd surprised everyone by showing up. And for

one night, Quinn had shared another with his daughter, Amber, who was a total sweetheart.

Lacey wondered if it mattered which room she took as hers during her stay. It was just temporary; there was no question of this being permanent. Maybe Duke thought he'd be able to convince her to take on her share, but Lacey had a plan. Sort of. She was going to take a few days off to refresh herself, and then she was going to spruce up her résumé and start applying for positions. Surely someone needed a person with an accounting degree to do their accounts payable or something.

There were logs by the fireplace but it was unlit, so she took a few moments to set up some kindling and light a match. It took a while for the dry wood to catch, but when it did Lacey was pleased with herself. She'd check the fridge, maybe make some coffee or tea and chill in front of the fire for this afternoon. She added a stick of wood to the growing flames and wished she'd worn a thicker sweater. Which reminded her that she hadn't brought in her bags…

A loud thump startled her, making her jump as she pressed her hand to her heart. The door opened down the hall, followed by stomping of feet and a general commotion. When she stepped around the corner, she saw two of her suitcases standing guard at the bottom of the stairs, and Quinn's retreating back as he went to her car a second time, retrieving her last suitcase and an overnight bag.

She wished he'd just left it alone. She didn't want to be beholden to him for anything. Ever.

He stomped in again and put down the bags. "Your

hatchback was unlocked. I saw the bags through the window, and…"

"Thank you, Quinn. I was just going to get them. I appreciate you bringing them in."

Her polite voice seemed to take him off guard and he stared at her for a moment. "You're welcome."

The civil exchange made for an uncomfortable silence between them. A log snapped on the fire and he raised his eyebrows. "You built a fire?"

"It was a little chilly in here. I thought I'd make some tea, get settled, that sort of thing."

"Right." He lifted a finger to his hat. "Well, I'll be off. I'll be in the horse barn if you need anything, and by the time I take off for the day, Duke will be back."

"You have to pick up Amber at day care," she supplied, smiling a little. It was hard not to smile when thinking about the little chatterbox—even if it did cause a pang of sadness in Lacey's heart. It was totally unfair that Amber was left without a mother and Quinn without his wife. By all accounts, Marie Solomon had doted on her child and been a perfect mom. Something Lacey would never be.

"Yeah. Anyway, I'd better go. Work won't do itself."

She shut the door behind him, then scooted to the office window and watched him walk across the yard, long strides eating up the distance between the house and the barn. He'd touched his hat, such an old-fashioned, mannerly gesture, that she was momentarily nonplussed. She wasn't sure they even made men like that anymore. Certainly Carter had never been like that. Not unless there'd been an audience, and then he'd been all chivalry and sweetness. But when they were alone? The walls went up between them again. By the time they'd divorced, she'd been relieved—even if she did still blame herself for how it all went wrong. She'd held on too tight, fought too hard and driven him away.

Then again, there was a limit to Quinn's chivalry. He hadn't offered to carry her bags upstairs, had he? Just put them inside the door and expected her to get on with it. She was glad. She was a big girl and could look after herself. Including making a few trips up and down stairs to transport her luggage.

She was huffing and puffing by the time the last bag was settled in what she assumed was the master bedroom. The heavy pine furniture was solid and sturdy, the quilt on the top she suspected was homemade—perhaps by her grandmother, Eileen? She was a little sad that she didn't know, that the connection to the Duggan side of the family had faltered so much after Lacey's father's death. All in all, this was her new temporary home and she felt like a square peg in a round hole.

But she'd make the best of it. She always rallied after being kicked around, and this time was no different. She sat on the bed, fell back into the soft covers, and stared at the ceiling, wondering exactly where she should start.

Quinn had known she was arriving today. He'd thought it would be later, that he'd finish his work in the house and be gone outside by the time she arrived and they could avoid that awkward first meeting. Lacey Duggan had every right to be at Crooked Valley—she owned a third of it.

It was the fact that she didn't value it that got under his skin. She'd rather sell the place and be rid of it entirely. The only reason she hadn't pushed for that solution to the inheritance dilemma left by her grandfather,

Joe, was that Duke had come home first and wanted to make a go of it. The whole family looked at Duke as some hero…a military vet with a permanent hearing disability who stepped in when everything went wrong.

Quinn had been skeptical, but he'd liked Duke right away. Humble and not afraid to admit he didn't know what he was doing. Willing to learn and work. Ready to lead.

But Lacey? That woman had waltzed in here at Thanksgiving and come right out and told Duke that he should unload the place. As if it and the people who worked it and loved it meant nothing.

Things had to be really desperate for her to agree to move in for a while.

He opened the front door to Sunshine Smiles Day Care and let his troubles drift away. It smelled like sugar cookies and fruit punch and there were happy squeals coming from the playroom. He smiled at the young woman at the front. "Hey, Melanie."

"Hey, yourself. Amber's helping clean up from after-school snacks. I'll get her."

His daughter was the light of his life. She attended preschool for half days and spent the balance of the day at the day care. There were times he felt guilty about the amount of time she spent with people other than a parent, but it couldn't be helped. Being a single dad was a hard job. He'd had to get good at things like pigtails and bows. There'd been a lot of tears before he got a handle on the tiny elastics and learned how to make a bow so that the ribbons didn't sag and droop. Marie had always done the little girly things. She'd known Amber's favorite colors, foods and preferred toys, sang to her at night and read her favorite stories. It wasn't that

Quinn hadn't been involved—of course he had. But Marie had been the anchor. The details person, the one who held them all together.

He still missed her every damn day. And not just for the details and day-to-day jobs he'd had to assume. He missed having someone to laugh with, missed hearing her breathing when she slept, her voice when she called out for him to do something, the way she ran her hands through his hair. He was damned lonely and struggling to get through every day.

"Daddy!"

He smiled suddenly as Amber came charging out of the playroom. "Hey, princess! How was school?"

"It was good. We gots to paint pictures of our favorite thing to do in winter."

He knew what hers was, but he asked anyway. "And what did you paint?"

She twirled in a circle. "Skating!"

Quinn's skating expertise was limited to hockey skates and a pond scrimmage now and again. This year Amber had wanted to learn, so for Christmas he'd bought her little white figure skates and signed her up for weekly lessons at the rink in town.

"Nice," he commented, reaching for her backpack while she shoved her arms in her coat. "Come on, let's go home and get some supper on."

She was jamming her hat on her head as she peered up at him. "Can we go see Duke and Carrie? I want to show them my picture."

"Maybe another time." Quinn swallowed, thinking about Lacey being at the house by herself tonight. She'd looked sort of…lost, he thought. It didn't really matter that he wasn't overly fond of her. Losing your job was stressful, especially when you didn't have a backup plan. She'd been making ends meet on a mediocre salary. He knew how upset he'd be if he lost his job and had Amber to support.

Maybe he was being too hard on Lacey.

"Please, Daddy? I haven't seen Duke all week." She pouted prettily as she took his hand and they walked to the door.

"Duke was still out in the pasture when I left. He might not even be back yet. Maybe tomorrow."

"Okay."

He helped her buckle into her booster seat in the backseat of his truck and then got in and started the engine. "Hey, pumpkin? Do you remember Lacey, Duke's sister? The one that was here for Thanksgiving and Christmas?"

He looked in the rearview mirror. Amber was nodding vigorously. "The pretty lady," she announced. "With the long red hair. Like Ariel."

Quinn blinked. He wasn't sure that Lacey looked like Ariel from *The Little Mermaid*, but there was no question that she had gorgeous hair—when she didn't have it all pulled off her face and shoved into a tail or bun or braid. He'd only seen it down once, but Amber had hit the nail on the head. Her hair was long and thick, a rich burnished color with just a hint of natural wave. Even disheveled in the morning, as he'd seen her on Christmas Eve, it was stunning.

"Daddy? What about her?"

He was pulled back from his musings. "Oh," he replied, turning at a stop sign. "Just that she's going to be staying at the big house for a while. I know I take you with me a lot, so when you're there you're going to have to be extra good. It's not just you and me now."

"But Lacey is nice. She played with me lots."

"But she might not want to entertain you all the time, sweetheart. Do you understand?"

Amber shrugged. He could see the exaggerated movement in the rearview mirror and his heart gave a sad little thump again. The gesture was so like Marie. Amber had parts of Marie that she didn't even realize, because her memories of her mother were already beginning to dim. They should have had Marie longer. She should have been here through all of this. They were like a jigsaw puzzle with pieces missing. Pieces that could never be replaced.

"How about spaghetti for supper?" he asked, suggesting one of Amber's favorites. There had to be at least one more container of frozen sauce in the freezer. It wouldn't take long to thaw it and cook some noodles and throw some garlic bread in the oven. Cooking was something else he'd learned to do over the past year and a half.

"Spaghetti! Yum! I'll help!"

He smiled then, pushing the maudlin thoughts aside. He might miss Marie, but he was still a lucky man. He had a job he loved, a roof over his head and a daughter he adored. They could muddle through the rest if they had each other.

Lacey, on the other hand, would be sitting at the ranch house tonight all alone. And for the first time, he truly felt sorry for her.

Chapter 2

Lacey was up, showered, and dressed by the time Quinn arrived just before eight. She'd made a point of setting the alarm for six-thirty, though it hadn't mattered. She'd awakened shortly after five, cold, and had thrown another quilt over top of the blankets in an effort to warm up. By six she gave up trying to go back to sleep and got up, cranked up the heat and ran a hot shower.

Now she had her laptop open, a cup of coffee beside her, and her glasses perched on her nose when she heard the truck drive in and the door slam.

There was a knock on the door.

Frowning, she got up to answer it. Maybe it wasn't Quinn arriving for the day? When she put her eye up to the peephole, she could see his scowly face on the other side. What the heck?

She opened the door. "Quinn. Why on earth did you knock?"

He stepped inside, bringing a gust of icy air with him. "You live here now. I don't have any desire to walk in and take you by surprise."

Her face heated as the possibilities of "surprise" sank in. "Well." She took a step backward as he toed off his boots. "Thanks, but this place is really more yours than mine." She realized they needed to set some boundaries with each other and it might as well start this morning. "Tell you what. During work hours, this place is yours. You should be able to come and go as you please and not worry about knocking."

"It's a ranch, Lacey. Not exactly a nine-to-five job."

Did he always have to be so contrary?

"I realize that. But you have to admit, most days you come and go at regular hours. Let's say…between eight and six, you've got free run of the place and I'll work around you. The rest of the time, it just takes a knock. Okay?"

He gave a short nod. "Okay."

She smiled. "Good. Now, do you want some coffee? I put on a pot and I shouldn't drink the whole thing or I'll be bouncing off the walls by noon."

He looked surprised that she'd asked, and his face relaxed a little. "That would be good."

"What do you take in it?"

"Cream and sugar."

Same as her. Go figure.

She retrieved a mug from a cupboard while he put a lunch bag in the fridge. When he turned around he noticed her laptop on the dining table. "What are you working on so early?" he asked, accepting the steaming mug from her hands. The pads of his fingers brushed against her knuckles.

She withdrew quickly, alarmed that the thoughtless touch felt so intimate. "I'm sprucing up my résumé. Then I'll log on to the Wi-Fi and start searching the job sites and boards. I'm a CPA. Surely someone between here and Great Falls could use my considerable accounting skills." She waggled her eyebrows, trying to keep the mood light. Maybe he could at least give her points for trying.

"I could ask around."

Another surprise. "Why would you do that?"

He took a sip of his coffee and looked at her over the rim of his cup. "The faster you get a job, the faster you can resume your old life."

The whisper of intimacy disintegrated. "Harsh."

"We both know you don't really want to live here, Lacey. No sense pretending otherwise."

He was right. But it didn't mean she hated it entirely. "You realize that you give me crap for judging ranch life but you do the exact same thing with me? You're just as prejudiced, you know."

Quinn looked slightly alarmed at that assessment and put his coffee cup on the island. "What?"

"I'm just saying, that sure, I've made it no secret that this is not the life I'd choose for myself. But you're judging me for that. Quinn, I respect that this is your home and your livelihood and you like it. But just because it's not for me, and I know it, doesn't make me less than you, okay?"

He stared at her for a long moment. "I just got schooled," he admitted. "You're right. I shouldn't judge. You just…"

"Drive you crazy?"

"Yeah."

"You push my buttons, too." Their gazes connected and that strange intimate feeling happened again. She swallowed. "It must be because we're so different. Oil and water."

"I'm sure that's it."

Another heavy silence. Finally Quinn picked up his cup. "I need to make a few calls before heading out again. And you look like you need to get back to your work. I'll see you later."

"Sure." She folded her arms around her middle, still a bit chilly. "Quinn, one more thing. Do you always keep it so cold in here? I woke up at five this morning darn near freezing."

He stopped at the entrance to the hall. "I never thought about that. We keep the thermostat turned down, just keep enough heat on to keep pipes from freezing, really. I use a space heater in the office."

"I don't mind turning the heat down at night, though maybe not that far down." She briefly considered an electric blanket, but that wouldn't solve the entire problem. And she didn't want to blast the heat in the whole house and run up a huge bill.

"I'll speak to Duke about it, maybe get some programmable thermostats," Quinn promised. "In the meantime, do you want me to light a fire for you?"

"I can do it. And I turned up the heat in these rooms anyway. Forget I mentioned it."

He walked away to his office and she resumed her seat at the table. Even with the heat on, she was glad she'd put on warm leggings and the long sweater. Her coffee was gone before long so she got up and refilled her cup then went back to it.

She was just prettying up her margins and spacing when she looked up and saw Quinn at the end of the hallway, putting on his outerwear. He didn't realize she was watching, and she let her eyes roam over his long, strong legs and wide shoulders as he put on his boots and jacket. Then his hat and a heavy pair of gloves… and her mouth watered.

Maybe they did get along about as well as cats in a sack. But she was still woman enough to appreciate a fine male form and it was hard to find fault with Quinn's.

She hurriedly glanced down at her monitor as Quinn looked back towards the kitchen. It wouldn't do to get caught staring. They could hardly agree on anything. Heck, at Christmastime they'd argued about the correct way to mash potatoes, for heaven's sake. If he had the smallest inkling she found him physically attractive… well, things were already super awkward around here.

"I'll be back in later to grab my lunch," he called, and he was out the door before she could reply.

Surly, she thought. That was the problem with Quinn Solomon. He was surly. It was hard to like a man who hardly ever smiled.

She wondered if he'd smiled more before his wife had died, and her heart turned over a little at the thought. Whether she liked him or not, losing his wife and the mother of his daughter had to be terribly sad. He must have loved her a lot…

She and Carter hadn't had that sort of love. She'd thought they had, at first. But when put to the test, they didn't have what it took for a successful marriage.

She pushed her glasses up her nose and focused on the spacing of her résumé. There was no sense worrying about a past that couldn't be changed. The only thing she could do was look to the future. There were days when even that was difficult, but she had a clean start now. It was up to her to make the most of it.

She was in the middle of bookmarking employment sites where she could upload her CV when Duke blustered in. Without knocking. Ah. Big brothers. Funny. When Quinn had knocked, Lacey had felt *she* was imposing on *him*. When her brother entered without knocking, his sense of entitlement got on her nerves a little.

"You made it." He shrugged off his coat and hung it on the hook.

"Yesterday, as a matter of fact. Thanks for noticing." She sent him a cheeky grin, making sure to face him straight on. Duke's hearing was compromised, and he often watched lips to fill in any gaps of clarity, especially if his head was turned a bit the wrong way.

"I was going to come over last night, but Carrie and I didn't finish until late. By the time supper was over, we were tuckered out." He'd removed his boots and came into the kitchen in his stocking feet. His face got this weird, soft, moony look about it. "Especially Carrie. I keep telling her not to overdo it, but she's stubborn."

Lacey liked Carrie a lot. The former foreman of the cattle operation, Carrie had fallen for Duke hard and fast when he'd come back to Crooked Valley. Now she and Duke were married and she was expecting his baby. Duke was so happy and protective, and Lacey was happy for them. Even so, their happiness and future plans did serve as a painful reminder of the life she would never have. The dream of an adoring husband and a house full of kids was long gone.

"Is Carrie feeling okay?" Lacey sat back in her chair and took off her glasses, putting them on top of her paper tablet.

"The odd morning sickness, but nothing major. And she's tired a lot. Otherwise, she's great." He pulled out a chair and sat down, resting his elbows on the table. "I can't wait for the ultrasound. We'll get pictures and everything."

It was like a knife to the heart, but Lacey never let on. No one except their mother knew that Lacey'd had to undergo surgery—the kind that prevented her from ever having children.

"I'm glad you're so happy." That, at least, was the truth.

"And you're here. That makes me happy." He grinned at her, his blue eyes sparkling at her. "I always love having a little sis around to torment."

"Don't get your hopes up. I appreciate the place to stay, but I'm not really interested in becoming a rancher. Gramps was crazy to split this place up the way he did."

Duke tapped his fingers on the table. "I used to think that, too."

"Well, you're not me. I'm not a rancher. I belong behind a desk somewhere, working with columns of numbers. Not shoveling manure or whatever it is you guys do outside all day."

Duke laughed. "I forgot you're such a girlie girl."

"Yes, well, you haven't exactly been around much the last few years." She realized that sounded a bit harsh, so she tempered it a little. "You were deployed, Duke. I don't blame you in the least. But you must realize that life went on while you were overseas. We all went our own ways."

She let him off the hook and smiled. "Anyway, I do really want to say thank-you for letting me crash. Losing my job was a big blow. I was living paycheck to paycheck and really couldn't see how I could keep up with the rent on the town house."

"What about Carter? Doesn't he pay you any alimony?"

She nodded. "Yes, but it's not much. Carter's alimony is peanuts, really. He's got his own troubles. I wouldn't ask him for anything more."

"You'd be within your rights. He walked out on you and left you with everything—including all the debt."

As Lacey thought about how to answer her brother, she got up and poured him the last cup of coffee from the pot. She put it down in front of him and then put her hand on his shoulder.

"It was a mutual decision, Duke," she said softly. "It just wasn't working. We were both unhappy." She didn't feel like mentioning that the debt Duke spoke of was mostly due to her and all her medical tests and treatment that weren't covered by her insurance. "I just want you to know that I appreciate the chance to stay here while I figure out what's next."

Duke smiled down into his coffee.

"What?"

He looked up and his eyes crinkled around the edges. "You sound like me a few months ago."

She knew Duke wanted her to take on her third of the ranch. If she did, and if they could convince Rylan to take on his third, the ranch stayed as is. But if they didn't…well, Duke would either have to find a way to buy them out of their thirds, or the place would be sold. It was an annoying thing, what their grandfather had done in his will. And it would have been much easier to brush off if Duke hadn't decided to stay on.

"I'm not taking on my third, Duke. I'll help you in any way I can, but not that."

Duke took a long drink of his cooling coffee. "Well, there's lots of time to think about it. What are you doing today?"

His whole dismissal sent out a message of "give me time to change your mind" and she ignored it. "I'm sending out my résumé, seeing if I can find any leads to a new job. It's not an ideal commute to Great Falls, but spring will be here soon and the bad weather is mostly done. I can do it for a while, until I build up some financial reserves. And who knows? Maybe I'll find something closer."

"Have you seen Quinn yet?"

She raised an eyebrow. "Of course I did. He was the welcoming committee." She smiled saucily.

"Oh, great. You weren't too hard on him, were you?"

She gave him a swat. "So much for family loyalty. What about how grouchy he might have been to me?"

Duke's frown deepened. "Was he?"

"Of course not." No matter her issues with Quinn, she wouldn't put Duke in the middle of it. He relied on Quinn too much. She wasn't here to stir up trouble.

"Hey. If I had one reservation about you staying at the house, it was that you'd be sharing space with Quinn. I know you don't get along. I don't know why, but you don't. I'm hoping you can coexist peacefully."

"We've laid out some ground rules." She sat back down at the table.

"Well, try not to kill each other. This place doesn't run without him." Duke raised his cup, drained what was left of his coffee, and stood. "Thanks for the coffee. I'd better get back."

"Anytime. This is your place, after all."

"No, it's yours. For as long as you want it, Lace." He put his hand over hers on top of the table. "I mean that. I wasn't around a lot, definitely not when you were going through some rough times. I'd like to be there for you now."

The backs of her eyes stung and she nodded through blurred vision. "That means a lot, Duke."

"Right. Better be off." He went down the hall and put on his gear again. "Oh, Lace?"

She looked up.

"Maybe next time you can have some cookies to go with that coffee? Carrie's on a 'no sweets' kick with the pregnancy. And somehow her kale chips just aren't cutting it for me."

She couldn't help but smile. "I'll see what I can do," she replied. "Now go, so I can find a job, will you?"

With a wink he disappeared.

Lacey turned her attention back to the document on the screen but didn't really focus on it. Instead she was thinking about what Duke had just said, and thinking about how it felt to be here. It felt good. It felt…right. Somehow being with family, having that support, was exactly what she needed.

She just had to be careful not to get too used to it, or use it as a crutch. This time she was making her own decisions and standing entirely on her own two feet. At least if she relied on herself, she wasn't being set up for disappointment.

* * *

Jack, one of the regular hands, was out with the flu so Quinn spent the rest of his morning mucking out stalls in the horse barn. It was a job he actually enjoyed. The slight physical exertion kept him warm and he usually talked to the horses as he worked. Even the scrape of the shovel on the barn floor had a comforting sound to it, and he worked away with the radio playing in the background, just him and his thoughts.

He had a lot of thoughts, as it happened. Most days it was about what needed to be done at the ranch, or worries about being a good single dad to Amber as she got older. He already knew far more about Disney princesses and ballet slippers and hair ribbons than most dads. And it wasn't that he minded. It was just…he knew Marie would have done a much better job. A little girl needed a mom. And Quinn wasn't sure how to solve that, because he wasn't really interested in getting married again.

Not when it had hurt so much the first time.

Thankfully he had Carrie and Kailey. Carrie was around even more now that she and Duke were married, and Amber loved spending time at Crooked Valley. Kailey was Carrie's best friend and lived at a neighboring ranch. Between the two of them, they provided Amber with some great girlie time. On Sundays, too, they visited with Quinn's mom, who lived in a little one-bedroom apartment in Great Falls. She'd moved there after his dad had died and she had a vital, happy life in the assisted-living complex, and help with the arthritis that sometimes made her day-to-day living a challenge.

Visits and special time were great. The girls were great. But they weren't her mother, and Quinn couldn't

help but feel like he'd somehow let Amber down even
though Marie's death had been a freak accident. A heart
defect that had gone undetected until it was too late.
One morning she'd been laughing with him over breakfast. Two hours later she'd just been…gone.

At noon he ventured back to the house and lifted his
hand to knock at the door, then pulled it back again.
Lacey had said to come and go as he pleased, and he
should. This was, after all, a working ranch. He was
pretty sure she wasn't going to be running around the
house in her Skivvies at twelve o'clock in the afternoon.

The thought gave him pause, because he pictured
her that way and his body tensed in a familiar way. Oh,
no. That would be too inconvenient. He had no business thinking about Lacey Duggan in her underwear
and even less business liking it.

He reached for the doorknob and resolutely turned
it. He stepped into the foyer and heard a radio playing, heard a soft female voice singing along. He was
transported back two years earlier, when he'd still had
the perfect life, and the joy he felt coming home to a
scene much like this one. There was the sound of something opening and closing, and the rattle of bake ware.
The aroma of fresh-baked cookies reached him and his
stomach growled in response.

After hanging up his coat, he wandered to the kitchen
to get his lunch out of the fridge. He'd just go eat in the
office, out of Lacey's way. It was a lonely-sounding
proposition but he realized that if he stayed in her little
sphere of existence, they'd probably end up arguing.
They always did.

"Don't mind me. I'm just here to get my lunch."

He forgot that she had music on. That she probably

hadn't heard him come inside. But he remembered now as she squeaked and jumped with alarm, jerking the spatula which held a perfectly round, warm, chocolate chip cookie. The cookie went flying and landed with a soft splat in the middle of the kitchen floor.

"Cripes, Quinn!" Her brows pulled together in annoyance. "Do you have to creep up on a person like that?"

She looked so indignant he had the strangest urge to laugh. "I wasn't trying to be quiet. I came in like I always do. I guess you didn't hear me because of the music."

"Whatever." She bent to pick up the cookie, which broke into pieces as she lifted it off the floor. She put the remnants on the counter and then went for a piece of paper towel to wipe the little dots of melted chocolate from the tile.

Quinn went to the fridge and took out his lunch bag. "Well, if it's any consolation, they smell great."

He turned around and headed back towards the hall.

"Where are you going?"

He paused and looked over his shoulder. "I was going to eat in the office."

"Is that where you normally eat?"

He didn't know how to answer. He usually grabbed his lunch, made himself a coffee, used the microwave if he had leftovers to heat. Today he had leftover spaghetti, which he'd planned to eat cold.

"I assume your lack of a fast reply means no. You normally use the kitchen, don't you?"

He sighed. "Sometimes."

"Truly, Quinn, I don't want you to alter your routine for me. Pretend I'm not here."

It was pretty hard to pretend because she was there, with her burnished curls caught up in a ponytail, her blue eyes snapping at him. He noticed, not for the first time, that she had the faintest dusting of freckles over the bridge of her nose. Duke was thirty, so that had to make her, what, twenty-eight or so?

Twenty-eight, with a career job behind her, married, divorced. Quinn was thirty-three, and he knew exactly how life could age a person so that numbers were insignificant. He tried to remember that Lacey had faced her share of troubles. Duke had made it plain that the family wasn't too impressed that her ex had walked out on her.

He went back and put his lunch bag on the island, unzipped it and took out the plastic container holding his lunch. "Do you mind if I use the microwave?"

She rolled her eyes. "What did I just say?"

Saucy. At least she was consistent.

He popped the container in the microwave and started it up, then stood awkwardly waiting for it to beep. Meanwhile, Lacey finished removing the cookies from the pan and began dropping batter by the spoonful on the parchment.

His stomach growled again.

When his meal was hot, he took it to the kitchen table—no laptop in sight now—and got out his knife and fork. The pasta didn't look as appetizing as it might have. He was an adequate cook only, but he was getting better. Trying new things now and again. The trouble was that by the time he got Amber from day care, he had to cook stuff that was relatively fast if they hoped to eat before her bath time.

He was nearly through when Lacey put a small plate beside him and a glass of milk.

"Uh, thanks," he said, looking up. She was smiling down at him, and for the first time there was no attitude in her expression.

"I'd be pretty heartless if I didn't offer you fresh cookies," she said. "Besides, I don't dare eat them all myself. I'm counting on you and Duke to eat the lion's share."

She went back to the sink and ran soapy water to wash the dishes.

Quinn bit into a cookie and sighed in appreciation. God, the woman knew how to cook. He'd realized that at Thanksgiving and then again at Christmas when she'd bustled in with all her bossiness. He and Amber had both enjoyed the home-cooked meals they'd shared here at the ranch. It had actually stung his pride a little when Amber asked if they could go back to "Uncle Duke's" because Lacey was there and doing a lot of the family cooking along with their mother, Helen.

"They turn out okay?" Lacey called from the sink, her hands immersed in the water. "I didn't have my recipe with me and went from memory."

He bit back a sarcastic comment. Why did she push his buttons so? Instead he reminded himself that she'd gone out of her way to be nice. To be accommodating. "They're delicious," he replied honestly. "Maybe the best chocolate chip cookie I've ever had."

She dried her hands on a dish towel, then grabbed a cookie and her coffee cup and joined him at the table. "Can I tell you a secret, Quinn?"

They were sharing confidences now?

"Um, sure. I guess."

She bit into the cookie, chewed thoughtfully and swallowed. "I bake when I'm stressed. I think it's a combination of things, from focusing on something other than what's going on, to the process of making something and maybe even the aromas. They're comforting smells, you know?"

He did know. He missed them around his place, and the absence of them sometimes made his chest ache.

"You're stressed?"

She broke off another piece of cookie. "Of course I am. Know what they said when I packed up my desk at the office? 'Oh, no, who's going to bring us treats all the time?' I mean, it's been better up until a few months ago, but when Carter first left…"

Right. Carter. That was the bastard's name.

"When Carter left it was weird, being all alone. We'd planned to be together forever, you know?"

His last bite of cookie swelled in his throat as a heavy silence fell over the table.

"Oh, God," she whispered, and to his surprise she put her hand on his arm. "I'm so sorry. That was so thoughtless of me. Of course you know."

He forced the cookie down and looked up at her. Her eyes were soft with sympathy and understanding and her hand was still on his wrist. Something passed between them, something that, for a flash, felt like shared grief. It was gone in the blink of an eye, but it had been there. He got the feeling that she understood more than he realized. Still, could divorce be as bad as a spouse dying? As bad as a child without a mother?

Lacey pulled her hand away. "I'm sorry," she repeated. "It's been so quiet here that I've talked your ear off. I should let you get back to work."

He cleared his throat. "Yes. Thanks for the cookies."

"Anytime. They'll be in Grandma Duggan's cookie

jar if you find yourself snackish." She gestured towards a stone crock that she must have unearthed from somewhere, now sitting on the counter next to the toaster.

"Will do."

Quinn put the lid on his dish and shoved everything back in his lunch bag, then put it in the fridge, empty, where he'd collect it at the end of the day.

Back in the office he pulled up a spreadsheet and tried to wrap his mind around the numbers in the columns, but nothing was fitting together right. His focus was shot. He kept getting stuck on the look on Lacey's face when she admitted she using baking as a coping mechanism. She'd looked lonely. Vulnerable. Feelings he could relate to so easily that when she'd put her fingers on his sleeve, he'd been tempted to turn his hand over and link his fingers with hers.

Ludicrous. Crazy. Duke Duggan's sister, for Pete's sake. His boss's pain-in-the-butt sister who hated anything to do with ranching.

With a frown he tweaked the column again, fixing the formula at the end. It wouldn't do to start thinking of Lacey Duggan in a friendly way. Certainly not in a kindred spirits kind of way.

A few hours later he heard her go out the door, heard her start her car and drive away. He let out a breath. Working here while Lacey was living at the house was going to be tougher than he thought—and not for the reasons he expected.

She wasn't back yet when he got his lunch bag from the fridge and left to pick up Amber. But when he got home, and as supper was cooking, he opened the bag to take out his dirty dishes. To his surprise, the container that had held his lunch was perfectly clean, and a little bag was beside it, full of cookies. A sticky note was stuck to the front. "For you and Amber," it said.

Quinn swallowed. Lacey had to stop being so nice, trying so hard. She was going to make it difficult for him to keep disliking her if she kept it up.

Chapter 3

Lacey had only been at Crooked Valley three days when she got her first phone call, asking her for an interview. A company in Great Falls was looking for someone to do their payroll. When Quinn came in for lunch on the day of the interview, she was running a lint brush over the dark material of a straight skirt. For some reason little bits of fluff kept sticking to the fabric, and she wanted to look perfect.

Her head told her it was just an interview at a manufacturing company, not a high-powered lawyer's office or anything. Neat and tidy business wear would have sufficed, but she was determined to put her absolute best foot forward. She'd brought out the big guns: black pencil skirt, cream silk blouse, patent heels.

She was turning into the kitchen from the downstairs bath at the same time as Quinn entered from the hall.

Both of them stopped short, but Quinn just stared at her. "Oh. Hi." He sort of recovered from the surprise but his expression plumped up her confidence just a little. It was definitely approval that glowed in his eyes for the few seconds before he shuttered it away.

"I have an interview this afternoon," she said, grabbing some hand lotion from the windowsill above the sink. She rubbed it into her hands as Quinn opened the fridge. "In Great Falls."

"That's good news," he answered, but now she noticed he was avoiding looking at her.

She frowned. Maybe she'd misread his expression before. "Do I look all right, Quinn? Should I maybe wear a different top or something? Are pearls a little too much?" She touched the strand at her collarbone. They were her grandmother Eileen's pearls. As the only granddaughter, they'd automatically gone to her. She rarely wore them, but it seemed appropriate somehow now that Lacey was living in the farmhouse. Like a good luck charm.

"You look fine," he answered.

Her frown deepened. He hadn't looked up when he said it, just stuck his lunch in the microwave and set the timer.

"I was hoping for something more than fine. More like, 'Wow, let's hire this one on the spot.'"

He turned and looked at her then, his face set in an impersonal mask. "You look great, Lacey. Very professional." He paused. "Very pretty."

It might have meant more if it didn't seem as if it pained him to say it.

"Thanks," Lacey replied, and then felt a bit silly.

She hadn't really been fishing for a compliment, but it felt that way now.

She wanted a splash of color, so she transferred her wallet and necessary items from her black purse to a turquoise handbag. "I made a coffee cake this morning," she said, doing a check for her car keys. "It's under the domed lid. Help yourself."

The microwave dinged and Quinn took out his lunch. "You trying to fatten me up with all this baking?"

"Not much chance of that." The words came out before she could think. She'd noticed Quinn's build. A little on the slim side, and she wondered if it was because he found it hard to work and be a full-time dad and do all the household things that needed to be done. "Like I said, I enjoy doing it. And I don't really have anyone to cook for. Duke's started coming in for coffee break each morning, and sometimes Carrie comes with him, but she's really watching her diet with the baby and all." Once again, the little pang of envy touched her heart but she pushed it away.

She'd never have a big family to cook for. She might as well accept it.

She took a minute and looked at Quinn. Really looked at him, and wondered what it must be like to lose a spouse and try to raise a small child on your own. Certainly he was doing a good job, but at what cost? She noticed he didn't smile all that often, and his eyes had lines at the corners. He wasn't that old, either. Maybe midthirties at the most. It seemed more like life had aged him.

"Quinn, how's Amber doing?"

He shrugged and twirled some spaghetti noodles

on his fork. "She's fine. Likes preschool. Does okay at the day care."

"It must be rough, bringing her up on your own."

He looked up at her sharply. "We get by."

"Oh, of course you do. I just thought that…" She hesitated. What was she thinking, anyway? She didn't really want to get involved with Quinn's life, did she? They'd sort of formed a truce since she'd moved in. Less criticizing and arguing, and that was good. Still slightly awkward, but good.

Truth of the matter was, Lacey was lonely. She didn't know anyone in Gibson, didn't have contact with colleagues since she was out of work, and she was going just a little bit stir-crazy here at Crooked Valley.

"I just thought that since cooking for one is a real pain, maybe I could send some food home with you. It's stupid. I make a recipe and then end up either freezing or throwing out half because it's more than I can eat."

"Didn't you cook for one before?"

She did, but it was different. "To be honest? I froze some, and I often gave some to a neighbor. She was elderly and alone and struggled to cook for herself and eat enough."

Quinn's eyes snapped at her. "So what, Amber and I look like we need charity, is that it?"

"No!" She twisted her fingers together. "I didn't mean that."

"We get along just fine, thanks." His lips were set, and Lacey dropped the subject. She hadn't meant to insult him or imply he was, well, lacking in any area.

"I'd better get going, then," she said quietly, and picked up her handbag.

"Good luck. I hope you get it," he answered, but his

voice lacked any warmth and the encouragement stung. Sure he hoped she got it, so she'd be out of his hair. Message received loud and clear.

She reached for her coat and keys and left him sitting there at the table. Maybe he was lonely and bitter but she didn't have to be! She was starting a new chapter in her life, and Quinn Solomon was not going to bring her down.

But fate had other ideas that afternoon. The directions that had seemed so clear earlier were suddenly not, and she got turned around. It was five minutes after her scheduled appointment time when she pulled into the parking lot. In her rush, she snagged her panty hose getting out of the car and there was no time to change or take them off, just hope that it wouldn't be visible once she was seated.

She stopped outside the office door, blew out a breath, rolled her shoulders, pasted on a smile and walked in.

"Hi," she greeted the receptionist. "I'm Lacey Duggan, here for the interview?"

The receptionist looked at her over the top of her glasses. "Just have a seat for a minute. Can I get you anything? Coffee?"

If she were any more hyped up she'd explode. "Maybe some water? That'd be great."

The woman returned with a small glass of water. Lacey removed her coat and hung it on a nearby coat tree and she reminded herself to calm down. It had only been a few days. This was her first interview. She took a sip of water and at the same time, her cell phone buzzed in the purse on her lap. It startled her enough that she jumped, and splashed water on the front of her silk blouse.

For the love of Mike.

An office door opened just as she was reaching in her bag for her phone. She dropped it back into the purse and stood up as a friendly-looking woman came out and smiled at her. She would get herself together and ignore her bad luck so far…

"You must be Ms. Duggan. I'm Corinna Blackwood. We spoke on the phone yesterday." She held out her hand and Lacey shook it.

The head of HR. And she looked approachable. Maybe Lacey could turn this around.

"I tried to call you about an hour ago," Ms. Blackwood said, stepping back. "I'm sorry you drove all this way. We filled the position earlier this afternoon."

Lacey swallowed, so surprised she didn't know how to respond. "I see." She licked her lips and tried not to sigh. "I drove in from Gibson. I must have just missed you."

"Yes, I spoke to someone at your home number. He said he'd try to reach you. I'm assuming he was unsuccessful."

Lacey felt her cheeks heat and struggled to keep her composure.

"I'm very sorry to disappoint you, Ms. Duggan."

Lacey blinked and got herself together. She called up a smile. "Me, too, but perhaps you can keep my résumé on file? In case anything else comes up in your accounting department in the future."

Ms. Blackwood's face lightened. "I certainly will. Can we offer you a coffee or something?"

"I'm fine," she answered, trying to mask her disappointment. "But maybe I'll leave you my cell number as well as my home number."

Ms. Blackwood seemed to appreciate the wry sense of humor and nodded. "Give it to Jane, here, and she'll put it on your résumé. It was nice to meet you."

They shook hands again, and then Lacey found herself back outside the office door.

She walked across the parking lot, the winter air freezing against her legs. Stupid shoes…she'd worn them for vanity and now it was for nothing and she was freezing her toes off. She turned on the car and finally looked at her phone. There were two text messages, one from Quinn and one from Duke.

The first one said Call home as soon as you get this. Q.

The second was the one that Duke had sent while she was in the office. Did Quinn get in touch with you?

She texted Duke back right away and let him know she was on her way back. Then she texted Quinn and simply replied that she'd just received his text and thanks.

Quinn already knew, then, that she didn't get the job. Great. She loved looking like a failure in front of him.

Worse, his truck was still in the yard when she got home. She would have preferred to lick her wounds in peace, but apparently today was just not her lucky day. Wearily she turned the key in the door and walked in, only to hear the television going and some very girlish laughter.

Amber was here.

Lacey tried to be annoyed but she couldn't. Amber was a total doll, clearly more like her mother than her father. She smiled easily and had gorgeous curls that set off a pair of impish blue eyes. Lacey shut the door and put her handbag on the first step of the stairs, then slipped off her heels. The office door to her right was closed; Quinn was probably in there working. She went through on stocking feet and found Amber sitting at the table, coloring some sheets that Lacey guessed were from school, and watching cartoons.

"Well, hello," she greeted. "Whatcha got there?"

"Lacey! Daddy said you were here!"

To her surprise, Amber hopped down from the chair and hugged Lacey's legs.

Suddenly the day didn't seem so gray.

"Okay, okay. No day care today?"

"Miss Melanie was sick today. Daddy came to pick me up after school, but he said he had some work to do first so I could watch TV." She looked up at Lacey, her eyes troubled. "Is that okay? You live here. Maybe Daddy should have asked p'mission."

God, if the kid were any more sweet she'd be made of sugar. "It's perfectly fine. You go ahead and carry on with the coloring. I'm going to change out of my clothes, okay?"

"But why? You look pretty."

Now there was a compliment that was heartfelt and Lacey smiled a little. "Why, thank you. But I think I'll put on something a little more comfortable so I can cook some dinner."

Instead of getting back in her seat, Amber followed Lacey down the hall to the stairs. "What are you going to make?" she asked, and Lacey hid a smile.

"If you were me, what would you make for supper?"

Amber followed her up the stairs. "I would make… fried chicken and 'tato salad."

It sounded like a strange order, and Lacey looked down at her companion. "Really?"

Amber nodded. "'Cause it's Daddy's favorite only he doesn't know how to make it and I'm too little."

And just like that Lacey's heart did a little turn. Quinn and Amber did the best they could. It wasn't hard to forgive him for his earlier sharpness. After all, he'd tried to pass on the message right away and it was her own fault she hadn't gotten the text. That she'd gotten lost.

"Now, what a coincidence! I was just going to make that!"

Amber turned her head sideways and peered up at Lacey as they reached the top step. "What's a coinc'dence?" She struggled over the word.

Lacey smiled. "Well, it's like taking two things that aren't related at all and connecting them together."

"Like me and my best friend, Emma? We're not related but purple is both our favorite color."

Bad grammar and all, Lacey was enchanted. "Well, sort of like that."

Amber actually followed her right into the bedroom and plopped up on the bed while Lacey went to the closet for a pair of sweats and an old hoodie. Not sure how Quinn would feel about Amber's intrusion, she did a quick change right in the closet and came out in her comfy clothes.

"Ta-da! Presto chango!"

Amber fell over on the bed in a fit of giggles.

"Amber? Where'd you go?"

"Uh-oh," the girl whispered, crawling off the bed. She stuck her head out the bedroom door. "I'm up here, Daddy."

"You're not supposed to wander around upstairs. You know that."

Lacey was right behind her. "That's okay. She came up with me."

Quinn's face changed, adopting that impersonal mask again that Lacey was starting to hate. "Oh. I didn't know you were back." He looked at Amber again. "Don't you go bothering Lacey, now."

"Sorry, Daddy."

Lacey put her hand on Amber's curls. "It's okay. I had a cruddy afternoon and Amber's a real ray of sunshine."

"You're sure?"

Lacey nodded. "I'm sure. Tell you what." She squatted down beside Amber. "Sometimes when you come over, I might not have time to hang out. If I tell you that I'm busy, you'll respect that, right?"

Amber's little head bobbed up and down. "I won't get in your way."

Lacey got the feeling that Amber's life revolved a little too much around being out of the way. Her heart ached for the little girl. Lacey wasn't a stranger to that sensation, either. Being the middle child in a single-parent home, she'd often felt invisible. Superfluous.

She held out her hand and they went down the stairs together, with Quinn waiting at the bottom. She could tell by the set of his jaw that he was tense about it. "Amber, why don't you go tidy up your crayons? Then you can help me in the kitchen if you want."

"Yay!" Amber raced off, while Lacey faced Quinn at the bottom of the stairs.

"You don't have to babysit her," he said quietly, so

his daughter couldn't hear. "She's used to amusing herself while I finish up."

It hurt a little to say, but she did it anyway. "Quinn, I like kids. Amber's sweet. I mean it. If she's in my way, I'll speak up. But you know I had a rotten afternoon. She really did perk it up."

"You didn't get my text, did you?"

She shook her head. "Not until after I'd gotten lost, ripped my panty hose, spilled water down my front and was told the position was already filled."

He laughed then, a dry chuckle that made her smile. "I know. It sounds ridiculous," she added.

"I'm sorry," he offered, and this time she knew he meant it.

"Ah well, it was my first nibble and it's only been a few days. Something will turn up."

"Yes, it will." His gaze was warmer as he looked at her and there was a moment where she got the feeling they almost…understood each other. But that was nuts. Oil and water. That's what they were…what she had to remember.

And she remembered the way he'd told her she looked pretty and got a little whoop-y feeling in her stomach.

"I'd better finish up," he said softly, and for the briefest moment his gaze dropped to her lips. Oh. Oh, my. She sucked in a breath.

"Okay."

Quinn left her standing there, still reeling from the split second where he'd stared at her mouth. He couldn't be attracted to her. Couldn't have thought about kissing her. He didn't even like her!

She didn't like him, either, but if she were honest, the

thought had crossed her mind that kissing him might not be so bad.

The door to the office closed and she shook her head. Fried chicken. Potato salad. She'd better get on it if they planned to have a decent dinner.

Amber was as much a distraction as a help in the kitchen, but Lacey didn't mind. She cut up the potatoes and Amber put them in the pot, and then while they waited for them to cook, Lacey set the girl to work mixing dressing for the salad while she put together seasoning for the chicken. Together they decided on frozen corn for a side, with a dish of sliced cucumbers, Amber's favorite raw vegetable. Potatoes were drained and rinsed repeatedly in cold water to cool them down, and Lacey started frying the chicken while Amber poured corn kernels in a casserole dish for heating in the microwave. They agreed on celery and a little red pepper in the salad but no onion, and by the time Quinn came out of his office, the chicken was frying merrily in a pan, the salad was in a pretty scalloped bowl, and the microwave was running.

"What on earth is all this?" he asked, staring at the mess on the countertops.

"We made dinner! I helped! It's your favorite, Daddy. Fried chicken!"

She looked up at him so happily that Lacey could tell he didn't have the heart to scowl.

"Fried chicken? How did you know that's my favorite?"

"Chicken and 'tato salad! Everyone knows that." She rolled her eyes and Lacey laughed.

"You're expected to stay, you know." She said it

softly, holding a pair of tongs in her hand. "I made enough for all of us. This way you don't have to go home and worry about supper."

She could tell that Quinn was torn. After their conversation at noon, this was exactly what he said he didn't want. She lifted her chin. "It was Amber's idea," she added.

His gaze held hers. Momentarily she felt guilty for putting his little girl in the middle, but Amber was very hard to resist. Couldn't he see how happy his daughter looked right now?

"Amber, why don't you set the table? Do you know where everything is?" she asked, breaking the connection.

Amber nodded and raced for a step stool that allowed her to reach the plates and glasses in the cupboard. Lacey turned the chicken in the pan, putting the splatter screen over the top again to keep the grease from dotting the top of the stove. She heard Quinn behind her, helping Amber put things on the table in preparation for the meal.

It felt homey. It felt…like everything Lacey was sure she'd been missing. Only this wasn't her family. Not her husband, not her daughter, not her home. It was just pretend. Something to make her feel better, to fill the gap until she got her life in order again.

And if now and again it gave Quinn a hand, all the better.

When had she started caring?

The chicken was perfectly done and she removed it from the pan and put it on a platter. The salad was placed in the middle of the table, and she added a sprinkle of paprika for color, then put the bowl of corn on a hot mat and stirred in just a little bit of butter. "There," she said, stepping back. "All done. Let's eat."

She took the spot at the foot of the table while Quinn sat at the head, where he normally ate his lunch, and Amber was in between them on the side. Lacey watched as Quinn helped Amber put salad, corn and cucumbers on her plate, and then chose a drumstick for her to eat. Her eyes were huge as she looked at all the food and then, just as Lacey was about to taste her first bite of potato salad, Amber dropped her fork with a clatter.

"Daddy! We forgot to say grace!"

He put down his fork. "So we did."

Amber turned her face to Lacey. "Do you want to say it, Lacey?"

Lacey struggled to answer. Grace was not really her thing. They'd never said it at home at mealtime and she wasn't quite comfortable right now, being put on the spot.

"Why don't you say it, sweetie?" Quinn came to the rescue and made the suggestion.

"Okay." When Lacey sat still, Amber held out her hand. "We hold hands, like this," she said, wiggling her fingers.

Hesitantly Lacey took the little fingers in her own, and watched as Quinn held Amber's other hand. Her heart melted a little bit as Amber's eyes squinted shut.

Lacey was expecting a scripted blessing, sort of the "God is great, God is good" thing she remembered from vacation Bible school when she'd spent time here at Crooked Valley when she was little. But instead, Amber took a few seconds to think before she offered up a simple prayer.

"Dear God, thank you for fried chicken and 'tato

salad and for my daddy and for my friend Lacey. Amen."

When she was done she dropped their hands, picked up her drumstick and took a bite, utterly unconcerned.

But Lacey met Quinn's gaze and saw something there she wasn't prepared for. She saw beyond the ranch manager and her biggest critic and the single dad to the man beneath.

And that man made her catch her breath.

Chapter 4

January turned into February. Lacey had two more interviews and no callbacks, which was highly discouraging. After the dinner at the ranch, she hadn't seen Amber. Miss Melanie was feeling better and Amber went back to day care after school each day. Quinn made an obvious effort to stay out of Lacey's way, too—eating his lunch in the office, or taking it out to the barn and eating with the hands around the coffee break table.

Lacey got the message loud and clear. If Quinn had been feeling any attraction, he certainly didn't want to act on it.

She occasionally sent home dinner with him. Some sliced baked ham and scalloped potatoes, or a dish of chili, or a casserole of lasagna for him to share with Amber. Quinn always protested, and she always answered the same way: she wasn't going to eat badly just because she was cooking for one. He might as well take the extra because she was going to cook it anyway.

The fact that he reluctantly agreed told her that he was glad to have the help even if he wouldn't admit it.

One sunshine-y day she printed out a few ads and drove into Gibson, hoping to put them up at the supermarket and post office and anywhere else she might find a bulletin board. Truth was, her unemployment checks were covering her expenses so far, but her real problem was having too much time on her hands. She needed something to keep her busy or she was going to eat too many brownies and fancy breads and end up requiring a whole new wardrobe. Taking on odd accounting jobs wasn't ideal but it was better than nothing. The businesses in Gibson were small, independently owned ones rather than big chains. Surely someone would be in need of some bookkeeping help.

She pinned up her notice on the community board at the grocery store, the drugstore, at the post office and at the office that housed the Chamber of Commerce. Then she ventured across the street to the library in the hopes of posting one there, which she left with the librarian. At the diner, she grabbed some lunch at the counter and asked if she could leave one there. Before going home, she stopped at the town's one and only department store, looking for some new dishcloths and some replacement pairs of panty hose just in case she got any more interview calls. She stopped in front of a Valentine's Day display and smiled a little at the boxes of kids' cards generally featuring characters from the latest animated movies or TV shows. She picked up one set that was from Amber's favorite cartoon. Amber would probably have her first school party this year and give cards to all her classmates. On a whim, Lacey put the box in her basket and also snagged a few paper decorations and craft kits.

She was just adding a small bag of foil-wrapped chocolate hearts when she ran into Kailey Brandt, wheeling a cart full of towels that were on sale, cleaning supplies and a box of file folders.

"Lacey! Hey there." Kailey stopped the cart and smiled at Lacey, though Lacey thought she could see some strain around the other woman's eyes. "What brings you into town?"

"Oh, this and that," she replied, suddenly feeling rather awkward that she was still out of work.

"Paper Valentines?" Kailey grinned. "Amber's been around some, huh?"

"Not much. But I saw them and I couldn't resist. It's been a long time since I handed out Valentine's Day cards."

Kailey nodded. "If you were like the rest of us around here, you decorated shoeboxes for a mailbox and ate way too many heart-shaped cookies at the class party."

They both laughed a little. "Those were the days, right? Far less complicated."

"Tell me about it," Kailey said, her shoulders slumping. "I'm trying to keep the tax stuff straight and I ran out of file folders. I swear to God, I can work with ornery horses all day long, but doing paperwork is like the seventh circle of hell."

Lacey's ears definitely perked up at that, but it seemed presumptuous to offer her services during a friendly, neighborly exchange at the department store. She paused and then cautiously asked, "Have you considered outsourcing it?"

Kailey nodded. "A few times. I only took over a few years ago after my mom got thrown and hit her head. She does okay most of the time, but she struggles with numbers now and deals with migraines a lot."

"I didn't know. Your poor mom."

Kailey smiled. "She manages, and she just does other stuff. But she's slowed down a lot and Dad doesn't have the patience for accounting. That leaves me, unless I hire an accountant. The office in town is pretty expensive and I'd have to take the stuff there, you know? It's more trouble than it's worth, so I suffer. Usually not in silence." She laughed at herself a little.

It would be the perfect situation. "You know I'm an accountant, right?" she asked.

"Yeah, but I figured you'd be looking for something full-time. We don't have a huge operation, Lacey. It's just a few hours here and there, with a little more at tax time."

Lacey shrugged. "So? If I can do a few hours for you, and find some other businesses with the same needs…it would at least get me out of the house and doing something other than going crazy."

"I can't imagine wanting to do math rather than be in a barn," Kailey said. "Let me talk it over with my dad. How much would you charge?"

Lacey named her hourly rate—a little on the low side, taking into consideration that budgets were probably a little tight in a small ranching community.

"You're staying at the house? I'll give you a call. Because honestly, you'd be doing me a huge favor if I didn't have to worry about this stuff."

"Yep. If I don't answer, just leave a message and I'll get back to you." For the first time in weeks she felt a sliver of hope. Even if she ended up getting a position somewhere on a more permanent basis, she could manage a single client after hours.

At that moment Kailey's cell phone rang and she frowned. "Weird. Hardly anyone ever calls me. Most of the time they text." She dug around in her purse and found the phone. "It's Carrie. I hope there's nothing wrong." She answered it at the same time as Lacey's phone began to ring.

A strange feeling crawled through Lacey's stomach. She looked at her phone and saw Duke's number on the display. She swallowed as she hit the accept button. She hoped it was nothing with the baby. That would be terrible for them and a little too close to home for her.

"Duke? What's wrong?"

"Thank God I got you. Where are you?"

"In town, shopping."

"Can you stop by the preschool and pick up Amber rather than her going to day care?"

The crawly feeling intensified. "What's happened? Is Quinn all right?"

"He'll be fine. There was a fire at his place, though. He tried to stop it while he was waiting for the fire department."

Gibson was so small that the department was volunteer-based. Response time could be slow…

"Is he hurt? What about the house?" Dread spiraled through her. Please let him be okay, she thought. And poor Amber. She didn't need any more upheaval, either…

"The house will be fine, eventually. Quinn kept it confined to the kitchen area and the department got there in time to knock it down. It'll need gutting, though. And Quinn…he got a few burns. He's on his way to the hospital now."

She lowered her voice. "How bad, Duke?"

"Not that bad," he assured her. "But he needs proper treatment and the burns are going to be tender for a while."

She closed her eyes, thinking of Quinn in pain, picturing him trying to fight the fire all on his own. Stupid, brave man.

"I'll get Amber. Should I come to the hospital?"

"No." Duke's voice was firm. "I don't know how much she remembers from when Marie died, but there's no need to freak her out. Just take her back to the house after school. I think she's done at noon."

Lacey caught Kailey's worried gaze and knew they were getting the same information.

"Don't worry about it, Duke. I'll take care of it."

"Thanks. We're going to head in to the hospital now."

"Then come to supper at the house. I'll cook for everyone. Amber can help and it'll be good to keep her busy. She likes helping in the kitchen."

"You're a gem, Lace."

Gem, huh? Truth was, she was more worried than she cared to admit about Quinn and she would benefit from being occupied. "Don't worry about it. Just text me with updates, okay?"

"Can do."

She hung up at the same time as Kailey and they looked at each other. Lacey wondered if her face looked as worried as Kailey's.

"You heard the news," Kailey said quietly.

"Yeah. Duke asked if I'd pick Amber up after school. I hope he's right, that Quinn's burns are minor."

"Me, too. Gosh, that family has been through enough."

Lacey remembered what it was like to lose a parent at a young age. And she remembered how frightening it was to think that something might happen to the one left behind. "This might be the perfect day for some Valentine's Day planning," Lacey said tightly.

"I've got to head home for a bit, but I offered to help the guys with the chores tonight. That way Duke and Carrie can look after Quinn."

Lacey had nearly forgotten what it was like to live in a small town, but the current crisis reminded her. "Listen, I'm going to cook for everyone. You're welcome to stay too, if you don't have to rush back home."

"Thanks." Kailey tucked her phone back in her purse. "I'll play it by ear, see when things get finished." She reached out and squeezed Lacey's arm. "Give Amber my love, okay? She's a sweetie."

"I will. See you back at the ranch."

Kailey rushed off to pay for her items and Lacey checked her watch. She still had some time before she needed to pick Amber up from school, so she added a few more craft supplies to the cart, and then threw in what she guessed to be the right size pajamas and set of yoga pants with a matching shirt, just in case Amber needed a change of clothes. Once she'd paid for those, she headed to the grocery store and picked up whatever was missing from the pantry for tonight's supper. There would be at least five of them to eat, six if Kailey was there, so she picked up a large roast and an extra bag of carrots. Fresh green beans were on sale, and she bought whipping cream and a bag of apples. On the way out, she snagged a couple of bottles of red wine. Once her groceries were stowed in the trunk along with her other purchases, she found it was nearly dismissal time and made her way to the school.

It worked out perfectly. She got there just ahead of the lunch bell. She explained the situation, and the young woman behind the desk said that Carrie had already called—she was on file as the emergency contact for Quinn. It wasn't until Amber had been paged to come to the office that Lacey realized she had no idea what to say to the little girl. She didn't want to be the one to tell her that there'd been a fire in her house. Quinn should be the one to do that. Amber was skipping down the hall towards the office. Lacey had to think of something fast.

"Lacey!" Amber came right up and gave her a hug.

"Just a minute. I need to see Miss J."

Politely Amber went to the young woman's desk. "Hi, Miss J."

The secretary smiled at Amber. "Miss Duggan is here to take you home today, Amber."

"I'm not going to day care?"

"Not today."

Amber looked over at Lacey. "But only Daddy or Carrie is supposed to pick me up from school."

Lacey went to a chair and sat down so she was more on Amber's level. "Carrie already called the office and said it would be okay."

"What about Daddy?" Amber's little face wrinkled with confusion. She was so delightfully innocent.

"Well, your daddy had to go into town for a while. But I went shopping this morning and I have a surprise in the car for you. We're going to spend the afternoon together."

"We are? Yay! I have to go to my classroom and get my stuff."

She turned around and gave Miss J a wave. "Bye, Miss J!"

While Lacey waited, the secretary got a binder from behind the desk and put it up front for Lacey to sign. "It's a sign-out log," she said. "I hope Quinn's all right."

"Duke said he'll be fine. I'm not sure what to tell Amber, though, so I'm going to hold off for a bit. We're going to make Valentines today and do some cooking."

Amber was back just as the lunch bell rang. "Okay Lacey, let's go!" she declared, her curls bouncing.

Once at home, Amber helped carry in the bags, chattering the whole time. "Did you bring my lunch?" she asked. "Daddy left it on the counter this morning. He said he'd go get it and bring it to me but he never did. He musta forgotted."

Lacey halted, her hand inside a grocery bag. Was that why Quinn had been home when the fire started? What might have happened if he hadn't been there? What if they'd lost everything?

"Lacey? You look funny."

She pasted on a smile. "Just thinking. I don't have your lunch, so let's make something. What's your favorite?"

"Grilled cheese!" Amber jumped up and down while Lacey wondered where she got all her energy. "With pickles!"

"Grilled cheese it is." She got Amber set up at the stove, standing on a step stool, armed with a spatula while the sandwiches fried, and Lacey put the groceries away, keeping a keen eye on her little chef. Amber did great, though, and Lacey cut up little dill pickles to go with their sandwiches and before long they were at the table munching. Once the mess was tidied, Lacey got out the Valentine's Day supplies which sent Amber into fits of rapture. Lacey found a shoebox upstairs in a closet and together they cut a mail slot in the lid and covered it with aluminum foil to make it shiny. After that Amber decorated the outside with red and pink and white foam hearts and stickers that had messages like "Happy Valentine's Day" and "Be Mine" on them. All in all, Amber was delighted with the result, but when it came to cleaning up the mess she lacked her usual enthusiasm.

Once the table was cleared of the paper and foil scraps, Lacey put on a few cartoons and Amber went to chill on the sofa. Five minutes later she was asleep.

Lacey checked her phone. Still no text from Duke.

She worked around the kitchen as quietly as she could, searing the roast and then putting it in the oven, peeling carrots and stemming the beans. Both were in pots on the stove when she started peeling potatoes, and her phone buzzed on the counter.

Her hands were damp so she dried them on a towel and reached for the phone. It was a text message, and her heart gave a little skip when she saw that it was from Quinn and not Duke.

How's Amber?

She typed back quickly. Fine. Asleep on the sofa. Are you okay?

Nothing serious. A few bandages. We should be out of here soon.

She didn't even get the reply typed when the next message came.

What did you tell her?

Lacey backspaced out what she'd been typing and simply responded, Nothing. Thought she needed to hear it from her daddy.

A pause. Then another buzz.

Thank you, Lace.

Why a simple thank-you made her eyes sting she had no idea. You're sure you're okay? she asked.

You worried about me? And then a winky face. Lacey frowned, feeling disturbingly transparent.

Amber woke from her nap, and Lacey typed back quickly. Amber's awake. Going to make dessert. Don't be late for supper. Huh. He needed to know that nothing had changed where they were concerned. She wasn't going to get all mushy and weird or let him off easily.

Except she was. She just wasn't going to give him the satisfaction of knowing it. Who knew what he'd do with that sort of information in his pocket?

Lacey had texted Carrie, requesting that Carrie let her know when they were about a half hour away. When the text came, Lacey and Amber were just taking the apple upside-down cake out of the oven. After that, Lacey turned on the vegetables while Amber set the table. By the time the entourage arrived, she'd put the roast to rest and was whisking red wine into the drippings in preparation for thickening it for gravy.

"Daddy Daddy Daddy!" Before Lacey could intervene, Amber went rushing to the door. There was a beat of silence, then Amber's shaky voice. "What happened to your hand, Daddy?"

Duke and Carrie appeared in the kitchen, their faces tired and drawn. "I don't envy him that conversation," Carrie said quietly.

She no sooner had it out of her mouth than Amber started crying. The pitiful sound filtered down the hall and into the kitchen where Lacey was stirring the gravy as if her life depended on it. Hearing Amber cry put a lump in her throat and tears in her eyes. Then the low tones of Quinn's response hit her square in the gut. How many times had he broken bad news to his little girl? Amber would be fine. Everyone was okay. But Quinn… it weighed heavier on him. It had to. Sometimes being an adult really sucked.

Duke disappeared down the hall and Carrie silently poured water into the dinner glasses. When Quinn and Amber came into the kitchen, he was holding her in his arms, his face tight as he tried to keep the bandaged parts from bumping anything. Amber's face was buried in his shoulder and Lacey knew without asking that he was enduring the pain because what his kid needed most right now was a hug and reassurance.

"Amber, honey," she said quietly. "Your daddy's probably really hungry. Do you want to help me put supper on?"

Amber's tear-streaked face peeked up at her. "My house got burned," she said in a devastated voice. "And my daddy got hurt."

"I know, honey." She reached out and put her hand along Amber's back, feeling Amber's pain, Quinn's, and her own, because despite the difficult day and circumstances, it hurt to know she'd never have this life as her own. "But know what? Everyone is okay. Your daddy's going to heal up just fine and we're all going to work together to fix things up like new."

Amber leaned back a little to look into her father's face and Quinn winced as she touched a spot on his forearm. "Daddy, are you going to die like Mommy?"

Duke had returned to the kitchen, but all three of them now had to turn away so Amber couldn't see their faces. Carrie gave a little sniff and Duke cleared his throat. And more than ever, Lacey understood a little better why Quinn could be so crotchety. He'd had a really rough go. Far worse than Lacey.

"No, honey, I'm not going to die. I just have some boo-boos on my arms. I promise they're going to get better and I'll be just fine."

"I love you, Daddy."

Oh, crap. Lacey couldn't take much more of this. She put down the bowl that was in her hands and slipped off to the bathroom to blow her nose. Inside the small bath, she took a few deep breaths. She'd been feeling so sorry for herself, so resentful. She couldn't have children. She'd lost her job, she'd moved back here. But she had a roof over her head. Family. She even suspected she could end up with a few friends—like her new sister-in-law, Carrie, and Kailey, and even Quinn, in a roundabout way. There were so many things in her life that were blessings. Maybe it was time she started appreciating them.

When she returned to the kitchen, Amber was putting dinner rolls on a plate and Quinn was sitting down, looking exhausted. Lacey could still smell the tinge of smoke on his clothing when she put a bowl of vegetables on the table beside him. All their things, she realized. Even if they weren't destroyed, they'd smell of smoke. Perhaps have water damage. She was doubly glad she'd picked up a few items for Amber.

Kailey came in on a gust of winter air and joined the party, bringing some much-needed high spirits. By the end of the meal, Amber was talking about the Valentine's box they'd made and the upcoming party in the classroom the following week. Lacey put Amber to work running the beaters for the whipping cream and they sat back and enjoyed the upside-down cake and coffee. Quinn took a bottle out of his pocket and shook a pill into his hand. Lacey got up and filled a glass half-full of water and handed it to him. "It hurts a lot, huh?" she asked in an undertone.

"Like the devil," he replied, wincing.

"I'm so sorry, Quinn." Before she moved away she put her hand on his shoulder and squeezed. Her fingers were sliding away when he reached up and grabbed her hand.

"Thank you. For all you did today. I can never repay you."

"No worries." She pulled her hand away, not wanting him to know how much the simple touch affected her.

"I mean it, Lacey. We had a few moments of upset, but she's taking it well. She feels safe here. Safe with you."

"I'm glad," she responded. "I know how important she is to you, Quinn. She's a great kid and you're a fine father."

It didn't even hurt to say, except perhaps in a bittersweet way. Her heart went out to both of them. The way anyone's would, she reasoned with herself.

Too bad she didn't quite believe it.

Chapter 5

Kailey went home and Carrie and Lacey tackled the dishes while Quinn and Duke got down to business.

"You'll stay here," Duke announced. "You can't go home until everything's been fixed up right. We'll contact the insurance company first thing in the morning. Hopefully it won't take too long. In the meantime, you and Amber are welcome to stay here. Right, Lacey?"

She didn't know why she hadn't thought of this. She'd assumed maybe they'd spend the night here tonight; it was why she'd bought Amber the pajamas after all. But move in? They'd be...roommates.

When she didn't answer, the silence grew awkward. "Hey," Quinn said into the quiet, "don't worry about it. I have options."

"What options?" Duke persisted.

"It's fine," Lacey agreed, even though she was far

from comfortable with the idea. Having the 8:00 a.m. to 6:00 p.m. rule was one thing. Having Quinn here 24/7 was quite another. She liked her privacy. Liked her freedom. She really wasn't in the market for a roommate. Plus, she was trying to say the right thing in the middle of being blindsided.

Except Quinn had just temporarily lost his home. This was Duke's place and he'd offered it to Lacey when she needed it. Why shouldn't he offer it to his manager and friend in his time of need as well?

"The Rogers kid is right on this road," Duke insisted. "I bet Amber can catch a ride with them in the mornings and still go to day care in the afternoons. Come on, man." He lowered his voice. "You know she's comfortable here. It would be less of an adjustment for her, you know?"

Lacey nodded, even though she had misgivings. "It's true, Quinn. There's lots of room here. And it's about what's best for Amber."

Maybe he wouldn't need this place for long. Or maybe one of her interviews would work out and she would be able to get out and get her own place.

"I hate imposing."

"It's not imposing," Carrie insisted. "If anyone else were in this situation, you'd do what you could to help and you know it."

"I don't even have anything for tonight." He sighed heavily. "I never even thought. All of Amber's stuff is at the house. And it is all probably smoke-damaged." He closed his eyes wearily.

"I've got spare toothbrushes at the bunkhouse. I'll bring them up," Carrie offered. "And you're close to the same size as Duke. I'll get you a change of clothes, and you can throw those ones in the washer."

"I bought Amber some stuff on impulse today," Lacey admitted. "Just in case she needed emergency clothes. I hope I got the right size. There are pajamas for tonight and an outfit for tomorrow. When she changes for bed, I'll wash up her clothes, too. I'll just throw some of mine in with them."

Quinn looked as if he'd aged ten years. "I don't know what to say. Thank you all. So much."

"As Carrie said, you'd do the same for any of us." Duke put his hand on Quinn's shoulder. "I'll go grab you a change of clothes."

"And I'll send up some toiletries. We'll worry about the rest tomorrow," Carrie said.

When they were gone, that just left Quinn and Lacey, and a tired-out Amber sprawled on the sofa with a book from her backpack.

Quinn sighed, got up from the table, went into the living room and sat beside her.

"So." He patted her leg. "I'm afraid we can't go home tonight, sweetheart."

Amber looked up. "But it's my bedtime soon."

Quinn swallowed several times and Lacey understood. The day was catching up to him and he was struggling to hold it together.

"What your dad means is that everyone is really tired and we were wondering if you'd like to have a sleepover here tonight." Lacey went closer and knelt by the sofa.

"On a school night?" The way she said it made it sound like the worst, most wonderful transgression.

"Yes, on a school night. I even picked out a pair of

jammies for you at the store today. If you want, you can have a bath in my tub and use my bubble bath."

"Really?"

"Yes, really."

Suddenly Amber frowned. "But I don't gots any underwear."

Quinn jumped into the conversation again. "What about the secret emergency pair in the pocket of your backpack?"

Amber's eyes lit up. "Oh, yeah!"

"So what do you think? Should we run you a bath?"

Amber nodded so quickly her ponytail bobbed up and down. "Bubbles! I love bubbles!"

She was off like a shot, running up the stairs and into the bathroom. Lacey treated Quinn to a sideways grin. "Did we ever have that much energy as kids?"

"We must have, though I don't remember."

He closed his eyes and she realized he must be exhausted. "You rest for a bit. I'll look after Amber."

"You're sure?"

"Positive."

He didn't even argue. Just let out a long sigh and kept his eyes closed. And that was what really worried Lacey. No smart remark, no protest…he was just letting her call the shots. It was so not like him that she guessed he was hurting more than he let on.

Amber loved the bubbles and after she'd washed her hair with Lacey's shampoo, Lacey wrapped her in an oversize towel and reached for the pajamas. They were light purple with pink and blue and yellow butterflies all over them and Amber was delighted, her chatter still going as she stepped into clean underwear and the bottoms. There was a brief reprieve as they pulled the top over her head but then she was off again, babbling about how tomorrow they'd have to go get her things from the house and get her teddy bears and toys. Lacey just let her go, because she didn't want to make any promises she might not be able to keep. She had no idea what sort of state the house was in.

Once the bath was over, though, it seemed Amber's insecurities returned. Carrie and Duke popped in briefly with the promised items but disappeared again. When Quinn announced it was time for Amber to go to bed, her eyes grew troubled and her face fell. "But Daddy, I don't want to go to bed yet."

"You need your rest for school tomorrow, pumpkin."

"But I want to go get my clothes and toys tomorrow."

Quinn's face tightened. "Honey, I'm not sure how that's going to work yet."

Tears swam in her eyes. "But I want my stuff! I can't sleep without Mary!"

Quinn sighed. "It's just a teddy bear, Amber."

"She's not! She's my favorite bear! I sleep with her every night!"

A teddy bear named Mary. Was it a coincidence that Amber's mom's name had been Marie? If Lacey's heart was aching right now, what must Quinn be going through?

"Would you like to borrow my teddy bear?" Lacey asked, heat blooming in her cheeks. She avoided looking at Quinn. A grown woman with a stuffed animal. She suspected he'd have some choice words about that.

"You have a bear?"

Lacey nodded. She wasn't even sure why she kept the damn thing. It was too hard to let go completely, she supposed. The soft brown bear with the red ribbon was something Carter had bought her when they'd first decided to try having a baby. They'd planned on giving it to their son or daughter as a first stuffed animal. As the months went on, she'd put the bear in the back of the closet. When everything had fallen apart, she probably should have gotten rid of it, but she somehow couldn't stand the thought of letting it go.

Amber might as well have it. At least it would be loved and not…well, not reminding Lacey of something that would never come to pass.

"I do. And you're welcome to have it."

Amber considered for a moment, and then went over to Quinn and crawled up beside him. "Daddy? Do you think Mary will be okay at home alone? I mean, won't she be scared sleeping all by herself?"

The tension eased in Quinn's face. "Honey, you know Mary has all sorts of stuffed animal friends keeping her company on your bed. She'll be fine."

"It's scary sleeping alone, Daddy."

Lacey saw him swallow. "Would you like to bunk with me tonight?"

The still-damp curls bobbed as she nodded. "Uh-huh."

"Let's go tuck you in, then. I promise I'll be up later."

"Promise?"

"Absolutely."

Lacey retrieved the bear and got an extra blanket for the spare bedroom. The bed was a queen, so there would be lots of room for both Quinn and Amber. There was no night-light, though, so Lacey left the light on in the bathroom so the upstairs wasn't pitch-black. Quinn came upstairs and once Amber brushed her teeth they tucked her in and Lacey tucked the bear in with her. It felt right, passing it on. Like something she should have done ages ago. On impulse she leaned down and kissed Amber's forehead. "Good night, sweetie."

"Night, Lacey."

"Go to sleep, baby." Quinn kissed her, too. "I'll be up soon."

"Okay, Daddy."

They left the door open, and made their way back downstairs. Quinn went back to the living room and sank into the soft cushions of the sofa, letting out a breath.

Lacey went straight to the cupboard above the stove and took out a bottle of whiskey that she assumed had once been her grandfather's before he died. She poured a healthy splash in two glasses and went back to the living room, handed Quinn a glass, and sat across from him on the love seat.

"Hell of a day," she said quietly, and Quinn nodded.

"Yep." He took a long drink of his whiskey and winced as he swallowed. "Gah."

Lacey did the same, felt the burn of the liquor heat her belly. "Are you sure you're okay?"

"This?" He lifted one bandaged arm. "It'll heal. I wish other things could be fixed as easily."

"Do you mean the house or your daughter?"

He drained the rest of the whiskey. "Both. Amber's had such a rough time. Our home was the one thing I could do to keep things consistent for her, you know? So she could see that not everything changed after Marie…" He paused and cleared his throat. "After she died. Now that's changed, too. I didn't want to tell her but there's a lot of smoke damage. Most of our things are ruined. A crew is going to have to go in there and do a major cleanup and the kitchen and downstairs bath will have to be rebuilt. Even then, those are just things. I hate that she's feeling so insecure again. That there's nothing I can do to keep her world the same as it was before."

"Except that you're still here and with her every step of the way."

"A kid her age doesn't get that. They see a change in routine, in familiar things, and fear. Tell me a fire wouldn't have scared the living shit out of you when you were four years old."

"I was six when a man in a uniform knocked on the door and told me my father was dead, Quinn. My mom moved us to the city. New people, new place, new everything. I know what you mean, but I also know that it meant the world to me to have my mom. Duke and Rylan were boys. They had each other. I was alone in the middle. I understand more than you think."

There was silence for a minute, and then Quinn reluctantly admitted, "I know you do. I'm sorry."

Lacey shook her head. "Don't be sorry at all. I'm not saying you're wrong. I'm just saying…" She searched for the right words. "Amber is lucky to have you, and even at her age, she knows it."

"She was afraid I was going to die like her mother. That damn near broke my heart."

"Of course it did. There's nothing worse than knowing your child is in pain."

Quinn winced as he shifted in the chair. "What would you know about it?"

Well, damn. Just when she let her guard down, thought she and Quinn were working together, bam. He knew exactly where to hit her so it hurt the most.

She finished her drink. Considered explaining and then decided against it. It was her private business, for one, and today wasn't about her. Quinn had a lot on his plate and she wasn't about to bring her drama into it. Another day she might have pointed out all she'd done to help and perhaps he could show a little gratitude. But not today. Not with something this big.

So she bit her tongue and instead asked about the house. "Do they have any idea what caused the fire?"

Quinn met her gaze. "Do you think Amber's asleep?"

It was an odd question, and she frowned at him. "Why?"

His voice was low as he answered. "I don't want her to hear."

It had been several minutes and the house was utterly silent. "She was exhausted. I'm sure she's asleep."

Quinn nodded. "Before school she came out with lipstick on and I sent her back to the bathroom to wipe it off. She must have gotten into some of Marie's things without me knowing. What I didn't realize was that she'd gotten out the straightening iron. The initial guess is that we left before she could use it and it got left on, since the fire seems to have started in the half bath. I can't think of anything else that would have done it." He scrubbed his face with a hand. "She misses her mom so much. Even now, after all this time. I know that. I should have checked before we left the house, but we were running late."

"You couldn't have known. Don't blame yourself."

His face hardened. "I'm sure as hell not going to blame her, if that's what you're getting at."

The whiskey hadn't done anything to ease his mood, and Lacey thought perhaps bed was a better idea. "I wasn't blaming anyone, and neither should you. That's why it's called an accident."

She pushed herself off the love seat and went to the kitchen, put her glass in the sink. "It's been a long day. I think I'll say good-night," she said, and headed for the stairs.

Quinn got up and followed her. "Lacey, wait."

She shouldn't have paused. She should have kept right on going, around the newel post and up the stairs to her room and shut the door. But she didn't. Her footsteps halted and he caught up with her. His fingers circled her forearm, turning her around to face him.

"I'm sorry I snapped at you," he said, his voice deep and low. "That was uncalled for."

She swallowed, unsure of what to say. "It's okay," she whispered, anxious to get away, terrified by how much she liked the feel of his hand on her wrist. Her breath came quick and shallow and when she looked up and their eyes met…

Let me go, she thought crazily. *Let me go because we can't do this.*

"It's not okay," he answered, and his hand tightened until she was sure he had to feel her pulse hammering against his fingertips. "You've done nothing but help today. You even thought to pick up things for my daughter just in case, and you cooked for all of us, and I know you must hate having us intrude on your space…"

"It's fine—"

"…and the first chance I get, I'm snapping at you."

"It's been a challenging day."

"And now you're making excuses for me. When what I should be doing is saying thank-you."

She was certain her heart was going to beat clear

through her chest when he pulled her closer and folded her in a hug. "Thank you," he whispered. "For taking care of my daughter as if she were your own."

Her eyes stung. His first words had been like a stab to the gut. But this…this was taking the knife and twisting it.

It was all she could do to not start crying.

"I don't know what we would have done without you today. She was so scared…hell, I was terrified. I walked in there and smelled the smoke and saw the flames and all I could think of was stopping it so we didn't lose what we had left of our old life."

He held her closer and she let him, because she could tell he needed to say it, to get it out in the open. It wasn't just Amber who'd been traumatized today. Quinn had been, too. His word choice said a lot, too. He was holding tight to the life they used to have. It wasn't the first time he'd said it. It was the life he'd had with Marie, when they'd all been a happy family. She had no business inserting herself into the middle of that.

Inserting herself? That was crazy, wasn't it? She didn't even like Quinn…

Except deep down she knew that was a lie. Yes, he got under her skin. Yes, she often felt inadequate when he was around. There wasn't anything he did poorly. But she did like him, or at least admire him. Too much for her own good. Too much for them to be living under the same roof and definitely too much for her to spend any longer in his embrace.

She gave a quick squeeze and then started to pull away. "But you are here, and everything is going to be fine. Just remember that." She stepped out of his embrace and smiled weakly. "Before you know it everything will be back to normal and this will all be behind you."

His gaze searched hers and she wondered if the whiskey had been extra strong.

"Back to normal. Right."

"I'm going to bed, Quinn. It's been a long day."

"Right."

"See you in the morning."

"Right again."

And still his gaze held her prisoner until she either had to break it or she was going to find herself in his arms again.

It was the reminder of Marie that made her back up a little more. His hand rested on the railing of the staircase and the plain gold band on his finger caught the light. It communicated their situation perfectly: Quinn Solomon was still another woman's husband. In his heart, where it mattered most. In that moment she was incredibly jealous of Marie Solomon. How lucky the woman had been, to know that much love and devotion.

It was foolish to be jealous of a woman who wasn't even alive anymore. What on earth was wrong with her?

"Good night," she whispered. And before she could change her mind, she turned and climbed the stairs without looking back to see if he was still standing at the bottom, watching her.

Chapter 6

Lacey put her job search on the back burner for a few days and focused on Quinn and Amber. If it felt a little too personal, she ignored it. She was merely someone in a position to help a neighbor. While Quinn dealt with the insurance company and all the other details about the house repairs, Lacey cooked meals, did laundry, and one day after preschool she took Amber shopping for a new wardrobe. The first stop, though, was lunch at the diner. Shopping with a hungry and cranky kid was not part of the plan.

Every small town she could think of had a family restaurant where everyone knew everyone else and the daily specials were practically memorized according to the day of the week. In Gibson, the diner had the uninspired name of the Horseshoe Diner.

Amber was practically bouncing as they went inside. "I'm gonna have a hot dog and a chocolate milk-shake!" she announced, her pigtails bobbing with each step. It was barely out of her mouth when she darted away. "Daddy!"

A jolt of something zipped through Lacey's body as her gaze followed Amber. Quinn was already at a booth, grinning at his daughter as if he hadn't seen her in days, rather than hours. Lacey was glad to see him, which made her a little uncomfortable. She'd thought today's lunch was just going to be her and Amber, not the three of them. She was trying to avoid the appearance of a family, which they definitely were not. But it was difficult when they lived under the same roof and as she started to care more and more for Amber. And for Quinn, a little voice in her head reminded her, but she pushed that thought away.

Pasting on a smile, she slid into the empty side of the booth. "I didn't realize you were going to be here," she said, putting her purse on the vinyl seat.

"I ended up having to come into town to sign some stuff," he replied. "I knew what time Amber was done, and I thought I'd meet you here."

"I want a hot dog, Daddy."

"Of course you do." He chuckled, the sound low and warm, sending ripples of pleasure over Lacey's nerve endings. Quinn really did have a great voice. Deep, quiet, but with a clarity and strength that…

Argh! She had to stop thinking this way. Instead she picked up the plastic menu and started scanning the of-ferings. She'd barely skimmed the first page when the waitress came over and asked to take their order.

"I'll have a hot dog and a chocolate milkshake,

please," Amber ordered clearly, and Lacey hid a smile. For a girl her age, she had a lot of poise.

"What would you like on your hot dog, sweetheart?" The waitress was smiling too, at this point. Amber was hard to resist.

"Just ketchup. Please."

"You got it. How about you, Lacey?"

Lacey blinked, unsure how or why the woman knew her name. "Oh. Uh…"

The woman grinned. "You look a lot like your brother. You were in here a few days back, too, putting up your sign." She gestured with her pen towards the bulletin board. "Strangers don't stay strangers very long in this town."

"Oh. Right. I'll, uh…" She bit down on her lip. "I guess I'll have the chicken salad on whole grain with a side salad instead of fries."

"You didn't say please," Amber piped up.

Lacey swallowed. "Please."

Quinn was trying not to laugh as he ordered a cheeseburger platter with everything on it.

As they waited for their food, they were saved from much conversation as Amber chattered along, filling the silence with tales from preschool and how Taylor Johnson picked his nose and wiped it on his shirt and Madison Jeffries had picked up a baby snake on the playground. When the meals came, Lacey felt immediate buyer's remorse as she looked at her plate. Oh, there was nothing wrong with her sandwich or salad, but the sight of the rich milkshake and the savory scent of Quinn's burger had her mouth watering.

She looked up and saw Quinn watching her with a lopsided grin. Then he deliberately picked up a French fry, dipped it in the dish of ketchup on his plate, and bit into it with enthusiasm.

"Tease," she muttered, before she could think better of it.

His gaze held hers and there was that zing again. She hadn't meant it that way, but it seemed innuendoes happened without her even trying.

She picked up her fork and speared a piece of cucumber. This was better for her. She'd be glad of her choice in the long run. Right?

"So," she asked, "everything okay this morning?"

Quinn looked over at Amber and then back at Lacey. "Things have a tendency to move slowly, if you know what I mean."

She understood completely. Paperwork and bureaucracy moved on their own time, not anyone else's.

"How's your coverage?" She picked up half her sandwich and took a bite, then dotted her lips with her napkin. Amber, she noticed, already had an adorable smear of ketchup on the side of her mouth.

"Adequate…but it'll be tight for a while." He frowned. "A single income already makes it tight."

He looked over at Amber, and Lacey wondered how much of his paycheck was eaten up by preschool fees and after-school day care. He had a good job at Crooked Valley, but bringing up kids solo was an expensive venture. She didn't need her accounting degree to figure that one out.

"Anything I can do to help?" she asked.

"You're already doing it. I saw the pile of laundry this morning. You don't have to do that."

"I'm home. You're working. I might as well be doing something and if it helps you guys out, bonus." She smiled at him. "I'm not used to being idle, Quinn. I mean it. It's no bother."

Still, a load or two of laundry and running some errands with Amber didn't feel like much help. Lacey enjoyed being with the little girl, who said funny things through the innocence of a four-year-old filter.

They finished their meal and Quinn paid the bill, then put on his hat. "Well, ladies, thank you for the lunch but I'd better get back to work."

"You can't go shopping with us, Daddy?"

Lacey grinned. She couldn't help it. Amber reminded her of a little Shirley Temple, hard to resist and twice as cute.

"Oh, I think that's best left to the women. You have fun and I'll see you at dinner."

"Lacey said she's making stuffy chops."

At Quinn's questioning glance, she elaborated. "Stuffed pork chops."

"Sounds good." They made their way outside into the sunshine and Lacey knelt down to help Amber get her thumbs into her mittens. When she stood up, Quinn was close. Too close.

"Thank you for this. I know you said it's no trouble, but I appreciate it just the same."

"You're welcome."

His hand was on the small of her back. She was sure it was just a polite gesture, mannerly. Gentlemanly. Still, the warmth of it seeped through her jacket to her skin.

Dry spell, she reminded herself. She only reacted to Quinn this way because she'd had such a big dry spell.

Even more disconcerting was the fact that he didn't seem to pick fights with her anymore. She sometimes missed the verbal sparring, but there had been bigger

issues to deal with than the right way to load the dishwasher or whether or not to fold the towels in halves
or thirds—the sort of thing they would have bickered
about before.

His hand slid away.

"I'll see you at home?"

She nodded, but it suddenly became clear. She was
acting this way because she was pretending. She was
playing house—with Quinn, with his daughter. But he
was not her husband and Amber was not her child and
it was certainly not her home…well, perhaps a third
of it was, but that really didn't matter. She was playing house, pretending to have the life she had always
wanted, but that had been taken away from her. She
would have to watch that. Stay rational. Put things in
perspective.

Crooked Valley was not growing on her. It certainly
wasn't a permanent solution to her problems. After all,
she couldn't live off her brother's goodwill forever, and
she wasn't contributing to the ranch so she didn't expect any of the returns.

Quinn kissed Amber's head and jogged away to his
truck. Lacey didn't want to get caught looking after
him, so she took Amber's hand and put on her cheeri-
est voice. "Okay, sweetie. Let's hit the stores."

Much to Lacey's relief, Kailey Brandt phoned and
said she'd like to meet to talk about some book work.
The past few days had been busy, but Lacey knew she
was getting too used to what were really housewife
duties and she wanted something more. The last thing
she needed to do was get in the habit of looking after
Quinn and Amber as if they were her family. Once

his house was fixed up, they'd be moving bac'k there and wouldn't need her anymore. Heck, they didn't need her now. They'd managed just fine, the two of them. It was her, needing to keep busy, longing to nurture, that kept her offering to do things for them. She was smart enough to know it. So the possibility of even part-time work was desperately exciting.

Quinn had driven Amber to school and was already in the barn when Lacey tucked her hair into a messy topknot and put on her coat and boots. It was February, quite cold outside, and she had to take a few precious minutes to scrape the frost from her windshield. The roads were decent, though, and it only took a few minutes to drive from Crooked Valley to the Brandt place.

Brandt Bucking Stock was clearly a profitable operation. The fences and buildings were large and well-maintained, with fresh paint and a general neatness that spoke of consistent care. Lacey compared it to Crooked Valley and frowned a little. Perhaps Granddad had struggled to keep profits up towards the end. It wasn't that Crooked Valley was falling apart or anything, but it lacked the polish and prosperity of Brandt. The little details that perhaps Duke couldn't afford.

She parked in front of the house and grabbed her laptop bag. Before she could even get out of the car, Kailey appeared on the porch, zipping up a heavy jacket.

Lacey got out and slammed the door. "Good morning."

"Hey," Kailey replied. "The office is in the main barn, so come on down. I'll show you what's what."

They crossed the yard, heading towards the biggest building, white with dark green trim and massive sliding doors on one end. They entered through a smaller man door, and as they walked down the concrete corridor past long rows of stalls, Lacey was even more impressed. Kailey's boots made clicking sounds on the floor and Lacey noticed the woman's purposeful stride. She envied Kailey in that moment—sure of who she was and what she was doing. The woman was perhaps a few years younger than Lacey, but with far more confidence and purpose.

The barn office was nothing fancy; white walls with some framed pictures of different horses that Lacey assumed were Brandt stock, a shelf of trophies and cups, two large metal filing cabinets and a basic desk, chair and computer set up with a printer on a side table. In no time at all, Kailey had brought up the accounting and banking programs. It was all straightforward and simple, and a program that Lacey was familiar with. Everything was linked to make tax payments and payroll deductions as well as print checks.

"You've got a good setup here," Lacey said, clicking the mouse and checking out different parts of the programs. "Nothing jumps out at me as being strange or set up incorrectly, which is great. You say you've looked after it up until now?"

Kailey nodded. "I took an accounting course and learned the rest as I went along. I just don't like it." She grinned, the freckles on her nose bunching up as she scrunched it. "I'd rather focus on the business of running the breeding program. I've got my eye on a new stallion, but I haven't convinced the owner to sell him to me yet." Her eyes twinkled at Lacey.

"I can come in once a week if you like. Take care of your invoices and billing, run your payroll biweekly, pay the expenses. Shouldn't take me more than a few hours each time, more or less depending on what's going on and how busy you are."

"That'd be great!" Kailey looked so relieved Lacey laughed.

"Tell me about it. It's good to know I've finally got a little work lined up. I'm hoping I'll get a few more calls from the flyers I put around town."

"I figured Amber would have you dancing to her tune by now."

Lacey chuckled, leaning back in the chair. "Oh, she does. But she's gone all day, you know. As much as I grumbled about Quinn, he's not bad for a roommate. Keeps his stuff picked up. Worries about Amber getting in my way. Actually, it's kind of weird. It's like he goes out of his way to be nice to me."

Kailey's brows pulled together. "That's just Quinn, though. He's a really nice guy."

"Not to me." At Kailey's astonished expression, Lacey backpedaled. "That's not what I meant. I just mean…when we met he found fault with just about everything I did. Now he's so polite it sets my teeth on edge."

"Quinn never likes to inconvenience anyone. He has a hard time accepting help. The last thing he'd do is make things difficult. I'm actually surprised he agreed to stay at the house at all."

"I'm pretty sure he did it for Amber."

Kailey nodded. "So she'd have some consistency and familiarity. Quinn doesn't *not* like you, Lacey. He's not like that. He's just very protective of the life he's built. It's no secret that you're not really into the ranch, and for Quinn, Crooked Valley is the one thing that makes his life here possible, so nothing else has to change. You can't really blame the guy for being defensive."

And now she was throwing that into turmoil by being so stubborn. She still didn't want to be involved with the ranch, but maybe there was a way she could work something out for a while and then sell her third to Duke. It wasn't just Quinn who had something at stake with Crooked Valley. It was Duke and Carrie and their unborn child.

Lacey sighed. "You're not like that with me, though."

Kailey shrugged. "It's not my business at stake. Anyway," she continued, "there's going to be a benefit at the Silver Dollar on Valentine's Day. A local band is going to provide the music for free and all the cover charge money is going to give Quinn a hand. Not that we've told him, mind you. He'd say no to charity flat out. It's a surprise. At least until it's so far arranged that he can't say no."

A benefit? For Quinn? Lacey thought it was a lovely idea. Though the idea of it being on Valentine's Day struck her as a bit funny. Quinn wasn't the kind of guy who was looking for romance. Not when he was still stuck in his perfect past life…

And then she remembered the way their eyes had met at the bottom of the stairs and got that swirly, tingly feeling.

"Is there anything I can do to help?"

Kailey grinned and perched on the edge of the desk. "I thought you'd never ask. We'd like to hold a raffle on the night. Carrie agreed to look after getting some items, but we'd need someone to look after the cash. You, being the money person and all…"

"I should be able to do that."

"Great. I'll tell Carrie."

"What about Amber?" Lacey zipped up her bag and looked up at Kailey. "If it's at a bar, where will she go?"

Kailey smiled. "We have that all figured out. Amber's going to spend the night with her grandmother in Great Falls. Quinn takes her up there most Sundays anyway. They'll be able to manage for one night."

"You've got it all figured out."

"It's been in the works since the fire. That's what we do here. Look after our own."

Lacey wondered if she was considered "one of their own" or if she'd been gone too long. Joe Duggan had been a big part of this community, but that didn't necessarily extend to grandkids who hadn't given him the time of day.

"Well, just let me know what you need me to do and when."

"Of course."

"When would you like me to start with the books?" Lacey got up from the chair and put her bag on her shoulder.

"Day after tomorrow? Payroll is next week, so you can get the hang of the system before that. If that works for you."

Lacey smiled. "Lucky for you, my schedule is pretty wide-open."

Kailey walked Lacey back to her car, but before Lacey got in, the other woman put her hand on the window. "Lacey…don't say anything about this to Quinn, will you? He's so proud."

"I won't."

"He's been hurt a lot. Thanks for trying to help him out. I know it means a lot to him." She fidgeted for a second, shifting her weight on her feet before meeting Lacey's eyes. "Look, I don't want to pry into what's going on over at the ranch, but he's a good-looking guy and you're young and pretty and you're spending a crap ton of time together. I wouldn't want to see either of you hurt, and honestly I think Quinn has a ways to go before he's over Marie, you know?"

Lacey's face burned hot. "It's not like that…"

"I'm looking at you, Lacey, and I'm seeing that it could be. Just be careful. There's a little girl to think of, too."

Lacey's chin went up. "I know that. And it's really not like that, Kailey. I appreciate you wanting to protect him…"

"Not just him. Both of you."

"Well, that's kind of you. But there's nothing to worry about. I'm not going to be staying at Crooked Valley forever and before you know it, he'll be back in his house and it'll all go back to normal."

She smiled. Tightly. Felt like a complete liar even though she meant every word.

"I'm sure you're right." Kailey smiled back at her. A genuine smile. It hadn't been a warning or a threat. Kailey was simply looking out for someone she cared about, with concern and not jealousy or anger. She was a really nice woman, and Lacey wondered why Quinn hadn't snapped her up in a hurry. Clearly they were very close.

But perhaps Kailey was right. Quinn simply wasn't ready. Maybe he wouldn't be, not for a long time. Besides, a man like him deserved someone like Kailey, who was in the same business and liked the same things and could give Amber brothers and sisters. She wasn't capable of any of that.

"I'll see you later," she said quietly, and got into her car as Kailey stepped back.

As she drove away, she wished she could muster some resentment for their young, pretty neighbor. But it was hard to resent someone who was one hundred percent right.

The meeting with Kailey and trip to the Brandt operation got Lacey thinking. Who had been looking after the Crooked Valley finances? Had Joe been doing it before he died? Was it Duke? Quinn? Was there a particular reason why the Duggan ranch didn't seem as prosperous as the Brandts'? She was home all day anyway. She could always take a look at the books.

She found Duke in the horse barn, in a stall with a big gelding who was currently standing patiently while Duke wielded a hoof pick. "Hey, brother."

He looked up briefly. "Hey, yourself. What brings you to the smelly part of the property?"

She laughed a little. Duke had never been one to mince words, mixing a bit of humor with the little barb of accusation. "Hey," she replied, "I don't actually mind horse smell. Much."

"Don't listen to her, Chief," he instructed the horse. "She doesn't mean to be insulting."

He let go of the foot and wiped the pick on his pant leg. "Seriously. What brings you to the barns? Is everything okay?"

She nodded, stepped back as he opened the stall door and came out into the corridor, latching the hasp behind him. "It's fine. I was over at Kailey's today. They're going to hire me to do some bookkeeping for them."

Duke's face lit up. "Hey, that's great!"

"Don't get too excited. I haven't had any other nibbles and it's only a few hours a week."

"Still. You have to start somewhere." He started walking down the corridor and she followed, all the way down to where the tack and feed were stored. There was a mini-office, nothing as big as at the Brandts', but with a bar fridge, coffeemaker, drop-leaf table and a few cast-off chairs, and behind that a half bath with a toilet and sink.

"You want a coffee?" he asked.

"Sure."

As Duke poured the black liquid from the pot—who knew how long the brew had been on the burner— Lacey grabbed a granola bar from a basket on the table. "Listen, Duke, I was wondering. Who does the books for the ranch?"

He turned around and put a mug in front of her, then took cream from the fridge and put it beside the cup. She added cream. A lot. It still barely changed the color of the coffee. She could hardly wait to see what it did to her stomach lining.

"Quinn, mostly. Apparently he was helping Joe with it for the last year or so, and took it on when Joe died. He's the manager. It made sense. Besides, I wouldn't know where to start."

He sat down across from her, took a sip of his coffee and winced. "Why? You offering?" His eyebrows went up hopefully.

"I thought I could take a quick look is all." She'd been hoping it had been Carrie or someone else paying the bills. Sure, she and Quinn had been getting along just fine. But if she started poking around in ranch business, she knew he'd have a few choice words for her.

It probably wasn't worth it.

"Never mind," she said, sitting back in the chair and eyeing the coffee with distrust. "I don't want to make waves. Quinn probably knows what he's doing."

"You worried about stepping on his toes?"

She raised an eyebrow. "Duh. We have this truce thing going on right now, considering we're living in the same house. It's for Amber's sake, really. I can just imagine he'd be really happy to hear me suggest improvements to the accounting system. Ten bucks says he'll say something like *we've always done it this way* and that'll be that. It's just…"

She halted, frowned.

"It's just what, Lace?"

She looked at her brother. He wasn't scowling. He was completely interested in whatever she was about to say.

"When I got to Kailey's, I could see the difference in the two places," she said honestly. "And it's not that Crooked Valley is run-down, by any stretch. But it doesn't look like the Brandts', either. It looks…tired. Is it because things fell behind as Joe got older? Finances? I just wondered if there was something there that could be adjusted so maybe…"

"I get what you're saying. It wouldn't hurt to have you take a look, anyway. Quinn's busy enough without having to do all the office work. If there's a way to make it easier…"

"No problem." She forgot her reservations about the coffee and took a long drink, shuddering at the bitter taste. "God, Duke. How long has that been on the burner?"

He shrugged. "I dunno. Since seven? Maybe eight?"

She pushed the cup aside. "Anyway, and it's not that I'm a big chicken or anything, but I think it would be better if you brought this up with Quinn. He's less likely to be defensive if it comes from you."

"I don't see why. If it were me, I'd be thrilled to have someone help out with the books."

"But it's not you. Look, Duke, this doesn't change anything. I'm still not interesting in owning a third of the ranch. Quinn knows it. It makes him defensive."

To her surprise, Duke stayed quiet. In fact, ever since she'd moved in, he hadn't pressed her about the owner-ship at all. Maybe he'd just been too preoccupied with work and his new bride and pending fatherhood that he'd let it go.

"Quinn loves this place. He's been here a long time."

Lacey huffed out a sigh. "He wasn't like that with you, though, was he? And you weren't going to stay here, either."

"I don't know what to say, Lacey. Besides, you guys seem to get along okay now."

"We came to a truce because of the current situa-tion." Which was the truth, but not all of the truth. Not that she'd breathe a word to Duke. Wouldn't it be em-barrassing for him to know that she actually *wanted* Quinn's approval?

Not that she'd admit it to anyone besides herself.

"If it makes you feel better, I'll talk to him about it later. Then the two of you can figure out a time to sit down and have a look at what's what."

"Okay. I'd better head back inside. Are you and Carrie coming for dinner tonight? I put pulled pork in the Crock-Pot. There's plenty."

"We'll see. I'll call up and let you know."

She was to the door before Duke's voice followed her. "Hey, sis?"

She turned around. "What?"

"Thank you. For looking after us, for looking after Quinn and Amber. For the record, Carter was a stupid ass to give you up. You care about people. You nurture them. He never appreciated that."

She swallowed tightly, touched by Duke's words, saddened, and on the verge of telling him the truth. But she couldn't somehow. Not that it was a big dirty secret or anything. It just made her feel like such a failure. Like such a…waste.

"Thanks, Duke. I really appreciate that."

"Anytime, shrimp." He winked at her, reverting to the nickname he'd given her when they were little kids. "I know I was gone for a long time, but I'm trying to make up for it now."

She'd forgotten what it was like to have a close family, to have a big brother to look out for her. It was a sweet, warm feeling. It stayed with her as she walked away and out of the barn. It was a feeling she dared not get used to, or else she might decide she didn't want to leave…

Chapter 7

Quinn made his way from barn to house through a bitter wind that sent snow stinging against his cheeks. He'd taken Amber to school since the forecast was for random snow squalls throughout the day, but damn, it was only February and he was ready for spring. By spring—real spring—his house should be fixed and he and Amber could move back into their own home. He still hadn't told Amber the truth about their belongings. Most of them were gone. The smoke damage had been too intense. She'd been so upset about the fire in the first place that he hadn't wanted to add to her distress.

But it was hellish at times, staying here at Crooked Valley. It reminded him of things. Reminded him of how it used to be when he was married. For nearly two years he'd raised Amber on his own. He'd gotten used to having to cook meals, clean the house, do the laundry in addition to everything else. It wasn't that he didn't do those things before, either. He and Marie had shared the load. Always.

Sharing was different than being the only one left. Way different. And the truth was, it was really nice to come in after a long day and smell supper cooking and find a pile of fresh laundry on his bed. He didn't want to get too used to it. Lacey Duggan certainly wasn't here to take Marie's place. No one could do that.

The snow had drifted over the front steps again so he grabbed the shovel and cleared them off before stomping up the steps. He wasn't looking forward to the next hour. Lacey might be Martha Stewart around the house but she was still the woman who was not sticking around, who cared little about the ranch that was his livelihood. He was worried about Amber, too. He didn't want her to get too attached if Lacey was only going to leave again. Amber had been through more than enough.

The number one thing he'd tried to do since losing Marie was protect Amber from any more pain. Lacey was nice, and kind, and he owed her a lot for all her help. But what was best for Amber had to come first. The strange feelings that kept cropping up had to be tamped down. He didn't want to "move on" and even if he did it wouldn't be with someone who wasn't planning on sticking around.

Which made the task ahead even more unpalatable. Duke had asked him to show Lacey the books, to see if she could lend a hand. Duke had asked before if they should get a bookkeeper, but Quinn had refused. They didn't need to spend more money when he could do it himself.

Once she saw that they were just riding the line between red and black, she wouldn't want anything to do with the ranch for sure.

He walked in the door and was greeted by a smell that brought his mother's sour cream coffee cake to mind. It only made him more grouchy. Lacey was always baking something tasty, making herself indispensable. Hell, Amber thought the sun rose and set on her and talked about her more than her preschool teacher, whom she loved. It was just like when Lacey showed up here at Christmas. Perfect Lacey this, perfect Lacey that. The big difference was he'd been biting his tongue the past few weeks because she'd helped them so much since the fire. It would be damned rude to be anything but grateful. And polite.

In stocking feet, he stepped into the kitchen and saw the cake cooling on a rack. Clean dishes were stacked neatly in a drying rack in the sink, a damp tea towel forgotten on the countertop. He picked it up and folded it lengthwise before hanging it over the handle of the stove door. And then she stepped into the kitchen, carrying an empty laundry basket, and his heart did this weird dance in his chest.

Yeah, there was this, too. And it was damned inconvenient. Lacey Duggan was beautiful. It wasn't like he could help noticing. Especially since they were living in the same house.

She smiled when she saw him and it was like the room lit up. For God's sake, he was an idiot. They wanted entirely different things. She turned her nose up at what he valued and still, he saw her in a pair of fine-fitting jeans and a soft hoodie with her hair in a ponytail and his stupid body responded like a damned teenage boy. On the heels of those feelings came the heavy drag of guilt. Marie had been the love of his life and he was still mourning her. It wasn't fair that his body and mind kept betraying his heart by focusing on someone new.

"I'll be with you in a sec. Duke said you wanted to meet this morning so I could have a look at the books."

"I have some time."

"Let me just put this away." She headed for the laundry room at the end of the hall. "Did you know I'm going to be doing some accounting for Kailey?"

Her voice carried back and he let out a big breath. "No." Come to think of it, she might have mentioned it last night over dinner, but he'd been too preoccupied to pay much attention.

She came back, tightening her ponytail as she walked. "My first work since getting laid off. Hopefully it'll turn into a few more jobs as word gets around."

"And then what?" he asked.

She shrugged. "I don't know. I'll have to decide when the time comes."

"Are you still looking for full-time work?"

She frowned at him. "Of course I am."

"And so what if you move? What will you do with those clients you've set up?" She was looking at him funny, like he'd asked a ridiculous question. But it wasn't ridiculous at all. "Will you just leave them high and dry when you take off for your next job?" *Will you leave us high and dry too?* he thought. *Will my daughter cry at night again because someone else she cares about goes away?*

Lacey stepped back. "Quinn, would you like to do this another time?"

"No. Let's just do it and get it over with."

He knew he sounded short, but he was frustrated, dammit. Frustrated at not being in his own home, frustrated at all the work there was to do, frustrated that nothing ever seemed to be permanent. Why the hell did things have to change all the time?

And through all that frustration was Lacey, so young and pretty and more cheerful than he deserved, and he was starting to like her. Too much. And one day soon, she'd be gone, too. It was startling to realize that his days would go back to being somewhat gray and colorless when that happened.

Goddammit. He'd fallen under her spell as surely as Amber had. His daughter wouldn't be the only one to miss Lacey when she left, or when they moved back to their house. And that wasn't what he wanted at all. He wanted things back to normal!

"Do you want some cake?" she asked gently. "I could make you a cup of coffee, take it into the office."

"No, I damn well don't want any cake."

Her lips hardened and her eyes snapped at him. "Fine. Let's get this over with, then. Should be fun."

It was easier to deal with snippy, angry Lacey. Far easier than when she looked at him with soft eyes and full lips and that hint of pink in her cheeks.

Get a grip, he reminded himself. *Like she said. Get it over with.*

They went into the office and he went straight to the desk and hit the power button on the computer. While the old beast was booting up, he went to the first filing cabinet.

"This is where you'll find the paper files and records of invoices and receipts. The top drawer is this year's.

Second drawer is last year's. Year before that was boxed up and put in the basement."

He shut the file cabinet door before she could really get a look inside. He'd forgotten how small the office was. And cold. While he logged on to the computer, Lacey went to the small space heater and flicked it on. "I see why you keep this in here," she said, rubbing her hands together. "It's chilly."

There was only one chair in the office, so she leaned over his shoulder to look at the screen as he brought up files. The scent of her shampoo swam around him, all soft and floral, and he clenched his teeth.

He resented her. He appreciated her. And, as she rested a cool hand on his shoulder as she looked at the screen, he finally admitted to himself that he wanted her. He didn't want to. All of it fed into this big ball of confusion that was centered in the middle of his chest, like a weight pressing down on his collarbone, making it hard to breathe.

He cleared his throat and tried to ignore her hand. "So this is what we've brought in." He clicked another icon and brought up a second sheet. "Our expenditures are in this file."

She stood up straight and stared at the simplistic columns. "You mean to tell me you've been doing all this in a spreadsheet?"

"That's how Joe had it set up. He showed me. He'd run it that way for years."

"Clearly. That program's version is ancient. Why didn't you upgrade to accounting software?"

Of course, another criticism. That was just what he needed. "I'm a rancher, Lacey. Not an accountant."

"The new programs are easy to use, and you don't

have to worry about copying and pasting stuff and making sure your formulas are correct. You enter it once, it posts it in the proper place and you can generate the right reports and everything. Heck, you can even direct file your taxes and stuff."

"And when would I have time to convert everything over and learn the program, huh? This is a working ranch. I've got my hands full just keeping things running around here and making sure we're in the black." He half turned in his chair and looked up at her. "At the end of the day everything balances. Isn't that what counts?"

"And that's great. It truly is. But…" She frowned at him. "I just thought…I'm staying here and not paying a bit of rent to Duke—"

"It's a third yours. Why would he charge you rent?"

"You take great pleasure in reminding me of that, don't you?" she answered, her words clipped. "I damn well know it's a third mine. You don't think I feel that pressure every day? That I don't feel some sort of obligation even though I want—" she broke off, shook her head. "Never mind. You wouldn't understand."

"Understand what?" He got up from the chair and faced her, his pulse quickening as the tension thickened in the small office.

"I need to stand on my own two feet! I need to stop feeling like life is happening to me and instead feel like I'm making it happen. I need to find my own job, pay my own bills, know that I'm not dependent on someone else for my happiness. For my…fulfillment."

They were incredibly different, so why did he feel like those words applied to him too? Particularly the part about relying on someone else for happiness.

"Is that what happened with your husband?" It was an intimate question but he asked it anyway. Just what sort of life had she had with him? He'd been putting snippets together here and there from what she said, from what Duke said.

"Yes. He checked out of our marriage and left me behind, picking up the pieces. And there were a lot of pieces. So I don't need reminding that I'm staying here on my brother's hopes that I won't leave, because once again it's not just my future at stake, it's his and yours and everyone else tied to Crooked Valley and if I can't figure out my own life, how the hell can I be responsible for someone else's?"

"Does it feel better to get that off your chest?" he asked, looking into her face. Her cheeks were flushed, her eyes sparked with anger and frustration. He shouldn't be finding her so attractive this way, but he couldn't deny his own body's response to her heightened state.

"Not really. You want to know why I asked Duke to approach you about the books rather than come to you myself? Because I knew this would happen. I know you don't think much of me, and you think I don't care. Whatever, Quinn. You've made up your mind, fine. But I was at Brandt yesterday and I couldn't help but compare this ranch to theirs and I wanted to know if the one thing I'm good at could help my brother. So sue me or yell at me or whatever. Just know that I'm not the one standing in the way here."

"Oh, that's rich." His blood heated again, annoyed by her accusation that any of this could be his fault. He'd been doing more than his share since Joe Duggan's health had started declining. He'd been thrilled when Duke had decided to stay on, because burning the candle at both ends and being a single parent was starting to take its toll. For her to accuse him of standing in the way of Crooked Valley's success was just ludicrous.

"I'll have you know I've been working this ranch for over ten years—"

"And that's great," she interrupted. "But heaven forbid you rely on anyone else, right? Or accept that someone might know more than you. Particularly someone you don't respect."

Her chest was rising and falling quickly, the sound of her breath audible in the silence that fell.

"You want to waltz in here and turn things upside down and then leave again. Excuse me if I don't get all excited about the possibility of having to clean up your messes."

"I don't want to turn things upside down at all! What are you talking about? I'm trying to help!"

Quinn stared at her and felt his frustration bubble up and over. There was just too much Lacey in his life all the time. In the morning when she made coffee and packed Amber's lunch for school. When she baked her stupid cakes and used her own stupid fabric softener on his clothes so he had her scent with him every damn day. Family dinners at night and the way she worked around the house while he took Amber through her bedtime routine. The little hesitation each evening when their eyes met and they said good-night before going to their separate rooms far too early, just to avoid time alone together…

"Maybe you could help a little less," he snapped. "I understand you're at loose ends and not working, but Amber and me? We're not your little project. We're not your surrogate family. So stop trying so goddamned hard to be indispensable to us. You're not Marie, so quit trying to be!"

She pulled back as if he'd struck her, her wide blue eyes filling with unexpected tears at the cruel words.

"Goddammit," he said as his control snapped. He stepped forward and cupped her head in his hands and kissed her, full-on, no holds barred, lips and tongues meshing in a furious, passionate dance.

Oh, God.

It had been so long since he'd held a woman in his arms, since he'd felt the softness of a female body pressed to his or heard a murmur of pleasure ripple through her mouth to his. She wasn't fighting him off, he realized, she was straining to reach him. Her fingers dug into his shoulder blades as she held him close and her teeth…oh God, her teeth bit into his lower lip, sending sparks of desire rocketing through him. He reached down, cupped one hand around a delicious buttock and pulled her against him, her gasp of surprise giving him a strange satisfaction as he ran his tongue over the seam of her lips.

He ground his pelvis against hers once, aching for her, but it was the one step that brought them both out of the passionate haze and into the present.

She pressed her hands to his chest—when had it started heaving like he'd been running? "Quinn," she whispered, her voice a mixture of wonder and apprehension. "What are we doing?"

He had to get a grip. "I'm sorry," he murmured, dropping his hands and backing up a step, needing to put some distance between their bodies in an attempt to clear his head.

"I…" She looked at him, her eyes wide and wary. "I never tried to replace your wife." Her lower lip quivered. "I know how much you loved her. Everyone says so. I swear I just wanted to help."

"I'm sorry I said that," he replied roughly, meaning it. "That's my own frustration and I shouldn't take it out on you." His own frustration indeed. It had been a year and a half. Why did he feel disloyal? It wasn't reasonable to think he'd go through the rest of his life alone. To think that he wouldn't care for someone again. That wasn't logical.

But once more, his heart got in the way. And once more, he realized that there was more than his heart at risk here. It was Amber's, too. Amber, who clearly needed her mother so much. If this went anywhere, and ended badly, she'd be so hurt.

"Then the kiss was…" Lacey's voice whispered through the room, soft and uncertain.

He swallowed. Admitting he was sexually drawn to her would be like dropping a match on gasoline. He was in no position to leave Crooked Valley and neither was she. There was really only one thing to do, and that was lie. Something he was never comfortable with, but which he knew was necessary for all their sakes.

"Frustration. Again, I'm sorry. It was unfair of me."

He would swear she looked relieved and disappointed all at the same time. Had she been feeling the same pull as he had? It seemed impossible, but she'd definitely participated equally in the kiss, practically wrapping herself around him…

Down, boy.

Accounting. He had to get back to thinking about numbers and columns.

"About the books," he said, turning around and looking at the computer screen which was now a floating mass of bubbles as the screensaver took over. "Have a look. Convert them if you want. When the time comes for you to go, I'll hire some part-time help to keep them up to date. Or maybe you can teach Carrie. As her pregnancy progresses and then after the baby's born, she'll be spending less time as foreman."

He didn't look at her again. Couldn't. He just spun on his heel and left the room, grabbed his jacket and boots and headed out to the barns. Anything to get some breathing room and get his head on straight again.

He wanted to say that the kiss had affected him the most. It would be easier, because it was purely physical.

But that wasn't what stuck in his mind right now. It was how hurt she'd looked when he'd accused her of insinuating herself into his life. And that told him one disturbing fact: more than his libido was involved where Lacey Duggan was concerned.

And that was troubling indeed.

Chapter 8

Lacey examined the expenditures column once more, matching them to invoices and looking at ways to streamline some of the administrative costs of the ranch. As far as operational costs, she'd made a list of potential items to ask Duke about, since she knew very little about the actual ranching aspect. Clearly Quinn wasn't interested in being involved, and she wasn't going to force it. Especially after that kiss.

She sighed, slid her hand off the mouse and stared blindly at the monitor. The kiss. It had been surprising, passionate, glorious, magnificent. She hadn't imagined Quinn had that kind of raw intensity, but there had been nothing soft or tentative about how he kissed her. It had thrilled her right to her toes, leaving her breathless and off balance.

Just thinking about it sent a spiral of desire whipping through her.

But Quinn wasn't interested. He was frustrated, he'd said. And unhappy with himself for doing it.

Way to make a girl feel great.

She inhaled deeply and put her hand on the mouse again, determined to get through this section of the accounting today. Quinn didn't want her here. He accepted her help because he needed it, not because he wanted it—or her. Fine. She'd clean up the books for Crooked Valley, and throw herself into her employment efforts again. Something that took her away from the house. If she were lucky, she'd find something in Great Falls and she'd be able to move out and really start over rather than feeling like a mooch.

Quinn picked Amber up from day care and for once the bubbly chatter of the little girl didn't lift Lacey's spirits. Supper was an unusually quick fix of what Lacey's mom had inaccurately called goulash—ground beef, macaroni and tomato soup. If Quinn noticed the change in effort, he said nothing, and Amber ate it up without a complaint, as long as there was lots of grated cheese to go on the top.

Quinn wouldn't meet her eyes.

After the dinner mess was cleaned up, Lacey disappeared back into the office. Once more, Quinn didn't interfere. If he assumed she was working on Crooked Valley stuff, all the better. Tonight she was sending emails and making phone calls about the benefit dance for Quinn. Before, she'd thought it was a nice thing to do, but after today, it meant that the sooner the money was raised, perhaps the faster they'd get back in their house and not be in each other's hair all the time. Right now Lacey was thinking if she had anywhere else to go…

But she didn't. So the easiest solution was getting Quinn back in his old place.

Amber popped in to say good-night, and Lacey's heart gave a bittersweet pang as she realized how much she'd come to love the little girl. She kissed her clean hair and said "Good night, honey."

Amber was nearly to the door when she spun back. "Lacey? Will you help me with my Valentines tomorrow? My teacher gave me a list with the names in my class but I's still learning my letters."

If things had gone according to plan with Carter, they might have had a daughter like this. It seemed like the muscles in her abdomen tightened, a reminder of what could never be. She could never carry a child of her own. God knows she'd tried. The hysterectomy had pretty much taken care of any of those hopes.

"Of course I'll help you," she answered softly, knowing she couldn't take her dissatisfaction with Quinn out on Amber.

"Our party is Friday," Amber added with a quicksilver grin. "I told my teacher I would bring cookies."

Of course she did. And she knew just how to wrap Lacey around her little finger, too. Not that Lacey minded. Not this once.

"We'll talk tomorrow. Your daddy is waiting to take you to bed."

"Okay. Night, Lacey."

When she was gone, Lacey put her head in her hands, bracing her elbows on the desk. What a mess. Why had she allowed her emotions to get involved? She was supposed to be here to start over. Not get attached to a family that was not her own. She'd worried about not getting along with Quinn at the beginning. Now it was…it was just too much.

She could do this. All she had to do was stay rational, logical. There was nothing wrong with liking Quinn's daughter. She was Duke's sister, after all. Even if she didn't take on her part of the ranch, she could be a part of the circle that made up Crooked Valley.

Except the circle as they all knew it might not even exist if she went her own way.

"If?" she murmured in the quiet office. Where had that word come from? Up until now it had been *when*.

Darn. She sat back in the chair and blew out a breath. Duke had been smart after all. He'd known, hadn't he? That once he got her here, in the house, it'd be hard for her to leave. Once she saw the people, the life…

He was sneaky, her brother.

She'd driven into the Brandt spread and found herself making comparisons. Gone headfirst into the books and gotten a fair picture of all that went into the running of a cattle operation. She cared. She cared whether it succeeded or failed.

And she didn't want to be responsible for it being sold out from under her brother, not when he'd made a whole new life here for himself. He had a wife. A baby on the way. And he was happy. Could she really ruin that just so she could be right?

After hitting save, she shut down the computer and went out into the hall, found her boots and jacket and started pulling them on. Upstairs a door closed and then Quinn appeared, coming quietly down the steps. Her heart jumped simply at the sight of him. He might be able to ignore what happened between them, but she could not.

"It's late to be going out," he said softly, looking back upstairs and then at Lacey again. She avoided meeting his gaze directly, not wanting to get sucked into the depths of his eyes. That happened all too easily.

"I'm just running down to Duke's for a minute. Leave the door unlocked. I'll lock up when I come back."

"Okay."

She zipped up her coat and pulled on a pair of thick mitts.

"About today…" he began, but she held up a hand.

"It's okay. You said what you needed to. I'm fine, Quinn." She couldn't help it, she met his gaze. "If anything, it woke me up to reality. So don't worry about it."

"Reality? What does that mean?"

She swallowed tightly, wondering what to say, how much to reveal. "I think we've both been wondering, don't you? Now we've got it out of our system. We can forget about it and move on. Focus on what's really important."

He frowned. "Like what?"

"Like Crooked Valley. Like me finding a full-time job. And you need to worry about getting your life back to normal. For Amber."

His cheeks flushed a little. "Yes, for Amber," he agreed. "I have to think of her first. I don't want her getting too attached to you if you're just going to leave again. She doesn't need disappointments."

It was honest but damn, it smarted. "Right. Well, anyway, I'm going to pop in and see Carrie and Duke for a bit. Don't wait up. Just leave the porch light on when you go to bed."

She sent him the most platonic, impersonal smile she could before turning the knob and pulling the door open. She closed it behind her with a soft click, inhaled the cold air deeply into her lungs.

The ground was hard under her feet as she made her way to the bunkhouse, which now served as Duke and Carrie's home. It was a small two-bedroom bungalow, big enough for the two of them, or even the three of them once the baby came. She knew Duke had plans to build a piece on as their family grew. She'd asked him once about moving into the big house since he and Carrie were planning kids, but they'd both agreed they liked where they were. Or so they said.

Carrie answered the door, a smile blossoming on her face when she saw Lacey standing there. "We were just talking about you!" she exclaimed, standing aside so Lacey could enter. "Duke was saying you were going to take a look at the books."

Lacey almost wished she hadn't said yes to Kailey's job offer, because then she wouldn't have asked about Crooked Valley and she could have gone on with her original plans. Funny how one thing could change everything...

Kind of like Quinn's kiss.

She put that to the back of her mind and smiled at her sister-in-law. Carrie wasn't really showing yet, though Lacey noticed she was wearing leggings and a baggy sweatshirt. Her waistbands were probably getting a little tight now that she was at the end of her first trimester.

Lacey would not be jealous. She would not be bitter. She would not.

"Is Duke around? I wanted to talk to you guys about something."

"Sure. We were just watching some TV, but it's nothing we're too interested in. Do you want some tea or anything?"

"I'm okay."

"Hey, is that Lace?" Duke's voice echoed from the living room.

"Yeah, it's me," she called back. Grinning, she toed off her boots and hung her jacket on a hook behind the door. "On second thought, Carrie, do you have anything stronger than tea?"

Carrie chuckled. "Not much. There might be a beer in the fridge."

"That works for me. I could stand to kick back for a bit."

The house was warm and cozy, Carrie's feminine touches evident in the decor. Duke was sitting on the sofa, the cushion next to him vacant except for a light blanket. They'd been cuddling in front of the television, and Lacey thought that was lovely.

"You," she accused, right off the bat, "are a sneaky devil."

He feigned an innocent look. "What did I do?"

She plopped down on a side chair. "You knew, didn't you? You knew that once I got here, I'd get roped into this place."

"Really?" He looked so hopeful she nearly laughed. Instead she let out a grudging sigh.

"Yes, really." Carrie came back with her drink. "Thanks, Carrie," she said, taking the bottle into her hands. "Anyway, I want to run some hypotheticals past you. Maybe there's a way we can find some middle ground so we both get what we want."

Duke sat up a bit. "I'm intrigued."

"Me, too," Carrie said, resuming her seat beside Duke.

Lacey wasn't entirely sure where to begin. "I'm just figuring this out, so don't assume too much, okay? What I need tonight is a sounding board."

"Okay," they both agreed, then looked at each other and smiled.

It made Lacey lonely, seeing that level of togetherness. She took a sip of her drink and licked her lips, searching for the right words to start. In the end, it came down to a simple truth.

"I don't want you to lose Crooked Valley."

"That's good to know," Duke responded, and Lacey blew out a breath.

"I think it's stupid, the way Granddad split this up, but there's nothing we can do about it. I don't want to be the cause of you losing it, Duke. You and Carrie love it here, and you're making your life here. I'm thinking there has to be a way for me to work the conditions in my favor, so the ranch doesn't get put up for sale and I don't have to wade my way through this place with mud on my boots." She looked over at Carrie and smiled. "Not that there's anything wrong with that, if it's your thing."

Carrie smiled back.

"Do you have any ideas?"

She nodded. "I think we need to have a lawyer take a good look at the will, for one thing. It will tell us how involved I have to be to meet conditions. I can't believe Granddad would expect me to be a rancher. I'm not even that comfortable around horses. But I'm good with numbers and computers. If being the ranch bookkeeper satisfies the terms, I'd be willing to stay on in that capacity. I think I could help Crooked Valley streamline some of the costs, and take advantage of a few tax breaks that I'm not sure Joe even knew about. It might give you some financial breathing room, especially as things need to be repaired and you're expanding your family."

Duke's brows lifted. "Lacey, that's great! I'd love that, I really would."

"I'm already doing some of the bookkeeping for Kailey's family, and I could do ours even if I got a full-time job somewhere close. Which brings me to the next bit."

"There's more?"

This was actually harder, she realized. She'd come to love the big house, the spacious kitchen, cozy fireplace, big bedrooms. "There's the question of where I'll live."

Duke's gaze held hers. "We're happy here. You should stay in the house."

But Lacey shook her head. "Duke, it's too big for just me. I mean, Quinn and Amber are there now, but that's not exactly a comfortable situation and they'll be going back to their own place when their house is ready. Besides, what if I find a job in the city or something? It's a long commute from here. Even finding a place on the other side of Gibson would cut fifteen or twenty minutes off my commute each way. You and Carrie should have the house. It's meant to be filled with kids and laughter and toys and family."

It hurt to say that last bit, even though it was true.

Duke's face softened, his eyes filled with understanding. "Lacey, I know it doesn't seem like it now, but you'll have that someday. Just because things didn't work out with Carter…"

"No, I won't," she answered firmly. Perhaps it was time to stop dancing around the subject. "Duke, you had to adjust to losing your hearing in one ear. It wasn't just the hearing, it was how it affected your life in the military. Your decisions that came afterwards. That was tough, right?"

"You know it was," he agreed. "I have to make adjustments all the time."

"And it won't ever be better, not even someday."

Carrie leaned forward. "What are you trying to say, Lacey?"

"The real reason Carter left…why things fell apart is because I can't have children. When I couldn't get pregnant, the doctors discovered endometriosis. We tried a few different things, but in the end I had a hysterectomy. I'll never fill the big house with kids, you see. It should be you."

Duke's mouth had fallen open while Carrie's face drooped with dismay. "Oh, Lacey, I'm so sorry." Her cheeks pinkened. "It must be so hard for you when I…" Awkward silence filled the room.

"I don't begrudge you one ounce of your happiness," Lacey whispered, her voice hoarse. "It's hard sometimes, but I'm really trying to move on. I don't want you guys to lose this place, and I'll help you keep it, but I have to take charge of my own life. Make my own decisions. So if I take on some of the office and administrative duties works, and if I can live off-site, we might be able to give this a go."

There were a few beats of silence before Duke asked, "What does Quinn think about this?"

Just the mention of his name made her muscles tense, in good ways and bad. "It's not up to Quinn. I know he's your manager, but the terms of the will and the ownership of the ranch is really about us."

"I value his opinion, Lacey. He's been doing this a lot longer than me."

She was rather tired of Quinn being held up as this paragon of perfection. It seemed like he could do no wrong. Perfect at his job, perfect dad, perfect husband. It was an impossible standard to live up to.

"Quinn is more than happy to pass on the accounting, that I can tell you for sure. As far as the rest goes, I know for a fact that what he really cares about is Crooked Valley and making sure he still has a job. This will take care of that. Or at least I hope it will." Quinn would be able to move back to his house, keep his job, support himself and Amber. Have the life he wanted to have.

Except he'd rather have it with Marie. His wife. Despite the kiss today, Lacey knew one thing for sure. Quinn was a long way from being over the woman he'd loved. After feeling like such a failure with Carter, Lacey wasn't interested in trying to compete. Quinn wasn't the only perfect one in that relationship and there was no way Lacey wanted to try to live up to Marie's memory.

She needed to find a job and a new place to live. Like, yesterday.

"I'll call the lawyer first thing in the morning, so we can iron out particulars. Then it's just a matter of getting Rylan onboard."

Lacey gave a wry chuckle. "Rylan, with his wandering feet? Good luck. He's not the settling down type."

"I never thought I was, either. Until I landed here. I think Granddad knew what he was doing more than we gave him credit for."

Lacey pondered that for a moment. "Do you think

we would have stayed here if Dad hadn't died?" Those days were a hazy memory for her; she'd been very young when their father had been killed in action. The ranch life hadn't been for their mom, Helen, and she'd moved into the city where she could work and provide for them all.

Duke shrugged. "Who knows? Does it matter? We're here now. And I, for one, am glad to be connecting with my family again."

"Even Mom and David?" It was no secret that Duke hadn't been a big fan of their mother remarrying.

"Even David. He ended up being a decent guy at Christmas. He makes her happy."

Lacey's eyes misted over. "Wow. Kudos to you, Carrie. Love has made this big lump into a bit of a marshmallow."

"What can I say?" Carrie replied, taking Duke's hand in hers. "He did the same for me. And someone is out there for you, too. I really believe that. The kids thing doesn't have to be a deal breaker."

"I'm afraid it does," Lacey answered, her voice suddenly brittle. "At least to some people."

"Then he didn't deserve you," Duke decreed. "You need a better man. Someone like…"

"Don't even think about saying it." She was terrified he would try to set her up or even worse, that *Quinn* was the name sitting on his tongue.

Duke just laughed. "Okay. Fair enough. Lacey, I'm really glad you came over. Glad you're willing to give this a shot. Thank you. I mean it."

She took another long drink of her beer and relaxed back into the cushions. "Honestly? Gibson isn't such a bad town. The people are nice. And now I have family here. Despite the employment situation, I could have landed in worse places."

Carrie laughed. "I had to convince Duke of that, too."

Lacey turned the bottle around in her hands. "Just one thing, though. Don't mention any of this to Quinn, okay?"

"Why?" Duke frowned, his brows pulling together. "I thought you said he was onboard with you doing the accounting?"

"He is. It's just…complicated. We don't see eye to eye on a lot of stuff. I'd rather just not get into it until I know for sure what I'm doing, you know?"

Carrie and Duke shared a look that Lacey couldn't quite interpret, but she could tell they were hesitating. "Look, it's been challenging being roomies, okay? I came to you because you're my brother. I need to figure this all out without Quinn putting in his two cents."

"And you think he would?"

She nodded quickly. "Oh, I know he would. He has opinions about everything I do."

She saw Carrie give Duke's hand a squeeze, and the topic was miraculously dropped. Instead, Carrie changed the subject to the benefit. "Speaking of, how are things coming along for the dance at the Silver Dollar? Kailey said you'd taken on getting some items for a raffle."

The conversation turned to planning the event and the three of them stayed up far later than was wise, but Lacey left with a full heart. Somehow, in the space of a few weeks, Crooked Valley had started to feel like a home. And she knew it had little to do with location and a lot more to do with family and acceptance. Maybe Granddad had known that all along, too.

Maybe Joe Duggan had been smarter than any of them had given him credit for.

Chapter 9

As resolved as Lacey was to keep her distance and perspective where Quinn was concerned, she wasn't so good at it when it came to Amber. The girl was just too cute, even when she got frustrated with writing the names on her Valentines and put down her pencil in disgust. They took a break and chatted about what kind of cookies Amber wanted for her class party. Quinn might puff and bluster about Lacey usurping Marie's place, but Lacey wasn't about to deny Amber a few cookies for her first Valentine's Day party. Quinn certainly didn't have time for it and grabbing ones from the grocery store just wasn't the same.

During the day, though, she worked in Quinn's office when he was in the barns, converting the accounts over to the new program. She spent one morning at the Brandt ranch, and met with two other prospective clients in town. Her full-time inquiries garnered two new interview appointments. Maybe the argument with Quinn was exactly the kick in the pants she'd needed to really find her gumption. Up until then she'd just been going through the motions.

Signs had gone up around town, advertising the Valentine's Day event, with no mention of the proceeds going to the Solomons. It amazed Lacey that the secret hadn't got out and back to Quinn, but he seemed to know nothing about it. The biggest challenge, it seemed, was going to be actually getting him to go. That bit was Kailey's job, a detail for which Lacey was grateful to have been spared.

February 13th rolled around and Amber and Lacey spent the afternoon making tiny heart-shaped chocolate shortbreads. As the cookies cooled, they decorated them with pink icing and left them to set a bit before packing them in cookie tins for the next day's event.

Lacey looked around the messy kitchen and realized it was going to be harder than she expected, leaving this house. It felt like a house should feel—warm and welcoming. Of course that could all change when Quinn and Amber left again. It wasn't really made for one person. If she moved out, and Quinn went back home, the big house would be empty again.

"There," she said, dusting her hands off on her apron. "That's the last pan in the oven. And there are extra. What do you say, should we taste test?"

"Yes!" Amber bounced up and down on her toes, then looked at Lacey speculatively. "How many extra?"

Lacey burst out laughing. "Enough for you to have two and no more or you'll ruin your supper."

"Okay." Amber made a close examination of the

cookies and plucked two off the rack. Lacey expected her to pop the cookies in her mouth but instead she hopped off the stool, came around the counter and handed them to Lacey. "These ones are yours," she stated, then popped back around to choose her own.

"Thanks," Lacey said, and waited until Amber was ready, then they took their first bites together.

Crumbs flaked away from the buttery cookie onto the floor. "Yummy," Amber said, breaking into a crumb-and-frosting smile. She licked her lips and looked at Lacey with pure adoration. "Lacey, I wish you were my mama."

The innocent words were a shock to Lacey's heart. A yearning so powerful, so pure, enveloped her and for a fleeting moment, she wished it, too. But being Amber's mom would mean being Quinn's wife and that simply wasn't going to happen. "Oh, honey," she murmured, and went over and put her arm around the little girl. "That is such a sweet thing to say. I can't be your mama, but I'll always be your friend, okay?"

"But why can't you be my mama?" Amber peered up at her with curious eyes. "You already do what mamas do. You wash my clothes and do all the cooking and tidy the house and make Valentimes cookies and you love me, too, right?"

Lacey sighed, so torn and yet happy, too. "I do love you. And don't you forget it. But to be your mommy, I'd have to be married to your daddy, see?"

Amber shrugged. "So marry my daddy." Unconcerned, she started putting decorated cookies on the bottom of the big tin.

How on earth could Lacey answer that? She was just trying to figure it out when the front door opened.

Great. Just what she needed. Quinn. Instead of answering Amber, Lacey went to the sink and started piling up dishes to be washed.

Quinn entered the kitchen, the top of his hair flattened from his hat, his shoulders looking impossibly broad in a soft denim shirt. "Cookies?" he asked, looking at Amber, sparing Lacey a brief glance before smiling at his daughter.

"Lacey helped me for my party tomorrow," Amber explained.

"I see."

Lacey heard the strain in his voice. Remembered how he'd told her to back off trying to replace Marie. She knew she should let it go but somehow couldn't. "Amber asked if I'd help her make cookies. It's her first Valentine's Day party."

The warning was issued: *don't make a big deal out of this, I did it for your kid.*

But Amber, being four, didn't sense the undertones and picked up a cookie. "Lacey said there's extras. Here." She pressed it against his lips, and with a laugh he opened his mouth so she could pop it inside.

He was still chewing when Amber went back to her cookie-packing and said, matter-of-factly, "I asked Lacey if she'd marry you and be my mama. Is that okay, Daddy?"

Lacey knew she should not feel quite so gratified when crumbs caught in Quinn's throat and he started coughing.

He looked over at her, eyes watering, crumbs on his lips and she struggled not to laugh. He would not find this funny. But he looked so comical, all red-faced and watery-eyed with the odd crumb flying out of his mouth when he coughed.

Amber, God love her, was waiting patiently for him to finish.

Lacey quietly handed him a glass of water which he took, drank, and finally breathed normally.

"So?" Amber persisted. "Can Lacey be my mama?"

Quinn's face flattened as his expression turned serious. "Honey, it's not that simple."

Amber's little eyebrows puckered in the middle. "It's easy. You ask her to marry you and she says yes and then she's my mama. Lacey said she would marry you."

Lacey's stomach clenched but she kept her voice soft and soothing. "Sweetie, that's not what I said. I said that while I love you, I can't be your mama because I'm not married to your daddy. We'd have to love each other for that to happen."

Amber's eyes filled with tears. "You don't love my daddy?"

Oh, God. She went to the child and knelt down in front of her. "You have the best dad ever, Amber. But we are just friends. We're not...like the princess and that ice guy in the movie you like so much, know what I mean?"

"But I want you to!" The tears in Amber's eyes spilled over and Lacey's heart broke. It was hard to be mad at Quinn for his stance the other day. This sort of thing was exactly what he was trying to avoid. She only wished he'd believe her when she said she wouldn't hurt Amber for the world.

"I know," Lacey answered softly. "And you can't know how happy it makes me to know you would like for me to be your mom. It's the biggest compliment ever. But like I said, I don't have to be your mama to be here for you. Right?"

Amber nodded halfheartedly.

Quinn came over and said quietly, "Come here, chicken." When Amber turned, he hefted her up into his arms and folded her into a quick hug. "So, are you okay now? Do you understand what Lacey said?"

She nodded, tucking her head into the curve of his neck. Quinn looked at Lacey over top of Amber's head. Lacey was sure she'd never seen him look so bleak.

He reached into his jacket pocket. "Look what I picked up today. Do you want to watch it?"

Lacey saw the red cover of a DVD case and recognized it as the Charlie Brown Valentine special. "Oooh, a Valentine's Day DVD!" she exclaimed, perhaps a bit too brightly but desperate to change the subject and mood. "Go put it in, sweetie. You can watch it before dinner."

"Okay." Amber took the case from her dad and made her way to the living room, where, like most kids her age, she was completely proficient in running the DVD player.

"What the hell was that?" he whispered, low enough for Amber not to hear but enough for Lacey to detect the ire in his voice.

"I had no idea, I swear. One moment we were baking cookies and the next she sprung it on me. I was trying to explain when you came in."

"Where on earth would she get such an idea?"

It burned that he considered the idea so utterly implausible. Was she really that terrible? That unattractive and unappealing?

"I certainly didn't put it there," she responded, with a

fair bit of acid in her voice. She turned away and went to the sink, flicking on the taps to run water for the dishes, hoping he couldn't tell how much his words stung.

But the running water only served to camouflage their voices as Quinn followed her. "This was what I was afraid of. She's too attached to you. And now she's going to get hurt."

"I would never hurt her! Wow, you must really think a lot of me."

"Hey, I know you're not staying around. You're only here temporarily, and then you'll be gone and where will Amber be? Hurt. She needs stability, not someone who is in her life and out of it again."

Words sat on her lips, begging to be spoken. It was entirely possible she would be staying in Gibson or at least close by for the foreseeable future.

And then she looked at Quinn and the defensive expression tightening his face and she understood. He wasn't just talking about Amber. It wasn't Lacey who was in and out of their lives, it was Marie. And because Marie had left them both, he didn't trust anyone to stay.

He didn't want any disappointments, either. Which meant that maybe, just maybe, he cared for her more than he was letting on.

Her anger towards him dissipated.

"Yes, she needs stability," she agreed softly. "Which is why she has you, and Duke, and Carrie and Kailey and everyone who has always been a support to you."

"But none that she's latched on to like you," he answered, turning a bit so that his back blocked them from Amber's view.

"Quinn, I don't know what to say. Except even if

we don't live in the same house much longer, I'll still care about her and want to see her and be there for her."

"Until you leave."

"What if I didn't leave?"

His eyes widened. "What do you mean?"

She peered around his shoulder and saw Amber engrossed in the show. "I mean, even if I'm not right here, at Crooked Valley, I've decided to stay in the area."

"When were you going to tell me?"

She met his gaze. "When I had figured out all the logistics." In other words, without his input and opinions, which always seemed to cloud any sort of clarity she managed to achieve. There was something between them. The kiss had proved that. Whether or not it ever went any farther was up in the air. This was one decision she had to make on her own, for the right reasons.

She could see the wheels turning in his head. The two of them, in the same town, either snapping at each other or gazing into each other's eyes like idiots, just like they were doing now. She'd thought of it, too, and didn't have the answers.

"I care about your daughter, Quinn. I know what you said about getting too close, but I couldn't say no when she asked for help with the cookies. Please don't be angry at me for that."

"I'm not, and I'm sorry I snapped at you. The truth is, I'm angry at myself for not being able to spare her disappointments. As a parent, the worst thing ever is seeing your child in pain." He sighed. "You'll understand that someday when you have your own."

But she wouldn't. And there was one little girl who'd like to have her for a mom and she couldn't do that, either. What little composure she'd been hanging onto, crumbled.

"Lacey? Did I say something wrong?"

She shook her head quickly and turned back to the dishes so he wouldn't see the distress on her face.

But he wouldn't let it alone. Leave her alone. "Now you know why I said what I did the other day…"

"No," she replied, starting to lose her cool. "No, I don't. I'm not trying to be your sainted wife, Quinn. I wasn't then, I'm not now. And the last thing I want is to be compared to her, okay?"

And then her heart stuttered a bit, because she was afraid if he did compare her to Marie, she'd come up sorely lacking. Her ego had taken a big enough beating when she wasn't "woman enough" for Carter. If Quinn actually verbalized her inadequacies to her face, she'd fall apart a little. Or a lot.

She bit down on her lip and scrubbed at a mixing bowl, hating that after everything, his opinion still seemed to matter. It wasn't fair.

"I'm just trying to protect my daughter," he murmured, "from getting hurt more than she already has."

She turned glistening eyes to him. "And I resent that you think she needs protecting from me. That either of you do. Just go, please. Let me clean up this mess before her show finishes and she sees me upset."

He left her alone and she nearly wiped the finish off the dishes, she scrubbed so hard with the dishcloth. By the time Amber's show was finished, the kitchen was spick-and-span and Lacey had to get out. If Amber said anything more about motherhood, Lacey was pretty sure she'd lose it. And she definitely wasn't up for another emotionally-charged conversation with Quinn.

She found him in his office and stuck her head in the door. "I have plans in town for supper. You and Amber can take something out of the freezer."

"We'll be fine," he answered briefly. "We managed before. You don't have to worry about us."

She wasn't sure if it was meant to be a reassurance or a brush-off, but she knew how it felt. *We don't need you. We're fine without you.*

You don't matter.

"Bye," she replied, and stepped away.

One of the hardest things she'd ever done was walk away from the house that evening, but she knew it was necessary. It was time to put some real distance between them all. One thing was for sure. As much as it hurt Lacey, she'd rather that than cause any more pain to the precious girl inside who'd lost enough already.

The last thing Quinn wanted to do was go out for Valentine's Day. How he'd been roped into attending some cockamamy dance at the Silver Dollar, he wasn't sure, but it definitely seemed like the universe was conspiring against him. His mom had called and asked if Amber could come visit and sleep over today, because she had plans on the weekend and wanted to do something special for Valentine's Day with her granddaughter. He couldn't say no—Amber loved visiting her grandma. But that left him alone on the most romantic night of the year. Torture for singles. He'd planned on grabbing a frozen pizza for his supper and hiding out at the house. Hopefully without Lacey in his way.

Now he was patting on some aftershave and tucking his favorite blue-and-white-striped shirt into clean jeans, making sure the cuffs were buttoned over his forearms. The bandages were gone, but he was still a little self-conscious about the pink scars on his skin, which would fade more but never really go away completely.

He wished he was better at saying no. Kailey had called. She'd had plans to go to the dance at the saloon and her date had cancelled at the last minute. Her argument had been that it was less pathetic to go as friends, as they'd done before, than sit home alone. When she learned that Amber was already cared for, any argument he might have put up didn't have a leg to stand on.

Even Lacey had plans. She'd gone straight from a job interview to dinner with friends. At least that was what her note said.

He turned off the bathroom light and sighed. Maybe it was better to get out tonight. He had to start doing that more, and at least with Kailey there were no expectations. What else was he going to do, sit home and wallow? That would only lead to thinking about a certain stubborn woman with coppery curls and snapping blue eyes. Why couldn't he get her out of his mind?

Kailey wasn't quite ready when he arrived at the Brandt spread, so he waited in the kitchen, talking to her mom and dad about their latest ideas on sires for their breeding mares. Quinn listened carefully; developing Crooked Valley's bucking stock was part of his job and one he wished he was better at. When Kailey finally came out of her room, Quinn found himself wishing he had a dynamite stud in his stable. That would make all the difference in the world, but coming up with the capital to buy such an animal was a big sticking point. The ranch simply didn't have the money right now.

"You ready?" Kailey asked, grinning widely.

Quinn shook his head. "Whooeee, girl. Ain't I the lucky one."

"If I thought you meant that, I'd go put on a pair of ratty jeans," she replied while her parents laughed. She was wearing a cute denim miniskirt, cowboy boots and a red plaid fitted shirt, the whole thing highlighting her curves while still being cute and modest.

Too bad Kailey was like a sister and didn't do a damned thing for him otherwise.

"I'll be having to give a good number of boys the stink-eye tonight," he said, frowning for effect.

She laughed. "Right back atcha. Is that a new shirt?"

He shook his head. "Nope. Anyway, let's get going." He said good-night to Mr. and Mrs. Brandt and they were off to town.

"The Dollar doesn't usually have a real dance on Valentine's Day. I wonder why they're doing it this year?"

Kailey shrugged and looked out the window. "Maybe they thought it would bring in a better crowd to make it official," she suggested.

Indeed, when they got to the saloon, the parking lot was packed. "Holy cow, are you sure you want to go in here? The floor will be crowded." He'd been to the Dollar several times since Marie's death, but tonight felt different. He was…nervous. And he didn't quite know why.

"Drinks are half-price until ten. Come on, Quinn." She winked at him. "We don't have to stay that long."

"Isn't that Carrie and Duke's truck?"

She squinted. "I believe it is. See? It's going to be fun." Instead of waiting for him to open her door, she hopped out of the cab. "Let's go!" she called. "My legs are freezing here!"

He truly hadn't suspected a thing. Not until the moment he stepped inside the bar and a cheer went up. Perplexed, his gaze was drawn to a banner above the bar: *Have a Heart: Benefit for Quinn and Amber Solomon.*

His throat hurt when he swallowed and heat rose to his cheeks. Jesus. Charity? That's what tonight was about?

Duke appeared at his side. "Put away your pride for one night, Quinn," he suggested, leaning close to be heard above the din. "Your friends and neighbors are all here to give you a helping hand."

Quinn looked at his friend. "I don't know what to say."

Duke smiled at him and clapped him on the back. "You'd do the same for anyone else. Just enjoy the night, okay?"

Kailey was grinning at him broadly. Carrie came over carrying a bottle of his preferred beer.

He remembered how many people had rallied around him after Marie died, bringing food and offering to take Amber places to give her life a little joy. Gibson was like that and it was one of the reasons he loved it here. But damn, he hated that twice now he'd needed help.

His gaze shifted to the area where the pool tables were. Instead of the clack of cues and balls, the green felt held an assortment of items. He could see some sort of cellophane basket done up, a mannequin head wearing a sparkling necklace and one of Junior Ellerbee's custom saddles that generally went for a big wad of cash. What the hell?

And there was Lacey. Not at dinner, but in a bottle-green dress that brought out the red tints in her hair, a pair of supple brown cowboy boots on her feet. Lord above, but she was pretty, and as she smiled at a young cowboy looking at the jewelry, Quinn caught his breath.

Damned inconvenient. He was starting to understand his unease. Somehow he'd started to move on, hadn't he? He'd been holding on to Marie's memory for dear life, just to get through. But now something else… someone else…occupied a good deal of his thoughts. He wasn't sure if it was a good thing or a bad thing, but he knew for damned sure it was uncomfortable, and a little frightening.

"Don't just stand there like an idiot," Kailey urged, nudging his elbow. "Go mingle. Say hi. See what's up for grabs at the silent auction."

Silent auction. So that's what Lacey was doing.

He took a long swig of beer and made his way through the crowd as the guest band started a rousing rendition of "Mud on the Tires" and couples formed up on the dance floor. It took quite a while for him to reach the sheltered area of the pool tables, as he was stopped every few feet by neighbors and well-wishers. By the time he reached Lacey, he wasn't sure if he was embarrassed and humbled or warmed by the generosity of the people of Gibson—or both.

"Dinner with friends, huh?" He had to speak loudly to be heard over top of the music and laughter.

"I did have dinner with friends. With Carrie and Duke and a few other people who chipped in to help set up. Roy made sure we had lots to eat." She patted her stomach and smiled. It was no secret in town that the cook had an eye for pretty women and a penchant for big portions. It made the Dollar a popular place to grab a bite.

She looked up at him hopefully. "So? What do you think?"

He couldn't deliberately douse the spark of hope in her eyes. Not without being a total jerk. "It's a bit overwhelming," he admitted. "Wonderful, but difficult, too, you know?"

"I do know. It can be hard to accept help. Almost as hard as asking for it."

She knew something about that, didn't she? His gaze clung to hers for a few more moments and he felt that strange sense of kinship with her that kept cropping up. That is, until someone jostled him from behind, pitching him forward. Lacey reached out and caught his arms, her fingers tightening around his biceps as his chest pressed against hers.

Color stained her cheeks and she bit down on her lip…he had the ungodly urge to pull her the rest of the way against his body and kiss her again. Which would solve absolutely nothing. Besides, they were in a crowded bar. Not exactly private.

And if they were in private? Would he act differently?

She let go of his arms and stepped back, but the shy blush was still on her face. Oh, he thought he might. Which was why it was good they were in a crowded, noisy room.

"Do you want to see what we've got for silent auction, Quinn? The items are open for bid until ten, and then we're awarding the prizes." Her eyes lit up again, and he realized that they were a different color blue than usual, darker, with a hint of green picked up from the hues of her dress.

"Sure."

She led him along the tables, pointing out a gift basket from the local salon, a weekend stay at a hotel in Great Falls, handmade silver jewelry from Joey Cartright, a silversmith right here in town. Being a ranching community, there were gift certificates from the feed store, a pair of custom boots from Lamont Leather and Western Wear, and the biggest item of all, Junior's saddle. He reached out and touched the intricate detail on the leather and once again felt humbled and unworthy.

"This is too much," he said, looking down at the current bid. It stood at fifteen hundred dollars.

"Why?" Lacey tilted her head and looked at him curiously. "Quinn, you're a big part of this community. Do you know how special that is? It's amazing how people help each other here. You've had such a rough time the last few years, but you're lucky, too. You belong here. This is your place and your people and they want to help you because they love you."

Did that include her? Because she was here and she was helping. The thought twisted something inside him. He was so attracted to her. Liked her. And yet every time she did something nice, something special, he got angry. He had to keep telling himself to stop comparing her to Marie. That no one could take Marie's place.

And then he got angry with himself for liking her so much and knowing that he shouldn't. Wasn't it disloyal?

"Sometimes it's just hard to accept help."

She laughed. "You're preaching to the choir. Do you think I was in a big hurry to come back to the ranch when I lost my job? I had to swallow a lot of pride, you know."

Another reminder that the ranch was something she'd

never wanted. If he could only remember that, perhaps he could forget about the rest. Like how tiny she looked in that dress, with the slim belt fastened at her waist. Or the way her lips were soft when they were pressed against his… God, he was getting so sick of fighting it. Wished there were fewer consequences to consider and that he could be free to just do what he wanted without having to worry about his decisions and how they'd affect everyone else. His daughter. Duke. Lacey.

Himself.

"These days," she continued on, as if oblivious to his turbulent thoughts, "I think being at Crooked Valley was meant to be. I like it more than I expected to."

"I told you." He smiled back at her politely, knowing he should feel glad she'd embraced life at the ranch. If Lacey took on her third of the ranch, they were that much closer to keeping it in the family and providing everyone with some security. Including him, and his job. Wasn't that what they'd all hoped for?

But then the flip side of that was knowing that if she did stay on, she'd be a part of his life. Perhaps on the periphery, but there, nonetheless. He'd have to get control of his feelings if that were to happen.

This wasn't even supposed to be an issue.

"I'm going to go mingle," he said, leaning forward just a little as another song started up and the noise increased. "I'll see you around."

Was that disappointment in her eyes? He rather thought it might be. But she simply gave him a little wave and turned her back on him, going to straighten one of the displays and talk to some of the ranch women who'd dragged their husbands out. He heard Lacey's bright voice ringing out over the clutter of music and conversation. "Ladies," she sang out, "you'll want to get your husbands to bid on this! Nothing says Valentine's Day like new jewelry!"

Chapter 10

Another hour had passed and Lacey was getting tired. She looked around the room, searching for Quinn. He was holding up a corner with a couple of ranch hands from a nearby spread, watching couples spinning on the floor. About a half dozen girls sent inviting looks their way, and Lacey felt a spurt of jealousy. But while Quinn urged his companions to take advantage with nods and elbows, he didn't seem interested.

Kailey was taking a turn on the floor with one of her old beaux, Colt Black, laughing at something he said. Even though Lacey had dressed up and made a real effort tonight, she'd never felt so old and out of place. She was not even thirty, for Pete's sake. But while time hadn't made her old, life had. If not old, weary. Too weary to get very excited for the bar scene.

Now Quinn was standing alone, holding up the

wall, and she made her way to his side. "Penny for your thoughts," Lacey said by his ear.

He looked over at her, his eyes shadowed. "You really want to know?"

She shrugged. "Try me."

He lifted one eyebrow. "I feel old."

She was so relieved, she started laughing. "Me, too!"

He rolled his eyes. "You? Come on."

"I dunno," she said, letting her eyes rove over the crowded dance floor. "The bar scene just isn't for me. I think I just lost the ability to be…carefree."

"You're young. Beautiful. With a lot ahead of you. You definitely shouldn't feel old."

Did he even realize what he'd just said? He'd called her young and beautiful, things she hadn't felt for a long, long time. But she wasn't about to ask him if he meant it, and open that whole can of worms. She just let the compliment sink in, let herself enjoy it for what it was.

"It's not like you're in your dotage, Quinn." She nudged his arm with her elbow. "How old are you? Thirty-five?"

"Thirty-four in June," he responded. She noticed he'd switched out his beer for a soda just as she had. She wasn't sure if they were both boring or simply cautious. Sometimes she longed to just cut loose, like she might have back in the old days. Oh, nothing too crazy, but without this looming sense of responsibility she always seemed to feel.

It was something that had absolutely nothing to do with age.

"You and I are old souls, Quinn. It's experience that's made us old, not years. And I think we've both had enough heartache for a lifetime."

He looked over at her. "You're comparing your divorce to Marie's death?"

Touchy subject, and she wasn't trying to downplay his pain, but that didn't lessen what she'd gone through. "No, of course not. Losing your wife was devastating, I'm sure. But I want you to think about something. Didn't you love each other until the end? At least you can say that. From everything I've heard, you had a beautiful relationship, one you can look back on without regrets. Me? Not so much. It's really hard to know that the person you promised to love forever—who promised to love you—chose to walk away. It's not easy to be rejected that way."

Quinn looked at her then. Really looked at her, with understanding eyes. "You loved him a lot."

"I did. I thought it would last forever. And then it didn't."

"But you get a do-over."

"And so do you. I think we both know that do-overs aren't as easy as they sound. You don't know everything about me, Quinn. Just as I'm sure I don't know everything about you. But I think we at least have that in common. Wounds can be slow to heal."

"Yes, they can," he agreed. What she didn't know was how much she was helping him heal his.

They were gazing into each other's eyes when Kailey bounced up. "Hey y'all, look who I found!"

Lacey turned her head and let out a happy squeal. "Rylan! Oh, my gosh, what are you doing here?"

Her younger brother grinned at her, picked her up and twirled her around. "Duke called me. When that didn't work, he sicced Carrie on me. I'm headed to North Dakota tomorrow, but I thought I could squeeze in a quick visit." He put her down and held his hand out to Quinn. "Sorry to hear about your place, Quinn."

Quinn shook his hand. "Thanks, Rylan."

"You should check out the auction items, Ry."

"I already did. That is a sweet saddle up for bid. Whoever made that has some serious talent."

"Junior Ellerbee," Lacey replied. "Well, then you should catch a few dances with a few pretty girls." Lacey gave him a nudge. "Don't be like Quinn here and hold up the wall all night."

He looked over at Kailey, who'd gone to the bar in search of another drink. "I'm not sure that's such a good idea."

"It's just a dance. Quinn, you want a refill? I think I'll join Kailey."

"I'm good," he replied.

Lacey grabbed another soda for herself and a beer for Quinn anyway, because he looked like he could still use some loosening up. And she grabbed Kailey, too, and brought her back to the group. Despite what Rylan said, he'd noticed Kailey for sure. It wouldn't hurt for him to give her a turn on the floor. The vibe between the two men was a bit tense, though, so Lacey pasted on her brightest smile and beckoned for Duke and Carrie to join them. In moments, the six of them were chatting away until Cy Williamson, the saloon owner, got up to speak when the band took a break.

"Hey, everyone," he began. "Thanks for coming tonight and helping out a neighbor...Gibson's own Quinn Solomon and that gorgeous little girl of his. As you all know, Quinn's house suffered serious damage in a fire a few weeks ago. Tonight's proceeds will go right to

Quinn to help him fix up his home and get life back to normal."

Cheers and claps echoed through the bar.

"And now, here are Carrie and Lacey to say a few words."

Lacey followed Carrie to the stage, and waited while Carrie said a few words about Quinn and thanked everyone for their generous donations. Kailey scooted up to hand Lacey a sheaf of papers—the bids from the silent auction. When it was her turn, she stepped up onto the low platform and took the microphone that Carrie handed her.

She scanned the sea of faces looking up at her and realized that this truly did feel like home. Like she belonged here, not just as Duke's little sister but as a part of the community. She owed a lot of that to Carrie and Kailey, who'd included her in the planning for tonight. But there was more, too. She'd made connections in town, either by running errands or shopping with Amber or looking for work. She'd had her co-workers at her last job, and her elderly neighbor, but none of them had contacted her in the weeks since she'd left Helena. The last time she'd been to the diner, however, at least three people had made a point to stop and chat and ask how things were at the ranch and with Quinn.

She really didn't want to leave. She wanted to be a part of this—permanently. It was a complete surprise, but there it was.

"Hi, everyone," she began hesitantly, her voice echoing through the mic. "I'm Lacey Duggan, Joe's granddaughter. I've got the results of the bidding right here in my hand, and some of you are going home with some wonderful items tonight. If I call your name, come to the stage at the end of the list to pay your money and pick up your prize."

She began with the gift certificates for stores around town, then moved on to the bigger items. Duke got high bid for the custom boots, while Dan Ketchum paid a ridiculous amount for the silver necklace and earrings, earning him a smacking kiss from his wife as everyone laughed.

"Now, for the saddle. I don't have to tell you all that this is a gorgeous item worth a lot of coin. Sincere thanks to Junior for donating it tonight. Junior, I can say with complete confidence that your saddle is going to be in very good hands. The high bid, which brought a whopping three thousand three hundred dollars, goes to Rylan Duggan."

Cheers went up and Duke gave Rylan a slap on the back. Quinn looked stunned. Lacey didn't even know Rylan had that kind of money, but he knew the rules. If the winner couldn't pay up, the item went to the next best bid. Lacey withdrew to the side of the stage and the chatter built up again through the room while canned country music played until the band returned.

She collected cash and checks and crossed items off the master list until finally Rylan was the last one there. He pulled out a roll of bills and started counting off in hundreds while Lacey gaped.

"Rylan. Where did you get that kind of money?"

He looked at her blandly. "Don't worry about it."

"You shouldn't be carrying around that much cash." She frowned at him, took what he owed, and saw he still had a decent-sized roll of bills.

He looked utterly unconcerned. "I didn't have time to go to the bank earlier today, that's all."

She pursed her lips together. She hardly ever saw her younger brother, and their relationship was tenuous at best. The last thing she wanted to do was antagonize him tonight, though alarm bells were going off in her head.

But she couldn't resist saying, "You're not into anything you shouldn't be, are you?"

Familiar blue eyes looked down into hers and his lips tipped up on one side. "Don't worry about it, sis. Nothing the IRS wouldn't approve of."

Why didn't that make her feel any better?

"Can I take the saddle at the end of the night?"

"Of course."

He went to turn away but she stopped him. "Rylan?"

He looked back.

"Don't be a stranger, okay?"

He frowned and came back. "What do you mean? Are you staying on at Crooked Valley, too? Man, I can't believe Duke convinced you. You were pretty adamant at Christmas."

"I'm still working it out. And I won't be staying on the ranch, just in the area. I've offered to take over doing the bookkeeping at Crooked Valley. I've already got a few clients in town, too. Kailey's family, for one. They're bucking stock contractors, you know."

Something flashed in Rylan's eyes but it was gone as quickly as it had come.

"I'm making a run for the NFR championship this year, Lace. Don't count on me being around much. I think I've got a real shot."

So he wouldn't be looking at taking on his third. Not before the first anniversary of Granddad Joe's death, anyway. She was surprised how disappointed she felt.

"Visit when you can, then," she suggested.

Kailey's laugh drifted over the noise of the crowd. "I'll try," he said, his gaze searching out the source of the laugh. He leaned in and kissed her cheek. "Thanks, sis."

When he was gone she rested her weight on one hip and frowned. Something was going on with her brother. She just wished she knew what it was. But then, Rylan had always been the hardest of them to pin down.

By the time she'd double-counted the money and stored it in Cy's safe, the party was back to full swing. Duke and Carrie were dancing, and so were Kailey and Rylan while Colt Black scowled at them from the sidelines. From everything Carrie said, this was a good thing. Her sister-in-law didn't seem to think very much of Colt and his on-again-off-again attention to Kailey.

Even Quinn had been dancing, with one of the waitresses that Lacey remembered from the diner. When the song changed, his popularity increased as he was snagged by Chrissy Baumgartner who worked at the library. Lacey liked her; the librarian was in her thirties, full-figured and with a smile that lit up a room. Quinn spun her around and they were both laughing and Lacey found herself grinning as she watched. It was good to see him smiling and not scowling. He was so handsome when he relaxed and had a good time.

She wished she didn't care so much.

The music thumped through the bar and Lacey leaned against a post, resting her head against the wood and enjoying the sight of so much merriment. Truth was, she cared for Quinn. She understood his pain, too. It only served to make her care more, but it was exactly the reason why nothing could happen between them again. She already knew what it felt like to be found lacking. There was no way on earth she could possibly live up to Marie's memory. It was plain to see that Quinn had practically made her into a saint in his mind.

When the song ended, she took him another beer. "Here," she offered, holding it out. "My treat."

He frowned. "I can't, Lace. Thanks though. I brought Kailey in the truck."

"I don't think you're going to have to worry about giving her a lift home," Lacey argued, nodding towards where Kailey and Rylan were talking. They only had eyes for each other.

"Is that wise?"

Lacey thought for a moment. She and Rylan weren't as close as they used to be for sure, and his money situation had definitely taken her by surprise. But she'd never known him to mistreat a woman. "They're both grown-ups. Kailey's smart and Rylan's a gentleman."

He nodded, but didn't look satisfied.

"Anyway, I can always drive your truck home if you want to have a few beers. It's no biggie if you want to cut loose a bit. When did you really get out and have fun last, Quinn?"

He shrugged. "Probably the same time you did."

He had her there. But he took the bottle from her anyway. "You're sure?"

"I'm sure. I don't mind being your wingman tonight."

"Thank you, Lacey."

"You're welcome."

"No," he contradicted, taking her hand and pulling her to the side, where it was marginally quieter. "I mean it. Thank you for everything. For your help doing this tonight, for your help with Amber, for all of it. I haven't always been fair to you. It's…complicated."

Her heart softened. "I know it is."

"I don't know how to do this." He looked over the crowd, took a long pull off the bottle, then looked at her again. "Do you know what I'm saying?"

Her heart started to beat a little faster. "I think I do."

"You see, I let myself get close, and then I get scared and then I push you away and I'm mean about it. It's not your fault." His gorgeous eyes delved into hers. "I've held onto my grief for so long, it's like an old friend. I don't know what to do without it, you know?"

Oh, mercy. Her pulse was fairly hammering now. Maybe it was the alcohol or the fact that the crowd and noise provided a measure of protection, but he was being all honest again.

"I do know. It's how you protect yourself from being vulnerable."

"And then I feel guilty when I…when we…"

He didn't finish the sentences, but it just took gazing into his eyes to understand the rest of the words. This would be so much easier if she didn't find him so irresistible…

She tried being flippant to lighten the mood. "Hey, are you admitting you like me, Quinn?" She sent him a dazzling smile.

But he didn't smile in return, just took her hand in his and squeezed her fingers. "More than is good for either of us, Lacey. And I'll be damned if I know what to do about it."

They stood there, in a little bubble of intimacy, oblivious to the people milling about. She squeezed his fingers back. "You could always ask me to dance."

A ghost of a smile flirted with his lips. "Miss Duggan, may I have this dance?" He rubbed his thumb along the side of her hand and a shot of pure electricity zipped up her arm.

"Of course," she answered. After all, what could happen on a crowded dance floor? It had to be safer than being cozied up here in the corner.

Quinn put his bottle on a nearby table and led her to the floor. Just as they arrived, the current song ended and they waited for the next one. When the opening measures began, Lacey began to laugh. "Oh, my. Are you up for this?"

The singer was doing a respectable imitation of Alan Jackson's voice in "I Don't Even Know Your Name" and couples paired up for a polka.

"Are you kidding? I was born doing a polka."

"Your poor mother."

He raised his arms in the correct posture. "Chicken?"

She laughed at the impish look on his face. He was so easy to like when he let go of the chip on his shoulder. "Not even a little bit." She stepped up and put her hand in his and her other on his shoulder. Before she could even catch a breath, he whirled her into the dance.

He was smooth. And he knew how to lead, too, sweeping her into the steps with surprising ease. It had been a long time since she'd danced like this and she felt a little rusty, but once they'd negotiated the floor in a full circle, she started to relax and get into the rhythm a little more. Quinn could tell, too, because he guided her into a spin that stole her breath and would have had her laughing if she hadn't had to shift into the steps right away.

She looked into his face and saw him grinning from

ear to ear, his eyes twinkling at her as he spun her in
a turn so quick she wasn't sure her feet even touched
the floor. They were good together, dammit. So good
that she just stopped thinking and threw herself into
the dance with a carefree abandon she'd forgotten she
possessed.

When the song ended, they were both winded and
laughing and clapping for the band, and Lacey noticed
that several faces were turned towards them and smiling. "That was so fun!" she exclaimed, pressing her
hand to her chest. "Oh, my gosh. I haven't danced like
that in years! Who knew you had it in you, Solomon?"

Whether it was the beer or the dance talking, she
didn't know, but she got a little thrill when he winked
at her and said, "You haven't seen all my moves yet."

Lord help her, she wanted to. They'd been doing this
on-again-off-again thing for weeks now. She suspected
it was because they both tended to overthink. To over-
feel. It was hard to do that when you were galloping
across a dance floor.

The next song was a line dance and Lacey laughed
and pulled her hair up into a ponytail to help cool her
neck. Quinn waggled his eyebrows as everyone lined up
for a tush push and the band launched right into the fast-
paced "Trouble." The steps were quick and light and
Lacey was treated to a fabulous view of Quinn's back-
side as he wiggled it from side to side midway through
the sequence. There were whoops and hollers from the
crowd and clapping from the sidelines as the lines of
dancers stomped their way through the song. When
had she last had this much fun? When had she allowed
herself to cut loose and just enjoy something? She piv-
oted, did the three-step and clapped, and laughed from

the sheer joy of it. Quinn looked over and grinned at her and she felt a strange sensation that in this moment, right now, she was exactly where she was meant to be.

With a final stomp the dance was over and the singer took a quick few moments to grab his water bottle. Quinn took Lacey's hand and led her from the floor straight to the bar, where they both ordered a water to help cool them down.

"Oh, Quinn! That was so fun. You're a great dancer."

"I haven't done that since…" His face clouded, but only for a moment. "Never mind how long. Thank you, Lacey."

"Anytime. I'm a bit rusty but funny how it all comes back to you."

"Tell me about it." His gaze met hers and she wondered what else they were rusty at—and if it would come back just as quickly as the dance steps.

She shouldn't be thinking that way.

The next song was a waltz. As soon as the opening bars started, Carrie and Duke, Kailey and Rylan, and most of the other couples moved to the crowded floor. Lacey looked at them with longing, but honestly the dance area was so jammed full of couples there wasn't much room to dance properly.

"Popular dance on Valentine's Day," he said, not looking at her.

"Seems like it."

He was quiet for a few seconds and then he asked, "Do you have a coat? I could use a cooldown. The water didn't quite cut it."

Butterflies began to flutter in her stomach. "I do. It's in the office."

"You want to get some fresh air?"

She nodded, feeling words strangle in her throat. "I'll just be a second."

The office was quieter, the sounds muffled through the thick walls, and Lacey took a moment to breathe deeply and consider what she was doing. Maybe it was all innocent. Maybe Quinn really did just want to cool off.

Maybe it was something more.

Or maybe she just wanted it to be.

Chapter 11

The air was crisp and cool outside the Silver Dollar, and Quinn and Lacey weren't the only ones to go outside. A few other couples left and a handful were outside taking a smoke break and chatting. Quinn took Lacey's hand in his and led her away from the entrance, around to the side of the log building, where it was quieter and more private.

At this point she didn't need to dance; her stomach was doing enough of a jig all on its own.

He let go of her fingers and put his hands in the pockets of his jacket, lifting his face to the sky. "It's a nice night. Not too cold. Clear."

Indeed, the sky was inky black, with the pinpoint dots of the stars winking down on them.

"In the city, sometimes the streetlights affect the visibility. I love the sky out here. It goes on forever." She let out a contented sigh.

"You hated it when you first arrived."

"I didn't hate it." She looked over at him. "I resented it. Big difference."

He smiled a little. "You don't like to be told what to do, do you?"

She smiled back. "What was your first clue?" She gazed up at the constellations. "It isn't just being told what to do. It's feeling like, I don't know, like I'm being shoehorned into something. Like I don't have a choice."

"You have choices, Lacey. Lots and lots of choices."

Didn't she just. And one was figuring out how exactly to proceed with the man beside her. Did she want to risk it? Or just back off? She'd probably get hurt in the end. There could never be anything serious between them, anyway. He'd made that abundantly clear.

"Does this mean we're going to stop fighting now, Quinn? It gets exhausting, treading on eggshells around you."

"I'd like to stop fighting. You make it difficult."

"I don't mean to be bitchy…"

"Not that, Lacey. That's not what I meant."

He put his hands on her shoulders and turned her to face him. The door to the bar closed and all was silent in the parking lot, except for the muffled sound of the second waltz in the set. His face loomed above hers, shadowed in the darkness away from the lights of the entrance, and she could see the little puffs of his breath in the air.

She rather thought he might kiss her, but instead he slid his hand down her arm to clasp her fingers and put his other hand at the small of her back, drawing her close.

Oh, Lord. Quinn Solomon was a romantic. He had

to be, because he was dancing with her in slow, narrow steps, beneath a winter moon.

It was impossible not to get caught up in the moment. She noticed everything about him—the way he smelled, how his cologne was magnified by the heat of his body after the fast dances, the roughness of his palm as it pressed against hers, the size of his body as it moved against her smaller one. With a little jolt of surprise, she realized that he'd put on weight over the past few weeks, lost that gaunt, lean look she'd noticed when he'd first arrived. A little sliver of female satisfaction warmed her, as she wondered if it was due to her home cooking. Maybe Quinn was right after all. She was a nurturer at heart. Liked to take care of people. Liked to take care of him.

She was treading into dangerous territory.

They were so close now that their coats were pressed together and his jaw grazed her temple, a stubbled caress that fuelled the fire of her desire for him. If their first kiss was anything to go by, Quinn had a lot of passion inside. Wrong or right, wise or foolish, she wanted to be the one to unleash it. She lifted her chin just a little, rubbing against him, a little nudge of invitation.

He nudged back, a silent acknowledgment, acceptance, and they embarked on a dance of anticipation so sweet that she held her breath, waiting for the moment when he'd finally give in and kiss her.

The tip of his nose was cold but his lips were warm when they finally descended on hers. Their feet stopped moving to the music, and Lacey lifted her arms, wrapping them around his neck to hold him close.

He did his part in that regard, his strong hand pressing on the curve of her bottom, an impassioned sound rippling up from his throat and sliding through her like an aphrodisiac.

Quinn, she thought. *Oh, Quinn.*

He put his other arm around her and lifted her up as if she weighed nothing at all, then walked forward until they were up against the rough logs of the saloon. With the wall behind her, he was able to press against her body and have his hands free. He put them on either side of her face and kissed her again and again until her knees went weak and she nearly forgot where they were.

The door to the saloon slammed and Lacey realized that things had gotten a little out of control when their bodies froze. It had been more than kissing—it was full-on making out. Quinn had been rubbing against her rhythmically, one hand had undone the buttons of her coat and he was cupping her breast through the thin fabric of her dress.

Thankfully Quinn shifted so that his body sheltered her from the view of the people leaving the bar.

"Jeez, get a room," one of them jeered, laughing, and she looked up at him. His eyes were nearly black in the darkness, but there was something else there, too. Agreement.

They had a whole big house to themselves tonight. All it would take was a ten-minute drive and they'd be free to do whatever they wanted.

She gulped, wanting it so badly she ached. She was terrified, too.

"It's up to you," he murmured, running one finger down her cheek in a soft caress. "I don't want to stop here. But I understand if you do…"

"You're sure?" she asked, her words a breathy sigh.

"You drive me crazy," he replied. "So damn crazy,

Lace. You have for weeks. I gotta do something about that or I'm going to explode."

Nothing he might have said would have been better for her female ego than that. A saucy grin tilted her lips as she took the leap. "Me, too. I don't want to think. I don't want to worry. I just want to touch you, Quinn. Really touch you without wondering if we're going to get caught."

He chuckled, a sexy, soft sound. "Darlin', getting caught is half the fun, don't you know that?"

"Take me home, Quinn."

With one last searing look, he backed away, grabbed her hand, and led her to his truck.

Because he'd been a little free with the beer, he handed Lacey the keys. It didn't seem super romantic or manly, but he hadn't abandoned all sense. She'd just adjusted the seat and started the engine when he spied another couple preparing to leave: Kailey and Rylan. Rylan was putting the saddle in the back and Kailey was hopping into the cab. As Lacey put the truck in gear, Quinn's phone buzzed.

I don't need a drive. You have a good night.

Kailey must have noticed their disappearance, but he found he didn't really care. Everything he did had been catalogued by this town. Just this once he wanted to do something impulsive and crazy without the worry of how it looked or what was appropriate. Didn't he deserve that? Hadn't he been through enough? For one night, he wanted to know what it was to live again rather than just go through the motions.

"Text message?" Lacey asked, turning on the blinker for the main road.

"Kailey. She left with your brother."

She spared him a quick glance and then put her attention back on the road. "It's Valentine's Day, Quinn. Romance is in the air."

"So it is."

"She's a big girl."

"Yep."

"Quinn?"

"What?"

"Why does this drive seem so long?"

The simple question had him questioning his sanity, because it made him want to pull the truck over to the side of the road and end the wait to take her in his arms. He clenched his fingers into fists.

The drive seemed to take forever and yet, somehow, only a few minutes and they were back at the house. There was a moment of hesitation when she cut the engine and they sat in the silence. Maybe she'd changed her mind. Maybe he should. He didn't want to give her false hope for the future. He couldn't honestly think beyond tonight. Beyond this moment.

But his thoughts were interrupted by Lacey, sliding across the seat, running her hand through his hair. That was all it took for him to pick up exactly where they'd left off, pressed up against the cold side of the Silver Dollar. His mouth fused to hers as he pulled her into his lap, the feel of her body warm against his.

"Let's get inside," he suggested, taking a precious moment away from her lips. Blindly, he undid his seat belt and opened the door, then miraculously got them both out of the vehicle without too much fumbling.

Quinn slammed the door and then picked Lacey up in his arms, heading for the house with long, purposeful strides.

"Quinn," she whispered against his neck, and the soft awe he heard in her voice made him feel about ten feet tall. He'd never been one for big romantic gestures, but damn, it had been a long dry spell.

Unlocking the door proved slightly tricky, but within moments they were in the foyer. Quinn put her down on the stair steps and knelt before her to take off her boots, his hand sliding down the smooth expanse of her calf. He removed his own footwear, slid off his jacket, took her coat and finally, finally met her gaze.

Her eyes glowed with heat and longing and his body responded. He hadn't wanted a woman like this in months. Not since…no. Dammit, he wouldn't think of that tonight. Tonight, the weight of the past would stay in the past. There was a beautiful woman in front of him, as eager for him as he was for her. He reached behind her and pulled the elastic from her hair, freeing the ponytail so that the copper waves fell about her shoulders. God, he loved her hair.

"Lacey." Her name was a low rumble in the quiet, dark house. "Are you sure?"

She stood up, standing on the bottom step, which put them eye to eye. Her hand rested against the side of his face. "All the times we argued and fought…that's passion, Quinn. I don't want to fight it anymore. I want to put it to better use. I want you to make love to me."

He took her upstairs to her room, to the master bedroom with its four-poster and thick mattress and soft-as-feathers duvet. Gazes locked, they undressed each other, no shyness, no false modesty. She was so beautiful, all creamy skin and slender limbs and that glorious mane of hair. When he took off his shirt, her fingers grazed his abdomen. "Oh," she said, biting down on her lip. Knowing she approved only fired his desire further.

They took their time, touching, kissing, caressing, until he couldn't wait any longer. "Do we need to take precautions?" he asked, hoping to God she was on the pill because he hadn't bought a condom in years.

Her startled gaze clashed with his, and then slid away. "No," she replied softly. "I'm good."

"Good?" Something didn't feel quite right about her response. He didn't want to kill the mood but he needed to be sure, too. He wanted to protect her. Protect both of them.

"I'm safe," she answered. "No worries there, Quinn. I promise."

Lacey was a lot of things, but she wasn't a liar and she wasn't manipulative. If she said they were safe, he trusted her.

As the February moon shone through the window, he let his gaze travel down the length of her lissome body once more. Then he closed his eyes and made her his, losing himself completely to pleasure.

Valentine's Day.

Lacey lay perfectly still in the bed, staring at the ceiling as dawn slowly broke. Beside her, Quinn lay on his side, his back to her, his breathing deep and even.

She had slept with her roommate, with the one man who drove her absolutely bananas, on Valentine's Day, that horrible, wonderful day that happened each year and made people crazy. This was a real first. And now she was wondering how to proceed. Should she try to extricate herself from the bed quietly, without waking him? She was stark naked under the soft sheets, but her robe was hanging on the back of the bathroom door. If she could reach it, she could at least cover herself...

Or should she stay? Wait for Quinn to wake up, leave first? She turned her head carefully, trying to be perfectly silent. Half of his back was visible above the edge of the sheet, and she gazed at his strong, broad shoulders, slightly freckled skin and a small scar that left a puckered pink mark right in between his shoulder blades. His hair was mussed, pushed to one side, but lying flat in the back.

A man in her bed. The first man since Carter. And Carter had been the only man since she was twenty.

She was hardly prolific in the sexual partners area. That wasn't a bad thing, but it did make last night perhaps slightly more important than it might have been if she tended to be more, well, casual about things.

He shifted slightly and she froze, but he settled once more, his breathing deep and rhythmic. His body warmed the bed, and her eyes drifted closed again, soaking in the moment. The truth was, she knew Quinn was unavailable. No matter what had happened last night, she knew for him it had just been about sex. Scratching an itch.

Hadn't it?

Carefully, she rolled to her left side, her body curling into the same position as his, but inches away so she wasn't technically spooning him. She wished she could. Wished she could curl up behind him, wrap her arm around his waist and rest her cheek against his back, drawing on his warmth and strength.

He'd been a wonderful lover. Attentive, intense, making sure she got her share of pleasure…and she had. More than once. It was funny how arousal took over, plunging them into the moment, where they'd been able to be utterly naked—not just with their bodies, but with their needs and feelings. Completely devoid of false modesty and lacking in self-consciousness.

There'd been a moment when he'd looked down into her eyes that she'd felt something click. Something she'd never expected to feel again. Tears stung her eyes now as she remembered how things had slowed down, how they'd savored each other. It hadn't been the rush of frantic sex.

It had been the slow burn of making love, just as she'd asked. But what Quinn didn't know was that they weren't just words to her. She really had made love to him, because she'd gone ahead and fallen *in* love with him.

Her throat tightened as she stared at the back of the man she wanted but knew she couldn't have. Her heart and pride had taken a beating after Carter left, but Quinn's had been utterly shattered with Marie's death. She was pretty sure he hadn't put it back together again, no matter what had happened between them last night. And the reason she knew was because he still wore his wedding ring. For some reason, it made her feel like she'd slept with another woman's husband. Maybe because, even though Marie was gone, Quinn still wasn't totally free.

Knowing she might never have another chance, she slid closer to him, until she was spooning him for real. Once he woke up, the spell would be broken. But even if it was for a few seconds, she wanted to know how it felt. She slid her arm carefully over his hips, curled against his warm body and rested her temple against his shoulder blade, breathing deeply to imprint the scent of him on her brain.

He sighed.

She closed her eyes.

It was several seconds later that he spoke. "Good morning."

"Hey," she answered. She felt exposed, naked beneath the bedding, but she was glad she hadn't sneaked away, too. These might be the last intimate moments they shared. Even if he thought they might pursue something, she knew that would change if he found out the truth.

"Some Valentine's Day, huh?"

She smiled against the soft skin of his back. "Beats a box of chocolates from the drugstore."

He chuckled, the movement brushing his body against hers in strategic places.

"Are you okay?"

He was trying to take care of her. Just like he had last night, even when there'd been no need.

"I'm fine, Quinn." More than fine.

He rolled over until he was facing her. There was morning stubble on his face, and she saw what her mom had always called "sleepy tears" in the inside corner of one of his eyes. But he was beautiful. He always had been. The difference was, she'd resented him for it before, especially when he found fault with her.

He'd certainly sung her praises last night, and she felt heat creep up her cheeks at the recollection.

"We should probably talk," he said quietly.

"I know." But then he was silent. After an uncomfortable pause, she suggested, "Do you want to go first?"

His gaze met hers, but she couldn't read what he was thinking. Not this time. "I should get up and get started on the chores first. Otherwise the boys'll be knocking on the door wondering what happened to me. That'd be awkward."

More awkward than this moment? Probably, she admitted to herself. No one needed to know what had happened here last night.

"Whatever you want," she said, trying to smile.

"Okay." He leaned closer and kissed the tip of her nose, and then moved away as if leaving the bed. But then he rolled back, braced up on an elbow.

"Lacey? Last night, when you said you were safe…"

Oh, God.

"…I just want to be sure you're okay."

It was a bit late to be sure now that the deed was done. "I'm positive," she replied, hoping he'd let the matter go. The last thing she wanted to do this morning was drop the bombshell that she couldn't ever have children. It was painful…and premature.

He smiled again. "Okay. I'll see you later?"

She nodded.

He slipped from the bed and padded—buck naked—to the bedroom door, scooting across the hall to his own room to get dressed for the day.

Lacey rolled to her back and stared at the ceiling. What on earth were they going to do now? They couldn't dance around each other forever, it would only make things tense.

The conversation she didn't want to have was inevitable…and necessary. There was no sense in being in denial about anything, because it only masked a truth that would eventually come to light.

Truth was, she'd let herself fall. For Amber, for Crooked Valley, for the damned town…and for Quinn Solomon most of all.

Chapter 12

Lacey was able to put off the conversation for several hours. She had a shower, tidied her bedroom and caught a ride into town with Carrie so they could get the proceeds from the benefit from the Silver Dollar safe and deposit it at the bank. Cy had graciously tallied up the entire amount complete with one of his deposit forms so all they had to do was pick it up. Lacey goggled at the total at the bottom. All told, the benefit had raised nearly ten thousand dollars for Quinn and Amber.

Carrie had a doctor's appointment, so Lacey offered to take it to the bank herself. Carrie stopped her at the door to the saloon as they were leaving, putting a hand on her arm.

"Lacey, are you okay today?"

Lacey looked up at her sister-in-law and friend, and saw real concern marring her normally happy face. "Of course I am."

"You're real quiet this morning."

"Just tired after all the excitement of the last few days." She smiled reassuringly. She hoped.

"You left your car here last night."

"Quinn had been drinking. I offered to drive him home."

"In his truck, not your car."

It was starting to feel a bit like an inquisition.

"I guess I thought he might need his truck this morning. For, uh, ranch stuff."

Carrie's eyes were a little too sharp for Lacey's liking. "How bad is it?"

"What?" She opened her car door and threw the deposit bag on the passenger seat.

"You can't kid a kidder, sweetie. I went through plenty of pains when I fell for your brother. Lots of doubt and indecision."

"Who said anyone's falling for...anyone?" Cripes, one mention of Quinn and she couldn't even form a proper sentence.

"So it's just sex? You're not in love with him?"

Lacey choked on her own spit and started to cough. "Jeez, Carrie. Blunt much?"

Carrie laughed a little before her face turned dead serious again. "Look, I saw you two dancing last night. I've seen the way you light up when you're together. The way sparks fly off when you argue. It's...familiar. I just don't want to see either of you get hurt."

"Me, either," Lacey admitted.

"And there's Amber to think of."

Lacey thought of Amber asking if she'd be her mommy and her stomach twisted.

"I didn't even say we slept together." She was rather proud how definitively that came out of her mouth.

"Oh honey, you didn't have to." Carrie looked at her with sympathy softening her features. "*Are* you in love with him?"

Lacey heaved out a sigh. "I don't know. And we need to talk, but I'm scared."

"He doesn't know?"

Carrie didn't have to elaborate; Lacey understood her meaning. "No. When I said he didn't need protection, he accepted it at face value." Her shoulders slumped. "God, he's really trusting, isn't he?"

"That's the thing, Lace. He's usually not. But he trusts you. That's a good sign, right?"

"Sure. Until I tell him the truth. Of course, he might be spending today trying to find a way to let me down gently. Maybe I should just tell him and let him off the hook."

"You think he won't be interested if he knows you can't have kids?"

She didn't answer, which she figured was answer enough.

"Do you want to be with him?"

"I don't know. I care for him. A lot. Enough that maybe the kindest thing would be to let him go. That way he can find someone he deserves. Someone who can give Amber a brother or sister. Maybe one of each. He's such a good dad and she's a great kid. They deserve that…"

"What a load of horse crap." Carrie made a disgusted sound.

"Carrie, I know you're happy with Duke and everything, but sometimes it's not that easy."

Carrie laughed out loud. "You think we were easy? Oh, my gosh. That's funny." She took Lacey's hands in hers and squeezed before letting them go. "Here's the thing. You went through hell, and the person who was supposed to be with you through it all bailed. Now you don't believe anyone will be there for you. But at some point you have to have a little faith, you know?"

What she was saying made sense. In theory. "I'm afraid my faith is in short supply."

Carrie frowned. "Well, don't give up. That's all I'm saying. Quinn might surprise you."

"Quinn's still in love with Marie."

"Is he? Or does he just think he is because he thinks he should be?"

All the questions were giving Lacey a headache. "Listen, Dr. Ruth, I've got to get to the bank and deposit this cash. And you need to get to your appointment and make sure that baby is doing okay. You can psychoanalyze both of us later."

Carrie responded with a lopsided smile. "I know. Duke told me not to interfere. I couldn't help myself."

This time it was Lacey who put her hand on Carrie's arm. "And I appreciate the thought. Just let us work it out ourselves, okay?"

"Okay."

Impulsively Carrie gave Lacey a hug. "You know, I always wanted a sister. Sorry if I get carried away and go overboard."

She'd let go and was heading to her old truck when she turned back around. "At least tell me one thing. Was it good?"

Lacey burst out laughing at the expectant look on Carrie's face. "That's for me to know and you to pon-

der," she called back, then got into her car. Despite the
meddling, she suspected she'd like having a sister of her
own, too. Duke had chosen exceptionally well.

Lacey worked herself up to talking to Quinn when
she returned home, but his truck was gone and she
found a note saying he'd gone to pick up Amber at his
mother's. Restless, Lacey did a load of laundry and
cleaned the upstairs bathrooms just to keep busy. She
started the makings of a beef stew, letting the meat
simmer with garlic and thyme and some red wine, then
poured a small glass for herself that she sipped while
making baking powder biscuits. Anything to keep busy
and not think too much about what she was going to say
when they were finally alone again. Maybe it would be
best to just let Quinn guide her. She'd gauge the situation as they went along.

It was going on five when the truck finally pulled
into the yard again. Amber came barreling inside,
straight to the kitchen, dropping her overnight backpack on the floor as she rushed to tell Lacey all about
the previous day's party, the Valentine's cards from her
classmates, and her night at Grandma's.

"Whoa, slow down, kiddo! Where's your dad?"

"He said he was going to look after the chores and
then he'd be in for dinner. I'm hungry."

Lacey laughed, but her heart gave a bittersweet pang.
The more Amber chattered, the more Lacey was sure
she had to tell Quinn the truth. It wouldn't be fair to
really start something with him and keep her situation
a secret.

The pan of biscuits came out of the oven and she put
them on a rack to cool. Then she eyed the wine bottle

again. She might need a bit more liquid courage to get through the hours ahead.

Quinn came in and washed up for dinner; Amber kept up sufficient chatter about her Valentine's Day party and her sleepover that Lacey and Quinn were spared having to make much conversation. After dinner, Lacey cleaned up while Quinn took Amber upstairs for her bath and to read stories. By eight o'clock, Lacey was fit to be tied, knowing the conversation was coming and unsure how it would go. Amber was overtired, too, and Lacey could hear a bit of a fuss going on upstairs as Quinn attempted to settle her in bed.

When he finally came downstairs, he looked exhausted. Maybe they should table talking until there was a better time...

"Wow," he said quietly, coming into the kitchen. "She was full of beans tonight."

"It sounds like she had an exciting time. And she's overstimulated and tired all at once."

"I know. I gotta say, though, when she starts with the whiny stuff, my patience dwindles pretty quickly."

Lacey chuckled and tucked some plastic dishes under the cupboard.

"Lacey, about last night..."

Here it comes, she thought. She schooled her face into a polite mask, a light smile with what she hoped was an "it's all good" expression.

"Now that Amber's home, it's probably not a good idea to...you know. Have a repeat."

Right. Discretion and all that. She didn't know whether to feel relieved or disappointed.

"Of course. The last thing she needs is more confusion and upset. After what she said the other night..."

"I'm just not sure that being…open with this is in her best interests right now. You're really important to her. To us. I just think we need to be careful, you know?"

Wait, what? Was he actually thinking of pursuing something with her? "Careful?"

He nodded. Met her gaze evenly, and the attraction to him spun through her core unbidden. All he had to do was look at her like there was nothing else around and she was a goner.

"Things were hard for Duke and Carrie. I know they're happy now, but she got pregnant so fast. It was really hard for them at first. I'm not sure what I want, Lacey. Until I know, until we know…"

She turned away, got down another wineglass, and poured a few ounces of ruby-red liquid in the bottom.

"Lacey?"

She gulped down the wine. In her heart she knew it wouldn't make this any easier, but she had to do something. Her hand shook as she put down the glass, the base of it clanking a little too loudly on the countertop.

"I told you, Quinn, you don't have to worry about that." Breathe, she reminded herself. Long, calming breaths.

"I know. But no method is a hundred percent."

She could do this. She had to do this. It was only fair to everyone for her to have full disclosure. "Well, there are a few methods that are."

She could have sworn she saw disappointment darken his gaze. "You mean abstinence. You really think last night was a mistake, then?"

"No!" She replied before she could even consider another response. "Quinn, no. Unless…unless you do."

Here she went again. Afraid to voice her own feelings, wants, needs. She'd gotten so used to holding things back, to calculating what to say to keep things from getting worse. She'd done it all the time when she and Carter were struggling, just to keep from having another argument. She was aware that she did it, but not sure how to stop.

"Let's go sit down," he suggested.

They went to the sofa and she perched on the edge, like a bird on a branch ready to flee at any moment. This was crazy. She was in love with him. Shouldn't she be throwing her arms around him, ready to explore what might evolve between them? Why couldn't she allow herself to be happy?

"Lacey," he said softly, covering her hand with his own. "What's wrong?"

She looked down at their joined hands. Willed the right words to come. Never in a million years had she imagined herself in this position. Not even after that crazy kiss in his office. This was different. Real. Terrifying.

Sad.

And that was it, wasn't it? She was sad. Sad that circumstances were what they were. Sad that nothing could be changed. She'd made peace with it long ago, but that didn't stop her from feeling like garbage about it.

"I didn't expect this," she began, staring at her knees. "We were always bickering. Finding fault with each other. And then I got to know you better."

"I got to know you, too." His voice was warm and affectionate.

"But you don't really know me, Quinn." She looked

up at him. "That's just it. You know the parts that I've let you know."

"I know your divorce had a profound effect on you. That it's been hard for you to bounce back from that rejection."

Bless him, he was trying. After being such a curmudgeon when they first met, the effort for tenderness and understanding only underscored how wonderful a man he was. "Oh, if it were only that." She sighed. "Honestly, Quinn, it's what led up to the divorce that really did a number on me. You had a brilliant marriage with Marie. I know that. A fool can see it. I can't begin to compete with that."

His hand slid from hers. "I won't deny that. We were really happy, and she was a wonderful wife and mom."

Lacey's heart sank even further.

"But Lacey, I never expected to feel like this again. Happy. Looking to the future, because I had something worth looking forward to. Something changed for me last night, do you get that? I took the first steps in moving on. I'm trying very hard not to feel guilty about it, or like I'm somehow betraying Marie's memory because the truth is she's gone and never coming back and I'm still here."

His gaze held hers. "Look, I'm definitely not ready to move fast. I don't think anyone could be more surprised than I am, but I'm not ready to walk away from us, either."

Oh, God. He was really making it tough. That he'd started to move beyond his grief…that it was because of her only added to her burden. She didn't want to be responsible for that. "I only wanted to help the both of you out."

"Are you saying you don't have feelings for me?"

She looked deeply into his eyes, wished she could say she didn't. It would all end right here. Clean break, move on. Could she lie that convincingly? But Quinn never gave her the opportunity.

"I was there last night," he murmured. "With you. Inside you. I don't think you're that good of an actress, Lacey Duggan."

She swallowed. "I have feelings, okay? I couldn't have been with you last night without them."

"So what? We were ships passing in the night?" The words were harder now, with an edge of hurt underlining them.

"I can't give you what you want, Quinn. I'm sorry."

Silence fell over the room, awkward and heavy.

After a few moments he spoke again. "What if what I want is you?"

The weight of the words pressed against her heart. "You are just realizing that there is a life out there waiting for you," she replied, her stomach a tangle of anxiety. "You're a family man—everyone can see that. You need a woman who can be the wife and mother you need. Don't you want brothers and sisters for Amber?"

"Maybe someday, but that's putting the cart a little ahead of the horse, don't you think?"

She shook her head, prayed briefly for strength and calm. "No, I don't. Because Quinn, I can never give you that. What I didn't tell you is that…that I can't have children."

She'd shocked him, that much was clear. His lips dropped open but no sound came out; his eyes widened with surprise. "So you see," she continued, "as much as last night was wonderful, I can't let you believe it was something it wasn't."

"Wow." His shoulders slumped a little as he let out a big breath. "I wasn't expecting that."

"I'm sorry, Quinn. Maybe I should have stopped things before they got…intimate. You were just kissing me and it felt so good and it had been so long since I felt that desirable. Wanted." She blinked, looked down. "That makes me sound opportunistic and a little vain."

"If you are, so am I."

She looked back up at him.

"Hey," he said softly. "You're not the only one who was suffering a crisis of virility."

"You carried me across the yard and…"

He grinned, a fleeting flash of teeth that reminded her of why she liked him so much. "And your face when I took my shirt off fed my ego."

Damn. They weren't supposed to be playing into the sexual tension here.

But the mood turned serious again. "Lacey, there are treatments you can try. I don't want to see you close a door prematurely. You'd be a wonderful mother."

Tears stung the backs of her eyes. "Thanks for the compliment, but I've been down that road, Quinn. I tried treatments and procedures. I had scarring from endometriosis. At first it was just the pain and I was on meds for that, but then when we kept trying to get pregnant, and nothing happened, I went on hormone treatment. In the end I had a hysterectomy. No amount of treatment can help me now, you see. I can't carry a child without a uterus."

There. It was out.

"When you mentioned about the birth control then… wow, you really meant it."

She nodded. "You need to understand that we married young. We had high hopes and plans for this great future. You know the type. A house and a yard and a few kids running around with the family dog. But there were no kids. No dog. I held on to that dream too tightly. Carter was a bit of a jackass for leaving, but I can't say he shoulders all the blame. My whole life became about hormones and fertility, I used up our savings and we didn't even have the joy of a great sex life to keep us going because I had so much pain. By the time I had the hysterectomy, the marriage was beyond repair. My last bit of false hope was gone. The last thing I want to do, Quinn, is give you that hope and then disappoint you in the end. You've been through enough."

She raised her hand and put it on his cheek. "I care about you too much. I probably should have been honest before, but we were arguing and then I thought the whole attraction thing was one-sided. It's not something I'm particularly open about."

"I'm so, so sorry," he answered, putting his hand over top of hers. "And to have Amber here, and Carrie pregnant next door…that must be so hard for you."

She shook her head, more touched than she cared to admit by his consideration. "Carrie and Duke know, and I would never begrudge my brother his happiness. At first it was a challenge, I admit. It was better after I told them."

"They knew."

"Yes."

Was he mad about being left out of the sharing circle?

She half wished he would be. It might be easier than dealing with sympathetic Quinn.

"I'm glad someone was there for you to talk to," he said. "Carrie's good at that. So's Kailey. They both listened to me often enough after Marie died."

She felt her heart clutch a little. "You have so much to offer, Quinn. You're a great dad and a good man."

"You do, too, you know."

"I'm not sure of that. My head tells me I'm still Lacey Duggan, that I still have…gumption in here somewhere." She pressed a fist to her chest. "My heart, though, isn't convinced. Logically I can tell myself that the surgery didn't make me less of a woman. But deep down, I feel like it does. And no one can change that."

Sometimes love was knowing when to let go. Lacey figured this was that moment.

His expression darkened. "Did Carter tell you that?"

He had. Not all the time, but when he got particularly frustrated. Lacey had felt like such a failure as a woman. Before the surgery, she'd been poked and prodded so many times it was ridiculous. There'd been hormonal swings and side effects, and sex had become mechanical. Even then, she'd held herself stiff, bracing for the pain that usually happened when they made love. She had felt totally and utterly betrayed by her body. When Carter had said he was done pretending, it had been a relief.

"I thought we would start over after the surgery. Get some counseling to put our marriage back together. Instead he moved out and started divorce proceedings right away. And he stuck me with the debt that we'd accumulated through all the treatments. You want to know why I had no emergency fund when I lost my job? I'm still paying those bills."

"He didn't help pay?"

"I was the one who pushed, so I was the one to pay."

To her surprise, he slid over on the sofa cushion until his thigh was pressed against hers, and he put his arm around her shoulders, urging her to lean on him. She didn't want to, but he was so warm and strong and she was feeling so drained from this whole truth thing that she wilted a bit, resting her head on his shoulder.

"Honey, I think you've already paid enough."

She wouldn't cry. She wouldn't.

But she was very, very close.

She turned into his embrace and let him hold her, let his steadfast strength give her a little bolster against all the hurt and disappointments. This was the problem with Quinn. If he were just a lover, it would be easier. But he was a friend, too. Sometimes they fought, sometimes they annoyed each other, but when the chips were down, he was the kind of man she could count on. Never before had she wished so fervently that she could be more perfect. Less flawed.

She sniffed.

He rubbed her back and said nothing, which was exactly what she needed.

When it had gone on long enough, she pushed her way out of his arms again. "Thank you," she whispered. "I needed that."

"I know." He smiled at her. "So. Where do we go from here?"

She frowned. "Nowhere, I guess. I'm sorry, Quinn. I just think this is better than really hurting each other down the road. There's Amber to think of, too. I think we need to be really consistent there. She's been through enough, and I know she's already attached."

"Lots of thinking on your part."

"It's nothing you haven't already said. Besides, it's better this way."

"Better for who?"

Don't make this more difficult than it already is, she thought. "For everyone. You'll see. We should…just go on being friends. Besides, before long your house will be ready for you to move back home. Maybe this just happened because we spend so much time together already. We've been playing house, you know? But it's not reality."

It sounded good. Even if she didn't quite believe it herself.

"If that's what you want." He sounded resigned and she tried to regret being with him last night. Tried because while she knew it would have been smarter, she couldn't quite bring herself to feel sorry for how amazing it had been to feel that cherished and loved once again.

"I think it's best."

He put his hands on his knees, pushed himself to standing. "I guess I'd better get some shut-eye, then. Lots to catch up on tomorrow."

He was about to pass her on his way to the hall, but he stopped and knelt before her, putting his hands on her knees, his face just below hers so she couldn't avoid looking into his eyes.

"You have so much to offer, Lacey. Don't let anyone tell you differently. You got that?"

She was in danger of sniffing again, but was saved when he got up and walked away. His footsteps sounded in muffled beats on the stairs, and still she sat there, not quite sure what to do with herself. Water ran in the upstairs bathroom, the toilet flushed, and the floors creaked a little as he went to his room and shut the door.

She had to get up, move, go to bed. Tomorrow was another day.

It was all fine until she went to crawl into bed. When she snuggled into the bedding, the scent of him wafted up from the sheets, an olfactory memory that immediately transported her to the previous night. A longing she wasn't prepared for pierced her heart, stealing her breath, until the tears she'd held back so valiantly in the living room came trickling down her cheeks.

All she'd ever wanted was a normal life. Nothing fancy. The love of a good man, a home to call her own, a family to love and care for. But she could never give Quinn the babies he wanted. The only thing worse than this feeling right now was knowing that she'd let down another man she loved.

Chapter 13

Quinn saddled up Big Turk, one of the geldings, and went for a long ride. He needed to get out of the house and into the sunshine. Amber was at a playdate with one of her classmates, whose parents would bring her home in time for dinner. Right now what Quinn needed most was wide-open space, fresh air and some perspective.

Turk was raring to go, dancing a little bit as Quinn held him back on the way to the east side of the ranch. There'd be time to let him loose once they got over the ridge and onto the flat part of the pasture. The sun was warm on Quinn's back, a harbinger of the milder spring temperatures to come. Soon the melt would start, calves would be born, the grass would green and sure, they'd have a few more snowstorms. They always did. But the hardest part of the winter was nearly over.

They hit the flats and Quinn gave Turk a nudge, both of them enjoying the run. It cleared away the cobwebs.

His mind kept going around and around, thinking about what Lacey had said. She'd raised a lot of questions about how he saw his future. A couple of months ago he would have said bringing up Amber in the house where she'd been born, and working at Crooked Valley, helping Duke make the place profitable again. Something had changed since Christmas. And that change was Lacey. Suddenly he wanted more.

Turk was getting lathered, so he slowed to a trot for a few minutes and then back to a walk again, heading to the top of a butte overlooking a creek bed. They crested the rise and Quinn took a deep, cleansing breath. Acres and acres of rolling pastureland spread out before him, the wide-open space awe-inspiring. Limitless.

He frowned a little. That's what Lacey had brought to his life. A sense of limitlessness, that there was more out there for him than his myopic vision. She had made him ask questions of himself, like what he really wanted out of his life. Before Lacey, he hadn't considered other children, but now…she was right. He wanted them. He wanted Amber to know brothers and sisters. He wanted a home with warmth and laughter and not just getting by. Lacey had given him that over the last weeks, bringing him back to life bit by bit. He'd let things go the other night because he'd known two things: he needed to think about what she was saying, and she'd made up her mind and nothing would change it, at least at that time.

The big question was, what was he going to do about it now? There was no escaping the fact that Lacey couldn't give him those children. But the home with warmth and laughter? Someone to share his life with, to talk to at the end of the day? He could see all those things with her. He had put all of his energy into his daughter, but even he could see the difference in the dynamic when Lacey was around. There was an ease to things when Lacey was added to the equation. A sense of rightness that had been missing when he and Amber had been muddling through.

Maybe, just maybe, if he could convince her to give them a try, they could look at other options for building their family.

Good heavens, was he really thinking about a future? Marriage? It seemed premature, and yet, in his situation, he didn't really know how to do casual. Any woman he dated—and Lacey was the first—had to be viewed as a potential mom for Amber. That's just how it was when you were a single parent. It was a package deal. His heart gave a little thump when he realized that Lacey and Amber had gotten along awesomely from the beginning. She was kind and firm and fun, and his daughter, who had once been insecure, had started to blossom just from being around her. If only Lacey could see the miracle she'd accomplished!

Quinn turned Turk around and headed back towards home. He was facing the wind now, and he turned his collar up against the chill. The plain truth was that despite fighting it at every turn, he'd fallen in love with her. Valentine's Day hadn't been about scratching an itch. It had been about starting a new chapter of his life—a chapter with her in it.

What Lacey needed was someone to counteract all the cruddy hogwash that Carter had fed her. The whole thing about him deserving better and her being less of a woman was bull. It wasn't like it was her choice to be sick. He'd like five minutes alone with her ex-husband to set him straight. But seeing as that wasn't likely and probably wouldn't help matters anyway, he figured that he needed to find a way to help her rebuild that confidence the way she'd rebuilt his. To let her see that she could have those things. That she deserved them.

It wasn't until he was nearly to the barnyard again that he came up with an idea. He'd need Amber's help, of course, but that wouldn't be a problem. His daughter would love this particular job.

He took a half hour to settle Turk and then he headed to his office to make some phone calls.

Quinn pulled in to the driveway and looked over at Amber. She was practically bouncing in her seat, anxious to get out and see the puppies.

"Okay, so you need to remember that this puppy is for Lacey, right?" He wanted Amber to be part of it, but wanted her to be prepared for the fact that the dog would be living at Crooked Valley and not at their house. He didn't expect it would be too rough because Amber spent a lot of time at the ranch and could see Lacey's dog often.

"I know, Daddy, I know. Come *on*!" She struggled impatiently with the seat belt crossing her booster seat. With a laugh, Quinn reached back and helped and she was out of the truck in a jiffy.

Sue Bramstock had a litter of puppies for sale and Quinn had remembered Lacey talking about planning the house, kids, picket fence and dogs. Well, she had the house, if she wanted to keep it. The Crooked Valley big house suited her to a tee. Instead of picket fences, there were corrals and pastures, and Quinn couldn't do anything about the kids. But he could get her a dog.

He took Amber's hand and they made their way to

the house. It took longer than he expected, because Amber got sidetracked by the chicken coop and fence, and had to go watch the hens peck around with their necks jutting back and forth. The rooster crowed and she giggled as she stood on the bottom rung and peered over the top. "Why don't we have chickens, Daddy?"

He'd never considered it. "I don't know."

"We should have chickens. They're funny."

One hen came over and looked them over with a beady eye, her head tilted to one side as if to say "What are you lookin' at?" Amber giggled.

The Bramstocks were the kind of farmers who were self-sufficient. They made their living with beef, but they also kept chickens, a few hogs and had a giant vegetable garden in the summer. He remembered years ago when Eileen Duggan had kept a huge garden. Joe had never found the time or the motivation to keep it up after she died.

"Come on, munchkin. Let's see the puppies."

"Okay." She took his hand again and hopped off the fence, and they went up the stairs to the front door and knocked.

Sue answered the door with an apron covering her jeans and sweatshirt. "Quinn! Good to see you. Come on in."

It smelled like apple pie in the house and his stomach growled. But he was soon distracted by a series of yips and shrill barks.

Sue grinned. "I've got the pups in the mudroom while I bake. There are four of them, about fourteen weeks old, and mature enough they are getting in my hair and under my feet. If you want to scoot over to the side door, I'll meet you there."

Quinn and Amber did indeed scoot. The ground was soft from the mild weather and the snow mixed with mud under their feet. Quinn got Amber to stomp hers off as best she could before they stepped inside the mudroom where Sue's husband, John, left his outerwear and boots.

"Oh!" Amber squealed at her first glimpse of the puppies, which were bigger than Quinn had expected. She dropped to her knees, utterly fearless, and was immediately mauled by brown-and-black bundles of fur, complete with pink tongues ready to kiss their new admirer.

He couldn't help but laugh.

"They're a little excitable yet," Sue said. "But housetraining has been going pretty well. They're smart dogs."

"You said they're a shepherd/retriever cross?"

"That's right. So they'll be a good size, but a really nice temperament. I love them." Sue reached down and gave the mama a pat. "Xena here is so loving, but when a stranger comes in, her guard dog tendencies take over. I like that. I feel safe, but she's not an aggressive dog. Know what I mean?"

"I do." And he liked the idea of Lacey having a protector, especially when he wasn't there anymore and she was in the house alone.

"Daddy, this one likes me!"

Three of the puppies were roughhousing in the middle of the floor, but a fourth was climbing into Amber's lap. His fur was a dark tan color, with black markings around his eyes, ears and feet. "He's a handsome boy, that's for sure," Quinn agreed.

Amber hugged him close and he certainly didn't seem to mind. "He's funny. And his paws are huge!"

"He'll grow into them," Quinn answered, knowing that they wouldn't be puppies for long. Already they'd lost the little-ball-of-fur look to them.

Another one jumped up on Amber's lap, kissing her face. "Can we get two, Daddy? Please?"

Oh, no. Quinn shook his head. "Remember. Just one today…"

"For Lacey. I know." Her face fell a little. "But I love this one, too. And she is his sister. Sisters and brothers should be together, shouldn't they?"

It was hard to argue with that. "Honey, we can't have two puppies at the ranch."

"Why not?"

He was scrambling for an answer when she was distracted with playing again and he was saved. He looked over at Sue, who was watching him with an amused expression. "I know," he said, sighing. "I have a hard time saying no."

"She's a good kid, Quinn. And I understand how hard it is. I think it's got to be even worse when you're a single parent."

He nodded. "Look, our house should be ready in a few weeks. Any chance of you holding the girl until then?" He kept his voice low, so as not to give Amber any false hopes.

"I can probably do that."

"Just don't let on to Amber. We're still staying at Crooked Valley while the repairs are being done. She'll get her puppy fix there for a while. Probably more than she realizes."

"No problem." Sue and Quinn went over details like

what dog food she was using and how much, if he had a crate and leash and all the other things he'd need. The crate he'd borrowed from Kailey's family, who kept a couple of border collies. The leash and collar he'd bought in town at the department store, along with a couple of ceramic dog bowls.

He took along the little bit of paperwork from the vet so they had a record of vaccinations, and the recommended age for neutering. Amber crawled out from beneath the mob, begging for the honor of sitting with the puppy on the drive home.

In very little time, they were back out in the truck, the puppy secured in the crate on the front seat, which Quinn had pushed all the way back. Amber was pouting, but when they got to Crooked Valley he clipped on the leash and let Amber take the pup for a quick pee before introducing him to Lacey.

He was suddenly nervous. He picked up the puppy and carried him to the front door, then opened it, because since that first morning the door had been unlocked during the day. He was hoping to tell Lacey himself, but Amber raced ahead, muddy boots and all, crying out "Lacey! Lacey! We gots you a puppy!"

Lacey came around the corner, tugged by an excited four-year-old. Her eyes got huge as she saw Quinn with the puppy in his arms. "You really did. Holy shit."

Amber halted abruptly. "You said a bad word."

Lacey's cheeks flamed. "Sorry."

She was immediately forgiven and Amber smiled again. "We got you a puppy, Lacey! Isn't he cute?"

Still she didn't say anything, and Quinn felt a sense of unease slide through his body. Maybe this hadn't been the smartest move. "Amber, can you go to the truck and get the bag of stuff?"

"Okay, Daddy!" She opened the door and then looked back at Lacey. "Wait'll you see the dog bowls me 'n' Daddy picked out."

She slammed out of the foyer.

"Quinn?"

He swallowed. Hard. "He's a shepherd/retriever cross. Three and a half months old, partially house-trained and guaranteed to be a sweetheart."

Tentatively she reached out and touched the soft fur. The pup wriggled excitedly, so Quinn put him down on the floor but kept him on the leash.

"Why would you do this? A dog?"

He stood up again, met her gaze. "You gave up everything. You said it yourself…the house, the kids, the dog and the picket fence. But you don't have to, Lacey. This can be your home, you see? The fences are here… maybe not the picket ones you imagined, but they're your legacy. And the dog…he'll be great company for you. You've lost enough. I just wanted to give something back to you."

To his relief, tears gathered in the corners of her eyes. "Well." She laughed, emotion filling her voice. "You are a man of surprises, Quinn Solomon. That's a lovely thought. Truly." The pup pulled on the leash and gave a sharp bark. "But a puppy?"

"If you really don't want him, I guess I could take him back to Sue's." Or his house. He was pretty sure Amber wouldn't mind, but he was still disappointed that his gesture wasn't welcome.

"Oh, it's not a case of wanting! He's awfully cute."

She smiled hesitantly. "I just...I've never had a puppy before. I have no idea what I'm doing."

"Never?" Relief rushed through him. Was that all?

She shook her head. "I always wanted one, but Mom was afraid of dogs."

"Well, this one's yours if you want him."

They shared a long look, and then Lacey sat down on the stairs. As soon as she did, the puppy rushed over and started to climb up on her.

She gathered him up on her lap, started to laugh when he began licking her face...and then got a strange look of horror.

Amber rushed back in with the shopping bag.

"Um...we're going to need some paper towel," Lacey suggested, putting the dog on the floor again. "And I need new pants."

"Eeeew!" Amber wrinkled her nose. "Bad puppy!"

Lacey laughed. "Aw, he was just excited. Puppies pee a lot. If he's going to stay here, you're going to have to keep your eye out for puddle accidents."

"Yuck!" Amber suddenly seemed disenchanted.

"He's a baby," Lacey explained. "Do you remember when you had to be potty trained?"

Amber nodded, though Quinn wondered if she actually did remember such a thing. "Well, doggies have to be house-trained so that they go to the bathroom outside. I might need your help with that."

"You need me to help?"

Lacey was winning over his daughter like a champ, not that she needed to try hard. It was so clear to him now. There was a reason she'd come here. And that, as far as he could tell, was to put a little sunshine back into his life. He wanted to be able to do that for her, too.

"Sometimes. Especially if I'm busy. And puppies have a lot of energy. He might need some playtime with toys, so he doesn't chew things."

"I can play with him!"

"Well, phew. That's a load off my mind, kiddo." She laughed. "But first, could you grab the roll of paper towel?"

Amber rushed away.

"You have a real way with her," he said, down low.

"Kids are people, too. They like to feel needed and important. As far as the dog, I don't know if I want to thank you or strangle you." The pup was sitting pretty as you please now, still on the leash. "But he *is* awfully cute."

Quinn stepped forward, ignoring the pull of the leash. "Lacey, you deserve to be happy. Stop punishing yourself."

"Quinn, if you did this to change my mind…"

Had he? He didn't think so. Though perhaps he had, just a little. Not to blackmail her, of course not. He wasn't into trying to buy someone's affections. But if he could make her see that the kid thing didn't matter…

"I did it because I didn't think you'd do it for yourself. And because a dog can be a great companion."

"Because I'll never have my own kids."

Frustrated, he heaved out a breath. "That's not what I said."

"Here you go, Lacey!" Amber came back with the towels, ripped off a few sheets and handed them over.

"Thank you, sweetie." Lacey wiped up the little puddle on the stairs. "I'll be right back. I need to change into some sweats or something."

She disappeared up the stairs, while Quinn waited

at the bottom, not sure how to handle her latest accusation. All he'd wanted to do was give her something she'd always wanted. To see her smile.

Why did women always have to invent motives for everything?

Chapter 14

Lacey's hands trembled as she pulled the sweats out of her dresser drawer. A puppy! Of all the romantic gestures she might have expected, this was the last thing she would have thought of. But there he'd been, standing in the doorway with the most adorable puppy she'd ever seen cuddled in his arms.

She was scared to death. Puppies were a lot of work! She didn't have to have owned one before to know that. But she was also incredibly touched. It was only the knowledge that Quinn wanted more kids that held her back from falling into his arms. The temptation was there, but in the end she knew the truth would come out, just as it had with Carter. They'd pretend it didn't matter until they couldn't pretend any longer. She wasn't sure she could stand to watch another man she loved walk away.

She peeled off her jeans and hung them over the shower rod to dry and pulled on the soft sweatpants. They'd have to get the dog settled and then think about dinner. It would serve to take her mind off her latest failure: she'd been told she'd hear by today about the job she'd interviewed for last week. The phone had been silent, so she assumed that the position had been given to someone else.

Back downstairs, there was a clanging sound coming from the living room. Quinn was assembling a wire dog crate, and Amber was dancing around with the dishes in her hands, wondering where would be the best place for "puppy" to eat.

Lord help her, it felt like a real family.

The enchantment with the "real" family evaporated quickly. Amber didn't want to go to bed before the dog, but wanted to stay up until they decided on a name. Quinn put his foot down, which resulted in the tears and wails of an uncharacteristic tantrum. Lacey's ears were still ringing when she took the pup outside for what felt like the tenth time. At bedtime, she put him in his crate in the living room, but she wasn't in bed five minutes when she heard him whining and crying. Quinn heard it too, and suggested that the puppy might need company. There was no way she was sleeping on the sofa, so Quinn took the dog, crate and all, and moved it to her bedroom.

She was nearly asleep when the whining started again. Lacey was half-tempted to let him out of the crate and on the bed, but she didn't want to get into that habit. Finally, she turned on the radio on her phone that was plugged into the dock, and set the volume low. That, at least, calmed the puppy.

At four in the morning the whining was more of a yelp. She pushed on her slippers and clomped downstairs with him, reaching for the leash on the hook by the door and letting him outside. Aggravated, she stared at Quinn's closed door with a fair bit of hostility. The reality of puppies was very different than the idea of all that cuteness.

She'd gone back to sleep, but when Quinn got up at six-thirty, she stuck her head under a pillow to blot out the sound of the shower. Pup heard the noise and started bouncing around in the crate. Where on earth did he get all the energy?

She didn't let him out of the crate until she'd had a quick shower and had pulled on a pair of comfortable jeans and an oversized hoodie. Once more, she trotted outdoors with him on the leash, then came back in just as Amber was coming down the stairs.

"Can I feed him? Please?"

"Sure. Be my guest." Amber could feed the dog while Lacey made much-needed coffee.

"Come on, dog." Amber sent Lacey a disapproving look. "He needs a name."

"I'll decide on one today, I promise."

"I can help." She set her chin defiantly.

Lacey hesitated. It was as plain as the nose on her face that Amber was already in love with the dog. That she was feeling proprietary. Had Quinn truly thought this through? What would happen when they moved back to their house and the dog stayed here? Could she really do that to Amber? In her head she knew it probably wasn't smart to give in because she felt sorry for the little girl. But her heart…how could she let Amber start to get attached and then break them up?

Quinn came down the stairs and took one look at her before veering off to the side.

"Rough night?" he asked, his voice innocently calm.

"You could say that."

"Aw, he just needs to adjust. He probably missed the other dogs last night. New place and all that."

"Great." She took a sip of her fresh coffee and closed her eyes for a moment. Amber was chatting away to the dog as she put a scoop of food in the bowl. "Quinn," she said quietly, "what happens when you move back home? She's going to hate to leave him."

"We talked about it. She knows she can see him whenever she's here."

"You think that's going to be enough?"

He frowned. "Don't worry about Amber. Anyway, we need to stop calling him 'dog' and 'puppy.' You come up with a name yet?"

She had, though she felt kind of silly about it. "When I was a kid, I read this book that I loved. There was a dog in it, and he was always getting into scrapes but helping people out. I know, it sounds lame, but he was great. His name was Ranger."

Quinn laughed. "I think I remember that book. The dog was even a shepherd, if memory serves."

"He was." She felt a little sheepish. Really, a kid's book? But there it was. "I always thought if I got a dog, I'd call him Ranger."

"You're sentimental," he observed, a grin tugging at his cheek. "Who'da thunk it?"

"Smart-ass," she murmured.

"What do you think, Amber? Lacey's going to name him Ranger."

Amber wrinkled her nose. "I like George."

Quinn caught Lacey's eye, then looked at Amber. "Well, Lacey gets to do the honors because Ranger is her dog, right?"

"I guess." Amber looked so crestfallen that Lacey couldn't help but offer a compromise.

"What if his middle name is George? You have a middle name, don't you?"

Amber nodded. "Amber Marie. After my mama."

It was impossible for Lacey to remain emotionally immune to the situation. "So what if we called him… Ranger George Duggan? What do you think?"

Amber giggled. "That's a long name for a dog."

"He's an important dog."

"Can I take him outside?"

Quinn looked at Lacey for permission, which she gave. "Okay," he agreed. "But on his leash, and only for fifteen minutes. When I call you to come in, you need to come in. You have to get ready for school."

"Yes, Daddy." She patted her leg. "Come on, Ranger!"

Lacey was sure that the pup had no idea that he was supposed to answer to that name, but he sure found chasing after Amber entertaining.

When the door slammed, Lacey was relieved for the reprieve from commotion. Quinn poured his coffee and smiled at her. "So," he said softly, "am I on the naughty list this morning? I know he was up in the night."

She thought for a moment but shook her head. "No. I know I'm going to love him, Quinn. Hey, if I'd had kids, I'd be up in the night, right?"

She asked it brightly but Quinn frowned. "Lacey, I've been thinking. Is there really no way? I mean—" his cheeks turned ruddy. "You uh, still have your ovaries, right? Have you considered a surrogate?"

She wished he wouldn't push for alternatives that no longer mattered. Did he honestly think she hadn't thought about these things?

"Do you know how much that costs?" She ran her hand through her hair, her fingers catching in the tangles. "There are the regular fees, legal fees, payments to the mom each month…we're talking thousands and thousands of dollars. I'm still paying off the bills from before. We didn't have that kind of money and I certainly don't now."

"I had no idea."

"I do. Believe me, I looked at all the angles."

"Adoption?"

She turned away, opened the dishwasher and began unloading it just to have something to do. "By the time we got to that part, Carter had had enough. I'm not sure he would have gone for it anyway. Not his flesh and blood, you see. And it can take years to get a baby."

"I see."

"You do?"

"Uh-huh."

She straightened and met his gaze. "And what exactly do you see?"

"I see you've given up. Truth is, I can bring home a puppy, I can tell you that you deserve happiness and I can say or do a hundred different things, but none of it is going to change your mind if you aren't open to changing it."

Her chest started to cramp. "Quinn, you know you want children."

"I have a daughter. Would I like more? Of course. But if it didn't happen? Shit, Lacey. A month ago I was sure that I'd never fall in love again, and now I have and what's standing in my way isn't grief or guilt or my feelings but your stubbornness!"

Had he really said he'd fallen in love? With her?

"It's been too fast. You don't know what you're saying."

"Let me know what the proper amount of time is to fall for someone. You know I wasn't looking. You know I went out of my way to be aggravating."

"You're still aggravating."

He stepped forward, grabbed her upper arms, and kissed her.

When she got over the initial surprise, she knew she should push him away. This wasn't helping at all. Instead she felt herself soften, lean into the kiss, open her lips beneath his. It felt so right, so perfect. The last thing she trusted was anything that seemed perfect, though, so she indulged in one last kiss before stepping back and out of his arms.

"What are you trying to prove?" she accused softly.

"That this is real. How we feel is real. And that I want to try."

Her heart hurt, both from longing and from the inevitable pain she knew was coming. "I can't, Quinn. I've been down this road before. I know you mean what you say right now. Eventually, though…"

"You won't even give us a chance."

"I'm sorry. I've been through this before and I care

about you, Quinn. I'm not sure I could go through it a second time, and I would fully expect to."

He just gaped at her. The word *coward* raced through her mind but she shoved it away. She wasn't a coward. She'd simply learned her lesson, learned not to idealize situations and saw them for what they were.

"That's a real no, then."

She smiled weakly, but there was little warmth in it. "Were you really trying to soften me up with the puppy?"

He took a step back. "I was hoping you would see that you didn't have to give up. I guess I didn't realize you already had. I should have known. I'd given up for a long time, too."

And would he again? She hated that she might cause him pain. That for the first time since his wife's death, he'd cared about someone, about her, and she was turning him away.

Better now than later, that little voice inside her whispered.

But she said nothing.

Quinn's face flattened as he shuttered away any more emotion. "Crews are working on the house this week. You'll only have to put up with us for a little while longer and then we'll be out of your hair."

She swallowed, hurt at his withdrawal, knowing she had no right to be. "There's no rush to leave, Quinn. You know you're welcome here. You have as much… no, more right to this house than I do." Her lip quivered and she bit down to stop it. "I can always stay with Duke and Carrie for a few weeks if me being here bothers you. If it's too awkward."

"I doubt you want to take Ranger there. It was a stupid idea, wasn't it? I can see if Sue will take him back."

A dull ache penetrated her stomach. "No, don't. I want to keep him. If that's okay with you."

"Fine. I'd better get Amber in to get ready for school." Conversation over.

He was halfway down the hall when she called after him. "Quinn?"

He didn't answer.

"I'm sorry," she whispered, knowing he probably couldn't hear her, full of regret.

It took ten days for Quinn's house to be ready to move back in. Lacey stayed out of his way as much as possible, and he stayed out of hers. They stayed civil so that Amber wouldn't notice anything was wrong, but she kept herself busy with some of her accounting jobs, looking after Ranger and visiting with Carrie a lot in the evenings.

She took phone calls intended for Quinn about the delivery of new furniture to replace that which had been damaged in the fire. New sofa, love seat, new beds for both him and Amber. It was almost March when he broke it to Amber that they would be moving back home the following day.

"Yay!" Amber cried out, her spoon clattering to the table, splattering pudding on the tablecloth.

For all her "will you be my mom" talk, Amber seemed to personify the sentiment that there really was no place like home. She seemed excited that she would be back among her familiar things—whatever had been salvaged from the smoke damage.

After dinner, Quinn disappeared with Amber to

pack. Lacey cleaned up the kitchen and felt a sorrow open up inside her at the thought of being alone in the house.

Then again, she wouldn't really be alone. Quinn would be back to venturing in and out, as the ranch office was still in the house. But Amber would be gone, too. And the sensation of going to bed at night and not feeling so all alone.

She looked over at Ranger, who was curled up in a ball on the leather sofa. She hadn't had the heart to make him stay off the furniture, especially since there was no fabric upholstery. She went over and sat beside him, pleased when he unfurled his warm body and stretched, and then rested his chin on her lap. She stroked the soft fur and found her throat clogging with tears. Maybe this was why Quinn had brought Ranger home. Because he knew they were leaving and he wanted her to have some company.

He really hadn't had any faith in her. It stung that he'd been right about it, too.

The next morning Lacey got up early to make a final breakfast for Amber. Her favorite was chocolate chip pancakes, so Lacey mixed up the batter and started frying them off while bacon snapped and sizzled in another pan. Amber came skidding into the kitchen with an excited grin. "You made pancakes?"

"I sure did. Do you want to find the syrup?"

Together they set the table, while Lacey tried to ignore the sound of Quinn going in and out, taking their bags to his truck. She'd hated the fact that he was moving in and now she hated to see him go. Yes, even though they'd reached an impasse lately, the house would seem unbearably empty without him and Amber here.

His spot at the table would be vacant.

She wouldn't smell his soap and aftershave in the bathroom anymore.

Instead of off-tune whistling, there'd be nothing but silence.

She grabbed the spatula and flipped the pancakes on the griddle as Quinn came in to grab a quick breakfast before hitting the road.

"I'm going to miss Ranger," Amber said a few minutes later, her mouth stuffed full of pancake.

"And I'm going to miss your help." Not exactly, but she would never tell Amber that. Sometimes kid and dog made more mess than they solved, but she wouldn't have traded it for anything. "You can come back to see him anytime, though. Have playdates!"

Amber giggled. "That's funny. Puppy playdates."

"We'd better get going," Quinn said firmly, putting his knife and fork on his plate and taking a last swig of coffee. "Thanks for breakfast this morning, Lacey."

Ouch. So impersonal. In such a rush to leave... "You're welcome. It's the least I could do."

He refused to meet her eyes. Amber collected her plate and, like the angel she was, started to take it to the dishwasher.

"Just leave it, I'll clean up. Your daddy's in a rush." A rush to get away from her. Either he was still really angry about what had happened, or she'd truly hurt him. She didn't like either option very much.

Amber took a minute to stop and hug Ranger, who was sitting beside Lacey's chair, hoping for a scrap of something to fall to the floor. "'Bye, Ranger. See you soon. Be a good doggie."

"What about me?" Lacey asked. "Do I get a hug?"

"O'course!" exclaimed Amber, barreling forward and wrapping her arms around Lacey's neck as Lacey leaned down. "I love you, Lacey." As if that weren't enough, Amber placed a sweet, smacking kiss on Lacey's cheek.

Quinn was right. Get out and get out fast, preferably before she embarrassed herself. For a moment, her gaze lifted and met Quinn's. There was no escaping the pain in his eyes. He wasn't leaving unscathed, either. But it was for the best. Wasn't it?

"Come on, Amber. Gotta get you to school and then unload the boxes."

"Coming, Daddy!"

She raced off to put on her boots and jacket, and Lacey followed, despondency leaching into her body, making it feel heavy and sluggish. She loved him. She truly did. She loved his strength and kindness and ethics and honesty. She loved watching him play with Amber, or help her with her letters, or any of the other things that required patience and love since he'd taken on this single-parenting gig. And it was for that reason alone that she let him go. Someone out there would make him happy, give him more children to spoil. Give Amber the opportunity to have brothers and sisters.

Amber ran to the truck and Quinn got her fastened in, then came back to the door for one last duffle bag.

It was in his hand before he looked up at her, standing by the banister.

"Well, this is it," he said, his voice betraying no emotion. "Thank you, Lacey, for sharing your space with us. You must be glad to be getting the house to yourself again."

Really? Did he actually just say that? It made her a

little bit mad that he could reduce what had happened here the last month to her wanting her space back. "That's it?" Her tone was brittle. "That's all these last weeks have been? Like you're checking out of a hotel?"

The crests of his cheeks pinked. "Don't make this harder than it already is."

"Then don't pretend that it's something it's not." She huffed out a breath. "Or rather that it's nothing when it was something."

Anger flashed in his eyes. "You refuse to let it be something. So it's just better this way. We can go back to me working in the office when I need to and if that's a problem I can talk to Duke about putting an office in the horse barn. There's room."

"You're punishing me."

He shook his head. "No, Lacey, I'm trying not to punish myself. Big difference."

Before she could reply, he nodded. "Gotta go. Amber's waiting. Thanks for everything."

He turned and walked away.

She stared after him until Ranger noticed the open door and made a run for it. The sound of his claws on the floor alerted her and she neatly stepped aside, blocking his path. Then she shut the door.

Chapter 15

It was as if someone had taken all the color out of her life.

There were no little pink-and-purple piles of clothing to be picked up, hardly any dirty dishes and no more coffee breaks at the kitchen table. What had initially been peace and quiet and order was now dull and silent and lonely. Ranger kept her busy and she clung on to caring for him like a lifeline, taking him for long walks around the ranch, enjoying the fresh air now that spring was around the corner. He started chewing her slippers, so she made a trip to the pet store for some better chew toys to keep him occupied. In the evenings, he often hopped up on the sofa with her as she watched TV. There was just one problem. Every time she looked at him she saw Quinn, standing in the doorway with a hopeful look on his face, Ranger in his arms.

For the millionth time, she wished things were different. She wished they could just have a normal life with the normal progression of things: fall in love, get married, have children. No bumps in the road, no…

She sighed, put her hand on Ranger's warm coat. No sacrifices or gut-wrenching decisions. Why did life have to be so complicated?

A week passed, then another. Lacey worked on the ranch books, then hung out her shingle for doing taxes as the season was in full swing. It kept her busy most days, papers spread out on the kitchen table. When she had a lull, she drove over to the Brandt spread to catch up with the monthly accounting.

Once more she was struck by the prosperous state of the ranch. It was so put together, so tidy and cared for. If she could do anything for Crooked Valley, she hoped it was find ways to save Duke some money so he could afford to make the little upgrades and give the place some polish. She'd discovered that the bucking stock side of the operation wasn't carrying its weight, and she wanted to speak to Duke about some options for either making it profitable or shedding themselves of the liability. Maybe talking to Kailey would help, too. The girl knew her business.

"Hey, girlfriend." Right on cue, Kailey stuck her head inside the office. "Saw your car out front and brought you some coffee."

Lacey let out a breath and smiled. "Thanks. I could use another cup."

"Not sleeping well? You look tired." She put the mug on the desk.

Lacey raised an eyebrow. "Gee, thanks for the compliment. Actually, the dog keeps me up a lot of nights. Though he's getting better."

"He's a cutie. I saw him when I was over to see Quinn a few days ago about one of the mares."

"You didn't come in?"

"Your car was gone," Kailey explained. "You know, you'd think Quinn would be happy, being back in his own place again. But a sorrier sight I've never seen. He's practically moping around."

Kailey's voice was a little too innocent, her gaze a little too knowing. Lacey took a sip of her coffee. "Don't start," she warned.

"Come on." Kailey sat across the desk from Lacey and rested her elbows on the scarred wood. "What happened with you two? Valentine's Day you couldn't keep your eyes off each other, and I bet that extended to your hands, too."

Lacey's cheeks heated.

"See? I'm right. We all figured things were headed in a new direction and honestly, I was really happy about it. He's not the kind of guy who should be alone forever. He's too wonderful."

Yes, it was well established that Quinn was practically a saint. "Then you marry him," Lacey snapped.

Kailey sat back. "Whoa. First of all, Quinn and I are friends. Always have been. Kissing him would be like kissing my brother. Yuck." She frowned at Lacey. "Second, what the hell is with the marriage thing? Did he ask you? Oh, my God. He did, didn't he?"

"No, he didn't," Lacey replied. "Thank God."

Kailey scowled. "Girl, what's wrong with you? Quinn's an amazing guy. And you know it, so what gives?"

Lacey deliberated for a moment. Truth was, other than Carrie, Kailey was her only other real friend here in Gibson. "It's just better this way," she hedged.

"Better? Better how? And Amber…she loves you. All she talked about was helping you cook and Lacey this and Lacey that…"

Pain sliced through Lacey's heart. It wasn't just Quinn she missed, it was Amber, too.

"I can't have children, Kailey." She closed her eyes and just let out the words.

She heard Kailey blow out a breath. When Lacey opened her eyes, Kailey was looking at her with sympathy softening her gaze.

"I'm sorry, Lace. I shouldn't have pushed. I had no idea."

"It's not something I talk about," she admitted. "I told Carrie and Duke a while ago. I told Quinn after Valentine's Day."

Kailey wasn't stupid. She put things together quickly. "When things got to a point where he needed to know."

"Yes." She gave a small nod.

"Oh, honey."

"Don't." Lacey held up a hand, determined not to get weepy. She proceeded to fill Kailey in on the painful details of her condition. "It is what it is. So now you see why Quinn and I can't be together."

Kailey's brows pulled together. "No, I don't. Not really."

"Quinn wants more kids. I could see it, and I called him on it. It's no sense pretending it doesn't matter. We'd just be fooling ourselves and then one day we wouldn't be able to ignore it any longer."

"Like you and your ex?"

Lacey looked into Kailey's eyes. "Yeah. Like that."

There was a moment of quiet while Kailey considered her next words. But if Lacey was expecting understanding or sympathy, she was way off base.

"So you're just giving up?" Kailey sat back in her chair, her lips pursed. "Do you know how hard it had to have been for Quinn to even care about someone again? What he's been through?"

"Of course I know!" Lacey bit down on her lip. "You don't think I've thought about it every day? How losing Marie destroyed his life and how incredible it is that he cares for me? You don't think this hurts?"

"Then fight for it. If you love him, why can't you fight for him?"

"Because I can't stand to think of the look in his eyes when he tells me he can't do it anymore. Just thinking about it makes this giant hole open up inside me, Kailey."

"And what makes you so sure he will?" Kailey leaned forward, pressing.

Lacey didn't know what to say. She was afraid, pure and simple. Afraid of letting Quinn down. Afraid that everything Carter had said to her the day he left would be true. That if she hadn't fought so hard, maybe she wouldn't have strangled their marriage to death.

"Kailey," she said softly, painfully. "I fought for this for years. I did treatments, surgeries, you name it. I fought for the family I couldn't have and in the end I drove my husband away. I made him hate me."

It was a few seconds before Kailey answered, but then she reached over and touched Lacey's hand. "Honey, have you considered that you fought for the family, but you forgot to fight for him?"

She took some time to think about that. Had she been so obsessed with a baby that she'd forgotten about her husband? What if he hadn't cared about it as much as she had? She'd been so worried about the status of her uterus that she'd forgotten to consider the status of her relationship with Carter.

She knew how to fight. But what if she'd just been fighting for the wrong things?

Kailey cleared her throat. "Sweetie, isn't Quinn worth fighting for? If he's not, then it's better this way. But if he is...what the hell are you doing sitting here?"

"I can't give him babies," Lacey reminded her, a catch in her voice.

"He has Amber. It's not like you're telling him he'll never be a father, and even if it was, don't you think that when you love someone, you love all of them? Not just the good stuff. What you have to decide is if you trust in him, if you believe in him enough to fight for the two of you. He's not Carter. You can't judge all men by the one man who let you down." Something passed over her face, something Lacey thought looked like pain but it quickly disappeared. Kailey pressed on. "At some point you have to have a little faith."

The idea was scary enough that Lacey's chest started to tighten and it was hard to breathe. She knew how to fight hard. She also knew how to lose, but in the end, would she always look back and regret turning him away?

That, finally, was the one clear answer. Of course she would.

"I might have already blown it," she whispered, cradling her head in her hands. "He's barely spoken to me since moving out."

"Because he's hurting. Lacey, I saw his face that night at the dance. I saw how it was between you. It's special. Don't throw it away out of fear. You were the one who sent him away. You've got to be the one to ask him to come back."

"How do I do that?"

Kailey finally smiled at her. "Three little words, sugar. That's all it takes."

Lacey wasn't sure how to get Quinn alone so they could talk. At his place, Amber would be in the way. At the ranch they ran the risk of being interrupted by Duke or one of the hands, and for this sort of conversation she wanted privacy. Time.

She finally found an opening when Carrie stopped in for tea on Thursday morning. As they chatted over chocolate chip cookies, Carrie revealed that Jack, one of the hands, was out getting his wisdom teeth pulled and that Quinn was working the horses all on his own this week. Carrie had offered to step in and take up the slack, but Duke was playing protective daddy now that she was starting to show.

So that was why he'd stayed away and not been in the office all week. Lacey was relieved it wasn't because he was avoiding her even more. The topic switched to Lacey, however, when Carrie let her know that the lawyer had called and as long as Lacey was running the office part of the ranch, the terms of the will were satisfied. Now she just had to decide if she wanted to stay on at the house or find a smaller place in town. For now, not paying rent was a good option.

It seemed like Carrie stayed and stayed and talked nonstop. Finally she left and Lacey raced to the bathroom to freshen up. She'd just go down and ask him to come to the house later when he had a break or something. She swiped on some lipstick and tidied her ponytail, swished on some mascara to brighten her eyes just a bit. Satisfied that she was acceptable, she put Ranger in his crate as a precaution against accidents, pulled on a jacket and a pair of boots and made her way to the horse barn.

The barn was warm and smelled of horses and hay, two scents that Lacey didn't find that unpleasant. Perhaps the outside of the barn looked a little neglected, but inside it was clean and tidy, with swept concrete floors and nothing piled up or lying around. She found Quinn in a stall, running his hands over the sides of a dappled mare. "Hey, there," she said softly, not wanting to startle either of them.

Quinn's head came up sharply at the sound of her voice. He hadn't heard her come in, but only because he'd been lost in thoughts about her again.

The past few weeks had been so weird. He'd thought by going home he'd be able to get into his old routine again. That it would feel right and this thing with Lacey wouldn't be so…present. But he'd been very, very wrong. To his surprise, home didn't quite feel like home. The new paint and floors looked different, the furniture brand-new. The bits and pieces of Marie that had been there were gone, and he realized he'd kept it exactly the same all that time in an effort to hold on to her. Like a shrine. And now it felt like he didn't belong there anymore.

He'd been living at home and wishing he was back at Crooked Valley. The only thing he'd been able to sort out for sure was that Lacey needed time and space to sort things out. He hadn't been able to move on until he was ready, and he wasn't going to push her, either. The one thing Lacey didn't expect was for him to stick around, because Carter hadn't. But Quinn could be a patient man. He hadn't given up on her yet.

And now she'd come to him. He kept his voice mellow. "What are you doing down here?"

"I came to see you. To see if we could talk."

"I'm shorthanded today." He hated to admit it, but there really wasn't a lot of spare time with Jack being out.

"I know. That's why I came to the barn."

"I don't follow." He stood and gave the mare a pat on the rump. "Good girl. You and the little one are doing fine."

The mare was expecting, and he realized that all around Lacey there was evidence of new life and reproduction and it had to be hell on her, especially when she'd wanted it so much.

"I knew you'd be alone, Quinn. I didn't want us to be overheard or interrupted. Maybe you can come to the house for a while."

"I'll try, but it might not be until later. I'm handling everything alone with Jack out today, and then I have to go get Amber." He tapped the mare's foreleg and she lifted it obligingly for him to examine the frog. He was deliberately playing it cool, but he wasn't going to be able to hold out for long. She looked so pretty, so nervous standing there fidgeting with her hands, that he really just wanted to pull her into his arms and tell her it was all going to be okay.

* * *

Lacey knew she deserved to be put off a bit. She'd been the one to close down any hope of them having a relationship. With nerves tangling over and around in her stomach, she remembered the moment he'd said he was falling in love with her.

She'd thought it impossible. A disaster...rather than a miracle. She wondered if at any time during her adulthood she'd stop being so blind.

"Just tell me what you need," he said.

Three little words. Perhaps not the three Kailey meant, but they were three that would answer his question.

"I need you."

He straightened, dropping the hoof, the mare forgotten. "What did you say?"

She wouldn't cry. She would not. Blinking furiously, she repeated the words, hope pushing against the fear in her heart. "I need you, Quinn. I can't go on this way. Nothing's right anymore."

He stepped away from the mare and came to the stall door, unlatching it and coming out into the hall, then closing it behind him again. "What are you saying, Lacey?"

She lifted her chin. "I guess I'm asking if it's too late for us."

If she expected him to fall into her arms, she was mistaken. In fact, she couldn't read his face at all, and she was suddenly very afraid that she'd missed her opportunity. That it really was too late. And she had no one to blame but herself.

"You were pretty clear a few weeks ago when you told me we were done. What changed?"

"I meant it, at the time. I'd spent a lot of energy fighting for what I wanted for years, and I lost. And then when I had something to fight for again, I was too afraid to go after it."

"And how did you come by this miraculous revelation?"

Oh, Lord, he was really holding his ground. She'd hurt him when she'd turned him away, hadn't she? And he was going to make her work now.

"Quinn," she whispered, on the verge of tears.

"You need to say it," he said firmly. "You need to, Lace."

It was time she rose to the challenge and became the kind of woman he deserved. She looked at him, standing across from her, and knew that he was right. She had to try. The idea of life without him was so utterly and completely empty.

"Kailey set me straight. She's a good friend, and happens to be pretty smart."

His face softened the tiniest bit. "Yes, she is."

And then she took a deep, fortifying breath.

"The thing is, Quinn, I was so afraid of losing you down the road that I couldn't bring myself to take a chance on us. And that wasn't giving either of us nearly enough credit." She gave a small sniff as emotion threatened to overwhelm her. "I'm miserable without you, Quinn. I miss hearing your voice telling Amber to be quiet in the morning. I miss seeing you across the dinner table. Hearing you laugh at a show on TV or talking about work even though I don't understand most of what you're saying. I love you, Quinn. I don't know how it happened, because you drive me crazy. But when you kiss me I feel alive again and when we made love

I knew what it felt like to be home and it scares me to death. Scares me because I want it so much, and it's so precious and fragile and the very idea of believing in us and then possibly losing you tears me up inside. I'm afraid to have faith, Quinn. But I love you. That I can't change."

She never expected to see tears in his eyes but they were there, glistening at her as she finished her speech. His voice was raw when he replied, still standing a few feet away, not touching her, but reaching her just the same, the way he always seemed to. With his heart.

"I had faith once, too," he said hoarsely, "and had it shattered. I didn't expect to love you, either. And maybe you were right before. Maybe it's easier for me because losing Marie broke my heart, but I wasn't left, I don't know, disillusioned, like you were with Carter. There was no blame to be passed around. Just an empty hole in my life. A cloud hanging over me until you came along and brought the sun with you."

"We used to fight all the time."

"Not for long." His lips turned up just a little. "Just enough to flirt without admitting we were doing it."

He was right. They'd been playing this mating game from the start.

"Do you think we can start over?" she asked, unable to keep the thread of uncertainty out of her voice.

"I've been miserable without you," he admitted. "Amber's grouchy because she misses you, I'm grouchy because I miss you, nothing seems right. Home just isn't home anymore, Lacey. It really is where the heart is. And I'm afraid I left my heart with you."

For a man who didn't make pretty speeches, that one was pretty damned good to her mind. But she had to be absolutely sure, get everything out in the open, no surprises.

"Quinn, you know what I can and can't offer you. I understand, and want you to be a hundred percent honest."

He came forward then, put his hands on her upper arms and squeezed. "It doesn't matter that you can't have children. You, me and Amber...we can be a family. I would never, ever turn you away for that, or make you feel that you were somehow lacking. There's nothing wrong with you. Nothing except the fact that you're too damned stubborn to take a chance. I hope that's changed."

She nodded. "I have to learn to trust again somehow. I figure a good starting point is the man I love. The most admirable man I know."

"Don't let Duke hear you say that," Quinn replied, but a smile broke out over his face. "God, it's so good to touch you again."

"Kiss me, please? I'm dying to kiss you, Quinn."

He needed no other prompting. His arms came around her as he claimed her with a kiss, his lips warm and firm and commanding. By the time they broke it off, she was quite breathless and weak-kneed.

"So we start over?" he asked hopefully.

She nodded. "We start over. We could begin with you coming to dinner with Amber tonight. I've missed her, too."

"I have to make a run home first," he said. "Say six-ish?"

"Sounds perfect."

Reluctant to let him go, she stepped into his embrace again, wrapping her arms around his ribs as she pressed her head to his chest, the rough fabric of his jacket against her cheek. "I'm sorry, Quinn. Sorry I was so stupid and scared."

"It doesn't matter," he murmured, kissing the top of her head. "You're here now. We'll make it work, Lacey. I promise."

After several long moments, the mare came to the door of the stall and stuck her head over the door, wondering what the fuss was about. Lacey laughed and Quinn lifted his hand and gave the soft muzzle a rub. "Jealous," he accused, but the lines around his face had relaxed. Lacey felt like a load had been lifted from her shoulders. That together they could do this thing.

"I'd better go decide what to make. It sucks cooking for one." She didn't want to leave his side but knew he had work to do.

Besides, this time she knew he'd be back. With Amber and her delightful chatter. The house would be full again—full with the people she loved.

"Whatever it is, it'll be delicious. It always is."

She went to pull away but he grabbed her hand and yanked her back, quickly enough that she fell into his arms with a laugh. The laugh died, though, when he treated her to a long, lingering kiss that left her wanting all sorts of things that shouldn't happen in the middle of a horse barn.

"I love you," he murmured before letting her go.

"I love you, too," she answered.

Chapter 16

For the past month, Quinn had been happier than he could ever remember being. But right now, his nerves were completely shot.

First of all, he'd had to make Amber promise to keep their secret, and he had no faith she'd be able to do so. For added security, he'd made the drive into the city and dropped her at his mother's place, which had required a quick and, he was sure, unsatisfactory explanation.

Then he'd stopped for flowers…again, in the city, because the only shop in Gibson to carry flowers was the grocery store and wouldn't that set tongues wagging? A dozen pink roses sat on the truck seat beside him. Right next to a little red envelope and a bottle of champagne.

He was so out of practice with this stuff.

Her car was in the driveway. At least that was good, because he wasn't sure what he would have done if she'd been out. Once he cut the engine, he peeked at his reflection in the rearview mirror. His brows were pulled together, forming a wrinkle at the top of his nose. He relaxed his forehead to erase it, then flicked a hand over his hair, fixing an invisible stray strand. Then he ran his finger under his collar, which felt far too tight, buttoned to the top. The knot in his tie was slightly askew, and he tried to straighten it although it refused to lie perfectly flat.

He was starting to sweat, so he figured he should get out of the truck and just get on with it.

It was ten minutes to six. The longer spring days meant that the sun still shone benevolently on the fresh grass that had greened up beautifully after the snow had melted. He left his jacket on the seat as he opened the door and then reached back for his bounty. One step after another, up the few stairs to the porch, where he hesitated.

The "rules" were that the door was unlocked between eight and six each day. But lately those rules had ceased to matter. He came and went as he pleased, stopping midday to share lunch, for coffee breaks, for dinner and movie dates. And it had been wonderful.

But it wasn't enough. So tonight he knocked on the door instead of walking right in. It seemed appropriate.

Ranger started barking his head off, the sound growing louder as the dog raced through the house to the door. Quinn could hear Lacey's voice telling him to hush, and then she opened the door.

The sight of her greeting him with a smile never failed to steal his breath.

"Quinn! I wasn't expecting you tonight."

"Surprise," he said, finding it easier than he expected

to smile at her. Yeah, he was nervous, but seeing her somehow made everything all right.

"Those are for me?" she asked, her face lighting up with pleasure.

He handed her the roses. "Yes, they're for you."

"What's the occasion?"

"Do I need one?" He followed her inside and shut the door. Tonight he'd worn his suit pants and dress shoes, not boots. When she had the flowers in her hands, she finally noticed he'd dressed up.

"Okay, now I know something's going on. Because I'm in sweats and you're all dressed up."

"I think you look beautiful." He truly did. There was something so soft and natural about her when she was like this. Her hair fell in waves over her shoulders, and he longed to sink his fingers into it and hear her say his name in that soft, husky way she did when they were alone…

But his hands were full. And there were things to say first.

"I've been doing taxes all day. I'm not wearing any makeup. You're deranged." She moved to the sink to fetch a vase and fill it with water.

"I just…I realized we never had a real Valentine's Day."

She stuck the roses in the vase and turned around, holding the vessel in her hands. "Um, really? Because I have some pretty romantic memories from Valentine's Day." She smiled at him wickedly.

"I never got you a present."

Her cheeks had turned a becoming shade of pink to match the roses and he marveled once more that he could be so lucky twice in his life. Lord, he loved her.

For her kindness and her vulnerability and her strength and the way she nurtured their relationship and his family. All leading to this moment.

He stepped forward, put the champagne on the counter and took the vase from her hands. "So," he said lightly, "tonight you get champagne and flowers. You get to be treated like a princess. Oh, and Amber also realized she'd left you off her list of Valentine's card recipients and asked me to give you this."

There. That had sounded casual and breezy, right? He hoped so because his heart was pounding painfully as he handed over the little red envelope.

She took it and smiled, then her face grew puzzled. "There's something in here with the card," she said, feeling along the outside of the envelope. "I wonder what she's put in here, the sneaky thing."

She had to open it soon. He'd forgotten how to breathe.

Lacey slid her finger along the seal and opened the envelope, then pulled out the little card with her favorite Disney couple on the outside. She laughed. "Of all the fish in the sea, you're the one for me! Of course. Ariel and Eric."

She turned the card over, and he watched her face as she read the words he'd helped Amber print on the back side.

Will you marry my Daddy?

Her gaze lifted to his, surprised, confused, amazed, and he hoped beyond hope, happy. Without speaking, she reached into the envelope and took out the ring he'd purchased last week when he'd started to put this plan into motion.

Her lip started to quiver, so he stepped forward, took

the ring from her fingertips and held her left hand in his own. "Lacey Duggan, will you marry me?"

At her quick nod, he slid the ring over her finger, where the diamonds winked up at them both, sealing the promise.

"Yes," she finally whispered, her voice hitching. "Oh, Quinn. It's beautiful."

"Just like you," he replied, lifting her hand and kissing her fingers. "I want us to be a family. Officially, forever. Amber already loves you like a mother and I'm wild about you. Life's too short to spend it apart. I want us to soak up every happy moment we can."

She was really crying now and he smiled indulgently, pulling her into his arms. "Shh," he soothed, cupping his hand over her head. "Today's a new start for us. I don't want you to cry. I want us to celebrate."

She stood back and swiped her fingers under her eyes. "I never thought I'd be this happy again," she replied. "It's almost too much to believe." She hesitated, like she wanted to say something but wasn't sure she should.

"What is it?" he asked, hoping she wasn't coming up with some roadblock to stand in the way of them getting married.

"It's the ranch. I know you just moved back into your house, but…" Her blue eyes pleaded with him. "I love this house. I never expected to, and it needs a family to make it a home. Would you and Amber consider moving in here?"

He barely gave it a moment's thought. Yes, he loved his house, but it was part of a past life that didn't exist anymore. He'd only kept it to give Amber some consistency, to feel like something in her life hadn't changed after her mother died. These days, when he thought of home, it was wherever Lacey was, and that meant Crooked Valley.

"If it's okay with Duke and Rylan, it's okay with me. You realize it means you're gaining one little girl and another rambunctious dog, right?"

He'd fulfilled his promise and Amber had been the proud owner of a shepherd cross named Molly for the better part of a month.

Lacey's grin spread. "Yes, but instead of one person and one dog there'll be three people and two dogs. Better ratio, right?"

He wasn't about to argue.

They were in the middle of kissing again when the house phone rang. They were going to ignore it when Quinn realized it was his mother's number on the caller ID.

"Hello?"

"Did she say yes?"

Leave it to Amber to be impatient. "Just a minute and you can ask her yourself." He put the phone on speaker. "Okay, darlin'. Go ahead."

"Lacey?"

"Yes, Amber?"

"Are you going to be my mommy now?"

The look on Lacey's face was something he knew he'd remember forever.

"I sure am, pumpkin." She reached over and took Quinn's hand in hers. "I sure am."

* * * * *

When Laurel Hudson is found—alive but with amnesia—no one is more relieved than Adam Fortune. He will do whatever it takes to reunite mother and son, even if it means a road trip in extremely close quarters. Will the long journey home remind Laurel how much they truly share?

Read on for a sneak preview of the final book in The Fortunes of Texas: Rambling Rose continuity, The Texan's Baby Bombshell by Allison Leigh.

He'd been falling for her from the very beginning. But that kiss had sealed the deal for him.

Now that glossy oak-barrel hair slid over her shoulder as Laurel's head turned and she looked his way.

His step faltered.

Her eyes were the same stunning shade of blue they'd always been. Her perfectly heart-shaped face was pale and delicate looking even without the pink scar on her forehead between her eyebrows.

Her eyebrows pulled together as their eyes met.

Remember me.

Remember us.

The words—unwanted and unexpected—pulsed through him, drowning out the splitting headache and the aching back and the impatience, the relief and the pain.

Then she blinked those incredible eyes of hers and he realized there was a flush on her cheeks and she was chewing at the corner of her lips. In contrast to her delicate features, her lips were just as full and pouty as they'd always been.

Kissing them had been an adventure in and of itself.

He pushed the pointless memory out of his head and then had to shove his hands in the pockets of his jeans because they were actually shaking.

"Hi." Puny first word to say to the woman who'd made a wreck out of him.

Still seated, she looked up at him. "Hi." She sounded breathless. "It's…it's Adam, right?"

The pain sitting in the pit of his stomach then had nothing to do with anything except her. He yanked his right hand from his pocket and held it out. "Adam Fortune."

She looked uncertain, then slowly settled her hand into his.

Unlike Dr. Granger's firm, brief clasp, Laurel's touch felt chilled and tentative. And it lingered. "I'm Lisa."

God help him. He was not strong enough for this.

Don't miss
The Texan's Baby Bombshell *by Allison Leigh,*
available June 2020 wherever
Harlequin Special Edition books and ebooks are sold.

Harlequin.com

SPECIAL EXCERPT FROM

LOVE INSPIRED SUSPENSE
INSPIRATIONAL ROMANCE

*They must work together to solve a cold case...
and to stay alive.*

Read on for a sneak preview of
Deadly Connection *by Lenora Worth,*
the next book in the True Blue K-9 Unit: Brooklyn series,
available June 2020 from Love Inspired Suspense.

Brooklyn K-9 Unit officer Belle Montera glanced back on the shortcut through Cadman Plaza Park, her K-9 partner, Justice, a sleek German shepherd, moving ahead of her as she held tightly to his leash. She had a weird sense she was being followed, but it had to be nothing.

Justice lifted his black nose and sniffed the humid air, then gave a soft woof. He might have seen a squirrel frolicking in the tall oaks, or he could have sensed Belle's agitation. Still on duty, she kept a keen eye on her surroundings.

"No time to go after innocent squirrels," she told Justice. "We're working, remember?"

Her faithful companion gave her a dark-eyed stare, his black K-9 unit protective vest cinched around his firm belly.

They were both on high alert.

"It's okay, boy," she said, giving Justice's shiny black-and-tan coat a soft rub. "Just my overactive imagination getting the best of me."

She had a meeting with a man who could have information regarding the McGregor murders. The DNA match from that case had indicated that US marshal Emmett Gage could be related to the killer.

The team had done a thorough background check on the marshal to eliminate him as a suspect, then Belle had been assigned to meet with him.

Justice lifted his head and sniffed again, his nose in the air. The big dog glanced back. Belle checked over her shoulder.

No one there.

She slowed and listened to hear if any footsteps hit the strip of pavement curving through the path toward the federal courthouse near the park.

Belle heard through the trees what sounded like a motorcycle revving, then nothing but the birds chirping. Minutes passed and then she heard a noise on the path, the crackle of a twig breaking, the slight shift of shoes hitting asphalt, a whiff of stale body odor wafting through the air. The hair on the back of her neck stood up and Belle knew then.

Someone is following me.

Don't miss
Deadly Connection *by Lenora Worth,*
available June 2020 wherever
Love Inspired Suspense books and ebooks are sold.

LoveInspired.com

H HARLEQUIN

*Heartfelt or suspenseful,
inspiring or passionate, Harlequin
has your happily-ever-after.*

With new books published
every month, you are sure to find the
satisfying escape you know you deserve.